A Compelling Novel of Love and Greed Set in the Decadent Atmosphere of Nazi-Occupied Paris

Summer 1941: The Louvre, the Jeu de Paume, and all of Paris—especially its art and beautiful women —are the spoils of the hated Nazi victors as they trample France under the boot of the Third Reich.

In this treacherous web of avarice and betrayal, Claude Le Brun—aristocrat, member of the French Resistance, and second-in-command at the great Jacobi Gallery—masquerades as a collaborator for the art-starved Third Reich in an attempt to forestall the rape of France's priceless art heritage.

Le Brun is up against the ruthless ambition of Hermann Goering, who needs the art treasures to repay a debt of failure, and the savage lust of General Von Banheim and his right-hand man Sergeant Raeder— who are after not only art but elegant Parisiennes as well. What's at stake is art, freedom—and Le Brun's love affair with beautiful heiress Sara Jacobi . . .

THE PLUNDERERS

THE
Plunderers

Franklin Coen

BALLANTINE BOOKS • NEW YORK

Library of Congress Catalog Card Number: 79-14289

ISBN 0-345-29166-2

This edition published by arrangement with
Coward McCann & Geoghegan

Manufactured in the United States of America

First Ballantine Books Edition: December 1980

For Monique

PART ONE

House 71: June 1945

THE WAR, THEY SAID, was over, but slow-moving clouds on the deeply pigmented sky had made a chiaroscuro of the mountain road, and from the top of the hill machine-gun fire erupted out of the shade, killing Rood, who was sitting in the lead jeep with Lieutenant Goldfarb.

The shots sent the three jeeps in a hurry to the shoulder, the occupants diving for cover in the woods. *It's hell to have to die at this stage of the thing,* Sergeant Mack was thinking, huddled behind the trunk of a husky pine. *Corporal Rood must have been damn mad.*

Mack didn't have to give any orders beyond a quick hand signal—the 3rd Army had no unit more competent. Rafferty and Ullman were already scrambling up through the trees with a bazooka—might be a tank emplaced there—and the rest of his men were concentrating small-arms fire on the crown of the hill. Minutes later they could hear the hiss and bang of the bazooka, followed by the splattering noise of a grenade.

After a short interlude they could hear Ullman yelling and see him waving from the top.

Corporal Rood was arranged on the rear seat of the third jeep and the small column proceeded upward, Goldfarb himself taking over the wheel of the lead vehicle.

Dammit, Mack said to himself. *My luck to get assigned to this scummy detail.* "No worry about firefights," *that smug replacement captain said:* "The goddam krauts are finished." *Screw you, Captain!*

Finished were the two dirt-blackened, steel-helmeted bodies beside the smashed machine gun. SS from the

3

collar insignia. Mack had been warned by other squad leaders that SS troops in small bands were still working these mountains. He watched while Rafferty and Ullman got into the middle jeep. But Goldfarb was edging forward, giving him a view of the terrain beyond. The lieutenant, whose uniform looked too big for him, who couldn't weigh more than a hundred-thirty soaking wet, seemed not to care what might be lurking in the next roller-coaster dip. Including land mines or, say, another SS suicide squad with an operable anti-tank gun. Crazy gray ghosts! How long could they hold out?

But Goldfarb was nuttier than anyone. Or stupider. One hand on the wheel, he was gesturing with the other to Mack. "There it is, Sergeant. Straight across the valley. That burnt-out clearing. No more than two miles. See it?"

Mack saw the clearing and a pointed rooftop and a huge stone chimney jutting out of the side of the mountain across from them. But how in hell could Goldfarb be sure that was what they were looking for?

"Okay, but for Crissakes, let's not go barging in, huh? Might be another committee waiting for us."

And Sergeant Mack, glancing back at Rood, spat a solid globule past Goldfarb's right ear. "You know, Lieutenant, that kid never went to a museum in his whole fuckin' life!"

Lieutenant Goldfarb had designed *his* life to be spent in museums. After graduating from Harvard with a masters in art, he had gone on to an internship at the National Gallery in Washington. It was from the gallery several years later that he'd been commissioned by the OSS for special duty in Germany—the Art Looting Section, designed to seek out those Nazis who had done such an efficient job of plundering the great masterpieces of the occupied countries.

In charge of actually laying hands on the art when found, of the protection and salvaging of artistic monuments in war areas, was another organization—the Monuments, Fine Arts and Archives Section, G-5, under SHAEF. Only a week previously, the G-5 boys had scored a great coup, finding an enormous salt mine only a few miles away in the Austrian Alps, where apparently the bulk of Hitler's war treasure had been stored for safekeeping from Allied bombing.

Priceless works of art were being found tucked away in the caves, Goldfarb had been told, trucked daily to the major repository in Munich. Already unearthed were Michelangelo's "Madonna and Child," important Rembrandts, the wonderful Ghent altarpiece by the Van Eycks, even several paper cartons filled with the Rothschild family jewels. And this was virtually only the first child's shovelful of recovered loot. Literally thousands more pieces stolen from Jews throughout the world, from national collections, and from famous private collections, were waiting to be surfaced from the vast salt caverns.

With all this happening around him, Goldfarb was in a state of perpetual excitement. Commissioned too late for combat, given hasty and superficial training near Washington, he had been flown to Paris, then on to Frankfurt, and to Munich. Here he had hung around, allowed to sit in on interrogations if he kept his mouth shut. The flow of Germans volunteering to come in and give information was amazing. Art dealers mostly, and minor museum officials, with knowledge of masterpieces acquired either by agents of Hitler or Goering, everyone anxious to reveal the real culprits, set the records straight.

Ten days in Munich and Goldfarb got an unusual break. The Art Looting Section had taken over a chalet not far from Berchtesgaden, for the purpose of questioning key Nazis rounded up in that area. The advance post was a gingerbread affair on the main street of the postcard alpine village, called House 71, and it was already paying off; the investigative officers in charge, Jim Jackson and Arnold Sherman, had hooked a very big fish indeed. Hermann Goering's number one art adviser and agent, Ernst Kröler was talking, it appeared—and the Nazi blueprint for plunder was beginning to emerge.

Jackson and Sherman were therefore being recalled briefly to Munich for initial debriefing while a new team of Captain Thomas Packard and Lieutenant Harold Goldfarb were to get their asses out to House

71 and complete the job of keeping Herr Kröler warm and cooperative.

Packard, an OSS veteran, was to operate under the guise of an art historian like Goldfarb.

The first appearance by the new men at House 71 was a total bust. Kröler, middle-sized, middle-aged, a man you would lose in a crowd but a very cool customer any way you looked at him, possibly miffed at being handed over to a junior team, was not exactly forthcoming as advertised. Other than confiding a few well-known generalities about the Reichsmarschall's unscrupulous activities, he was politely uncommunicative.

On the second day a frustrated Captain Packard suggested a postluncheon stroll in the pleasant garden, which seemed to hang in space under the surrounding peaks. The day was warm and in the mountain stillness a distant hammering could be heard—someone's first tentative blows at reconstruction. Having lunched splendidly, consuming a bottle of excellent Gewürztraminer, Packard and Goldfarb were not in a combative mood. But a question of pride was at stake: what in hell could they report to Munich?

Obviously determined to break the spell, Packard, a beanpole of a Yale man with a theatrical manner, led the way to the shade of the gazebo where he whipped out a folder of papers from his hip pocket, thrusting it under Kröler's nose.

"Now listen, you bastard—you know what this is. You know it isn't complete. It's within your ability to complete it for us. Or take the consequences!"

What the file contained was a list of paintings, sculptures, rare furniture, and other art treasures recovered from a dozen or more freight cars found unguarded on tracks near Hermann Goering's chalet not far from House 71. Also included were descriptions of lesser treasures in Goering's chalet when the first elements of the 3rd Army reached it. What surprised Goldfarb about Packard's flaunting of the list was that the previous team had suggested it remain classified for as long as possible, specifically as a check against Kröler's continuing reliability.

"So how about it: Goering was the biggest crook in Christendom—you, yourself, admitted it this morning. Where's the rest of the loot hidden?"

"But there *is* no other loot, Captain," Kröler said. "Everything of value was removed from Carinhall for protection against air raids. If time permitted, the Reichsmarschall would have moved them again, perhaps to another salt mine—there are many around here, you know."

"Are there? Tell us about them."

But Kröler continued to maintain that infuriating posture of innocence. "If you'd like, I could take a look at your inventory. Perhaps I could then be one hundred percent sure."

"Oh, no you don't!" said Packard, snatching the folder away, as if Kröler were really going to make a grab for it. "For God's sake, how dumb do you think we are?"

"It appears to me, Captain," put in Goldfarb, "that Kröler is giving us nothing but crap. So let Munich take him over—the boys there have the techniques."

Kröler's bland, colorless eyes were suddenly opaque.

"Please," he said. "Your colleagues have already questioned me about that list, without being willing to show it to me. If I could verify that what's down there is the lot; or on the contrary, that you've missed a few items, so much time and anger could be saved. You'd know what to search for, wouldn't you?"

A bumblebee flew into the gazebo, landing on Packard's sleeve. Packard brushed it recklessly away.

"All right," he growled, handing Kröler the list. "Here. Take a good look."

Kröler sat down on a bench and spread the pages on a wooden table.

The distant hammering stopped, started again; the bumblebee made another foray out into the hot sunshine; Kröler read on, handling the pages carefully.

Finally he was finished.

"Well?" asked Packard.

"All the principal acquisitions seem to be posted here. I'm not omniscient of course. I may have missed one or two . . ."

There was a curious change in Kröler's manner.

Goldfarb, watching him, decided it was as though the man wanted to tell them something but didn't know how to do it. *Could I be imagining things?* Goldfarb wondered.

Kröler had given the papers back to Packard. He was lighting a small cigar. His hands—again, was Goldfarb reading him right?—shook slightly. "You're sure you picked up everything at the chalet?"

Packard was sure as hell. "Neither Jackson nor Sherman is blind."

"They found the subcellar?"

"They found it. It contained ordinary household silver."

"The gymnasium?"

Goldfarb intervened. "You think it possible they did overlook something?"

Kröler made the classic shrugging gesture with open palms.

Goldfarb had a flash. *We did miss something, but for reasons of his own Kröler's afraid to tell us—or not to tell us. Afraid of the consequences either way. The man was looking on that list for something he didn't find. And now he's in an awful dilemma.*

"Would another trip to Goering's chalet be worthwhile?" Goldfarb asked.

"There's a pretty view from the terrace," Kröler answered. "Not as stunning as the panorama from the Eagle's Nest. But you *could* look around again."

"Maybe we'll allow Goldfarb the afternoon off tomorrow," Packard said. "Let him take the tour. You and I, Kröler, can carry on here with the birds and the bees."

". . . never went to a fuckin' museum in his life," Mack had said of the dead corporal. He and his men were mad as hell. Mack started to communicate with his walkie-talkie, but out of Goldfarb's hearing.

Goldfarb felt the barb deeply. Sergeant Mack was right. Whatever they found at Goering's chalet—if they found anything—how could it be worth Rood's life? But he believed in art. Art, it had been said, was the conscience of man, the inner light. To renew and preserve that incandescence was a continual uphill struggle.

"Let's get on with it, Sergeant," Goldfarb called, hitting the gas. The jeep spurted over the crest.

No guard had been left at the chalet, and local souvenir hunters had taken everything of possible value, including the toilet fixtures, bricks from fireplaces, and paneling from walls. And then someone had applied the torch; the building was a burnt-out shell.

Kröler had been right about the view. From the terrace, which fronted the vaulted living room, one could see Austria, a rolling carpet of pine tops, interspersed with lakes catching the sun-fire like carelessly tossed sapphires.

But Goldfarb did not find it beautiful. His mood was wrong. He was filled with hate at the thought of bastards like Goering, only there was no vengeance he could take against the view or this ruin of a building.

There was another structure, one-storied, on the plateau alongside the chalet.

Goldfarb and Mack, along with Rafferty and Ullman, went to take a look. It had been a gymnasium, it appeared, from the few broken fixtures still on the walls, although there were several offices there, too. In one of these—not a piece of furniture in it, filthy, scavenged like the main house—they found the floor littered with papers. *My God, we've struck it rich!* Goldfarb thought at first. *Goering's archives! So that was what Kröler was hinting at.*

He grabbed up handfuls, examining the papers by flashlight. They were household accounts, receipts and expenditures, scrupulously kept by a Goering steward, of possible interest only to a sociologist. Goldfarb, however, leaving nothing to chance—possibly some kind of code had been used—ordered Mack to have the stuff collected and taken back with them.

They were all pitching in, picking up every scrap, when an ominous, high-pitched whine stopped them. On its heels came an explosion almost overhead, shaking the building.

"Mortar!" Mack shouted. They hit the floor but within seconds Rafferty and Mack were up again and

9

at the blown-out windows, Mack shouting something unintelligible into his walkie-talkie.

Another whining sound and this time the shell knocked off a corner of the house. It seemed a miracle to Goldfarb they weren't all killed. It was, except for the incident on the road, his first exposure to enemy fire, and he was scared out of his wits.

A third mortar shell, shaking him badly, crashed into the far side of the building. A deep, ragged gouge appeared at the end of the large room, apparently down to the foundation.

Mack and Rafferty and Ullman at the windows were firing at an unseen foe, and Goldfarb could hear the sound of a machine gun rattling from the chalet, behind the men with the mortars.

Mack was beckoning fiercely.

Legs unsteady, Goldfarb obeyed, joining him, looking out the window over his shoulders.

He saw a handful of soldiers in dirty gray-green flopping to their stomachs between the gymnasium and the road. More staccato firing and the figures appeared to melt. Presently a dozen GIs appeared around the corner of the chalet, slowly reconnoitering the dead Germans.

In their building, Mack, Rafferty, and Ullman were standing back, lighting up cigarettes.

"How'd you like that?" Ullman asked Goldfarb.

Mack was grinning. "Goddamn—I thought those bastards would never get here!"

"What bastards?" asked Goldfarb, still confused.

"Second platoon, Lieutenant!"

"Second platoon?"

"There had to be more than those two on top of the hill, and I knew their friends would be tailing us —so I just called for a little backup."

"We were just the bait," said Rafferty.

"You might have told me," Goldfarb said in a voice which came out as a strangled snarl.

"You'd have shit in your pants," Sergeant Mack said politely.

He and Ullman and Rafferty, arms loaded with Goering's household accounts, slipped away laughing.

Alone, Goldfarb wasn't too unhappy with his bap-

tism by fire. *At least I didn't actually disgrace myself,*
he thought. *The sonsabitches!*

He walked over to take a look at the mortar damage.

The splintered hole in the floor was larger than he
had imagined, a good twenty feet or so in length, half
that in width. But he could now see that a secret basement of some kind had been opened up by the explosion.

Peering below didn't help—it was black—but then
he remembered the flashlight, beaming it into the
jagged recess.

My God!

Lying down there on dry, solid flooring, was a
great piece of ancient marble, enormous wings thrusting out from a prone, draped body, stationed on a
boat-shaped pedestal.

One

THE ARMORED TRAIN slid into the yards of the Gare
de L'Est in Paris. It was barely dawn, August 1941.
Immediately behind the engine, which was protected
by thick steel plating, was the armaments car, manned
by an elite unit of the Luftwaffe. This unit was
equipped with antiaircraft guns as well as armor-
piercing cannon and machine guns set in revolving
turrets.

Two service coaches followed with bunks, mess
compartments, and recreation rooms.

Now came the Reichsmarschall's section, four
coaches specially built for his use: coach number one
with bedroom suites, gymnasium, and a study where
he could work. Coach number two, dining salon and
kitchen. Coach three, an elegant salon for state recep-
tions, including several small chambers for private

conferences. Coach four, a large war room, plus a communications center filled with sophisticated electronic equipment.

Throughout, only the finest woods had been used for interior walls, marble for the lavatories; no expense had been spared in workmanship. And the Reichsmarschall had seen to it that paintings and sculpture met the eye everywhere; in the third coach in the salon he had hung some of the best of his growing French collection, including several especially fine Bouchers.

The train, which bore the code name ASIA, was actually a highly functional headquarters on wheels, and served to carry Hermann Goering back and forth on the Continent, wherever duty beckoned.

The final car, a flatbed, was manned by additional Luftwaffe troops, completing protection front to rear. All undersides of the coaches were heavily plated; the engine, with an elliptical front like a bullet, gave the entire train the look of the next century. Rolling through the conquered countryside, it provoked an impression of speed, power, and impregnability—all of which, in fact, it had.

By order of Major Klaus Kruger, Goering's personal aide, the train that morning was to remain where it was until the first engineer was ordered otherwise. Kruger knew the Reichsmarschall had a long day ahead of him and could use his sleep, and the yards would surely be quieter than the depot proper.

At six-thirty he was forced to order Goering awakened, using the intercom to reach Maida Thaler, Goering's nurse, who accompanied him whenever he left Berlin, although the rumor was that even in Carinhall, Maida was in residence whether Emmy Goering liked it or not.

"He could do with another hour," Maida told Kruger.

"So could I. Get him up," Kruger replied briefly. He knew how long it took to get his boss prepared, able to cope with what lay ahead. "There's a staff meeting scheduled for nine," he added. "And, Frau Thaler—"

"Yes?"

"General Galland and staff will be present. It would help if your charge is . . . alert."

"Don't worry about it," snapped Maida, hanging up.

Bitch, thought Kruger, knowing how he'd like her to end up but also what he'd like to do to her first.

Maida Thaler wasted no time on Kruger. At times she felt he had the brain of a cuckoo clock, but that, too, was needed. Kruger kept the mechanisms of command oiled, the train on the tracks.

Shivering, for it was drizzling outside, she still couldn't help her excitement; after all, they had arrived in Paris. Anything could happen in Paris. It was nice that she'd be here alone, that Theodor, her husband, was stationed in Holland; perhaps by now Theodor had found himself a little Dutch girl. She smiled at the thought, bending over the basin to brush her teeth. She scrubbed vigorously, sponged under her armpits, tugged her mop of curly black hair into some sort of shape, wondering for the thousandth time if she shouldn't dye it blond, sat on the corner of the bed to pull on her white stockings. Her legs were good, but the rest of her was too trim; she needed to be plumper here and there, but ironically she had trouble putting on weight. A pity. Emmy Goering was blond, statuesque. The German men approved—a woman should have substance.

She turned in the full-length mirror opposite the bunk, examining herself. At least her breasts were large and firm. She didn't have much to complain about. She knew enough men, high-ranking officers even, who would like to get their hands on her.

In the corridor, there was only Heinrich, Goering's valet, standing at an open window, smoking a cigarette, gazing out at the blurred city skyline. Seeing Frau Thaler, he pulled back, forcing her to squeeze by in front of him to reach the Reichsmarschall's suite.

"Bastard," she hissed at him. Even through her starched uniform she could feel his erection.

The Reichsmarschall was already on the massage table when she arrived, his silk pajamas and robe

13

flung across the unmade bed. Half covered with a sheet, he nodded curtly to her. "I've been waiting."

"Kruger was late in calling me," she answered. "Besides, I thought I'd give you a few extra moments. How did you sleep?"

"Not well, Frau Thaler."

Nodding sympathetically, she removed the sheet, telling him to turn over. He did so with difficulty, presenting his huge pink backside. He was really immense. Finding a bottle of his specially perfumed oil in the cabinet across from the table, she began to massage his back and neck with her thin, strong fingers, gently, then more vigorously, evoking small moans of pleasure. Finally she ordered him onto his back again and began to dig into his stomach in wide circular patterns. This wasn't as pleasing, and he mumbled, "Frau Thaler!"

"It is what the doctor ordered."

"The hell with the doctor!"

"Yes, Reichsmarschall."

He nodded, wearing a little smile. He was a pleasant, generous man with those he liked and trusted, actually easy to get along with.

"Did you take your medicine?"

"To be sure, Frau Thaler."

Almost accidently, her hand brushed his penis. Then again. Then she bent over him. The Reichsmarschall smiled. "I have a full morning, *Liebchen* . . . thank you . . . you may call Heinrich. And, Frau Thaler . . ."

"Yes, Herr Reichsmarschall?"

"You should see Paris. Walk a bit. It's quite safe. Last year when we took it—when the Führer was here—I strolled alone on the Champs-Elysées in the late afternoon. It was very beautiful. A fine memory."

"But the French are vicious people."

With an effort, Frau Thaler helping to boost him, the Reichsmarschall sat up, dangling thick, heavy legs from the table.

"Yes, they're vicious. But so are we when necessary —and we're their masters!"

She laughed and started for the door. "I shall not

14

go walking," she said over her shoulder. "You may need me. I'll be within call."

The war room was full of talk and cigarette smoke; at a buffet a steward served hot coffee and schnapps. But an abrupt cough from near the door and the mood in the room suddenly altered. Goering had entered. Emphasizing the importance he was giving the briefing, he was uniformed simply; a gray tunic with white piping, slightly darker-toned trousers, and only the most important of his decorations, including the Collar of the Annunziata, given him by the King of Italy. On his feet, however, he wore elaborate but comfortable deerskin moccasins from Norway on which bright red swastikas were embroidered.

He gave a soft "At ease" and a comradely nod to the ranking men clustered in front of the long operations table. With Galland, commander of the Luftwaffe in the west, he shook hands. However they may have felt about him, Goering was relaxed with these people. They were his own, and like them, he had earned his wings. In the first world war, while most here were children, he had been a *Jagdflieger*, a fighter pilot, a member of the original Richthofen squadron. He had shot down twenty-two Allied planes, once returning to base with sixty bulletholes in the fuselage of his plane and several in his stomach.

And in the end he had been put in command of the Richthofen squadron, having been awarded the Zaehring Lion with Swords, Iron Cross first class, and other medals before receiving the most coveted, Pour le Mérite. Oh yes, he'd been a dashing, romantic fellow, and half his present size.

"You've been waiting long?" he asked Galland politely.

"An opportunity to assess the latest reports," Galland replied, indicating the huge map of the coastline which took up most of the table. Galland was a tall, bony officer, the angularity extending to his face and his manner; he could be like a broad-bladed knife. But he was tough and competent and, it was said, unafraid to stand up to the Reichsmarschall.

"Yes, of course, the latest reports," murmured Goering, frowning.

Galland nodded to a young officer near him. "Proceed, Captain Schacter."

Schacter had a pointer and a voice like a race announcer. He began to indicate the squadron strength at the Luftwaffe airfields depicted on the map table, as well as the number of planes involved in the night's action and their targets. Britain, a bilious green on the map, was pocked with small, flaming red plaques; one showed the areas bombed and, supplemented by Schacter, the damage inflicted.

"London," said Schacter with finality, "will not soon forget last night."

There were smiles on the faces of the junior officers in the railway car. Not on Galland's.

"And our losses, Captain?"

Schacter's hesitation was fractional. Galland had given him no signal. "Sixteen fighters. Nine fighter-bombers."

"The enemy?"

"Twenty six, confirmed, not counting probables."

"Permit me, Reichsmarschall, but if we hit their airfields with enough shit they won't get the stink out easily," put in Riehl. He was a full colonel, Galland's adjutant, a short, blunt man who had risen from the ranks. Goering knew him as a competent officer. "God knows how many planes were destroyed on the ground."

"And that," added Schacter eagerly, "does not take into account the damage to war plants in the target areas." His pointer tapped half a dozen spots on the table. "The destruction was certainly extensive."

The statement was capped by a murmur of agreement; without doubt the raid would have to be considered a notable victory.

Goering felt them waiting for his approval. He did not give it. He walked past the position table where a large crystal jar had been placed on a console. The jar was full of small white tablets. Removing the lid, Goering popped one into his mouth, as if treating himself to candy. Returning to the men at the position table, he studied the board in deep concentration.

"The Führer will be most gratified," he finally said, as if not a moment had passed. "This phase of our activities is of great concern to him. It is the Führer's opinion that England is on the verge of collapse—that she can withstand so much and no more—that she must not be allowed to catch her breath. Now is not the time to call it quits! Have I made myself clear? We must fight unrelentingly! And in the air!"

In the silence Galland shrugged his shoulders, to his intimates a sign of suppressed anger. Of all people, Goering was aware that the figures given him by Schacter were lies. One could only hope Hitler's intuition about Britain was correct, but he, Galland, had to send up planes and men. It would help if his superiors had a realistic notion of his problems.

Galland itched to say something of this openly, so that his staff could see he wasn't knuckling under without a struggle. But Galland, feeling sour-stomached —too much coffee probably—kept silent. *What good would such a protest do? Particularly with the Reichsmarschall back on the pills. My God, he's eating the damn things openly now! In front of the entire staff! Does he imagine they think it's a bowl of mints?*

"Some of my pilots," Galland said slowly, "could do with relief. They've been flying night after night without any rest."

"They shall have rest—we'll give them leave at home or in Paris. Who loves them more than we do? But when the job's done! *Now* we show our stamina! Let's see who's the first to cry 'enough'!"

Applause.

He put his hand on Galland's shoulder; he wore only one ring today, a large emerald set in a heavy gold frame. He turned Galland, their backs to the others, so that they appeared to be scrutinizing the position board. "I have affairs in the city here for most of the day, but by evening my train will be at your advance headquarters. When they come home from the enemy I'll be at your side to welcome them, eh, Galland?"

Climbing into his staff car outside the train, Galland paused. A small convoy of civilian vehicles was approaching along the access road to the yards. It stopped a little distance from the train. There were several Mercedes and a Hispano-Suiza roadster, in excellent shape, its chassis and chrome work gleaming. The occupants hustled out of their cars toward the train where Major Kruger's security car waited to examine their credentials. They all carred briefcases; the one man in uniform, a sergeant, ungainly, with thick eyeglasses, carried a large flat package.

Galland's eyes followed the man from the Hispano-Suiza—first, because the automobile itself was unique enough to have attracted his attention, and second because unlike his companions, who wore business suits, the fellow had scorned protocol and dressed in slacks and suede jacket with a knotted silk scarf—almost, it occurred to Galland, the garb of a pre-war aviator. A Frenchman, clearly, tall, thin, and, like his car, elegantly handsome. His papers having passed muster, he disappeared with the group into Goering's salon coach.

"His goddamn art people," Galland heard Riehl behind him say bitterly. "If he spent half as much time—"

"That's enough!" Galland interrupted sharply. "We have our own work cut out for us, Colonel. May we proceed with it, please?"

The painting that Sergeant Hans Raeder took from its wrappings and placed on the easel was a Delacroix, a good-sized oil depicting a royal hunt of uncertain period or place. The focus of the work was the wounded and bleeding boar, freely handled but with such virtuoso technique that its death agony was like a blow to the viewer's heart.

The men gathered around it, pulled back as Goering entered the salon. He had changed uniforms, if what he was wearing could be called a uniform. Actually it was a white satin blouse in the Russian style, but with epaulettes.

The *"Guten Morgen Reichsmarschall!"* in chorus was barely acknowledged as he hurried to the easel.

He was munching on a cake. At his side his short,

barrel-chested valet Heinrich carried a tray on which there was a pot of coffee, a creamer, and more cakes.

"One of his best, as you can see, Reichsmarschall," murmured Ernst Kröler behind him.

The other arrivals, the Frenchman; Kröler's assistant Eckmann, a middle-aged Austrian who never opened his mouth; and the sergeant, an enigma with cold, steel-gray eyes, remained to one side, out of the way.

"The boar is magnificent, *mein Gott!*" Goering exclaimed. Reaching toward Kröler, he was given a magnifying glass with a wrought-silver handle. Proceeding from top to bottom, he began to examine the canvas minutely.

"His brushstrokes, his color . . ." he whispered admiringly. "Can you believe it?"

"Exactly," said Kröler.

"Undoubtedly genuine."

"I would swear it," said Kröler. And, with what was intended as a chuckle: "If it isn't, our friend here will answer for it!"

For the first time, Goering turned to regard Le Brun.

The Frenchman was in his early thirties. He had the ascetic look of an arrogant young prelate, except for the unexpected rakish quality lent by his slightly hooked nose. But when he smiled, it was clear he could be charming. "The Jacobi galleries haven't sold a fake since they went into business," he said directly to Goering.

"The Jacobi?" Goering asked, surprised, with a serious look at Kröler.

"The House of Jacobi and most other galleries have been Aryanized—but not officially," Kröler explained. "In the case of Jacobi we've not gotten around to putting someone in charge."

"There is still stock? Paintings?"

"Nothing exceptional," volunteered Le Brun. "Except of course in the foreign branches—London, New York, Buenos Aires. Unhappily not available to us here. Our French pieces, as you know, have been expropriated from the bank vaults. You have them all."

Goering motioned to Heinrich, who passed him another cake. "Some good things in that collection, particularly the Fouquets," he mused. "Rosenberg has set aside the best for the Führer's use, destined for the new museum to be constructed at Linz where, as you know, Hitler was born. You've nothing at all left in Paris?"

"Only some unimportant furniture in the family house here on the avenue Foch."

Goering continued his appraisal of Le Brun. With a motion toward the Delacroix: "And this, then?"

"From my own collection. The centerpiece, you might say."

"For which you want a fortune. How many hundred thousand marks?"

"For which I want not one mark. It is my gift to you."

Goering continued to study Le Brun, then suddenly grinned and waved them all to chairs in a rough semicircle around the easel.

"What is your position at Jacobi's?" he asked Le Brun.

"I was a junior partner."

"You are Jewish?"

"To my knowledge I have no Jewish blood. Aaron Jacobi simply . . . liked me. He had no sons. Only two daughters. The older, Erica, and I were friends. I think he would have liked—"

"You have a title?" Goering interrupted.

"My brother is Count Guy Le Brun. So I suppose even though not of their faith, Aaron Jacobi considered me a—"

"A catch," said Goering. A bark of laughter. The others laughed too, except for the sergeant in the corner and Le Brun, who looked uncomfortable.

"But you didn't marry this older daughter?"

"She was killed in a plane accident. And I'm afraid you're wrong. He thought of me simply as someone, a protégé, who—when he was gone—could carry on the business."

"The younger daughter?"

Le Brun shrugged. "In London, I think, with her

20

father and mother. I've no further contact with the family."

Goering's glance shifted to Kröler, whose nod was slight but emphatic, then unaccountably to the corner of the salon where Sergeant Hans Raeder stood quietly. The sergeant made no sign whatsoever.

Goering turned back to Le Brun; for his own reasons, he appeared satisfied.

"Tell me, this Jacobi house in Paris—it's occupied?"

"By a few servants."

"Paid by whom?"

"By me."

"Awaiting the family's return?"

"France will be at the disposition of the Third Reich for the foreseeable future. I cannot imagine a Jewish family returning."

"Then why have you kept it up?"

"It is a beautiful old house, Reichsmarschall. Some might consider it a national monument. I would hate to see it go to ruin."

"How much would you say it is worth? Fifty thousand?"

"Oh, much more, Reichsmarschall!"

"Then you wouldn't be unhappy to receive it in return for the Delacroix?"

Le Brun was on his feet, his voice calm. He didn't appear to be in awe of Goering. "I did not offer the Delacroix with a return in mind. It was a mark of my admiration for—" Abruptly, as if suddenly aware of his situation, he broke off. That charming smile lit up his face. "I'm a fool, Reichsmarschall. Such a gift would of course make me supremely happy!"

There was amusement in the coach. Even Sergeant Raeder allowed himself a gritty cough of laughter.

"Good. We will naturally be grateful if you keep your eyes open for us. A generous finder's fee for whatever Jewish works we've missed. And there'll be other sources you'll run across. For knowledge of which, naturally, we'll pay top money. Kröler, arrange for Le Brun to take over the Jacobi firm officially. I will sign whatever documents are necessary."

"Yes, Reichsmarschall."

Goering made his way to a side table on which sat

21

a jar of white tablets identical to the one in the war room. Again the Reichsmarschall popped one of the tablets into his mouth. What was exceptional about these pills was that they kept him in a serene mood without impairing his ability to think or to make decisions. Turning, he nodded affably to the Frenchman, dismissing him.

Le Brun, who had not brought a briefcase, not even a topcoat against the rain, bowed slightly to Kröler, a small gesture to Eckmann, and was gone.

Waiting until he could hear the voices of the outside guard ushering Le Brun to his car, Goering motioned to Sergeant Raeder.

Raeder immediately approached the easel and began a thorough examination of the Delacroix, even removing it and studying the back of the canvas. Finally, after what seemed an interminable appraisal, he stepped back.

"Authentic."

Goering nodded. "I'd heard of it. One of his greatest. I've always wanted it. Value?"

"Over three hundred thousand."

Goering smiled. "Thank you, Hans." To Kröler: "Your Frenchman is no fool. However, he knows what he is getting in exchange."

"That is certainly true."

Goering crossed to the sofa and sprawled on it. He was beginning to feel drowsy. "For that matter, the Jacobi paintings picked up in the bank vault may *not* be all the family had. I've heard rumors of a really important collection. Our clever Monsieur Le Brun would know of it."

"The thought had occurred to me," said Sergeant Raeder. "In fact, I'd bet on it."

"So would I," said Kröler. "A *major* collection."

"Follow up on it, eh?" said Goering. "Both of you. Hans, you especially, will keep a watch. A close one. Only not *too* close, you understand? I like this Le Brun, I must tell you. But I too believe there are things hidden . . . in the man, behind that careful front."

"As you wish, Reichsmarschall."

Goering nodded, pushing himself to his feet. He

took one more look at the Delacroix. He yawned hugely. There was really no limit to the art he could accumulate, he decided. He would have the most valuable collection in all the world.

"I'm tired, gentlemen," he said. "Been up and about since before dawn. Kröler, later—early this afternoon—I'll try to manage the Jeu de Paume. Inform General von Banheim and the others. You'll have some beauties set aside for me, right?"

Kröler made a short, stiff bow.

"Heinrich, send Frau Thaler to my compartment."

He yawned a final time and, swaying slightly, made his way to the corridor.

Two

SARA JACOBI WAS DETERMINED to go back to France— to fight in the Underground, she told her father.

"Do you really believe the Resistance needs you?"

"They can use everyone. I can ride a horse. I can pilot a plane. I can shoot a gun. I can even type."

It brought no smile.

"You're a child."

"Twenty-two," she answered tartly. "An ancient twenty-two."

"You look half that!"

"Dammit, that's no compliment!"

Aaron sighed. It was a working tenet not to waste energy on a losing cause. But this was one fight with his daughter he would not allow himself to lose. Again he said, "You'd be risking your life, and for what?"

"Do I have to repeat it? For France!" And instantly regretting it, too late to recall the high-flown phrase, she added, "I could perhaps arrange to have the collection sent over here to you."

His jet-black eyes, the light glinting on them, held her fixed. "Do you imagine I would risk your life for the collection?"

"No, Papa."

"Then try to be reasonable. As a Jew you'd be in mortal danger the moment you set foot on French soil. Anyone recognizing you on the street could well be the one to reveal your presence to the authorities, French *or* German. Remember, you're my daughter— how they'd love to get their hands on you!"

"I could alter my appearance. I'm clever at such things, Papa. I'm an artist, you forget."

"You're a fool if you think you could get away with such a fragile deception for very long. And a conceited child if you believe that joining the Underground will make any difference in the eventual outcome for France."

This only made her angrier. His smallness, she had often thought, had perversely given him more leverage where it was needed: he could overwhelm with the unremitting strength of his resolve.

"There's another course of action open to you. An alternative. I had lunch with General de Gaulle yesterday." Almost off-handedly, he went on, "I've put certain sums of money at his disposal; I've provided various links with the Jewish establishment in England that can prove valuable to him and to Free France. Your mother has accepted a vice-chairmanship of a French-American fund-raising group . . ."

His voice fell away while she waited.

They were in the library of the mansion in Belgravia that Aaron Jacobi had leased for the duration. It was large, formerly the residence of a newspaper baron, and furnished in what a decorator had considered "modern"—big, ugly, square pieces that antagonized the old wainscotted walls, the lovely recessed windows, offended the stately dimensions of a fine Edwardian home. Aaron, for his own reasons, thought the place suitable, if not sublime, and had balked only at decorator-chosen works of art. These had immediately been replaced by paintings from the back room in the Jacobi gallery located in the West

End—a lovely early Renoir hung over the fireplace in the study where they now sat.

But the cream, ah, the cream of the Jacobi collection was still in Paris, Aaron had kept reminding them for months—a half dozen priceless Picassos of the Pink and Blue periods, four superb Cézannes, unbelievably, six Monets, a Manet, a Vuillard, a Matisse, so many others. In speaking of what remained behind, what he had been unable in the last hectic days to take out safely, Aaron's voice would falter, his soft, piping tones color with emotion.

Not because of its value. Aaron did not try to conceal the fact that even without the collection he was a very rich man. But the Paris paintings, no question about it, were close to his heart; he had put the collection together lovingly over the years, using all his resources and knowledge to find only the best, planning, Sara guessed, ultimately to will it to his adopted country—perhaps even to provide the funds for the construction of a wing in one of the national museums to house it.

"The point is"—Aaron roused himself from his reverie—"he's promised to find you a more . . . rewarding job."

Sara had been working for the past four months in the secretarial pool of de Gaulle's London headquarters. The work was mostly typing and filing endless reports having, as far as she could determine, no importance to the outcome of the war; she worked exclusively for people at the bottom of the ladder, and whatever excitement trickled down to this layer you could put into an eyecup.

"What kind of a job?" she asked bluntly.

"He doesn't know yet. Possibly an assistant to one of his top officers—at least a position close to the heart of things. Translating, perhaps. Confidential work. He agrees you're being wasted . . . your English is excellent, you're reasonably bright, you know how to keep your mouth shut, you're a very pretty girl. . . ." He smiled at her innocently, this complex but finally single-minded man who was her father. "You'd be an asset actually, and of course you'd be fighting the enemy as well!"

25

"Still at a desk."

"Not the same one, I assure you. And think of the type of man who'll pass by—the march of events. You'll be in the thick of things, Sara. Naturally, it's for you to decide. . . ."

He paused, trying hard to appear objective.

She could hear cars tooting outside; the late-afternoon traffic boiled around the square at this hour. Wartime London, she'd discovered, was noisier and quicker-tempoed than Paris. Like its sister town, it was militarily oriented, but fortunately it could speak its mind. It was dirtier than Paris, however, and bore the raw scars of blitz-bombing—a tragedy, the fine buildings, the city blocks already destroyed.

"Well?"

"I'll think about it, Papa."

She couldn't remember when she had last lied to him; she was lying now. She felt a stab of guilt, he looked so damn weary. It mustn't be easy being her father.

"How about a sherry?" she asked.

"Whiskey."

His smile had strengthened, though. "Let's not tell your mother about . . . all this. The mere idea that you . . ."

"All right," she agreed at once. "But Papa, listen, whatever I do, I have a strong sense of survival. You mustn't worry, really. You mustn't always think of Erica. *I'm* not Erica!"

She was at the buffet, pouring him his scotch. She gave herself a pony shot. Neat for both of them. She walked back with the glasses.

He hadn't responded to the thrust about Erica, although he had understood. Erica had been the center of Helene Jacobi's life; Sara believed her mother hadn't yet recovered from the loss, perhaps never would. If it had been any easier for her father, it was because he had loved his daughters equally—or as deeply—and thus wasn't totally bereft.

"No, you're not Erica."

"She was as tough as I am. You couldn't push her around either. We were both your daughters."

A melancholy grin peeked out of the small dark

face. Unexpectedly he raised his glass. "To my daughters here and there."

"Here and there," said Sara, drinking.

And then, a subject she had resolved not to bring up, came willy-nilly to her lips. "Claude Le Brun, Papa . . . have you heard from him?"

"How could I?"

"I thought perhaps with your connections . . . you practically run your own secret service . . ."

Aaron knew her very well.

His eyes were searching her face. "What do you know?" he said abruptly.

He had gotten to his feet, not taking his eyes from her—she was a head taller, as was her mother—suddenly fierce and demanding. "What do you know, Sara. Tell me?"

"He's gone with them," she said. "You remember Jonathan Court?"

"Which one is he?"

"The Foreign Service man who comes around . . . blond . . . the one you say smiles too much . . . liaison with our office."

"Yes, well?"

"Jonathan read it in a secret report from Paris. It just happened. I didn't know whether to tell you. Claude's become close to Goering. And Papa, listen, he's agreed to take over the House of Jacobi, the gallery, the entire business!"

She hated being the bearer of these tidings.

"Traitor. Ingrate!" he snarled.

"It will soon be official. Even our house on the Foch. Their Aryan representative."

Her father had gone to the bar for a refill. She hoped that telling him had been the right thing . . .

They had made an odd pair: Aaron, the dynamic Austrian Jew, self-educated, with his flair for acquiring invaluable art, and Claude, the young French aristocrat with a parallel ability—but hardly Aaron's acquisitive drive, until now, apparently. Still, he and Aaron had communicated beautifully over the years: if not with the stormy, symbiotic stress of a father-son relationship, then with the rapport of teacher-pupil.

27

And Claude had been brought into family intimacy by the tragedy they all shared.

"Jonathan's information could be wrong, but I think it's probably true, Papa. The report says Claude sees Kröler, Goering's man, regularly . . . a General von Banheim . . . they're all thick as thieves."

Her father whirled to face her, his black eyes blazing.

"Jew haters, all of them! You *see* what the danger would be if you went to Paris."

This was a turn she hadn't foreseen.

Quickly she answered, "It's academic, isn't it? But I can't imagine Claude doing me any harm!"

"Suppose *they* ordered it? How could he refuse them?—a man who's already sold us out?"

But she saw that the hurt had gone deep—beyond concealment, harking back to Erica, as well as to whatever emotional involvement he had in Le Brun. *Investment,* she thought. *What a revelatory word!* You did not *invest* in people; the word smacked of a demand for monetary return. And her father hadn't expected anything from Claude Le Brun, she was certain—anything beyond a clear-cut loyalty. Le Brun had been a younger man with whom, for special reasons, he could communicate within the sphere reserved for family. And, say what you will, males needed males, as women their own, on all sorts of special levels.

But she came back to it; he would not show it openly to her, but he was badly hurt, literally sick at the knowledge of Le Brun's defection.

She must nullify it, make him well again.

She had had to tell him, but by the same token she had the responsibility to verify it. Rumors about people in France floated over the Channel like clouds of insects—this one, that one, was collaborating, was Laval's or Pétain's bedfellow. Hardly a prominent Frenchman still in Paris went untainted. And so often the reports turned out to be entirely false. Perhaps so with Claude Le Brun!

Erica had loved him. Erica, for all her recklessness, was no fool. Could she have loved so vile a betrayer?

No, Sara thought, never! But then, she thought, perhaps *yes*, and then who is the idiot?

Offhandedly she asked, "Does Le Brun know where the collection's hidden? I assumed he did."

"You assumed wrong. I never told him. Was afraid the knowledge might come back to haunt him. Torture, whatever! Not knowing, you see, would keep him reasonably safe." Her father's lips dipped at the corners. He said—with irony, she thought—"Don't imagine he's grateful now, do you? I'll wager he's ready to dig up the garden with his fingernails to find it."

"You never even told *me* where you've hid it!"

"Didn't want you to know, either, *Liebchen.*"

"They can't get their hands on me in London. You're not imagining that?"

He shrugged. *Life*, the gesture said, *keeps no promises.*

They had another drink together, talking about the war. The German advance into Russia was slowing. But the Wehrmacht, the pundits were saying, would regroup and steamroll into Moscow. Aaron Jacobi didn't agree. "The Russians use bodies like cordwood. They'll build a mountain with them, too high for the Nazis with all their tanks to climb."

Sara thought her father for once was guilty of wishful thinking, but he smiled his secret smile. "You'll see, my love."

Her mother swept in from an afternoon reception, ravishingly dressed, looking like Sara's older sister, an elegant self-possessed woman of Roman-Jewish descent. Sara, in fact, had inherited Helene's slightly aquiline nose, her long black hair, her quick graceful movements.

"What are you two up to?" Helene demanded. She had a positive instinct for sniffing out conspiracies—no family secret was ever proof against it.

Without waiting for an answer now, confident that whatever was being withheld would shortly be revealed, she crossed and kissed Aaron on the lips, Sara on the cheeks. Kicking off her shoes, she folded herself into a deep chair with a sigh. A stranger, making a snap judgment, would have judged her vain, frivolous,

29

a social butterfly, Continental to her skin. Occasional lovers, perhaps on the side.

She adored Aaron. But she had one consuming weakness or—strength: she had to be in the middle of everything, to be, if at all possible, the boss. This trait had been aggravated by the powerlessness she'd felt at the loss of Erica. Now she was driven by the need to keep active, never to pause, never to think, never to remember.

"They want me," she announced, "to go to New York."

"I don't like—" began Aaron.

"For a month perhaps. I told them not a day longer! Military transport, quite safe they assure me. Aaron, *chéri*, I can do a lot of good. You know too well how I can squeeze money out of people." The deep-throated laugh. "Particularly from the Americans. The committee's quite frank about that—that would be my special area. They're anxious for my answer."

"I'm sure they are," Aaron said without enthusiasm.

"Why don't you come with me?"

"Impossible, you know it."

"So you won't be alone. You'll have Sara to keep you company."

"Yes," Aaron answered with some satisfaction.

According to the identification papers in Sara's purse, prepared with meticulous care by Jonathan Court's people, she was Marie-Anne Courbel, born on the outskirts of Tours in a development spawned in the year of her birth by the opening of an automobile parts factory. Somehow Jonathan Court, vaguely connected with the Foreign Service, had, in a matter of days, been able to learn that this insignificant village had suffered a disastrous fire, the *mairie* burning down along with all its records.

While copies of essential documents had undoubtedly been made, one could not say with absolute certainty that Marie-Anne's birth certificate had not been lost, that she had never been properly registered at birth. Actually, within a week a card would be inserted in the files at Tours, certifying to her existence and to the untimely death of her parents in that terrible fire.

For now, she sat and shivered in the stern of an open fishing boat while its inboard engine, caterwauling like an angry animal, slammed the vessel into the maw of a hard-running sea. She had wanted to fly in; she was a good pilot, had already qualified for her license. She had pictured herself dropping neatly onto a small, tree-lined meadow one evening while her copilot, with a wave of a gloved hand, took over the controls, the plane taxiing off, lifting like a moth in the moonlight on its flight back to England.

Simple.

Or she could have been parachuted in. Surely her father, if he had chosen to cooperate, could have arranged that with Churchill.

But Aaron Jacobi, asleep this moment in his bed in London, presumably peacefully asleep, had no knowledge that she wasn't secure in her own room two doors down the corridor and wouldn't know differently until the morning when the letter, or note—it had been purposely brief—would face him on his breakfast tray. *Terribly sorry, Papa. Must go down my own road. Will be very careful. A big kiss to Mother. S.*

She had no idea how Aaron Jacobi would take it; indeed, what options did he have? With luck, in the morning, when he'd read the note, she'd be in France.

Tonight that seemed as far as the moon.

Jonathan Court had driven her to the village just beyond Dartmouth, cursing himself for being such a damn fool as to cooperate in this insane affair. He would hold himself responsible for the rest of his life if anything happened to her. And if it didn't, it would be a bloody miracle! Besides which, of course, for the stunts he had pulled, military execution was too lenient. He'd by hanged by his testicles.

She leaned over and kissed Jonathan on the lips, told him for the umpteenth time what a dear he was, that it was going to be lonely in France without him. And in a way she wasn't lying; he *was* a dear, and she *was* extremely fond of him, even though with that Guardsman's mustache set above his honest, flawless face he didn't look as if anything but gears

31

and levers functioned inside. Not at all true. Jonathan was actually reasonably emotional, wept at the news of the death of old army pals, kept trying to bed Sara with cheerful determination, and did not lose his good humor when sent home with his colors struck. He was obviously held in high esteem by his superiors at his office at Whitehall, and, witness tonight, was not above sticking his neck out for the woman he loved.

He had insisted on this route. If the journey across the Channel was far longer from Dartmouth, it definitely offered safer passage. The Dover-Dieppe line, while shorter, held the danger of constant surveillance by German patrol boats, as well as by the Luftwaffe.

The two Breton fishermen risking the voyage had been promised very good money—Sara had given Jonathan an enormous bundle to disperse as needed—but this in no way sweetened their attitude toward their passenger. Why in hell did she want to go back to France? Was she a teenage Mata Hari?

The skipper stowed in a locker the one bag she had brought aboard, thrust a heavy yellow slicker at her, and motioned toward a slatted cockpit seat. With the clanking engine throttled, the Breton then transacted his business with a patently miserable Jonathan bundled in coat and scarf alongside his battered Humber which, for all its faithful service, looked far more fit to withstand the elements than the open dory. A thick envelope in his hand, the skipper then jumped back aboard, and they were away, toward the harbor's mouth, Sara able to throw no more than a desperate farewell wave to the man on the quay.

Jonathan answered with a quick jerk of his arm and a melancholy grin, willing to bet he would never see her again.

For the next several hours Sara shared that view.

At dawn, they had barely passed Guernsey, a dirty-gray sky overhead, the Channel still a hostile, battering force. Luckily for them, the skipper told Sara, having lost some of his surliness, once they were under way few Nazi patrol ships would range this far south in such foul weather, and patrol planes were not likely to be cruising overhead.

They gave her a pail, but she confounded them by

disdaining it. Sara was a reasonably good sailor, although there were moments when she was not sure she could hold out.

But at midmorning, to Sara's astonishment, the long, wide-open boat chugged past the occupied battlements of St. Malo and tied up to a stone wharf at the small town of Dinard, across the water abreast an incoming high tide.

Stiff-legged and numb with cold, Sara stumbled onto the wharf and turned to thank the men who had brought her. She had no chance; the little boat was already backing away, losing itself in the sea traffic beginning to develop behind them.

"Your name, please," the woman said.

She had materialized beside Sara out of the cold, raw morning. She was dumpy and wore a floppy hat, under which Sara could see a Breton's red-cheeked face. The eyes, clear as a child's, were examining Sara with unabashed curiosity.

"Marie Courbel."

"I'm Madame Procat. Let's get out of here. We're completely exposed." Turning, the woman plodded up the stone landing, then turned up the long road toward the town, which sat peering down at them.

Sara had been in Dinard once with the family, years before. Facing St. Malo across the estuary of the Rance, it had been a pre-war favorite of British weekenders. While hardly rivaling the Riviera towns in weather, its fine position on the cape, its gray stone-houses, tennis clubs, casino, long, wide beaches, its holiday-oriented visitors had given it a scintillating, light-hearted air.

Now Sara saw it empty and melancholy, the only humans in sight, a pack of children in swimsuits and heavy sweaters, a handful of men busy with the boats below.

Madame Procat, if that was her real name, was hardly out of breath when, after passing the Grand Hotel, they reached another small, disreputable Victorian hotel—all balconies and fluted embellishments and badly in need of paint. HÔTEL RIVAGE, the sign said.

Inside, Madame Procat made for the desk without

delay. A woman who could have been her twin appeared from an inside doorway, crossed to the counter, and unceremoniously shoved a register at Sara to sign.

"And your papers, please," the woman said.

Handing over her ID, bending to sign, Sara paused.

A soldier had emerged from an elevator across from them. Freshly shaven, in a field-gray uniform, he nodded pleasantly at the woman behind the desk.

"Good morning, Frau Ricard," he said in quite reasonable French.

"Good morning, Corporal."

He almost stopped at the sight of Sara, looking her over brazenly.

"Good morning, Fräulein."

She managed a nod.

Jauntily he was at the exit and gone.

Sara turned back to the register. It had been her first German. She felt slightly sick but at the same time strengthened. Men were men; she'd manage.

With a firm hand she signed "Marie Courbel" and took the wooden-handled key the woman gave her.

Turning to ask Madame Procat what the next step would be, she saw her headed for the door. Pivoting back to the desk, she could see the other woman disappearing into the office.

Carrying her valise, Sara entered the elevator cage and was rocketed to the second floor.

Eighteen was the corridor's end.

Waiting there for her in the room, as tall and big-boned as her Breton fisherman, but older, stood a man, his great frame half-blotting out the window light. Sara's heart lurched. Then he turned. Prince Kilkanov.

So Aaron Jacobi had smelled it out, she knew at once, had bowed to the inevitable, working all along with Jonathan Court—the deceitful bastard!

For a moment her fury at both of them overwhelmed her.

Then, with a laugh, she called, "Mischa!" and rushed forward like a child into his arms.

House 71 : June 1945

HAVING SENT WORD to Munich about the find at the Goering chalet—he had understood the statue had been recovered by the French (a puzzler!)—asking for a special detail to remove it as quickly as possible, Goldfarb also requested some historical information on the Winged Victory. He was sure of the details but felt he ought to play it safe.

Word came back that a team would be dispatched the following morning to take the statue back to the main repository. Received, in addition, was the following brief summary:

Victory of Samothrace, considered the greatest masterpiece of Hellenistic sculpture. The Goddess (or Nike) looks as though she has just descended from the prow of a ship. The wings spread wide and the figure leans forward against powerful head winds that whip the folds of her garment.

Discovered in 1863 by the French Consul Champoisseau, it is ascribed to a Rhodes sculptor of the second century B.C., Pythokritos. The left wing, right breast and pedestal are restorations. About eight feet in height, the statue is sculpted in Parian marble, from the Island of Paras, located in the Aegean sea.

Ernst Kröler swore he had no knowledge of it, claiming he hadn't the faintest idea how Goering had stolen it or how it had come to be hidden in the gymnasium.

Obviously a lie.

Goldfarb, having discussed strategy with Captain Packard, decided to play the waiting game, turning the questions to Goering's Paris activities.

"In the beginning," Kröler said agreeably, "it was, as you can imagine, mostly a matter of organization. Alfred Rosenberg was in charge for the Führer, nominally General von Banheim for the Reichsmarschall, although my participation was, of course, crucial.

"The great Jewish collections were seized at once. These collections were taken to an annex of the Louvre, the Jeu de Paume. You know it well, I'm sure, the small museum at the near side of the Tuileries, facing the place de la Concorde. It was used by us as a storage and shipping depot. Virtually every important work of art that passed through our hands was first evaluated at the Jeu de Paume, photographed there, then shipped on to Germany."

"What personnel did you use for the job?" asked Packard.

"German art experts, a few young French curators we considered friendly to us, some of our troops, even Jewish labor in the shipping department."

"The French, I'm told, had emptied the Louvre proper before your arrival."

Kröler laughed. "What do you suppose? When we arrived in Paris the cupboard was bare. The treasures of the Louvre had long before been crated and trucked down to secret hiding places, mostly in the châteaux of the Loire Valley. But I'll tell you something: Reichsmarschall Goering was nobody's fool. Months before the war even started he had our people in Paris. Undercover men. When we arrived we *knew* where everything was hidden. Every single piece we cared about!"

"Including the Winged Victory?" asked Goldfarb.

Kröler looked at him with contempt.

"Including the Winged Victory, Lieutenant. Along with the Venus de Milo and the cream of world painting and sculpture. The sculpture, which seems to interest you so much, was stored at a château south of Tours—Valençay."

"Why didn't you just drive down and scoop it up?"

"Because, Captain," said Kröler dryly, "Valençay was in unoccupied France, nominally under the jurisdiction of the Vichy government. There was, of course, an even more important consideration: if Operation

Sea Lion, the invasion of England, was to take place, it was vital that the French fleet at Toulon be available to us, or at the very least, neutralized. The Vichy government, whatever you may think of it, made the decision to use the fleet as a *quid pro quo*. Plunder the National Art, they told us, and all discussions concerning the fleet would be terminated at once. Hitler had no choice."

"Or Goering," put in Goldfarb.

"Or Goering," nodded Kröler.

They were in the dining room of House 71. Sunlight flooded in through the windows, burnishing the oak of the table into gold. Kröler sipped at his coffee. "But Goering wouldn't be stopped," he said quietly, remembering.

"How was that?" asked Goldfarb, pouring more hot coffee from the ceramic pot into Kröler's cup.

"He couldn't stand the idea of all that superb art down there, just out of his reach. Drove him crazy. So we plotted to get it, Goering, Hans Raeder, and I."

"Sergeant Hans Raeder?" asked Packard, consulting his notes. "Oh, yes, a young soldier Goering relied on for technical advice. One of your assistants."

"Oh, much more than that," said Kröler. "Sergeant Raeder was more important than that. Yes, Captain, believe me, Raeder was key."

Three

SERGEANT RAEDER BELIEVED in giving complete satisfaction. And thus far, he had done well for himself. In the back of the bureau in his comfortable suite on the top floor of the Hotel Hamilton, rue de Rivoli, a small but elegant hostelry formerly a haven for English tourists, he had taped a leather pouch containing two hundred thousand marks, with plenty more to fatten the pouch on the way.

Raeder had, of course, to observe the limitations of his rank. *This is my disguise, my armor,* he thought with satisfaction. Who among his superiors could be jealous of a lowly sergeant? Who in the Gestapo, should it ever come to that, would even bother to observe the comings and goings of someone so unimportant? Excused from ordinary military duties and petty details, yes; otherwise a very faithful servant of the Reichsmarschall's, a dutiful clerk annotating the acquisitions along with dozens of other clerks, a well-greased cog in the machinery.

In some respects he suffered.

Rarely could he allow himself to be seen in the finer restaurants. He could not be permitted the pleasure of frequenting the expensive bordellos; for that matter he couldn't even be caught escorting any of those elegant and expensive women up to his rooms; that was the kind of thing that could draw attention like a lighted window in a blackout.

At all times he had to present the picture of a mediocre drone when actually underneath lived a virile athlete who had barely been beaten out for the saber championship of his university at Leipzig.

Take, for instance, the morning meeting on Goering's train. Le Brun's cool, controlled responses to the Reichsmarschall had infuriated Raeder. With rank, Raeder would have kicked his balls in. He had taken an instant and visceral dislike to the Frenchman. It wasn't simply a question of nationality. And, from what Raeder had been able to gather from dealers around Paris, Le Brun was considered thoroughly professional. It was that subtle air of superiority that outraged the sergeant, perhaps because in him it seemed natural, inbred.

Raeder hardly thought of himself as a peasant: his father had been an affluent merchant, a man with titled friends. No, Raeder knew damn well what it was that pissed him off about the Frenchman: it was Le Brun's woman!

Her name was Mallou. She was the star of Chez Jeannot, Paris' most popular *boîte*. Jeannot, a talented entrepreneur of indefinite sex, had no bias against men in *any* uniform, and every night those who could afford the astronomical tab jammed the tiny club. Once Kröler had made Raeder put on civilian clothes and had taken him along. Raeder still couldn't get that night out of his mind. She was tall, with jet-black hair worn to the shoulders, and eyes just as black that burned out of her white, satiny skin. She was perfect, Raeder thought, beautifully built, with gorgous legs, completely revealed by a daring dress, split to the thigh, and encased in the sheerest of silk stockings. In a low, throaty voice, Mallou sang songs of forsaken love like Piaf, but with more elegance; there was nothing of the Paris waif in Mallou.

As they had left Chez Jeannot's that night, a number of brandies after her act was finished, they saw Mallou with a companion. She was climbing into a long, open car. Kröler saw it was an Hispano-Suiza; and the owner, Mallou's escort, was a Frenchman, Claude Le Brun.

Raeder hadn't the slightest notion who Le Brun was then, nor did he care, even when Le Brun and Kröler exchanged brief greetings; all Raeder had eyes for was Mallou. There was something at once sensual and arrogant about her—the kind of woman he'd like to have in his bed.

He thought it fate, leaving the Gare de l'Est this morning, that the man Goering had ordered put under surveillance was Le Brun. But what made his blood race—what made him abandon his usual caution, gunning the staff car out of the yards on that wet, rutted road—was where the assignment promised to take him—to the woman. And, depending on what was going on—if she and Le Brun were involved in something threatening to the Reich—he, Raeder, would gladly show that long-legged bitch a trick or two. . . .

The rain had almost stopped when he reached the place de la Concorde. He turned his car over to the doorman of the Hôtel Crillon. Standing at the northwestern end of the great place, the Crillon had been almost completely taken over by Wehrmacht staff. Only a few old French clients were allowed to retain their quarters.

Accosted by the duty officer at a desk in the lobby, Raeder found himself going through the familiar routine, flashing the letter from Goering that practically accorded him general officer status. The duty officer read the letter twice before reluctantly nodding to the armed soldiers blocking the area.

Elevator to the fifth floor.

The sergeant on duty, recognizing Raeder, waved him on by.

Right turn to General von Banheim's suites.

Colonel Bocke, von Banheim's adjutant, said, "No, Sergeant. Apologies, but the general is indisposed. May I help you?"

The general, Raeder could see through the French windows opening onto the terrace, was having a late breakfast with a lady. Von Banheim, considered one of the most handsome of the occupiers, with a perpetual Riviera tan, was in a silk dressing gown; the lady wore something chic but warmer. The awning had been drawn over the terrace, which gave a magnificent view of Cleopatra's Needle, the Chamber of Deputies, the Jeu de Paume, and Paris traffic which, even in these perilous times, was brisk.

Envying von Banheim, not so much his view, but his lifestyle, Raeder told Bocke what he needed. Bocke made notes with a small gold pencil as Raeder explained.

"Don't worry about it," Bocke said, closing his notebook with a snap. "This office is a model of efficiency. By the way, we hear Herr Goering is in town."

Raeder helped himself from a cigarette box on a coffee table. The suite had just been redone for von Banheim and was resplendent with its red damask wallpaper and antique furnishings.

"Very much in town," said Raeder. Colonel Bocke had long ago come to terms with Raeder's real status; the two men found it to their mutual advantage to cooperate.

"When?" asked Bocke.

"My guess is around two o'clock. Jeu de Paume."

"The general will be there."

"He'd better be."

"Not easy to get him away from that one," Bocke said with a sigh, indicating the terrace. Raeder wished he could see her face; all he could tell was that she was young, blond, and had a long, lovely neck.

Bocke referred once more to his notebook.

"I gather the Reichsmarschall considers this assignment important. Who is this Le Brun?"

Raeder shrugged. "Another art dealer."

"I see. Well, *au revoir*."

"Heil Hitler," said Raeder.

Four

RETURNING FROM A MEETING with Ernst Kröler on the details of the Jacobi transfer, Le Brun tiptoed through the bedroom and into his dressing room to change; for the rest of the day an old pair of slacks and a comfortable shirt would do. Once the rain stopped it would be hot and muggy. He hated Paris in August.

But, despite his care, on his way out he awakened her.

She sat up at once, not bothering to pull the sheet up around her. Rarely did Mallou do anything without intending to, so that caught in the morning light filtering through the yellow voile curtains, her hair cascading down, breasts high, firm, ripe, she presented the picture she wanted; let Le Brun resist it!

"Where are you going?"

"To market, my sweet."

"To buy me what?"

"To buy you your heart's desire!"

He smiled at her; she didn't return it. "You left before it was even light. Woke me up. Where have you been?"

"I'm sorry, *chérie*," he said quietly, standing by the bed.

"I don't like what you're doing. I don't like your friends. You should stay out of it."

He shrugged.

She regarded him for a long moment, then beckoned toward the cigarettes on the nighttable. He reached for one, lit it for her with his Cartier lighter, gave it to her.

She took a long, deep puff, surveying him sadly. "You'll get caught one day. They'll stand you up against a wall and shoot you. You'll bleed ice water."

"I don't know where you get all those ideas. My friends are perfectly innocent. Painters. Artists—mostly bad ones. Even a few shopkeepers who happen to sell amateur paintings. You mustn't imagine I'm involved in what you're thinking." He sat on a corner of the bed, his face smilingly impenetrable. "Thoughts like that are not only dangerous to me, they can involve you. You're too smart not to know where they can lead."

His amiability did not fool her. Abruptly, Mallou pushed away the sheets and on her knees was across the bed, at his side. "Don't go yet, Claude."

He hesitated, got to his feet, bent to kiss her, draping the sheet around her again. "We'll make up for everything tonight. I promise. You're the most beautiful woman in France."

He seemed enormously tall, looking down at her. "I've an appointment with Georges to smooth out the transmission of the Hispano. And you know how tough it is these days to get Georges even to answer the phone."

She was furious, yet somehow she covered it up with a short laugh. "Jesus Christ!"

He appeared oblivious. He kissed her again and left.

She knew damn well it wasn't the Hispano. They had been together over a year, and although he was gentle and loving she couldn't get inside him, not for one goddamned minute. He gave what he wanted to give, not one iota more. "You and that *merde* of a car!" she shouted. "That's all you've got, Le Brun. That car and a cock!"

He might have been grinning, she couldn't tell, but

he was out of the bedroom before she could be more insulting. He hadn't even bothered to look back.

The Hispano was parked on the street below his apartment on the avenue Montaigne, close to the Rond Point of the Champs-Elysées.

Le Brun started up, as always appreciating the latent power there at his disposal, even though he was feeding the gas slowly, watching the RPM build on his tachometer before moving from the curb. The problem with the car wasn't the transmission, which was smooth as silk, but one of an environmental mismatching; this machine was designed for long, hard, fast runs on country roads, not for the stop and go and puny speeds of the city. He would have to take Mallou for a drive, maybe Sunday when Chez Jeannot was closed. Beg a special exit permit from Kröler. Let it out! Hit the floor with it!

As he pulled out slowly into traffic, checking his sideview mirror, a black Citroën edged into the street behind him.

On the rue St. Honoré, he saw that the Citroën was still following, having allowed several other vehicles to intervene.

Not a very good job of tailing, Le Brun decided: he had been remarkably free of surveillance until the Goering meeting on the train. With the embrace had come what? The kiss of death? He hardly thought so. Routine, more likely. *Make sure the new boy is firmly on our side.*

The rain had stopped. The sky over the city was a decidedly less ominous gray with a splash of pink visible in the west, which was clearing rapidly. *It could be a bomber's night,* he thought irrelevantly. *London again? Mother of God!*

Past Châtelet, the Hôtel de Ville still nominally in French hands. *Goddamn vipers!* He swung left, then right, then abruptly into the gaping black entrance of a sizable garage.

Georges, jockey-sized, eagle-beaked, cleaning his hands on cotton batting, emerged grinning out of the gloom.

"Le Brun! How goes it?"

"Followed," said Le Brun, climbing out of the Hispano.

Georges looked sharply at Le Brun. "No problem,"
he said. "Henri!"

A mechanic in filthy overalls, at least three times
Georges' size, straightened from under the hood of a
car and plodded over. Georges jerked a shoulder toward the street. Henri nodded, walking Le Brun to the
garage entrance where the two stood a moment in
plain sight, Le Brun making gestures that could be
interpreted as an ordinary dialogue between mechanic
and car owner.

"The Citroën three cars up," said Henri after a second. "The man with the ferret face and the tan raincoat. I can smell the bastard from here."

"You're probably right," said Le Brun, not looking
right or left.

"You want him taken to lunch?"

"*I'm* going to lunch," said Le Brun. "I want him to
think you're checking out the carburetor during that
time. And by the way, it could use checking out. You
did a lousy job last week."

Henri laughed. "I could take care of him easily.
One less *Boche!* Good deed for the day."

"Stick to the carburetor," said Le Brun.

On the other side of the garage was La Grandmère,
chosen because of its proximity and because, at the
time, there wasn't a better eating place in Paris.

Le Brun left Henri, walking openly to the restaurant. Only three tables were occupied. No Germans,
but it was barely noon. Vernet, the proprietor, greeted
Le Brun with just the right degree of warmth. "Your
reservation is upstairs today," he said, indicating a
flight of stairs to the rear. "But you prefer it there, I
remember. Quieter."

"Exactly, Vernet. Thank you."

Vernet led the way up the creaking stairs to a small
salon with room for only a handful of tables. Two men
were seated in a corner waiting.

Vernet retreated and Le Brun made his way to the
men, shaking hands soberly.

One, Arnaud, he had expected. Arnaud looked like
a scaled-down giraffe, neck towering over a stick of a

44

body and a too-large head. He had just returned from England, and appeared to be having a little trouble getting around.

The second man was Garnier, a deputy of the director of the National Museums of France. Garnier was slightly older than Le Brun, darkly handsome with an imperious manner that did not help him in certain patriotic circles, especially since he had decided to remain on as an important functionary in the Vichy government. Until this moment, in fact, Le Brun himself had not been sure where Garnier stood.

Apparently Garnier had been no more sure of him. With a gesture toward Arnaud, Garnier said, "Happy to see you here, Claude."

"We're all overjoyed to see each other," growled Arnaud. "Order something, Le Brun, and for God's sake let's get down to business."

A waiter appeared and Le Brun asked for the house specialty, *coquilles Mephistopheles,* heard Garnier congratulate him on taking over the Jacobi firm. "But it will automatically put you in my category," Garnier commented. "They'll tag you a collaborationist."

Le Brun shrugged, tasting the Pouilly Fuissé the waiter had poured.

"In any case," he said, "the Delacroix did the trick."

"If you think it was easy getting it for you—had to put an armlock on a certain curator," Garnier answered, grinning.

"I wish you two would stop congratulating each other," said Arnaud. "Garnier, tell him the other news."

"Rosenberg, egged on by Goering, is demanding a trade of a hundred pieces of art," Garnier said.

"Trade?" Le Brun asked, eyebrows raised.

"Call it what you want. We 'lend' them a hundred of our best, La Joconde, Vénus de Milo, Winged Victory, et cetera: they 'lend' us a hundred of *their* best. But I've seen their list. Hardly recognized anything. Junk!"

"And Vichy?"

Arnaud answered for Garnier. "So far Vichy has refused. But Vichy is losing patience with us. We're a bit too—"

"Chauvinistic," stated Garnier flatly. "Of course they still have the fleet as a bargaining weapon, but they'd prefer to use it to retain other favors. The truth is, Vichy is not very art-minded. Naturally I've warned the old man that once that art leaves France, it's the last we see of it. Loan, my ass!"

"Will Pétain back you?"

"For the time being, yes."

"What can I do?" asked Le Brun.

A thin wry smile. "You'll constitute our number one listening post close to Goering," said Garnier. "Although I'm sure Arnaud here has additional jobs in mind. I'll be playing for time, sending a man to Berlin for another list, begging for more prestigious works."

Arnaud stared moodily into his wineglass; Le Brun sipped at his.

It was the constant fear of everyone associated with the National Art, Le Brun knew, that finally the Nazis would simply cross into unoccupied France with a division of troops, a dozen convoys, and grab everything—all of it, the nation's treasure.

The waiter arrived with their food. The three did not let their apprehensions spoil their excellent lunch. They dug in hungrily.

When Le Brun returned to the garage, Henri was slamming down the hood of the Hispano and Georges, in his glass-framed office, was drinking red wine. In the back of the shop another mechanic was working with a heavy wrench at an engine block and swearing steadily.

Georges didn't intend to be disturbed. He waved and went on drinking. Henri came around, his hands black with grease. "Enjoy your lunch? Did anyone tell you about La Grandmère? Last week a customer found a rattail in the potage."

"Don't be cute," said Le Brun. "What about the *Boche?*"

"Would you believe it, you weren't gone two minutes before he drives in. Asks how much we charge for a tuneup. Georges tells him, but his eyes are busy everywhere. Doesn't do him much good. I'm really working on your fuckin' car. Pretty smooth now, by the way."

"My profound thanks."

"Only one thing."

"What's that?"

"The bastard isn't German—he's one of us."

Henri was suddenly serious. So the man was an undercover agent for the Milice, the police force organized by Vichy in collaboration with the invaders. No group in occupied France was more despised.

"He's parked around the corner," added Henri. "Waiting for you to continue your afternoon jaunt."

Georges came out of his booth. "Hey, Le Brun," he said. "We don't mind little favors for old friends, but next time you've got somebody on your ass, don't drop 'em off here. Agreed?"

"Agreed," said Le Brun. "What do I owe you for the work?"

"Nothing," said Georges. "We drained your gasoline tank; you've got just enough to get home."

There was a station behind La Madeleine that sold gasoline to people with the privileged cards—top Vichy officials, doctors, a few like Le Brun with special authorization from the military government in Paris. Le Brun barely made it and had the tank filled to the top.

The black Citroën was still tailing him as he proceeded up boulevard Haussmann, then across the Etoile to avenue Foch, where he parked.

The Jacobi mansion looked deserted, its great doors securely bolted. There weren't many private dwellings left on this part of the wide avenue, mostly elegant apartment buildings with some embassies.

Having pushed the call button, Le Brun waited. He knew he could be observed from a window on the top floor over the garage as well as from a peephole in the exterior gates.

It was a strange August in Paris, the traditional summer exodus canceled by the Occupation. People grumbled and made the best of it. They swarmed over the Bois de Boulogne; they sunbathed along the muddy, swirling Seine; they made small expeditions into the countryside, hoping to coax a scrawny chicken or a bag of potatoes from a farmer cousin. Anything to break the monotony of the ubiquitous rutabaga, the everyday substance of their diets.

Traffic this afternoon on the avenue Foch was light. Buses, an occasional private car, some military vehicles. Trucks with wood-burning attachments in the rear. Nearby, on avenue Victor-Hugo, people strolled still; the habit of "window-licking" was born in the Parisian, but the boutiques had only a fraction of their pre-war riches. Paris, Le Brun observed sadly, was like Marguérite, Lady of the Camelias, still very beautiful despite her illness, but slowly coughing herself to the grave.

A voice came at him from nowhere, actually a microphone hidden behind the immense brass door pulls. "Walk to the garage, Mr. Le Brun," it commanded.

A Judas door opened suddenly and Mischa appeared, cadaverous and shiny bald to his sideburns, but with a vigor that gave the lie to his beleaguered face. As always he was dressed in his butler's black bombazine with an immaculate starched shirt and a white bow tie. Mischa was the Prince Kilkanov, a world-class bridge player. He had been Aaron Jacobi's bridge partner for ten years; he was also major-domo of the household.

Mischa was distantly polite to Le Brun; he had already made clear where his loyalty lay. He would have signed the proverbial pact with the devil to have accompanied the Jacobis into, for him, a second exile. But the Princess Kilkanov had been incapacitated for years, confined to a wheelchair, and could not travel.

Now Mischa—no one associated with the Jacobis would have thought of addressing him by his title— led the way through another exit into the front courtyard and up the wide steps into the house. Closing the framed plate glass doors, he waited expressionless while Le Brun, caught by a sudden whim, moved inside the central reception area to stand at the foot of the grand staircase, gazing up as if waiting for someone to appear on the steps above. Le Brun seemed to break out of a cocoon of painful memories. Then he turned to Mischa. "It has just become official. I'm taking over the Jacobi Galleries."

"Official?"

"Here's a copy of the order. Naturally it includes this house."

"I'll be out of here tonight." Mischa announced at once.

Harshly Le Brun said, "You'll stay and run things for me. For when they return."

"You really expect me to believe they're coming back? And if they do, that there'll be anything left to collect?"

"It's not impossible."

"You tell me so."

"You're a fool," said Le Brun coldly. "Would you prefer that the family interests be managed by a stranger? A Nazi?"

"Better," said Mischa with scorn, "than you."

"Think what you like. I'll double your salary. You'll be able to pay for your wife's medical bills. You'll both be able to eat, along with half the Russian colony in Paris."

Mischa studied Le Brun calmly. The Russian had lived through many disasters. He was indeed a card-player, who was rarely without alternative moves. *You've trumped me.* Le Brun could almost hear the wheels turning. *But don't count me out. The game isn't over!*

"What about the staff?" Mischa finally asked; it was the closest he could come to verbal acquiescence.

"How many at present?"

"Three with the cook. Four with the gardener."

"Keep them on. I'll be moving in tomorrow with a friend. And, my dear Prince Kilkanov . . ."

"Yes?"

"I don't give a goddamn how much you hate me. I want obedience and impeccable service. Do we understand one another?"

Sunlight streaming through from a painted glass dome above them highlighted Mischa's Slavic cheekbones, the ice-blue eyes. He straightened, his beaten face abruptly younger. "Yes, master."

"I'll want an inventory of everything in the place."

"Naturally," said Mischa.

The beautiful paintings had been removed from the walls, as well as most of the first floor furnishings; it was remarkable how empty it made the Jacobi mansion look. Le Brun had been there briefly the week before to leave money for the servants, but had not had the time for a thorough tour. Now he marched doggedly from room to room, trying to evoke the spirit of times past, of the family. It was not easy. He kept hearing voices, not certain they weren't his own invention.

It had always been more than an ordinary house, of course; Aaron Jacobi had bought it from the daughter of one of Napoleon's generals. Very occasionally, Aaron would bring special clients here, once even a king, several times American "royalty," to consummate particularly lucrative deals.

Aaron Jacobi's success was made up of a superb eye for the best art and a master salesman's subtle skill. No one buying an expensive painting from him was sure that Jacobi wanted to get rid of it.

Le Brun's first meeting with Aaron was from the opposite point of view. Guy, Claude's brother, declaring a temporary cash shortage—the family was in wine near Troyes—decided to sell an heirloom, a painting by Géricault of a stallion that had belonged to the family's racing stable many years ago. As a recent graduate of the Beaux-Arts, an art historian, if just as knowledgeable of the more obvious joys of Paris, Claude was given the job of making overtures to some preselected dealers.

"What I want to know," Guy told him, "is just how much we can pick up in cash. Only one thing—"

"Yes, Guy."

"Don't conclude any deal until I approve."

Claude wouldn't have expected to, was in fact flattered that Guy trusted him this much. Guy was years older, head of the clan since their father's death, and Claude, although fighting him tooth and nail as a child, had come to respect him. If Guy was more conservative, his responsibility was great. He had a wife, children, a mistress; he had friends in high places. Being the younger brother of Count Guy Le Brun was no small *cachet*.

Aaron Jacobi was the third dealer Claude approached. The figures named by the first two were not far apart, in the area of fifty thousand francs. The painting had been on loan to museums; it had a known value.

The Jacobi Gallery was on the avenue Matignon. It specialized in the major Impressionists. The story went that Aaron Jacobi had seized on them before anyone, thus making his fortune. The story was apocryphal. Jacobi's father had become rich decades earlier dealing in antiquities; Aaron had used the available capital to buy all periods of art at rock-bottom prices, holding until the market soared.

A small, graceful man with a salt and pepper Vandyke, he honored the Le Brun name by having Claude ushered to an upstairs office, a working office really, with stacked canvases and much litter, where he had the Géricault placed on an easel. While hardly seeming to examine it, Jacobi kept up a gentle patter, asking Claude questions about himself, his schooling, his ambitions.

Claude had no ambitions to speak of. He considered being a Le Brun sufficient. He would have liked to be an artist if he hadn't discovered early on that his talent was limited. He lived for beauty in every form. He thought no one could do better than fashioning an existence designed to appreciate it. *Someday,* he thought, *I might open an art gallery of my own.* He said as much to Aaron Jacobi.

"Beauty," replied Jacobi, "can pall."

"How can a man like you say such a thing?"

Jacobi looked from the easel to Claude. Jacobi didn't usually waste time handing out platitudes to wet-behind-the-ears aristocrats.

"Because," said Jacobi, "there are times when beauty becomes unreal, when the soul hungers for rough texture, the shock of ugliness. Because—and I'm beginning to sound pompous—beauty can lie—like this picture!" He made a violent sweeping gesture at the painting. "You're either a poor student or a clumsy thief. Géricault never touched a brush to this canvas!"

Shocked to silence, throttling his anger, Claude stepped close to the easel. Gradually, as he cooled, he

51

began to see things he hadn't before—a small distortion in the foreleg of the horse; here and there a lighter brushstroke than Géricault's usual; other variations. In one corner the paint was thin, almost transparent. Suddenly it became clear to him, too. No, not a Géricault!

Unable to look Jacobi in the face, mumbling a goodbye, he seized the framed canvas, and hurried out of the office, down the stairs.

When he reached the family house in Montparnasse, his sister-in-law told him that Guy was at the racetrack.

There was a locked closet in the library, where for a hundred years the Le Bruns had kept their treasures. Lacking a key, Claude found a hammer and chisel, and heedless of the damage to the old oak paneling, pried open the door. In the back of the deep closet, along with old and broken bric-a-brac, objets d'art long ago forgotten, was a Géricault—the authentic one. Claude filled a tumbler with cognac and waited for Guy to come home.

Guy had had a bad day at the track, but as soon as he entered the library and saw the two "Géricaults" placed side by side against the wall, he began to laugh. "Well, goodbye to a thousand francs," he said. "That's what that genius painter friend of yours stuck me for the copy."

"Paul Dosser?"

"That's the one."

"Dosser's good," said Claude. "Only not good enough." Picking up the Géricault on the right, the original, Claude started off with it.

Guy bellowed, "Where the hell do you think you're going with that? Come back!"

"Go fuck yourself!" Claude shouted to him.

With one exception, he saw his brother again only at funerals.

The Jacobi Gallery on the avenue Matignon was closed by the time Claude got there, but the Jacobi residence on the avenue Foch had once been pointed out to him. He directed the taxi driver to it. Upon stating his business to a butler who spoke French with an

52

atrocious Russian accent, Claude was ushered into a salon off the central foyer.

A pair of exquisite Fouquets were on the wall, but what impressed Claude was the noise in the house. Someone was playing or practicing the piano, not bad at all, Mozart . . . a girl's voice was busy detailing an injustice at school, while, it seemed, its owner ran up and down the stairs that dominated the entrance. Elsewhere, protesting voices—women, and a man trying hard to be firm about something.

Are all Jewish houses like this? Claude wondered.

Aaron Jacobi entered the salon without warning. He hadn't changed a bit since the afternoon except that he was wearing a beautifully cut blue velvet smoking jacket. Everything he wore, Claude learned later, was made to order by Sulka, including his socks. He was smoking a cigarette in an ivory holder stained yellow with age. Apparently he held nothing against Claude. "What can I do for you this time, young man?"

Claude lifted the Géricault, holding it in front of him. "Please examine it carefully. You may have this one at your own price."

Jacobi looked, a single swift glance, then back to Claude.

"How much were you offered for the other?"

"Fifty thousand."

"And if I offered you twenty-five for this?"

"It would be yours."

"For God's sake, put it down there on the bench! I'll give you fifty-five."

Two girls, one about fourteen, with a chestnut braid and the face of a *gamine,* the other perhaps eleven, with long black hair, very solemn, stood in the doorway of the salon, staring unabashedly at Claude. A giggle from the older and they were gone; he couldn't be sure he had even seen them.

"Well?" asked Jacobi.

"Sold, of course, but you're paying too much."

"Don't worry about it. I'll get rid of it to an American for a hundred thousand. And he won't be cheated."

"May I apologize for my behavior this afternoon? You must believe me, I didn't know . . ."

Impatiently, Jacobi waved him silent. "Will a check in the morning be all right?"

"Certainly."

"Listen, Le Brun, I'm opening a branch in Rio. I'll have to send personnel there, which means I'll be short-handed here, at Matignon. Could use an apprentice like you. That's of course if you have any intention of working for a living."

"I hadn't decided my future plans," said Claude, "but it's kind of you to—"

"Think it over," Jacobi said. "No hurry. You know, looking at this Géricault again, I find it does not stir my blood. I realize perhaps I have nothing in common with it. Do paintings of racehorses do anything for you?"

The grand salon, stripped bare as a swimming pool, intricately marbled floor, fluted columns gold-gilded, pink angels on the ceiling, looked out past its wide terrace to the garden.

The garden this August day lay under a lowering sky, green, lush, heavy with perfume, stretching on and on, indecently large in the center of Paris.

Mallou would enjoy it, he thought, wandering through its alleys. She was a city woman, but the garden's sheer size, the opulence it suggested, would excite her. Its history. Josephine had once strolled through these gardens. Mallou would enjoy telling her friends that.

He followed a graveled path to a bench that sat behind a row of box hedges, a small, private bower. He had kissed Erica Jacobi here, wondering aloud what her father would think of this—Erica in the embrace not only of a trusted employee but of a gentile.

Snug against him, she had raised her head impishly. "Is that what you think of Aaron Jacobi—a racist? If I love a man and he loves me . . ."

"Did you say you loved a man? Did he say he loved you?"

She had pulled away at once, furious, her small, lovely face frowning. "Look here, Le Brun, nobody is standing over you with a gun. Nobody forced you

54

to kiss me like that just now . . . you're a know-what?"

"What?"

"A conceited, cowardly ravisher of young girls . . . a hit and runner!"

He laughed.

Erica always made him laugh. She was laughing, too, at herself. She folded herself into his arms once again and it was a long time before they broke apart.

Five

IT HAD BEEN in the last stages of the Civil War in Spain, the dark hours, the Republican forces crumbling under the sustained rebel attacks. Erica had just turned twenty, a slim kid with chestnut hair bobbed short, a boy almost, but not a boy—heads turned wherever she went, leggy, bright-eyed, and alert as a thoroughbred filly . . . daughter of Aaron Jacobi, Rothschild intimate, princess of the Rive Gauche, *enfant terrible* . . .

Political. No one could guess how much money she had wheedled out of Aaron to be siphoned to the comrades in Madrid. The party, she told Le Brun indignantly, would not accept her. Wisely. Don't tempt fate, don't anger the old man. So far he'd been tolerant, the golden child would grow out of it; meanwhile Jacobi suffered her (their) hand in his pocket.

Le Brun had picked her up on a late April afternoon at a Left Bank address, rue des Saints-Pères— MARCHÉ, a small, cardboard plaque on the lower landing informed the visitor. A new radical weekly, one of the numerous publications that sprang up in Paris like tropical plants each spring to die out by the end of summer, exhausted by the heat, done in by hidden genetic factors: so many factions, so many young, brilliant, angry protestors. . . .

They ordered apéritifs at Deux Magots while Erica

lazily spun out her story. *Marché* had offered her an editorship but would expect, *évidemment,* a generous contribution.

"They can go fuck themselves," Erica said.

She swore shamelessly. Somehow she equated it with maturity, with freedom.

"I told them that, Le Brun," she said now, giggling. "But they're babies, you know. Really very nice. And they truly believe in the struggle."

"And you will give them something?"

"I don't know. How much more can I bleed Papa, poor dear! And then there are more important causes, aren't there? More important than massaging adolescent egos. Including my own. You agree, *mon vieux?*"

He agreed smilingly, ordering another drink.

Away from her he'd continually rationalize that he *was* really ancient, thirty-one, far too old for her. But in her presence her intelligence, clear as a running stream, occasionally clownish, took over—and the age difference never seemed to matter, was hardly important.

Tilting her glass now, watching the shadows creep slowly toward their table, the chatter around them losing itself in the late-spring twilight, isolating them in a soft, intimate prism, she said, "I'm going to Nice tomorrow."

"Are you? Bravo . . ."

"Very important meeting. The Friends of Free Spain. Dubeucher invited me. André Malraux is flying in from Madrid to speak to us."

"He'll be inspiring."

"Why don't you drive me down?"

He caught her look, the large brown eyes impish, then not amused at all . . . steady, searching. "Look here, little girl . . ."

"Go to hell!"

"All right, big girl. Your father's in London. I don't think he'd jump for joy if his number one assistant ran off unannounced to the south for a holiday."

"And screwed his daughter."

"His barely-of-age daughter."

"You're a goddamn coward, Le Brun. A hypocrite."

"I have not," he stated, "transgressed the forbidden barriers."

"Bull," she said. "And a pure technicality besides."

Diplomatically he maintained silence, clicking the ice in his glass, staring her down.

"I think it's about time," she finally told him, "that you acknowledged certain truths about our relationship."

"Such as?"

"I'm not going to disappear. I'm going to be around."

He put the glass on the table.

"Thank God for that."

"Well, the gentleman *can* speak affirmatively!"

"But that doesn't mean—"

"It does, it does! Or I'll confound you and myself and really go away! I speak from the heart, Le Brun. Be a man and come to Nice with me."

She wore a wispy smile, it hung over her face like a veil of smoke. The smile made him afraid. Perhaps she *would* go away. The thought was intolerable. Suddenly he decided: to hell with her father, to hell with the job, with the difference in years. It all was of absolutely no consequence.

"I've bought that car I was telling you about."

"The Hispano?"

He nodded. "They're putting on new tires. I couldn't possibly pick you up before noon."

Her hand touched his lightly. She turned her young head toward the traffic on the Boul' Mich'; when she looked back he saw tears.

But then, without warning, she was straining upward, calling "Berthe!"

The woman stalking past the sidewalk tables on heels so high her walk was precarious waved back enthusiastically. "Erica!" A few years older than Erica, and undoubtedly a *putain*, but clearly a girl with her mind on her work. Waving graciously again, she was on her way, obviously to an important assignation, but not without bringing wide smiles from the tables around them. It was spring and her passing had heightened its bouquet.

"Isn't she beautiful?" Erica murmured.

They drove all the following afternoon and into the dusk, talking very little, bound together in a chrysalis of fear, anticipation, excitement—Arles for dinner, a bistro along the route, Le Brun eating little, Erica famished, eating for them both.

Le Brun thought to break the journey there.

"No, please," she had begged. "All the way to Nice, tonight—no stops, and a room overlooking the sea. Oh, and with a balcony. You promise, Le Brun?"

"I promise."

The Hispano was in fine condition, a great buy, he decided, delighted with it: its mahogany chassis was waxed to a warm, reddish glow, but more important, its finely tuned engine was responding perfectly to Le Brun's commands. It had belonged, the dealer had sworn, to a Corsican gangster from Marseilles—a drug smuggler. To Erica this gave it, of course, added *cachet*.

On the deserted night highway, Le Brun pushed the car to a crazy speed; the herb-scented Provençal air was a sweet perfume; they sang like idiots with the wind that rode the highway with them.

Triumphant, they pulled into Nice, down the boulevard des Anglais, with dawn unannounced, still lurking beyond the bulk of the Massif, elephantine behind the city.

The hotel room, as promised, had a balcony facing the sea.

Erica hardly noticed.

The next night, not having left the room in the interim, they attended the fund-raising at the municipal auditorium, the place packed with a combination of workers and intellectuals—a healthy distribution, Erica decided. Conundrum: why was the lazy, sun-drenched south, she asked, more loyally to the left than the industrial north?

No time for Le Brun to answer. The crowd was on its feet. On the platform had arrived the dark, handsome man they had come to see, the customary dead cigarette butt clenched between his teeth, as they, traditionally, clenched theirs.

He was not as persuasive in his speech as in his writing, Le Brun thought, but eloquent enough. He spoke of the war, the devastation the Fascist planes had wrought, the agony of the people; he told of the massacre at Guernica, the continuing heroic defense of Madrid. And he called upon them to call upon the Blum government to give aid to the people's army, the proletariat . . . to forego giving even one gun, one bullet to Franco's savage beasts.

A wild acclamation, a forest of raised fists . . .

At the party afterward in a restaurant at the port, Malraux's famous tic close up gave emphasis to his plea to help him raise funds for the planes that could still turn aside Franco's Falangists, could still save the day for democracy . . . Malraux's España air force, the international squadron he himself had set up which had bought time for the International Brigade —an air arm which was now in urgent need of replenishment. "Planes, my friends, planes!"

Erica pledged money of course. *Too much,* Le Brun thought. It wasn't that he didn't support the Loyalists. It was simply that he was a Frenchman. Money was not something you spread carelessly about, not even in the best of times.

Le Brun had been accosted unexpectedly, imprisoned in a corner by a paunchy, self-satisfied fellow named Louguette, a schoolboy chum of his brother Guy, who professed a smug surprise at his being there, a Le Brun supporting this damn potential commissar— imagine it! He and Guy were brothers, Le Brun replied, not necessarily political twins. As a matter of fact, he told Louguette, he himself was thinking of joining the Communist party, enlisting with Malraux in Spain.

This had an unexpected result. Louguette grabbed him by the shoulders, crying, *"Formidable!* I'll enlist with you!"

"We'll arrange it in Paris," Le Brun said, breaking away.

The place was exploding with revolutionary fervor, just short of a brawl. Should France jump in or not?

Erica, Le Brun saw, was standing in a corner with the man of the hour, both with drinks in their hands. Trust her to have captured him, or was it the other way around?

Le Brun recognized that he was suffering from an identifiable malaise: jealousy. An absolutely new, never-before-experienced emotion. Had he never before been in love?

And the little she-devil, spotting him, was now waving him over.

Not as tall as Le Brun, Malraux had a careless elegance, like a slightly down-at-the-heels member of royalty. "Knew your brother Guy," he told Le Brun.

My God, the second time within minutes!

"An idiot," answered Le Brun.

"Agreed," replied Malraux.

They grinned at each other with malicious enjoyment.

But serious again, Malraux spoke more about the war.

A charming man, Le Brun had to admit. The intellectual who had turned words into action, who had dared to bloody his hands in the fray. And what of Le Brun—of all these effete countrymen of theirs who still held back? Nothing actually spoken, no direct criticism, of course, but implicit in the challenge of the voice, in the darting black eyes.

As if aware of the tension, Erica had securely linked her hand in Le Brun's. "You've said that Fascist art, if such exists, leads to the aestheticization of war. Doesn't democratic art, by virtue of necessity, work toward the same end?"

Indignant, his passion burst over them.

"Of course not. Our fight—the cultural aspects of it—is completely different. We want a philosophy, political structures, and a hope that leads to peace, not to war!"

They had begun to dribble out of the restaurant, the union chiefs, the leftist civic leaders who had been given the special invitation to the reception. Almost everyone was drunk, drunk with excitement at the close contact with Malraux, with tales to tell in the morning as revealed to them by their friend Malraux, the tragic deterioration of the Loyalist position, and the desperate need—no crap, Malraux had sworn it —of assistance from France.

A fresh breeze blew across the face of the restaurant as they staggered out, men clogging the area around the doors, the smell of the port carrying over to them.

Le Brun was looking for the Hispano—he had parked it quite a distance down the quay—when the shots rang out. At first Le Brun had considered the noises harmless—balloons being punctured—but had there been any balloons at the reception?

Then he heard the indrawn breath from Erica, a swallowed sob of sorts really, and he turned: Malraux had just come out of the restaurant, and near him one of his unofficial guards was sinking against the façade of the building, blood and gray matter dripping from a head shattered by a bullet.

Several figures plunged forward, shielding Malraux, while a small man in a rumpled suit and close-cropped hair fired a revolver at a Citroën parked obliquely across the street.

Now another man joined the first, a larger gun in his hands, an automatic, Le Brun could see, adding his firepower to the assault.

Moments later, someone burst out of the Citroën, a small, frantic man, firing a pistol as he ran. Several yards of flight and then his chest exploded with blood as he stumbled and fell.

More bullets were now rattling against the side of the Citroën, and a man whose head had been visible in the front seat alongside the driver was no longer in view.

The firing stopped abruptly, the witnesses either prostrate on the sidewalk or on their feet, pressed stupidly for protection against the building wall.

A member of Malraux's bodyguard ran across to the Citroën and flung the door open. A man's head and torso tumbled out, a dark bundle in the semi-darkness.

"Go home, please—everyone go home!" a voice shouted with authority. It was a high-up member of the Nice police who has been a guest at the affair, a tall man with a brush mustache. Le Brun remembered his having stood close to Malraux most of the evening.

Malraux, it could now be seen, was being led off to a limousine not far from the crippled Citroën. He was chatting calmly with the men escorting him, as if what had happened was an everyday occurrence. *Well, in a way, probably it was,* Le Brun had thought at the time. *Even as sensitive a human being as Malraux could be brutalized in some respects by war.* Then Le Brun had decided: *How inane of me!—how can I possibly know what such a man is thinking, how he's reacting in his gut?*

"Le Brun," Erica whispered. "Please take me home."

At the hotel she drank a brandy and then seemed all right. *Erica's made of strong stuff,* he thought.

They discussed what had happened, speculating that the aborted assassination had been plotted by Falangists or Franco sympathizers in the city. How lucky that it had failed: Malraux was a national, perhaps even an international, treasure.

Le Brun tried to joke. Perhaps she was a little too impressed by the man—possibly a small, a very tiny infatuation?

She had been standing by the tall windows opening onto the terrace, but now she turned and put her hands on Le Brun's shoulders. "Listen, Le Brun. I admire him. I admire many men. I love just two, my father and the fool I'm looking at. Maybe one day we'll have a son I can love. But that will never happen if we stand here talking, will it?"

"No," he said.

It was not the same in bed as the previous night, when their lovemaking had been gentle and tentative, Le Brun conscious of her youth, acting despite himself as if he'd brought to bed an infinitely delicate, exotic creature. She, on the other hand, while utterly giving, had seemed fearful of exceeding the bounds of what she obviously considered womanly passivity.

Tonight was different.

The excitement of the Malraux meeting, the shooting, had fired them both: death had been experienced. The torment of a country glimpsed through the eyes of a poet, the end product of that tragedy through their own. They sought to come to grips with the meaning and terror of it; they sought this fiercely with their bodies.

Erica was the surprise. A burning ember, she came at Le Brun, touching, leaving, inciting, all tongue and flame, carrying him upward, farther than he had ever gone, by some magic holding him there, until the climax came for them both, leaving Le Brun wanting her, if it were possible, almost at once, again. And simultaneously furious with her—tricked.

"You're angry?" she asked him, sensing it.

"Yes."

Eyes closed, he was inert on the rumbled bed.

Bending over him, she kissed him lightly on the lips.

She giggled. "Much too experienced, you think."

He did not answer.

"Only a bad little girl, a woman of the streets would—"

"Yes!"

"Le Brun, turn around, look at me. You're my first man. Well, almost. There was André when I was fifteen. Once. It was not what you'd call a memorable occasion."

"I'm hardly interested in your adolescent affairs."

"A month ago I made Berthe a proposition."

"Berthe?"

"We saw her at Deux Magots the other day. The girl—well, you know her profession—gave me several nights a week. Charged me a damn fortune, if you want to know."

He was sitting up, staring at her. "In God's name, to do what?"

"To teach me what men liked, of course! How. All the tricks. Sooner or later I knew you'd weaken, I knew I'd get you. I wanted to be—reasonably okay. To be able to make you happy. Listen, Le Brun, it's to be for life, you understand. No screwing around with other women for you, so you deserve something satisfying, right? Expert—not an awkward, frightened, clumsy little bed partner."

"Jesus!"

"It makes sense, doesn't it?"

She was giggling, but abruptly she stopped and was silent, eyes studying him. "I made a mess of it, didn't I?"

"In a way," he told her. "In a way, no."

She got up from the bed, standing at the window, the lights from the boulevard making her seem transparent, ethereal, a sprite who had providentially flown in.

He rose and joined her. "When did I say I would marry you?"

She was gazing down into the empty street. Listlessly: "Didn't you? It makes no difference now, does it?"

"We can't possibly get married," he said, "until your father comes back from London next month. I wouldn't be party to such a dirty trick. No, next month at the earliest!"

There may have been a tiny smile on her lips, he couldn't be sure.

"Do you think we could get dressed and go out and find a place and have some breakfast?" Erica asked. "Tons of eggs and *petits-pains* and butter and marmalade and gallons of hot coffee. I'm absolutely starved!"

They spent another four days in Nice, then drove slowly home. Le Brun had made one stipulation: he would leave the Jacobi firm; he would not suffer being the employee who had married the daughter of the boss.

And she would live on what he could make—goodbye to being the fairy princess of the left, a donor to every down-and-out radical cause.

She hadn't liked that, but she'd accepted it, her small face upturned to his as he drove. "Yes, Claude. Anything you say. And you'll see how good I am at accounts. We'll live like nuns. No, that isn't right, is it? We'll live within our means; you're not to worry."

"Dammit," he growled, "we'll have enough. I've plenty of good offers."

"I'm sure," she said, putting her face up to be kissed. "And then you'll be for yourself, and the house of Le Brun will be even bigger than Jacobi—the greatest in France—and—"

"No, no!" he cried. "Who gives a damn about size? It's just that—"

"What?"

He was aware she was laughing, curling against him, "You shall live as you want, Le Brun."

He moved the car to the side of the road and took her in his arms.

"You shall live as *you* want, my Erica."

The next day they reached Paris and Le Brun drove her to the airport. She was to fly to London to tell her mother and father of their decision to marry.

At the boarding gate, she sought to remain with him until the last second, until the last passenger was checked in, and she had no choice but to get onto the plane.

He went out to the terrace that fronted the take-off and landing strips. A warm, drizzling rain had moved over the city and he had no raincoat, but it didn't seem to matter. The thin, flying rain gave taste to his mood; the wet air was caressing; colors had never seemed as vivid. The airport itself was intensely exciting.

He watched her plane taxi to the take-off sector, then turn and with a roar of motors blast down the runway. But suddenly, although it seemed to him to be happening in slow motion, he saw the plane falter, an engine inexplicably ceasing to fire, prop flailing like an exhausted runner.

The plane lifted, then fell back, moments later plunging into trees at the runway's limit.

While he watched, the plane exploded into flames and Le Brun's life with it.

Six

He rose from the bench, empty. The afternoon heat had become oppressive. He must tell Mischa he wanted the reflecting pool filled; the gardener mustn't be permitted to become careless.

Mischa's voice could suddenly be heard from the kitchen area, a scolding of sorts taking place; then the voices abruptly quieted, as if aware of a listener. Secretive.

Le Brun briefly considered taking Mischa into his confidence, then as quickly discarded the notion. It was dangerous from many angles. And then there were the legendary drinking bouts when Prince Kilkanov became a roaring lion, demonic, a revealer of all secrets.

"Claude," the voice said.

Brooding, his back to the house, he turned swiftly. It wasn't Erica, naturally. It was a girl with hair black as night falling over slim shoulders, with Erica's voice but without Erica's gaiety in her eyes, without Erica's jokes on her lips, but a solemn beauty that made her at what?—twenty-one?—twenty-two?—a woman.

"For God's sake, Sara!"

They stared at each other.

"Mischa didn't want you to know I am here."

"Since when does Mischa—"

He took her in his arms; she was trembling. He released her, standing back.

"I thought you were in London."

"I was."

"Your father?"

"He fought me, of course. I'm French. Why would I want to leave?"

"You're Jewish."

"My ID says I'm Marie-Anne Courbel. Roman Catholic from Tours. A very good ID, Claude."

"Still dangerous; they check."

She shrugged.

"Why did you come to Paris? That compounds the danger."

"I'd heard they'd taken everything. I wanted to see for myself. If there was anything I could save."

"Nothing. They've wiped us out."

"Us?"

It was sharp; her eyes never left him. He was startled, then he wasn't. But when she was a child he'd swung her around playing carousel; they'd had a private, special relationship, holding secrets in common. Adult ones. Such as how many lovers Angelle, the cook with the mountainous bosom, was having. Such as the fact that Mischa was one of them . . .

Erica had believed Sara had a monumental crush on him, would probably never get over it. Erica also said she didn't mind; that often happened with younger sisters.

Sara's look did not suggest affection now.

"You've taken over, Mischa says."

"That's right. I am now the Jacobi Galleries."

"But only caretaker. You told Mischa you'd give it all back one day?"

He didn't evade it. "No," he said. "No, Sara. I may have told Mischa that—but it isn't so."

"The fortunes of war?"

"Yes."

Her laugh was hard, a grown woman's.

"Your father," he said, "is a capable man. He'll have no trouble making a go of it. Besides, he has assets everywhere. I'm not worried about him."

She said nothing, shivered slightly despite the heat. "Do I have to worry about you turning me in?"

"No matter what you think, I'm not that much of a bastard. In fact, if you get into trouble you musn't hesitate to call on me. I do carry a little weight with them. I still think you ought to get out of the country, though. Are you still working at your photography? How could you in these times? It's a pity. I hate to see such talent being wasted."

"Go to hell, Claude," Sara said.

Turning, walking very erect, slowly as if afraid to stumble, she made her way away from him to the servants' quarters.

He watched until he could see her no more, then he lit a cigarette and went back into the house, into the grand salon.

He heard footsteps approaching, sounding sharp on the marble. It was Mischa, the butler, Prince Kilkanov.

"I'm leaving," Claude told him.

"The bedroom looking over the garden will be ready for you and your friend tomorrow," Mischa said. "I've scavenged furniture from the other rooms."

"Good. And see if you can get Sara out of Paris. You know as well as I do she's not safe here."

"It may be too late."

"How's that?"

"There's been a man watching the house since you got here today. From a Citroën across the street."

"Tan raincoat?"

"Until a while ago; he took it off. Is he one of your men, one of your new friends?"

Le Brun didn't respond, trying to decide how to handle this.

"He's been using a camera," volunteered Mischa. "He took pictures of Sara. I saw him."

Le Brun went cold. That complicated things. Sara Jacobi had been a figure in fashionable Paris. She had been on the cover of *Femme*. Her book of photographs, precocious but revealing a real talent, had earned respectable reviews, above and beyond her father's prominence.

"Look here," Le Brun said to Mischa, "that fellow outside is okay, won't use the pictures unless I tell him. Nothing to worry about, understand? But Sara must get away; the next time I might not be able to handle it."

Mischa looked sardonic, unconvinced, but there wasn't much he could do but take Le Brun's word for it. "I'll talk to her."

"Yes. There's really nothing to hold her here and she's in constant danger—try to convince her of that."

Le Brun walked through the half-empty house.

Mischa, on his heels, ushered him to the street, then went back in, locking the door securely behind him.

It was still hot and clouded, the air heavy; what Le Brun wanted above all was a long, cold shower.

The man in the Citroën was sitting in his car, sunk almost out of sight, sore-assed, Le Brun was willing to bet.

Le Brun got in the Hispano, nursed the engine into a proper mood, and pushed out into the light Saturday traffic, making sure the Citroën had time to glide into the stream behind him.

Just two blocks and Le Brun made a left, proceeding up several more streets before stopping in front of a *café-tabac* on Victor-Hugo.

It was crowded, the noise level high with a scratchy American record on the player—what did people do with themselves on a weekend afternoon in the occupied city?

Within sight of the window he bought cigarettes from a woman at the *caisse*. Tan Raincoat was taking no chances, and was walking toward the entrance. Le Brun might even then be slipping out the alley in back. But delaying a moment, he went down the stairs to the toilets.

There was the usual public telephone, and Le Brun waited by it until he could see his man. He was wearing a deep-brown summer suit, was heavyset with a fleshy pugnose. The man plodded down the steps, hardly giving Le Brun a glance, and moved past him toward the toilet.

Two customers came out buttoning their flies, talking, going up to the bar.

Le Brun followed them, taking his time. Sure enough, Tan Raincoat wasn't to be tricked, and climbed after Le Brun, almost on his heels.

Le Brun reached the top and began to run through the crowd toward the kitchen. Tan Raincoat made no pretense now, pushing and elbowing after him.

The kitchen was about the size of a large closet, and the chef and helper gaped at Le Brun who, grinning at them, slid through into the alley. Moments later, Tan Raincoat banged into a cart of dirty dishes, barely saved himself from a fall, and hurled himself onward.

Le Brun was waiting in the alley behind a stack of crates filled with empty wine bottles—partial concealment but all he could find when his pursuer staggered out.

In the momentary span while the man, service Luger in hand, canvassed the alley, Le Brun rose almost directly behind him, his own Luger, obtained for him a week previously by Kröler, pulled out of his pocket.

What Le Brun had in mind was a swift blow to the man's head, grab the camera with the shots of Sara in it, and dash for safety.

Tan Raincoat was too quick.

Whipping around, he wasted no time in getting a clear view of his target, and just fired at random where he thought Le Brun was standing, where the crates had moved. The alley echoed with the sound of exploding glass.

But Le Brun was some feet beyond and now, untouched, he pulled the trigger and kept pulling it, pumping bullets at close range into the man's body.

He was sure he had missed and would be killed by his opponent, who faced him in the sunlight, teeth bared, eyes dark and angry. But a few small steps and the man sank down silently, blood gushing onto his jacket.

At almost the same time, Le Brun was aware of the kitchen help, standing in the doorway as if watching a film, one with a skillet of onions in his hand.

Stepping over the broken glass to the dead man, Le Brun fished in his clothes and came up with a mini-camera, which he pocketed. Then, still ignoring the men in the kitchen door, he ran down the alley to the street and past the *café-tabac* entrance where he was parked.

Ten minutes later, he parked the car again just off the Faubourg St. Honoré and headed on foot for the place de la Concorde. If he knew his countrymen, the body would soon be carted far from the *café-tabac,* tossed unceremoniously into a deserted lot. Who wanted trouble with the authorities?

The bar at the Hôtel Crillon could be entered from a side street, rue Boissy D'Anglas, and Le Brun was glad to find it reasonably empty and serene, two young lieutenants with their girls in a booth, another pair near the door to the lobby, a drunken Luftwaffe major at the bar.

Le Brun took a single table against the wall and when the waiter came ordered a double brandy, grateful for the empty conversation around him, the Germans trying to communicate with the women in execrable French, the women, prostitutes was his guess, pretending to understand.

The waiter, the kind of rangy, blue-eyed specimen the Nazis like to call a typical Aryan, grinned at Le Brun, making a small derisive gesture toward the Germans. Le Brun smiled back companionably. The man had served him here before, he doubled as a bartender, they had once talked. He was a young American art student studying in Paris, a sculptor, a student, Le Brun seemed to recall, of the great octogenarian sculptor Brazin. Perplexing to imagine what an American was doing in Paris these days.

Le Brun had no time to ask; the waiter had been given a preemptory order by the major and had sped away to fill it. Le Brun himself, following a long therapeutic pull at the brandy snifter, went to the telephone booth in the lobby just outside the bar and dialed the Jeu de Paume.

Reaching the museum and getting Ernst Kröler at the other end of the phone were two different things. Couldn't she take a message? Kröler's secretary asked. The Reichsmarschall was in the museum and Kröler was understandably busy.

"No," insisted Le Brun. "It's extremely important. Herr Kröler will want to hear what I have to say. Please, you must believe me!"

After an interval Sergeant Raeder came on. "What the devil do you want, Le Brun? Weren't you told the Reichsmarschall is visiting?"

"Listen to me, Raeder," said Le Brun angrily. "You have your troubles, I have mine. There's been a leak."

"What kind of leak?"

"They've found out I'm working with you."

"And who are 'they'?"

"The Resistance, dammit! They've had a man following me all day. I had to kill him."

The silence on the other end was pregnant indeed. *"Had to kill him?"*

"Once those bastards smell you're collaborating, they play you like a violin."

Raeder got the drift. "I wouldn't worry, Le Brun. We'll give you protection if you want."

"Thanks so much! Might as well carry a sign saying I'm your boy. Sorry I bothered you. Just wanted you to know somebody inside your organization has a big mouth."

"It will be looked into, I promise you."

"My compliments to the Reichsmarschall."

Le Brun hung up, grinning.

Back at his table, he finished off the brandy, calling for another.

"Isn't your name Morgan?" he asked the waiter. "I seem to remember our talking before."

"McNulty," the young man said. "Tom McNulty."

"Not American? Look here, your secret's safe with me."

"Irish," the young man said with a correcting smile and the touch of a brogue. "From the heart of Dublin, sir. You've got the face right but have mistaken the name, I'm afraid."

"Artist, aren't you? Student of Pierre Brazin?"

"That much is correct, sir. Although haven't seen the old boy for months. You've got to do with art yourself, right? Dealer, could it be?"

"Dealer," said Le Brun.

"Thought so," said McNulty triumphantly. "Second brandy coming up."

An Irishman, considered Le Brun, could survive in Nazi Paris, whereas an American couldn't. The Irish and the Germans, some at least, had ties going back to World War I. That still didn't explain why McNulty, Morgan, if he were an American, had chosen to remain in France.

His drink arrived without covering conversation. Sipping in a more civilized manner, Le Brun began to feel his nerve ends go light, the brandy beginning to make the earlier events of the afternoon, while not reasonable, at least supportable.

So, at last, he was up to his neck in the war.

He could go home to Mallou now, she was probably awake. He wondered if he'd look any different to her after what he'd done to Tan Raincoat. If she'd notice. If it would be different making love. If it would be written on his body that he had killed a man. If he'd perform differently.

Mallou was convinced that he was an iceberg inside anyway, that he was not indifferent but actually uncaring about anything but the buying and selling of paintings. He was sorry she felt that way about him, but there was little he could do about it. He was not prepared to tell her about Erica. He didn't think he could ever tell anyone about Erica, except someday perhaps Aaron Jacobi. Now that was strange as hell, he thought: the notion of telling Erica's father!

But in some curious way it might bring solace to Aaron . . . he didn't know why . . . just a hunch.

And soon now in London, Aaron would be getting the news of the takeover. What face would he present to the world on that one?

Getting up to leave, paying his check, Le Brun consoled himself with that thought: if he wanted the approval of any man in the world it was that of that small, fragile Jew. Which brought him back to memories of Erica, and then, unexpectedly the very recent one of Sara trembling in his arms that afternoon in the garden. Before the hurt had crept into her eyes. *Christ!*

The sky was charcoal and deep pink, the color he loved best over Paris. It was slightly cooler, the shops were closing, and there were few French on the streets, mostly small packs of gray-uniformed, jackbooted soldiers on the prowl for women. Le Brun found there was nowhere he wanted to go, no one he wanted to see; he went back to the apartment and Mallou.

Seven

AT THE JEU DE PAUME, Sergeant Raeder, following his telephone conversation with Le Brun, placed his own call to Colonel Bocke, informing him of the death of the Milice agent.

Bocke was unperturbed, if anything amused that Le Brun had mistaken the detective for someone from the Resistance. Bocke did promise to give his Milice contact hell for not having assigned a more efficient undercover man.

The incident put Raeder in a foul mood. It crossed his mind that Le Brun might have known very well the dead man was Milice and had pretended otherwise—in which case score one for Le Brun. The man obviously was not to be underestimated despite that supercilious air, that gaunt, aristocratic appearance. On impulse, he phoned Bocke again.

"Forget the Milice," he said. "I'll contact the Gestapo."

"You know, Raeder, once those bloodhounds are in, they're in all the way. Is that what you want?"

Bocke had a point. Thus far the continuing struggle between Hitler and Goering for the cream of the stolen art had been kept out of official channels. Invite the Gestapo, even for a small job, and the floodgates might be opened.

"All right," Raeder conceded. "Have the Milice do the follow-up on Le Brun, but for God's sake—"

"Yes, yes! Put good people on him! Don't worry!"

Raeder, whose office was a cubicle in the basement, heard his buzzer, which meant an urgent summons from the main gallery. Deliberately letting them wait, he mounted to the first floor, a vast assembly line for

74

crating and shipping, and on up to the second, where selection, ownership, and designation were decided.

Here canvases, framed oils, drawings, gouaches, watercolors, statuary—the bulk of the loot of the *Einsatzstab* Rosenberg—were piled haphazardly against the walls, the area in the middle kept clear for the display easels.

In a special chaise, flanked by Rosenberg and von Banheim on folding chairs, sat Goering, peering at two paintings on easels in front of him, a Rembrandt and a Hooch. In attendance was the usual gang of curators, even a few commercial dealers from Berlin used by Rosenberg for special "transactions."

Spotting Raeder, Goering grumbled, "What took you so long? Herr Rosenberg believes our Führer would truly appreciate the Rembrandt, though it is perhaps not one of his best. The Hooch, I think, is a fine one, don't you agree?" He looked sharply at Raeder. "What we must make sure of here is that we don't shortchange anyone. The Führer is to receive the most valuable of the two, it goes without saying!" (Translation: *I want the Rembrandt badly. How are we going to pull the wool over Rosenberg's eyes and get it?*)

Aware of the game, Raeder took his own good time examining the paintings, it gave him special satisfaction that, with all the heavyweights present, Goering had called upon him.

In no time at all Raeder realized what none of the others had: the Rembrandt was not a Rembrandt! What had probably fooled everyone, including Kröler, was a combination of familiar benchmarks: the Old Testament scene typical of the master, the familiar warm colors, the oriental costumes. What should have given Goering's experts pause, however, was the knowle ge that biblical Rembrandts, many with forged signatures, abounded in museums from Amsterdam to Boston. This particular one, Raeder would bet, was the work of a Rembrandt pupil, Aert de Gelder, who could produce plausible copies every day of the week.

The second painting, on the other hand, a domestic scene done with great clarity of detail, was a genuine Hooch, a Dutchman who had many of the qualities of Vermeer without being a copyist. In Raeder's opinion it was close to a masterpiece, far more valuable than the other oil. He whispered his findings to Goering, all the while praising the Rembrandt elaborately and loud.

Goering nodded with great interest, reaching into his pocket for a large pillbox and placing one of the white tablets delicately on his tongue. "Thank you, Sergeant," he said in a clear voice. "But as I said, the Führer's choice must of course come before mine. If the Rembrandt is as fine as you say it is, he shall have it. I'll content myself with the Hooch. Unless, Alfred, you think the Führer would want that, too?"

Rosenberg, on Goering's left, dark complexioned with thinning hair, a hyperactive man who had trouble sitting still on a chair, bounced up, gratefully shaking the Reichsmarschall's jeweled paw with both hands. "I'm sure our beloved leader will be overjoyed at the decision. And of course, Hermann, *you* must have the Hooch. He would insist!"

Goering rose, beamed, slapped von Banheim genially on the arm. "Tell me, General, is female companionship in Paris becoming as difficult to find as good art? The latter seems to be in short supply lately."

Von Banheim wasn't fooled by the bantering tone; the barb was apparent to everybody. "The cupboard, Reichsmarschall, commences to look bare, I admit it. I speak of art, naturally."

Laughter and good spirits all around. Emboldened, the curators stepped forward to mingle with the celebrities. Coffee and cakes were being served on a long table near the easels. And some excellent schnapps from the Fatherland.

"I'm serious," von Banheim continued to Goering in an aside. "What else can we expect? We've already had the best of the Jewish collections. So what remains besides isolated finds like these"—a long, manicured index finger was aimed at the paintings on the easels—"while the really great pieces—the French National Treasure—remain frustratingly out of reach. Give me just one division, a free hand, and you'll see art! I'll dazzle you with it!"

Rosenberg was hopping from one leg to another

like a man with a urinary problem. "He's right. Ridiculous! Moldering away in those damn châteaux, hidden for all we know in damp cellars! Who can say what shape they'll be in when we finally do get hold of them!"

Goering headed for the table with the cakes. He dunked one in a coffee mug. "Considerations of state, gentlemen. Vital! The fleet! I spoke to Admiral Darlan only last week. Our French allies have their problems just as we do. We have to bide our time."

But he was the most impatient of all. On how many occasions had they heard him explode with fury at the treasures the French were withholding! He turned to an art dealer from Berlin, Frau Hilda Zetlin, a woman close to sixty and as grossly overweight as himself. "Would you believe it, dear lady, they've been able to conceal nothing from me. I can tell you exactly where each work is deposited, the exact château, almost the very room—the Brueghels, the Bouchers, Caravaggio, Goya, Raphael, the Titians!"

She nodded, smiling, bovine. The Zetlin was famous for her terrible taste and for her shrewdness; she had become a millionaire since the war started, finding and selling second-rate art at inflated prices to Hitler.

"Oh yes, and Le Nain, Fra Angelico, Rubens . . . the sculpture! Where do they hide the sculpture, Kröler?"

"At Valençay, Reichsmarschall."

"Valençay . . . the Venus de Milo. The Winged Victory. Can you imagine it?" He paused, turning to the others, splendid in his gold and beige uniform, causing them almost to catch their breath, his voice seductive, subdued: "Patience, comrades, and on with your work! It is of tremendous importance to the Reich! Heil Hitler!"

He was on his way out, Rosenberg at his heels, trying to fill him in on the new plan being put into effect —*"Aktion M"*—the seizure of furnishings of Jewish residences; *"Möbel"* being the German word for furniture.

Goering only half-listened. Rosenberg bored everyone. It was said the Führer would no longer grant him personal meetings; Rosenberg had to resort to lengthy memorandums.

Downstairs, Goering pulled up abruptly. On the wall, to one side of the exit doors, was a large poster in color. It showed the entrance hall of the Louvre, the main staircase with the Winged Victory looming above it, huge, dominating, magnificent.

The pause was only momentary, the Reichmarschall continuing through the doors only to be halted again immediately beyond, where gardeners were planting a sapling in front of the terrace and had tied off a rope across Goering's path.

Knee-high or more, it was not to be stepped over. And wisely, he made the decision not to risk loss of face by trying to jump it. Officers began to shout at the gardeners, who, confused and frightened, did nothing.

A step behind Goering, von Banheim drew his revolver out of its holster and, almost in the same fluid motion, fired, the bullet neatly severing the rope.

A moment for the feat to register, then a spontaneous burst of applause. After all, von Banheim had only his left eye—the other was glass, which made what he had done even more remarkable. Led by Goering, the group proceeded toward the staff cars with the old swagger.

Raeder, still on the museum terrace, saw Kröler beckoning to him. "The Reichsmarschall," Kröler told him, "wants you to accompany him. That business with the painting was very clever." Kröler's tone was brave, concealing the hurt at his rejection. "I simply did not think it an appropriate time to say so."

"Quite right," said Raeder, smiling.

The armored train powered through the soft August night, toward the west, toward the green of Normandy, all tracks cleared ahead of it.

In his dining salon, the Reichsmarschall was explaining his plan to exchange one hundred paintings from the Reich museums for one hundred works of art belonging to the French.

"They'll do their damnedest to thwart us, but in the end they'll have to accept it. Of course, we'll give them nothing but crap. Sergeant Raeder, you'll draw up a list of what *we* want. Take your time. I want their absolute best."

Raeder could see Maida Thaler watching him. Moments ago he had caught the woman eyeing von Banheim. Goering treated her like one of the family. A hot number, Raeder was sure. Tits that strained the powder-blue cotton dress; long, slim legs and firm buttocks. Sipping the fine Moselle, Raeder ventured, "Why not go down there and see for ourselves, Reichsmarschall? That way they pull no tricks; we *know* what we're getting!"

"You don't seem to realize," Kröler said, "that access is denied. According to the treaty—"

"Fuck the treaty," said Raeder.

Kröler retreated, shocked.

Goering did not seem bothered by Raeder's language. "What did you have in mind?"

"We let them know we're coming. We go in mufti. Very friendly. No troops. I don't think they'll have the guts to refuse you. It is simply to reassure ourselves that everything is in order, that they need no dehumidifying equipment from us, for example. No extra heaters or restoring supplies. We are really just being helpful."

Goering turned his head toward von Banheim, who was toying with a wine cork. "Not bad. And we take back a sample or two, eh? Like the Mona Lisa?"

Raeder's suggestion was neither taken too seriously nor ignored. They were stuffed with food, sleepy with fine wines, conquerors. Nothing was impossible. The heavy crystal candelabra shone on the table china, on their immaculate uniforms, on the gold of the decorations, on the bright ribbons they wore. The train slowed, going through a town, then they could feel it pick up speed again, whistling through the countryside. Exhilarating. "The only problem I can forsee," said von Banheim, "is security. I would want to be absolutely sure the Reichsmarschall is properly protected. With a small force and out of uniform, without ample firepower, that might be difficult."

"Impossible," said Kröler.

The Reichsmarschall yawned.

"I'll take a little nap. We have a long night ahead. Raeder, work on that list."

Raeder had Maida Thaler beneath him, writhing like a feral creature, half screaming as he entered, biting, tearing at his back with her nails, worrying the hell out of him. Goering's suite, she had warned in the beginning, was only several doors away.

When finally, taut as a bow, he climaxed, she shuddered the length of her body, then pushed him off. "My God, you've got some cock!"

"You didn't like it?"

She brooded, then laughed. "Seeing twice is believing."

"How about time to reload?"

He could have been asking the wall. She had started to work on him again; he had never experienced anyone so expert. "We've got to hurry. Pretty soon he'll call me and I'll have to go."

As he lay sated on the bunk, she began to dress, teasing him as she drew on panties and stockings, chattering nonstop. Goering planned one more day back in the city; perhaps they could meet at his hotel. *She* wouldn't mind if, of course, it suited Raeder. Why wasn't he an officer? He was well-enough educated, surely. Perhaps not as handsome or as well-born as General von Banheim, but just as smart, no?

He didn't respond to the bait. *God, what a bitch!* And she rattled away: the most handsome, really, wasn't a German, though. That French art fellow, Le Brun. Such a fine, sweet-spoken gentleman, didn't Raeder agree?

"Oh sure. And probably in his pants the size of a peanut!"

Turning on Raeder, she smiled smugly and was greedily on top of him. *A whore,* he thought. This time he gave her what she deserved, a sound beating along with it.

The long summer twilight was over, dark-blue ink leaking over the land, the moon hiding behind fast-moving clouds.

The armored train, lights doused, was a sleeping

dragon in the small station, except for the guards patrolling fore and aft.

They were not far from the Channel, the Normandy coast, and it was cool, almost cold. Goering, descending from his bedroom car with von Banheim and Kruger, wore a black leather topcoat.

Waiting to escort him to the airfield was Colonel Riehl. With the visitors at ease in the staff limousine, the squat little colonel delivered his report: three hundred fighter-bombers were over England this very minute, accompanied by every Focke-Wulf and Messerschmitt fighter plane they could get into service.

As they continued along the winding Normandy road, Riehl gave his own estimate of what might be expected from the night's work: England was in for a bloody nose, if not a severe body blow. "You can count on it, Reichsmarschall!"

Goering, who was usually ebullient, especially when extolling the exploits of his air force to Hitler, could be cynical enough on his own turf: "From your mouth to God's ear, Colonel"—a Jewish expression he had picked up from a friend of his wife and was fond of using.

The hours spent at the Jeu de Paume had served as an anodyne; the rape of art chased away all his worries. But now he was faced with reality again—his own problems within the hierarchy. Bormann and Goebbels, his spies had told him, were sniping at him at every turn. A particular target was his failure months ago at Dunkirk, made worse because he had convinced Hitler to order the Luftwaffe to finish it off. The damnable weather and failure! Then the mounting losses over Britain, escalating the need for an exploitable success.

But tonight could do it!

He fed himself a white pill, then quickly added another. He had one great bulwark: the people of Germany. The people loved their big, fat, jolly Hermann. All the others, even the Führer, acknowledged it; that was why they could go only so far in dealing with him. That was why the Führer had officially made him his number two man, his political heir.

In the speeding car von Banheim was making a

joke about Deauville being close by. Couldn't they stop for a little play at the tables? They all knew the casino was shut tight, but von Banheim said that, if the Reichsmarschall desired it, he would have it reopened especially for them.

Goering managed a smile.

And the heavens had cleared—a good omen. The clouds were scudding off, driven by a freshening wind out of the North Sea, the moon shooting into the clear like an enormous yellow beacon. "Our moon," exulted Riehl. "A wonderful victory, Reichsmarschall. You'll see I'm right!"

The operations room, sunk deep into the earth, was alive with lights, the quick laughter of the younger personnel, the steady commands of the higher ranks. Goering, sitting to one side, wanting to be out of the way, out of Galland's hair, was aware of the heady mood, the absolute confidence of success. Gradually, however, as news came in and a reliable overview of the raid emerged, he began to sense a dwindling of excitement.

The raid was inflicting damage, no question about that. London must be on fire. But at what cost? Airfields up and down the coast were rapidly filing their reports as those Luftwaffe planes still in the air struggled back to home bases.

Galland, at the far end of the room, chain-smoking, stalking the tiny confines of his command area, was himself no more than the nexus of a communications system—the recipient of the telephone information, the wireless, the parade of message-toting orderlies—helpless because once the raid had begun, Galland was basically an observer.

Goering signaled von Banheim; he needed a breath of fresh air.

Outside, at the entrance to the bunker, the wind whipping at their legs, Goering and von Banheim and Kruger watched a fighter-bomber make its approach down the runway. It was relatively undamaged. Pilots and gunners jumped out, full of talk, of extravagant gestures as the welcoming ground crew took over. Then, on their way down into the bunker for debriefing, they continued to relive the mission, missing the Reichsmarschall where he stood in the shadows, slouching past him still on their talking jag, the bunker swallowing them.

Another plane was trying to land. They could tell at once it was in trouble, and soon they could see why: fire had broken out on the starboard engine. No need for sirens. The fire-fighting crews were on standby.

The pilot was coming in short. Ignoring Goering, von Banheim began to curse. "Goddamn fool—bring it up, up!"

The nose wouldn't come up; the entire front of the big Junkers was ablaze, and now Goering was aware that Galland and half his staff were on the runway beside him, and others in addition to von Banheim were shouting to the pilot, some even praying.

The plane smashed into the ground almost directly in front of them, sliding, sliding, then flip-flopping, finally coming to rest. Then, wrenched by a sudden internal blast, it exploded, consumed by fire. There was no more cursing or praying, only the quiet crackling of the flames.

As soon as the bodies were removed, Goering walked over to the still-smoking wreck. Its body crushed, wings crumpled, the Junkers no longer resembled a flying machine but something else, something grotesque but strangely familiar. And then Goering realized what it was he was looking at—a blackened, distorted reminder of the Winged Victory, seen only that afternoon in the poster in the Jeu de Paume.

Galland had walked with him, Goering until now unaware of his presence. "We've taken a beating, Reichsmarschall, but nothing compared to the one we've inflicted. Colonel Riehl was a prophet for once: a dozen more raids like this one and I promise you they'll cry surrender! Just get me the planes!"

"You'll have them, General," Goering promised.

Back in the train, in pajamas and robe, he had Kruger summon von Banheim and Raeder into his quarters. Considering the haste in which they had dressed, the likelihood was that neither man had a stitch on under his uniform.

It would have made no difference to Goering. He had not taken one of the white pills for an hour. No need to. He was walking on air.

"I've decided to implement your plan," he told Raeder.

Raeder, who had been rudely awakened from a drugged sleep, for once looked blank.

"Our little trip into unoccupied France to the châteaux country."

Before von Banheim could protest, Goering swung toward him. "Work out the security and political steps, General. Contact Vichy. Use any threats necessary. I'm particularly interested in Valençay. And I'll let you both in on one thing: I do not intend to leave that château empty-handed."

They stared at him. Oddly, neither von Banheim nor Raeder suspected him of being drugged. Yet he was high as a kite, euphoric.

They saluted formally and left him, too bemused even to compare notes in the corridor.

Alone, Goering poured a large brandy and paced back and forth, snifter in hand, exalted by the grandeur of his vision. He would place his gift to them —to the German people—squarely in the center of Unter den Linden.

There, on the grand boulevard of the most important city on earth, his Winged Victory of Samothrace would stand forever, a symbol of his devotion to the Fatherland, and of its victorious march across the world.

House 71 : June 1945

PACKARD AND GOLDFARB decided to soft-pedal the questions about the Winged Victory. Unclear, of course, was whether or not it was the original.

The subject had obviously touched a sensitive area within Kröler's "fear zone."

They informed Kröler that Goering, in American custody along with Rosenberg, Schacht and Hess, von Neurath, Papen, would have to face a war crimes trial. "Others will be included," added Goldfarb. "Perhaps not as important, but all bear responsibility."

"You mustn't underestimate," Kröler told Goldfarb and Packard defensively, "how completely we were under their thumbs. And they could be ruthless, even with their colleagues."

Not looking up from his notebook, Packard said, "Be specific, Ernst."

Kröler helped himself from the bottle of bourbon; he had come to like bourbon and they'd discovered it served to grease these debriefings marvelously.

"We'll go back," Kröler said with the air of imparting the secret of the pharaohs, "to the Roehm Affair, the so-called Night of the Long Knives. Are you aware of it?"

Packard looked contemptuous.

"But are you also aware of the Reichsmarschall's part in it? A man who couldn't stand the idea of an animal suffering? A man who promulgated and enforced the most humane hunting laws of any country in the western world?"

"What exactly happened that night?" Goldfarb asked, gesturing Parkard silent.

"What happened? I'll tell you in detail. First you must know that Roehm, Hitler's earliest supporter and leader of the *Sturmabteilung,* the SA, was planning a putsch. He had assembled his storm troopers in various places throughout Germany and informed them to await his word.

"Roehm's mistake was in assuming all this could be accomplished without news of it reaching Goering.

"The inevitable of course happened. When Goering got word of it, he wasted no time, immediately informing Hitler. The Führer was terribly angry. Calling out a force of seven hundred gunmen, the Führer raced to Munich, then to the lakeside resort where Roehm was spending the night with his boys."

Packard was still, sipping his lemonade as if it were straight whiskey; Goldfarb sucked on his pipe.

"Surrounding Roehm's lodge, Hitler and his men

routed the whole lot out of bed—many out of one
another's beds. Most, like Heines, Roehm's second-in-
command, were marched naked into the forest where
they were shot. Roehm himself was driven into Munich and executed in a prison cell.

"But that was only the first part of it. Goering's
purge had just begun, he had his death lists in order.
No one friendly with Roehm in the past was safe. Nor
for that matter was any personal rival of a party
functionary. Old enmities, old jealousies, were everywhere punished—or you might say, rewarded! People
were butchered in their sleep. The gun, the blade, the
rope . . . for days the party, the country, lay in the
grip of Goering's revenge."

Goldfarb was fascinated. "These many then shall
die," he quoted. "Their names are prick'd. . . . He
shall not live; look with a spot I damn him."

"When finally Goering called an end to the blood-
letting," resumed Kröler, "his position alongside the
Führer was secure. I tell you all this so you will understand the kind of man you are dealing with when
he wants something badly enough. And remember
this: Goering's body was flabby, not his will. Murder
did not revolt him."

Eight

HE WAS STILL BEING TAILED, and this time by someone more adept. The new man was elderly, even a
little shabby, in a dark worsted suit and an open
collar. He hung well back, seemed to disappear for
long moments, then could be suddenly glimpsed again,
almost a shadow in a shop doorway.

Le Brun, who had been to a small gallery in the
neighborhood, walked briskly as far as the Palais de
Chaillot. At this time of year normally alive with

tourists, it was, except for a few guards, sunlit and empty. In its emptiness, it was uniquely exposed, its classic lines laid bare to Le Brun's appreciative eye, the Tour Eiffel looming across the river like an engineer's bad dream, powerful but not engaging. Le Brun remembered Aaron Jacobi's long-ago dictum about the impact of ugliness.

Turning, he climbed into the Hispano and was off back toward L'Etoile. The usual army of bikes, military vehicles, and buses gave the man assigned to follow him a hard time. But finally he emerged in the clear, not too far behind Le Brun, in a black Citroën; apparently all the Milice cars were Citroëns.

Making no attempt to elude the tail, Le Brun now drove down the Champs to George V, then over to avenue Marceau to Chez Jeannot.

He could hear the din from the club from up the street where he parked. The banging of a piano and then sudden bursts of laughter had attracted a woman and a couple of old men, who loitered outside the entrance.

"Whores," the woman muttered angrily before moving on; the men said nothing, obviously eager to slip in for a peek.

The club was no bigger than a *boîte*. A midget-sized stage. A midget-sized piano player named Fernando. Mallou and Fernando were working out refinements in a new number, while front and center Jeannot's chorus line was choreographing a routine.

Except for the work light on the stage, the club was cool and gloomy, chairs piled on tables, the smell of booze emanating from the woodwork—the place had been a saloon for years beyond memory.

Sitting in a chair halfway back, Jeannot spotted Le Brun and motioned him over. In his early fifties, Jeannot had bleached blond hair and a blond mustache that, surprisingly, seemed to go with a broad peasant face. A deep tan from quick trips to the South. Although he made no pretense of being anything but a *pédé*, the heavy muscular development obvious under the silk shirts he favored was a deterrent to bullies. Jeannot had worked as a youth on the railroad lines hammering ties; he was no one to fool with.

Up on the stage an argument was in progress between Mallou and one of the dancers who turned, and shouted passionately out into the darkness for Jeannot's intercession.

"They always bitch at each other like this," Jeannot said to Le Brun. "The best thing is to stay out of it."

In a moment the music was pounding again. Mallou, looking lithe and fit in her rehearsal clothes, waved at Le Brun without missing a beat in her song. Jeannot asked if Le Brun wanted something alcoholic.

"No, thanks. A *citron pressé* will do the trick."

Le Brun had watched rehearsals here before, and it was always the same: he found it impossible to say he was not watching six talented female dancers.

On stage the number finished, with Mallou doing a few fancy tricks of her own, while behind her the chorus was kicking high, flashing stocking tops, garters, and expanses of white thighs.

Jeannot and Le Brun applauded.

Laughter came back at them.

Mallou jumped down from the stage and came over to brush Le Brun's cheek with her lips.

"Will you take me to lunch?"

In her skin-tight leotard, sweated and moving without coquetry, she was even more desirable, he thought, than when in the nude. The tight cloth drew her into sinuous unity—breasts, sex clearly outlined—and then the long, beautifully proportioned legs.

"Terribly sorry," he said. "Business appointment. Someone claims to have come upon a long-forgotten Monet. I've promised to take a look at it."

"I'd forgotten you're the Jacobi *patron*," she answered sharply.

He ignored the tone. "Tonight, after your performance, we've been invited to the Crillon. General von Banheim is giving a party. Intimate—no ranks below field officer."

"Von Banheim? What a bore!"

"But you don't know him, do you?"

"The party, I mean. Very well." She kissed him lightly again. "Never fall in love with a goddamn businessman," she said to Jeannot. She was on her way to her dressing room, the chorus line working out again with Fernando, linking arms, calling out the count.

Watching Le Brun watching the "girls," Jeannot suddenly asked, "Which would be your choice?"

Le Brun smiled at the older man.

"They're all marvelous, Jeannot."

"You'd be amazed how the *Boche* officer corps delights in my darlings. How often they're invited to their intimate soirées!"

One of the performers detached himself, pulled off a blond wig, strolled languorously over to them.

"The routine is idiotic, Jeannot. It will lay an egg."

"It's superb, Philippe; it'll knock 'em dead."

"What in hell do you know?" Philippe said without rancor. Behind him the rehearsal was breaking up, Fernando gathering his music, the performers making their way into the gloom of the back.

"He's right of course," said Philippe to Le Brun. "The entire new show will be magnificent, with Mallou the crown jewel. If only the kid could sing—"

Kicking off his high heels, nursing cramped toes, he hobbled off after the others.

"They adore her really."

"Do they?" asked Le Brun. He was watching Jeannot watch Philippe. So this was the new one.

"Part Arab," Jeannot said. "A nice boy, really. And talented, the best of them."

"I could see."

"Smart, too. Keeps his eyes and ears open. Last night he told me—Marcel—he's the tallest one in the line, the red wig—the especially lovely legs—Marcel was a guest of your new friends."

Le Brun did not quite know what he was driving at.

"A Colonel Emil Bocke," Jeannot added.

"Bocke?"

"Oh, yes—another faggot."

Le Brun—it had happened often before—found himself saddened by the apparent need of men like Jeannot to run themselves down. He grinned, however, as if he had made a joke. "Von Banheim's adjutant, isn't he? Christ, you never know where these pansies will show up."

"This one is a *numéro*. Fancies the whip. Marcel, I believe, likes the other end of it. He's been invited to accompany the colonel on a little weekend trip . . . to the Loire Valley."

"Jeannot, that's unoccupied France!"

"Marcel has the brains of a goose. He thought Philippe would be jealous. Philippe's not going of course—he's performing."

Le Brun was staring at Jeannot. The treasures of France were hidden in the Loire Valley; this weekend excursion would hardly be confining itself to sightseeing!

Jeannot, who was probably *au courant* with every whisper in Paris, continued to smile innocently.

"Ah, but the Loire is so beautiful at this time of year . . . wouldn't we like to be going down there ourselves!"

Nine

THE TAIL WAS PARKED three quarters of a block up, on the other side of the street. As soon as he saw Le Brun appear he hurried into the Citroën.

Unconcernedly, Le Brun started the Hispano, swung away from the curb and headed for George V. There, with the Citroën taking care to remain hidden behind other cars, Le Brun abruptly hit the accelerator, reached the Champs-Elysées, shot across the boulevard, making another sharp turn, a left, and headed up toward the Etoile.

The Citroën, he could see in his mirror, was trying desperately to disentangle itself from the traffic issuing at George V and the people trying to cross the Champs. The driver was good, but not good enough to reach the Etoile before Le Brun was a quarter way around. And while the Etoile in wartime was not the Etoile with a thousand cars spinning around the great circle, it was still no place to be watching a vehicle a hundred yards ahead.

The Citroën had first to fend for itself.

The driver thought Le Brun had spun off into the avenue Hoche, but he wasn't absolutely sure: it might have been Kléber. He chose to cruise down Kléber, looking for the Hispano.

It had been Hoche, and moments later Le Brun had parked on a side street and was walking back to the Etoile. There he took the Metro to Châtelet and changed over to the Left Bank line. The noontime cars were fairly crowded, people preferring to attend to their business during the day rather than risk the danger of being caught out after curfew. Le Brun reflected that the Occupation had made people mute: the natural ebullience of his countrymen was more or less deliberately down-played in public, as if not to encourage in the Germans any sense of normality, the slightest degree of acceptance.

The Germans found this a constant goad. Le Brun saw this now in a young Wehrmacht soldier sitting opposite him. The boy's eyes sought his as if in friendship, or at least in the hope of Le Brun's acknowledgment of his presence, desperately trying to achieve minimal human contact. Le Brun was as indifferent to this as were the other Frenchmen around him. While the boy met no overt hostility, neither in the Métro car could he make eye contact with anyone. Stiffening, giving Le Brun an almost feminine look of disdain, he retreated into the arrogance of the conqueror.

Le Brun left the Métro at St.-Germain-des-Prés. The sun shone down through a nearly cloudless sky; the city lay in a midday stupor and he was thirsty again, wishing he had time to stop at the Deux Magots. The table Erica and he had always sought was empty; sheltered from the direct sun, it had an excellent view of the boulevard and the church and any movement within the quadrant. Suddenly he heard her quick laugh, felt the light touch of her hand on his, and oh, the voice . . . it rang in his ears, clearer to him now than the memory of her face.

Will you drive me to Nice, Le Brun?

He walked past the Deux Magots and found a *café–*

tabac down the street. In a corner, a shaded table. When a waiter finally appeared he ordered a coffee. In this quarter he was at home. Only a few streets away he had attended the Beaux-Arts; Montparnasse, where his family lived, was not too far. He could plot the position of practically every shop and gallery. It was *old* Paris, really. He had read somewhere that a wall in the Institut de France, just a few blocks away, along the quay, was an original wall of the city.

Past the table, he could see the *concierge* watering a geranium pot on a window shelf on the ground floor of a building opposite. The woman plucked off some dead leaves, then withdrew into the gloom of her apartment.

Le Brun knew these apartments well. Centrally located, romantically desirable, most were falling apart, dilapidated, victims of years of poverty and neglect. The paint was peeled, the plaster crumbling and yellow-stained from water damage, the plumbing ancient and barely usable, the floors crazily buckled. Le Brun had been sent to the very building across from him some years ago by Aaron Jacobi. An old man, a friend of a client, had some paintings to sell; Aaron, too busy himself and considering it an insignificant purchase, had dispatched his new employee. This morning's lie to Mallou reminded Le Brun now that the old man across the street on that long-ago day did have a Monet for sale, but did not know it.

The canvas was unsigned and the old man in a wrinkled blue suit told Le Brun simply that he had been willed it by a brother some time before. Whatever it was, the old man liked it, though. Weren't the colors good?

The colors were superb. Water, cool and shimmering —a river, caught in the rose-pink of dusk, slowly flowing past an old stone farmhouse. An early Monet but no inferior work, the brushwork already demonstrating inspired virtuosity.

The old man, who seemed half-asleep, waited patiently as he studied the canvas. Le Brun finally turned his head. "Do you know the name of the artist?"

"I'm told it's the work of one of the new young ones,

very popular they say, but it has no signature, does it, so what is it worth?"

It did not have to be signed, Le Brun had it on his tongue to say, not when it was so unmistakably the work of Monet. Any art dealer worth his salt could verify it, the signature was unmistakable in the style, the color, the brilliance of the technique.

The old man remained silent, while Le Brun considered his position. A coup in the making—buy it for a pittance, return to Jacobi in triumph, the masterpiece under his arm! A shrewd fellow that Le Brun, someone to watch, to promote!

The old man was still waiting; the words came out differently from what Le Brun had planned.

"Would you consider forty thousand francs?"

The old man's glance swung up to Le Brun sharply. The seamed, sagging face appeared to regain focus. The eyes were bright. "But without a name on it?"

"A Monet, monsieur, nevertheless."

"That's what they told me . . . I didn't really believe. Forty thousand? Yes, that doesn't sound too bad."

"You could try another dealer," Le Brun said.

"No." The voice was firm. "I like the one I have. Come here, young man."

An open closet. Stacked there three other paintings. The old man gestured, Le Brun carried them out. *Formidable!* A Cézanne Provençal landscape, structured in greens and browns; a Bonnard Paris street scene; a small but exquisite Rouault.

The ugliness of the flat heightened the beauty before Le Brun. His eyes skated desperately from one painting to the other; he fought for breath, finally lifting his gaze back to the old man. What was his name? My God!—yes, Ricard.

"Monsieur Ricard . . ."

"How much for the lot?"

The lot? Did he imagine he was selling some pieces of second-hand furniture?

"If you'll forgive me, sir, in your place I'd insist on at least one more appraisal . . . I can give you the name of another dealer . . ."

"You don't wish them yourself?"

93

"I'm not purchasing for myself, monsieur. I told you, remember? I'm an employee of the Jacobi Galleries."

"But you were empowered to set a price, no?"

"Yes . . . of course they'd no idea—"

"—no idea you would find paintings of such quality?"

Le Brun had sighed with relief. The man was not altogether naive.

"Exactly."

"I'm dying."

"What?"

"Oh, not before your eyes. But soon, quite soon. I've no time for 'other dealers.' Oh, yes, I have a list of them but no time, you understand? I have a granddaughter. I would like the money for her. Again, my dear Le Brun—it is Le Brun, isn't it?—give me a figure. The four paintings. *Now,* please!"

How can I? Le Brun had wondered. Not his money he'd be quoting. But suppose he left without the paintings? Suppose the old fellow turned around and sold them to the next name on his list? How would Aaron Jacobi react to losing such a buy? What would he think then of Claude Le Brun?

Then there was the matter of provenances. How could he be certain the old man wasn't selling him fakes. In this light, under these conditions! Mother of God!

Transfixed by the glowing thing he held in his hands, he walked to the window with it.

Ricard started to say something, but then coughed. He coughed for what seemed a terribly long time, his whole body racked. Then, with a supreme effort, he stopped and said, "The paintings belonged to my brother. He was David Ricard. You've heard of David Ricard?"

Indeed. David Ricard had been one of the leading wine merchants in Paris. Guy Le Brun had bought from him. David Ricard, if the old man was telling the truth, would have known what he was buying, so the provenances—the proof of authenticity, the history of the paintings—would rest in the wine merchant's good judgment.

Still a gamble only Aaron Jacobi should make.

He could see the old man was losing patience.

"Two hundred thousand," Le Brun heard himself saying. "For the four paintings, the lot."

"Your best?"

"Aaron Jacobi himself could offer you more . . . or less."

The old man laughed. The sound rumbled in his throat like pebbles tossed in a leather bag. "Done."

"What?"

"Sold."

An hour later, in his Matignon gallery office, Aaron Jacobi listened grimly while Le Brun revealed the offer he had made.

"Two hundred thousand?"

"You see, I—"

"You're aware," Jacobi interrupted acidly, "that you were representing the firm? I will have to honor the purchase, however badly you overpaid!"

"Yes, sir."

Picking up his silver-headed cane, placing his spectacle case in an inner jacket pocket, Jacobi silently headed for the stairs with Le Brun in tow. They took the firm's Bentley, Le Brun at the wheel, Jacobi in the front seat beside him, stiffly elegant in his black silk Sulka suit, lips compressed. *A cobra too is silent before a strike,* thought Le Brun, beginning to sweat.

At Ricard's building, Jacobi hopped out first, then realizing he did not know the apartment, imperiously waved Le Brun ahead of him, following up the worn, wooden treads to the third floor. Inside the apartment, beyond a quick searching appraisal of the shabby furnishings, Jacobi made no pretenses. A bare nod to Ricard on the couch, the old man apparently not at all bothered by the intrusion, and Jacobi made at once to the four paintings now ranged against the wall near the window

Le Brun watched his employer pick up each painting and hold it carefully to the light, suddenly unhurried. At last he had come to the Monet. This he cradled toward the sun, which barely topped the building across the street. He viewed the painting, it seemed, from every conceivable angle, turning it this way and that with increasing agitation.

Suppose I've made a mistake? Le Brun, despite his earlier confidence, couldn't help thinking. *And what makes me so goddamn sure I haven't?*

Jacobi appeared to be talking to himself, loudly and unintelligibly—in German, Le Brun eventually realized.

With infinite care, Jacobi now placed the Monet back with the others. The ultimate trader, his face giving nothing away, he faced Ricard. "You are satisfied with the price quoted?" he asked in his soft, fluted voice.

"Why, yes."

Nodding, Jacobi reached into his pocket, fished a small cigar from a silver case. From another pocket, a lighter, flame spurting. "You are right to be satisfied. My—colleague—has quoted you a very decent figure."

"Too high?" the old man asked with a touch of petulance.

"No," Jacobi said at once. "Fair to you, fair to us. The Monet, I must tell you, is magnificent. It is, in a way, a coup for us to get it. Le Brun, go to my bank and have the transaction completed to Monsieur Ricard's complete satisfaction. He is to be paid in the coin of any realm he chooses. Monsieur Ricard, I'll take the paintings with me now, if you don't mind. Every moment they remain in this firetrap places them in unacceptable danger!"

The Monet was to become one of the prize pieces in the great Jacobi collection. And the next day, a Friday, Claude Le Brun received a call from Helene Jacobi inviting him to dinner.

The Jacobis were not what would be considered orthodox Jews. They occasionally attended temple on the High Holidays, however, and their table, on Friday nights, did bear the seven-candled menorah; otherwise the service was princely, from the lustrous table linen to the gold-bordered Limoges. A family dinner, nonetheless, Le Brun sitting between Erica and Sara, Erica happily talking nonstop, making Le Brun describe every moment of the meeting with Monsieur Ricard—how he'd felt when he actually saw the Monet; how he'd *dared* the offer without proof of its being genuine. Why, if he had been mistaken, Papa would have had him garroted!

Laughter and more buzzing: the Jacobis did not separate their business from their personal lives . . . how could one with art? Each member of the family was aware of every sale, every acquisition; each had a favorite picture or objet d'art and screamed if Papa sold it—unless, of course, the price was considered advantageous.

Whatever the clamor, Aaron never lost his natural authority. Before dessert, a fine chilled sauterne being served, he mentioned, with no particular roll of drums, that he'd decided to send Le Brun to the New York gallery for six months to get an idea of the sort of paintings the Americans liked, the price structure in the States—an opportunity to improve his English.

Erica's euphoria was abruptly deflated. The family had planned to spend the summer at their Saint-Tropez villa, and she had made Le Brun promise to come down at least for a week in August, hidden at a hotel of course, although she'd work on Helene to invite him to use the villa's beach facilities.

Her father had paused, noting Le Brun's hesitation: perhaps the New York assignment—particularly during the summer months—was not to his liking. Did Le Brun imagine, or had Aaron's black, unreadable eyes also flickered over Erica?

"Oh, no, sir," Le Brun replied. "It's a marvelous opportunity. I'm grateful. My English will be even more grateful." He paused, suppressing a grimace of pain as Erica kicked him sharply under the table.

And then, with the sweetest of smiles, she had risen, excusing herself—exams to study for. What a bore all this endless chatter about the art business: art should have no prices; selling art was like trading in human souls!

Le Brun was furious with her, he remembered, not just for the pain inflicted, but for the rare sophomoric display. He was a serious businessman, dammit, and did she imagine her family could not see behind the tantrum? What could they think of him, pursuing an affair with their adolescent daughter?

They were laughing, Helene and Sara at least, Sara not quite up to looking at him; even Aaron Jacobi wore a tiny smile. Le Brun, who was not used to this kind of family interplay, tried gamely to pretend he had no idea what it was all about.

But Sara was the only one to speak. "Dear, dear Claude," she said, raising those big, black eyes—her father's eyes but larger—"you must forgive us, we've all an eccentric idea of what's funny. Savages, aren't we, Papa?"

"You might like to come down to Saint-Trop' for a few days before you leave," Helene Jacobi added placatingly. "As our guest, of course."

"Good idea," said Papa. "That way, while you frivolous women amuse yourselves at the beach, Le Brun and I can put in some solid working hours."

This set mother and father and younger daughter off again, not one of them making the slightest effort to control his or her hilarity.

Idiots, thought Le Brun, *absolute idiots!*

The next day, quite casually, Jacobi had mentioned at the office that there was a bonus involved in the Monet transaction. Would Le Brun prefer it in cash or in kind? Having no idea what Jacobi meant by "kind," indeed having expected nothing, Le Brun told Jacobi so. He had just done his job.

Ignoring the comment, Jacobi said, "Remember your Géricault, the one you sold me, the horse?"

Of course Le Brun remembered it.

"Well, I never did sell it. Don't know why. Never even put it up for sale. Perhaps I thought to keep it for an eventual trade. In any case, it's yours again."

Le Brun stared at Jacobi.

"Thought you might want to take it back to the family."

"My brother would have it on the market in ten seconds. I think I'll keep it in trust. At least for the time being. Do you mind if it stays with your collection—in the vaults?"

"Suit yourself. Pull it out when you want."

"It's a magnificent gift, Mr. Jacobi. I'm very grateful."

The dark little man wore the ghost of a smile. "It's a pleasure to give sometimes. Makes one feel wonderfully rich."

It had all happened in another life, Le Brun decided now, sitting in the *café–tabac* off rue Visconti. His watch showed precisely one o'clock. He had finished his coffee. The *concierge* across the street appeared again, oddly, to water her already-watered geraniums.

Le Brun left some change for the waiter and, making sure no one was loitering, watching, he crossed the street and walked through the doorway and into the *concierge's* apartment.

Garnier and Arnaud were already there, having entered from the rear alley connected to a court of a building down the street. With Le Brun's arrival, the *concierge* departed, loudly closing the door behind her.

A bottle of vermouth and three glasses had been left on the table in the tiny living room. Arnaud was the only one who was drinking. He was obviously agitated about something. "It must not happen again!" he was saying to Garnier as Le Brun joined them.

Garnier was trying to explain Vichy's position to Arnaud. "I grant you our resources are limited, which is why obviously, Pétain and Laval are trying to deal 'politically.' It's our only weapon, after all. The others want the fleet neutralized—at the very least they want economic cooperation; they want minimal interference in what they call their 'solution' to the Jewish problem. Fight them on these issues and they'll come down on all our heads with their gun butts! They'll take our bread, our lives. They'll take our women, they'll take our art!"

"Our art! That's all you *espèces de cons* think about!"

Garnier colored; he was not used to being talked to in this manner. Arnaud was, of course, a Communist. Unfortunately the Communists were the best-organized —at this point really the only—underground fighters to be relied upon. But there was no question about Arnaud's vulgarity and about the basic ideological differences he and his kind represented.

"A hundred thousand workers being sent to the Reich," Arnaud was saying, still gnawing on the same bone, "and you bastards say, 'Go ahead, take more!'"

"A hundred thousand volunteers! And at least they

99

go through our hands. We know their names, where they're being sent. We have some control."

"You have shit," said Arnaud.

"We're not meeting here to discuss national policy . . . we're here to discuss practical matters— the unimaginable amount of art being shipped out of the country, for example. Le Brun will verify it." Garnier cast a quick look at Le Brun.

"It's hardly a secret," Le Brun commented. Like Garnier, he was coldly angry. How to explain to a jackass like Arnaud that the great treasures of France represented not simply a source of money, but something infinitely more precious—the cultural heritage of a nation, a civilization?

"And it's hardly anything we can stop. What do you expect of the railroad people, the SNCF?" Arnaud said caustically. "The *Boches* are fiendishly clever. Between every four or five cars of art, a cattle car filled with Jews. Shall our railroad people lay dynamite on the tracks?"

"There'll soon be no more Jews for the bastards to send," said Le Brun.

"They'll find more, don't worry," said Arnaud. "Every day they discover some hiding in the cracks. And already the Gestapo is on to us. We will have increasing casualties."

They were silent, for once in agreement. As the Resistance grew, so did the Nazi force against it. And by the Resistance, one meant not trained subversives, but ordinary men and women throwing themselves into the work, risking their lives.

"Speaking of Jews"—Arnaud turned to Le Brun— "we picked up an interesting item from London."

"What's that?"

"Aaron Jacobi's daughter has been making discreet arrangements to sneak into France. The younger one. The older was killed some years ago. Damned curious. She may be here already. Sara Jacobi. Now why in hell would she want to come back?"

Le Brun looked coldly at Arnaud. "I wouldn't have the slightest idea."

"Well, I would," put in Garnier. "The Jacobi

collection. To recover it, perhaps ship it to safety in London."

"Jacobi," said Arnaud tartly, "may be as shrewd as they come, but he's no magician. That would take some doing."

"I agree," said Le Brun. "But if the girl is here couldn't she simply have returned for patriotic reasons, to fight for her country?"

"A Jewess?" asked Arnaud.

"She's an especially lovely young woman," said Garnier unexpectedly. "My wife knew her as a child. But I agree, the collection could be the magnet. God knows, Goering would sell his soul to possess it."

"Who wouldn't?" said Arnaud at once. Then, aware of their concentration on him, he added hastily, "To turn it over to the government, naturally. Don't deny you'd grab it, Garnier!"

"Only for custodial care," Garnier said stiffly. "I must point that out. It would still belong to Jacobi. Don't put us in the same category as Goering."

"Even so, if only to deprive *them* of it, I would think it's important we keep on top of this. Don't you agree, Le Brun?"

"Without question," Le Brun told Arnaud. But did the man believe he was fooling anybody? Wouldn't the Communists love to pounce on the collection! How long would it take them to sell it abroad? In Spain? Switzerland? And, with that much gold on hand, would there be any question which Resistance faction would remain top dog?"

Garnier, Le Brun sensed, was on the same wavelength. "Should you be correct, Arnaud," he said, "and the girl is back here for that purpose, she could inadvertently accomplish just the opposite of what she intends: lead the bastards to wherever the collection is hidden."

"Exactly my thoughts," said Arnaud smugly.

"All right," said Le Brun. "If Sara Jacobi is in Paris—and I doubt it—I accept her as my responsibility. One final thing: I've received a tip—I prefer not to reveal my source—that Goering plans a little weekend excursion into the Loire. Might be just a sightseeing jaunt, or he might have more ambitious plans."

Garnier was alarmed. "Are you sure of it? I'd better inform Vichy."

Arnaud laughed savagely. "Fat chance anyone in Vichy will move his ass. Unless it's to greet Goering at the border with caviar and champagne. Well, maybe assassination is a possibility."

Neither Garnier nor Le Brun commented.

"In any case," said Arnaud, "We don't know yet when it will be, do we?"

"No," said Le Brun.

"Well, time to take action when we do. Forget this damned art business, Le Brun. You pick up anything else in that viper's nest? Like worker quotes for Germany? Gestapo strength in Paris? For Christ's sake, anything up *my* alley?"

"No, sorry. If I do—"

"Yes. *If* you do," Arnaud said irritably. "Madame Chard!" he called loudly.

The *concierge* appeared too quickly; she must have been listening at the door.

The three men, having set up the cover for the next meeting, went their separate ways.

Le Brun decided he needed to stretch his legs, do some thinking. Arnaud's information about Sara Jacobi, while not dangerous so far, was alarming. The question: how best to use it? How to tell her? Press too vigorously and the girl was likely to overract, stay on to spite him *and* the Germans. As Erica would have done. Sound a bugle and a Jacobi would bet or fight. Aaron, who pretended to scorn the ambiance of the racetrack, the cult of the thoroughbred, was an inveterate gambler. As were his wife and daughters. Erica's loudest complaint against the world was the injustice done to women in forbidding them the glory of the battlefield. She had bitterly resented the fact that as a volunteer in Spain she would not, officially at any rate, ever be given a rifle. She wouldn't hurt a fly, but she'd gladly kill a Fascist, she claimed. Could she actually have pulled a trigger?

He was at the rue de Sèvres without having realized it. The afternoon was cooling off slightly, the clouds beginning to bank over the city in pillows of smoke. *It could be rain,* he thought.

Montparnasse.

Hesitating, he turned right, then paused. His family lived only a dozen blocks away. What would happen if he appeared at the door, rang, faced them? His brother Guy had joined Laval's staff, a Foreign Office appointment, was probably at the quai d'Orsay, which would leave his sister-in-law, a half-blind old aunt, and his young nephews. A brood of vipers.

He saw a Métro kiosk a street away and made for it.

Le Brun spent several hours at the Matignon gallery in the afternoon working with Pierre Lavoulière, a gray-faced man in his late fifties with a withered left hand. Lavoulière was formerly an assistant accountant. The senior accountant had gone with Jacobi. The rest of the staff, with the exception of three gentiles, had vanished weeks before.

Although von Banheim's people, Raeder specifically, had cleaned out the most valuable paintings, some pieces had been stored in a hidden vault below the gallery and a handful of reasonably good ones had been out on consignment.

The Jacobi Gallery would continue in business, that Le Brun had already made clear to Lavoulière, but on a highly restricted basis. Whatever business Le Brun could manage from this point onward would have to be based on wit and skill and the clout he possessed with Goering's group at the Jeu de Paume.

Actually he was in touch with Amsterdam and Brussels; there were people there he had met with Jacobi who would deal with him. It was possible he could come up with some desirable items from those cities to dangle before Kröler's eyes. And then in Paris he was already on to certain paintings—names of former owners unmentioned—that he was sure the Germans would snap up at handsome prices . . . the prices, he knew, had to be high or his bona fides would become suspect.

"Of course," said Lavoulière, when they had run through the current dealings, "if we could put our hands on the collection . . ."

"No, not the collection," said Le Brun mildly. Had to be careful about Lavoulière, who might already have been bought off by Kröler's organization—or could be at any instant. In a level voice Le Brun added, "Even if we knew where Jacobi put it, we'd have to offer it at once to Dr. Kröler. If you wish to continue to work for me, Lavoulière, kindly remember to whom we owe our loyalty!"

"Truly, truly," said Lavoulière, his head bobbing. "But that in itself would be a coup, wouldn't it? Reichsmarschall Goering himself would have to be pleased. Unquestionably it would make the firm's fortune all over again!"

The house on the avenue Foch was a short drive from the gallery.

A tail was on him again; they had probably staked out the Matignon, figuring he had to turn up there periodically. It was the same man as in the morning, the elderly, hangdog fellow in the threadbare worsted suit at the wheel of a Citroën. Le Brun wondered briefly whether the man had been reprimanded by his superiors for losing him earlier and if he resented Le Brun for the fact. Another traitorous Frenchman. *May you rot in hell!* Le Brun thought with sudden venom.

At the Jacobi house—now the Le Brun house—Mischa was in his street clothes, just leaving, he said, for the day.

"Don't let me keep you," Le Brun told him.

Mischa said he'd stay a few minutes.

He had set the Jacobi mansion to rights as he had promised Le Brun. The rooms on the ground floor had been cleared and scrubbed and polished, odd pieces of furniture removed and carted upstairs to the bedrooms, which now were fairly habitable—at least the two master bedrooms overlooking the gardens. The bathrooms were immaculate, tiles gleaming. "You can move in whenever you wish, monsieur," he told Le Brun who was making a quick inspection tour. "Fortunately the soldiers who came did not also steal the linen; you'll find there is plenty. Also the kitchen is fairly complete. Of course they took the silverware and the good dinner services."

Mischa could have been reading off the inventory of a house Le Brun was renting. But the ice-blue eyes hardly took Le Brun into account at all; they were focused inward on something exceedingly unpleasant.

"Thank you, you've been very efficient. I shall furnish only one of the lower drawing rooms, possibly the library. Mademoiselle Dumont, my companion who will move in with me, is not concerned with entertaining. She is a professional, as you may know, and a busy woman. Mischa, what I must speak to you about is Sara. You can detest me as much as you want, but you must listen to me now. Certain people know that the girl is either in France or planning to come here."

Mischa whirled to face him. "Who are these 'certain people'?"

"What's the difference? The Resistance today, the Gestapo tomorrow."

"What would they care about a young girl?"

"For Christ's sake, Mischa, let's not play games! It's the collection they're after."

"Or *you're* after!"

Le Brun grabbed Mischa's arm—it was like trying to take hold of corded steel. "Get her to leave Paris."

Mischa had yellowed, big-fanged teeth. They were showing humorlessly. "Tell a Jacobi what to do? I could better tell my uncle. He was an archduke."

"They'll get their hands on her eventually. Doesn't she see—?"

"What she wants to!"

The blue eyes locked on Le Brun, but were looking through him, the Prince Kilkanov thinking, measuring the odds. Finally he relented: "I will get her to talk with you. You will try and reason with her. If harm comes to Sara because of this meeting—"

With Mischa gone, alone in the big empty house, Le Brun would have wandered, haunted by one lovely, laughing ghost. But he had other business.

Off the large pantry between kitchen and formal dining room, was the stairwell. One stairway led upward to the family bedrooms, the other to two levels of cellars—the first, the laundry rooms, food storage, and the like; the second, smaller and stone-lined, housed old furniture, luggage, family paraphernalia, as well as the wine cellar. In the house of Aaron Jacobi the latter was of prime importance.

Le Brun switched on an overhead light. The racks, as expected, loomed empty, forlorn, the vintage bottles long since appropriated by von Banheim's looters. A large, empty room but clean and rodent-free, a tribute to Mischa's diligence. At the far end, a thermometer in a wooden case was screwed to the wall. Fifty-five degrees. Still perfect for a decent red, Le Brun saw, twisting and pulling the wooden case like a door handle with all his strength.

The stone behind the instrument slid obediently back. Revealed was an opening at a tall man's height, perhaps three feet in width. Inside was a heavy metal lightswitch. Le Brun yanked it down, illuminating a tunnel which ran into the distance.

He returned to the head of the steps and listened. The house above him was a tomb. Satisfied, he walked back to the tunnel, entered, and rolled the false stone door closed behind him.

Starting forward, on uneven paving, he heard small animals scurrying ahead; the rank earth-smell closed around him. Bolstered by bricks along the way, the roof had been planked, but a long time ago, and in places it was rotting. Roots had broken through and occasionally there was trickling of sewer water.

The length of a long city block later, Le Brun reached the tunnel's end, a massive wooden door secured by a beam set in iron slots. On both sides of the door stones had been set in mortar to bolster the frame. He dug a finger in a crack at eye height. A slab of mortar swung back on a rusty hinge; it was actually a painted wooden slab concealing a tiny pocket in the wall that housed a large iron key.

Removing the beam, Le Brun inserted the key, playing with the lock before it clicked within the mechanism and the door creaked open. He entered a pitch-dark chamber, but his exploring hand found a switch near the door. High-wattage lamps had been placed at intervals on the ceiling; the room was suddenly brilliant and alive before him.

Overwhelmed, Le Brun stood a moment on the threshold before shutting himself in.

No crumbling, dank, earth-smelling crypt. Plastered walls and a new brick floor. In one corner, a large humidifier hummed quietly.

Against the far wall, facing him, framed paintings were stacked; others had been placed side by side on a raised wooden platform.

Exactly seventy-eight, including the Monet he had bought for Jacobi years ago, as well as the works of Manet, Vuillard, Bonnard, Matisse, Vlaminck, Picasso, Rouault, Dégas, Van Gogh, Cézanne.

It would be difficult, Le Brun knew, to estimate the value of the collection, especially in these chaotic days. While scorning the painters as decadent, Goering and Hitler would have paid a fortune for the works, knowing they could obtain an even greater one reselling overseas. The future price when peace came, if it were to come, would be incalculable.

Ignoring his Géricault on an upper tier, he took the Monet from its resting place, setting it alone in a clear spot on the second tier. It was his favorite.

There was a small wooden table in the corner and a plain wooden chair. On the table was an ordinary account book in which were listed the paintings in the cave.

The caretakers of the collection had insisted on this.

A second account book was in Aaron Jacobi's possession in London, signed by a Father Gregory; the priest had also insisted on this second record—there must be no question later on of dereliction on his part, or on the part of anyone connected with his Church.

Le Brun sat on the chair and smoked a cigarette, wondering how he would manage it—to save what had been stored in this cave, this treasure—to slip it out of France, somehow, to England, to Jacobi.

He remembered the night Aaron had first brought him here.

It was a week before Jacobi himself had left with

107

his family, the Germans coming on fast, almost cutting it too close, Le Brun had then considered.

Days before leaving, however, the Prince Kilkanov —Mischa himself—had lugged the collection, painting by painting, through the tunnel to the church.

The tunnel between the Jacobi house and the church was no happenstance.

The house on the avenue Foch, almost a century and a half previously, had belonged briefly to the church, donated by a Russian diamond merchant as a fitting domicile for the bishop. The merchant had dreamed of the bishop's one day becoming patriarch of all the Russias, and of God and the patriarch rewarding him handsomely for his generosity.

He had the tunnel dug to serve His Holiness in inclement weather—or as a getaway in case the ardor of the revolutionary tribunals turned against the Russian churchmen who had made their first, tentative foray into this foreign city.

Father Gregory, for his part, had prepared the cave well in advance, installing the machine to keep the air dry (the workmen had been told that holy relics would be stored here), and building the scaffolding for the paintings.

Only two other priests were told what was going on, both scheduled to be transferred back to the Motherland. Mischa was not informed that Claude Le Brun had been let in on the secret.

"I trust him completely, it goes without saying," Jacobi had told Le Brun, "but for your sake the less he knows the better."

They had discussed the possibility of German occupation and how then to get the collection out of France.

Where would it be safe in that calamitous situation? New York? But New York was across the Atlantic. London?

"If France falls," said Jacobi, "England will follow."

"France won't fall," stated Le Brun categorically. Neither man believed it.

A pact was made between them. Le Brun would remain, and should the worst happen, play whatever role was necessary for survival. The goal: save the collection. From whatever sanctuary he finally chose, Jacobi would use all his resources to send aid, money, people, whatever was available. From Switzerland, perhaps. Italy. Spain. "They won't enter the war, any of them," said Jacobi contemptuously. "They'll stay neutral, wait it out, then pounce and gorge on the dead bodies."

Le Brun considered the older man cynical. If France collapsed, what countries would *not* be dragged into it? The world would be disarranged like a map cut into little pieces and scattered to the winds.

That night—*My God, it seems decades ago*—he thought, they discussed another problem. Would Jacobi tell his wife and Sara of the arrangement between Le Brun and himself?

No, Jacobi had answered promptly. If Le Brun didn't mind. Better for them to remain ignorant. Better for Le Brun. Later, when the collection was rescued, then . . .

Le Brun, still in shock over Erica, nodded obediently, not liking it. Would he always be so emotionally tied to this family?

They had tramped back through the tunnel. They reentered the wine cellar, Jacobi sliding the false wall of stone across it, concealing it. Then he looked around him sadly. "You select what you want, *mon fils,*" he said. It was the first time Jacobi had ever used the word "son."

"It will go to the *Boches* if you don't," Aaron added and he spat. It was the one vulgar gesture Le Brun had ever seen him make.

The *Boches* were already at the Belgian border, the blitzkrieg under way.

Le Brun had been working out future tactics in his mind. "I'll lead them down here *if* they get here," he said. "I'll invite them to take what they want."

"If you think it best. But what a waste." Jacobi was walking slowly past the wine racks like a defeated general saying farewell to the troops. Finally he paused at a special rack at the far end. Straightening, he held a bottle of brandy upright in his fist. "Napoléon '98.

109

We drink it now. At once." His smile at Le Brun suddenly had nothing of defeat in it.

They drank the bottle all right, Le Brun remembered. He would not have believed the dapper little man could hold so much.

The Monet, he considered, now, examining it in the cave, represented, somehow, the essence of its present owner, as if what the artist had sought to put on canvas—the fertility, the deep, tenacious richness of this tiny piece of French soil—also characterized the Jews, Aaron Jacobi.

Someone was fumbling with the lock behind Le Brun, the door leading up into the building above them.

Le Brun swung around, reaching for his Luger, then dropped his hand.

The man who entered was tall and bearded, in his early forties perhaps. He wore the traditional black cassock. The unique cross of the Russian Orthodoxy attached to a heavy gold chain lay on his chest. He closed the door behind him, locking it.

Father Gregory.

Le Brun did not have to ask what had brought him; a light signal had been devised to alert him any time the cave was entered.

"I was wondering when we would meet again," he said shaking Le Brun's hand.

"I'm constantly followed, Father. To have sought you out myself would have been to risk your involvement."

Father Gregory smiled and took a cigarette from the pack Le Brun held out.

"Any news from London?"

"Not directly. But surely Kilkanov has told you that Sara Jacobi is here in the city."

The priest's concern was immediate, his dark, liquid eyes troubled, as he hesitated, then bent to Le Brun's match.

"The Prince Kilkanov and I do not see each other very often."

"But surely some contact—" Le Brun said, surprised.

"The truth," Father Gregory put in dryly, "is that our friend is not much of a churchgoer. And with the

110

Princess immobilized . . ." He shook his head, struck by a more pressing thought: "Why has the girl come?"

"To play a part in the war, I suppose. To fight for her country."

"Nothing to do with the collection?"

Le Brun was firm about that. "She has no idea where it's hidden. Her father would not have permitted her to know. And I don't think Kilkanov has told her."

"She's tough, that one," the priest said. "Like her father in a way. Like her sister. I'd put nothing past her." His glance swept past Le Brun again, his ham of a hand extended toward the paintings. "I'm sorry to ask, but have you any possibility of moving them?"

"No. Not yet. Why?"

The priest's voice suddenly had a hint of harshness, of finality. "I don't know how much more time you'll be granted. I'm God's vicar here, not master. There are other priests. The existence of this room is of course known—but happily, not what's in it. The cover is that I'm hiding a whole storeroom of contraband foodstuffs, black market, because of my insatiable appetite." Father Gregory's half-smile at Le Brun broke suddenly into a grin, showing strong white teeth. *He is remarkably handsome,* Le Brun thought. He recalled Aaron Jacobi remarking on what the women had missed when the priest had chosen celibacy. "Actually," Father Gregory said ruefully, "I do have a healthy appetite, but it's because of my size, don't you think?"

"I could smuggle you in some food," offered Le Brun. "I have connections."

"Cigarettes," said Father Gregory. "Any brand. And should you find yourself by chance overburdened with butter and coffee and sugar and wine . . ."

They both laughed, the sound breaking against the stone walls, making them stop at once, guiltily. But from above, stealing through the crevices, another sound could be heard. Male voices in chorus, filtering down to them by some magic, growing in contained volume and purity like the resonance of a far-off organ.

111

"Rehearsing," Father Gregory said proudly, seeing the pleasure on Le Brun's face. "Jacobi would come to listen and perhaps pray, although he swore he was an agnostic. Did you know he was very generous with us for years? Before we had any way of repaying?"

The priest had turned, was staring at the paintings.

"It would be a pity to let the swine get their hands on them, wouldn't it? To allow them to be scattered, peddled in whatever markets they can find . . . and what for? Gold to buy more panzers!"

He looked back to Le Brun. The gruff, amiable giant had been transformed into a frightening, dominating presence. "Find a way to stop them!" he ordered harshly. "And quickly, Le Brun, eh?"

Making his way back through the tunnel, Le Brun paused abruptly at the Jacobi end, his heart in his throat: men were in the wine cellar! He could hear them moving about.

He reached for his gun, this time drawing it, then again stuck it back in his jacket. What good would it do? Unless of course they found the tunnel and came after him.

Closer to the panel, ear against it.

"Hurry, dammit!" he could hear someone saying. "The walls. Behind the racks. It must be somewhere!"

Sergeant Raeder. Le Brun could swear it was Raeder. Speaking French. The men with him had to be Milice agents.

"We've been here before, Sergeant. Found nothing. The whole house is clean. An entire day. A dozen men . . ."

"To hell with your dozen men. The floor as well. A secret room below, perhaps."

They had brought picks and hammers.

They were banging everywhere.

They would discover nothing by tapping the walls, Le Brun knew. The back of the panel had been reinforced by Jacobi's men to provide for this contingency. It would not ring hollow.

By the sound they were now concentrating on the stone floor.

"Suppose he comes back and finds us here?" the Milice officer asked.

112

"Why should he come back at this hour? Didn't you say your man had seen him leave?"

"Begging your pardon, Sergeant, he did not see him leave. He did see the lights in the house go out."

Stupid! Le Brun swore at himself. *Why did I do that? Inbred, French penny-pinching custom. Lights in daylight?*

"He assumed Le Brun had evaded him, perhaps by scaling the garden walls of the neighboring house. It abuts the side street. Vincent ran around to see, but by then, naturally, Le Brun could easily have left by the front door."

Raeder broke into nasty laughter.

"Suppose you were up against a real professional? How many dozen men would you need?

How can they take this shit from Raeder? Le Brun found himself thinking indignantly. *They are still Frenchmen.*

The sound of picks and hammers continued. Le Brun watched, the cold of the tunnel penetrating to his bones. He had switched off the lights; they might shine through an inside crack. Something brushed against his trouser leg; he kicked wildly, hitting air.

"People don't always hide things in cellars, you know, Sergeant," he heard the Milice man say.

"Well, then, you tell me where they hide them," Raeder answered sarcastically.

"Just the same," the other man said doggedly, "the way Le Brun eludes our tail strikes me as more than suspicious."

"Of course it's suspicious. But for the moment we find him a useful tool which is more than I can say for you. Okay—let's get out of here!"

They left presently, clomping up the stairs.

When he was sure they'd gone, Le Brun made his way up, walked through main salon and out into the garden.

Using the strategy the Milice agent had described, he climbed the neighboring garden wall, walked along it to its juncture with the cross street, then hauled himself over.

Pedestrians at the far end, no one else in sight.

Unhurriedly, he strolled toward the Champs-Elysées.

Le Brun went back to his office.

Lavoulière had news from Brussels—a Fragonard they had been negotiating for from a dealer, a man Jacobi and Company had dealt with on other occasions, was available.

"How much?" asked Le Brun.

"Three hundred thousand Reichsmarks."

"Offer two-fifty."

"He won't—"

"Try him," snapped Le Brun.

Lavoulière went out and Le Brun sat at his desk attending to neglected correspondence while debating a certain course of action. He had nothing to lose, he finally decided, to put in a call to Kröler at the Jeu de Paume. After the customary bout with Kröler's secretary, Le Brun was successful, Kröler came on the line.

"And how is our French *Kamarad* today?" he asked jovially.

Goering must be out of town, Le Brun was willing to wager. "Rotten, Kröler. I want to speak to the Reichsmarschall."

The easiness faded from the voice on the other end. "About what?"

"About harassment. I am constantly being followed. By squads of your secret agents. I demand that it be stopped at once. Another thing. Today your goddamn Gestapo—or whoever they are—broke into my house. Such behavior is inadmissable. It appears obvious the Reichsmarschall distrusts me and wishes to terminate our association."

The silence appeared interminable. When he spoke, Kröler seemed to be choking slightly.

"You were present when the house was broken into?"

"I had left, but neighbors reported seeing these . . . bloodhounds leave. So now I'm not only suspect by you people but also by the nice citizens on my street. What are they to think of the new owner of the Jacobi mansion? I repeat, am I to understand I no longer have your confidence?"

"Absolutely not," said Kröler firmly, regaining his composure. *That smartass Raeder!* "Believe me, Le

114

Brun, this office is absolutely ignorant of any activity against you. But you have my word it will be stopped as soon as I can make a phone call! You must know in what high regard Reichsmarschall Goering holds you!"

Le Brun allowed several seconds to pass, aware that Lavoulière had returned and was staring at him, mouth open, aghast at his audacity.

"Good. I accept that fact that this is none of your doing. And I admit it would pain me greatly to be separated from the Reichsmarschall—you're aware how much I admire him! By the way, something of interest has turned up: I am able to lay my hands on Fragonard's 'Dressmaker.' Are you familiar with it?"

"The 'Dressmaker'? Surely. Wasn't it in the Brussels museum?"

"On loan. It is back in private hands. Do you want it?"

"Without question." But Kröler had abruptly turned cool, assuming his negotiating stance. "If, naturally, the price is not exorbitant."

"Seven hundred thousand."

Lavoulière could not suppress an audible indrawn breath. Le Brun paid no attention.

"Five hundred thousand," barked Kröler. "We're not made of gold, Le Brun."

"Six hundred thousand," Le Brun countered, unimpressed. "You must allow me a small profit."

"A small fortune!" Kröler said after a pause. "But all right. Providing the Reichsmarschall does not disapprove."

"Will he want to see the work?"

"Not necessarily. He's enormously busy these days. However, he knows the painting and he'll be pleased. Congratulations, Le Brun. Keep at it. And let's try to forget the other little matter, eh?"

"Forgotten. I'll call again tomorrow when I know the Brussels arrangements. *Au 'voir.*" Hanging up, Le Brun caught Lavoulière regarding him with a mixture of admiration and dismay. "Did Brussels accept two-fifty?"

"Yes—but a three-fifty profit! Remarkable!"

"It's a Fragonard, not a piece of cheese. Any less

and they'd have no respect for us. Now who will you send to pick it up? I don't trust ordinary transport. Special permits will be needed for the border. Kröler's office will supply them. Wait—on second thought, I don't want to risk any slip-ups. You'd better make the trip yourself."

Lavoulière simply nodded, but his body, held stiffly at attention, demonstrated his pleasure and the awe with which he regarded his new benefactor. To think he'd be free of his wife and kids for a half a week! And in Brussels—a truly sophisticated city!

Le Brun was looking at his watch.

"All in your hands, my friend. Can you handle it?"

"You'll see," replied Lavoulière smartly, accompanying Le Brun to the stairs. In his excitement he couldn't stop talking. "So the *Boches* were giving you trouble. How cleverly you handled them!"

Le Brun gave him a half-smile. "It may be necessary at times, Lavoulière," he said, "to assert our independence. We can't let them walk all over us. But they're not bastards, they're our partners, our *allies!* Remember that! See you in the morning."

"In the morning," repeated Lavoulière humbly.

Ten

HE SAW HER, several hundred yards away, get off a bus and start across the esplanade toward the museum. She was wearing a simple cream-silk blouse; a blue skirt; practical, flat shoes; walking slowly, warily. Halfway to him she paused, as if looking toward the Tour Eiffel and the Champ de Mars. The sun, which was dancing between the dark masses of sky, sped into the clear abruptly, bathing her in light, and her head went up as if to drink it in. She bore herself with the same easy grace as Erica, he thought; but being taller, dark hair cascading down, she was more naturally elegant. She ought to tone herself down, somehow, he found himself thinking: dangerous in today's Paris to be so striking—hands could pull at an attractive woman from empty streets.

She had lit a cigarette and was continuing slowly toward the museum columns though he was fairly sure he was still concealed.

After another moment he stepped out where she could see him.

"Hello," he said, bending to kiss her. She pulled back as if stung. "Allow me to kiss you, please," he insisted quietly. "Suppose we're being watched? Why would we rendezvous here? Are we strangers?"

She bent her face toward his, allowing his lips to brush her cheeks.

I should be ashamed of myself, he thought. He had checked thoroughly before coming here—Kröler had succeeded in putting a stop to the surveillance—the tail had been removed. They were not being watched, he was sure.

But still I used this dishonest little trick to get close to her, he told himself angrily.

Inside the museum they were almost alone with the row on row of model ships within the glass cases. At the far end a father with two young boys. Nearer, a nicely dressed white-haired woman who seemed to be going methodically from one display to the next; Le Brun, scrutinizing everyone, wondered briefly at her interest—a cool, quiet sanctuary perhaps?

Sara had moved next to a case in the middle aisle which contained a scale model of the shipentine *Madeleine,* 321 feet with a gross tonnage of 3942, constructed in France in 1896, four decks and built of wood, although her diagonal framing was braced with iron, the plaque below the ship informed.

Le Brun almost lost the girl's first words: "Mischa insisted, otherwise I would not be here. I intend to listen politely. I hardly think your counsel is to be trusted."

"I expected nothing else. Listen, Sara, they know

you're here or will be. Only a fool would tempt fate by staying."

"Is that all you have to say?"

"Let me drive you down to the Loire. It's no trouble to wangle exit permits. The family farm would be reasonably safe—for a while, at least. And, being in the unoccupied zone, it didn't pass over to me."

"But it will. Sooner or later you'll get your hands on it, won't you?"

"Sooner or later." He shrugged. "The *Boches* will descend like a wolf on the fold—yes, it will pass to me . . . perhaps for five minutes! But for now it still belongs to the Jacobis, and we're playing for time."

"You or me? My father's paintings are long since gone from Paris. Both you and the filthy scum you work for can forget about them."

So she didn't know where the collection was hidden —although she must surely be working on Mischa to tell her. How long would he be able to hold out?

"I'm thinking of your life," he said flatly.

She wanted to believe him. She had been in love with him since the night he had walked into the house to meet with her father. Erica, she imagined, had known about it but considered it a passing crush. A schoolgirl's infatuation, Erica would have reasoned lightly, being all of three years older and so damned precocious.

Sara told herself that she hated Le Brun now. It was no use allowing the old, childish emotions to intrude. If any physical attraction remained, that was clearly separable and could be dealt with. She was not weak. On the contrary, she was able to cope with any problems that might arise in that department.

Le Brun was thinner than she remembered him, older decidedly, some gray strands in the raven-black hair. The slightly arrogant look was still there, but the widespread eyes were deep and brown, revealing the warmth of the man when he chose to show it.

She could read nothing in the eyes now but a hint of desperation, if it wasn't dissembled, which she told herself was certainly possible. He appeared to be searching not for exits but for entrances, a way to convince her of something very important.

118

"Are you interested in these ships? Over there is the barque *France*—a five-master, as you can see. Oddly, she was built in Glasgow at the end of the century." He stopped, then continued rambling: "The old system of recruitment in the French navy was horrible, by the way—particularly before Napoleon. Between the 'old' aristocrats and the so-called *'officiers bleus.'* It accounted, I would think, for our naval defeats. I practically lived here as a kid. You and Erica used to sail, I seem to recall."

Aware of the disjointedness, he stopped, smiling a little, abruptly tongue-tied.

Sensitive to his distress, she heard herself saying, "Yes, she liked to sail," and added, "I like to fly. I was about to get my pilot's license. I suppose I can forget that now."

The white-haired woman had left; the other family had lost itself in the rear of the museum.

Sara turned to Le Brun, suddenly serious. "Did you and Erica plan to get married?"

"What?"

"Were you and my sister about to be married?"

The question wrenched him back. "We loved each other very much."

She looked away from him quickly, silent. It could never happen now. On no account, ever, could she steal this love from her fallen sister; it would be the most disloyal of blows, unanswerable from the grave—the one she could never deliver.

In a way it made everything much easier.

"You must get out of the city," he was saying again; it seemed to him he had been repeating this endlessly.

"You don't have to worry about me," she answered in as distant a voice as she could manage. "Goodbye, Claude."

"Goodbye," he said unhappily.

Turning—no one to witness a kiss now—she walked briskly away from him down the aisle of glass cases and out of the building.

He followed slowly, in time to see her cross the place du Trocadéro—there were others now on the esplanade, the usual jackboots with their cameras, and here

119

and there the old, riding the benches, seeking the sun, sharp, dark eyes silently cursing the invaders.

She was gone now, perhaps aboard a bus that had paused briefly, then plunged into the traffic, headed up Kléber to the Etoile.

He found a cigarette and puffed deeply, annoyed with her for her stubborness even while—he could be objective—he understood and credited her mistrust. The rendezvous had after all been stupid; worse, fruitless. But her look, the *feeling* she had given him of Erica—the mannerisms, the voice—had grabbed hold. It took another several minutes for him to smoke the cigarette down, grind out the butt, look at his watch. Home or office again? He opted for the Matignon; he was not up to a bout, verbal or sexual, with Mallou.

The church, one of several Russian Orthodox churches of Paris, was close to the avenue Victor-Hugo, where the bus let her off.

Across the street from the church, an impressive domed structure sitting easily in alien territory, actually between Victor-Hugo and Foch, was a row of nineteenth-century apartment houses. It was at the first of these that Sara paused, pushed the outside door button, and let herself in. Nameplates in the lobby noted that the Prince and Princess Kilkanov occupied apartment 2 bis, rear. Walking through to the back of the building, Sara arrived at a small area with a service elevator.

The elevator took her to the top floor, a long corridor with a mansard roof, the length of the corridor punctuated by doors on each side all the way to the end. Each door opened to a tiny room consisting of a washstand, a radiator, a small window giving onto the roof opposite, and a bed. A communal bathroom somewhere in the middle of the corridor. The rooms, barely larger than the length of two beds, end to end, were occupied by the servants of the owners of the apartments below.

The room Sara entered, number 26, was even more cramped than the others, having been used for storage by the Kilkanovs, who had had no regular maid. Boxes, crates, even two steamer trunks, were stacked immediately at the entrance, giving Sara barely enough room to slip between and reach the bed. Squeezing past it now, she could see the church between a split in the buildings opposite, the dome catching the weak, lemony sun. It was no more than a block away from their house on Foch, an octagonal building with a small-windowed clerestory to permit light.

It was a small church, really, wearing a gold onion crown. A square clock and a gold mosaic of Christ Pantocrater graced the central façade.

She knew the inside well, having been there many times as a child with Mischa and Mischa's wife, Sonia. When Sonia was still able to walk.

Her father had been on good terms with the bishop and the priests. The bishop had come to dinner on occasion, and she imagined that Aaron had donated money. He genuinely enjoyed the Russian Orthodox service, he had told his daughters.

Thinking of him, knowing he had been right as usual about this desperate adventure, deepened Sara's depression. The knowledge assailed her that coming back here was a romantic escapade at best—that she was a silly young woman to think for a moment that merely facing Claude Le Brun would magically produce a convincing set of facts contrary to her father's information.

Le Brun was a traitor . . . to his country, to her father. A Fascist, an opportunist, as Aaron Jacobi had said. Sara Jacobi in Paris could do little but confirm the fact.

Then what further reason to stay? To work with the Resistance? What use could they possibly make of her?

Find the collection? Bring it in triumph to London? Not unless she could get hold of an airplane, a secret airfield, a pilot, accomplices willing to risk the consequences. And even then, first to be able to break down Mischa—get him to reveal the location—get him to break his promise to her father, come over to her side.

She turned from the window and the church and,

standing in front of the small mirror over the wash-stand, began to experiment with her hair. By combing it severely back she achieved a slight change, but not good enough.

Perhaps, she thought, *a wig. A mouse-brown wig. And glasses. The Princess Kilkanov will help. Old frumpy skirts, old, bulky sweaters. Reduce the chance of seeing one of the kids I know—my God, I know half of Paris!—spotting and hailing me on the streets.*

She sat on the bed and began to cry.

Stop it! she told herself angrily. *To hell with Claude Le Brun.* She was her own woman now, no longer ridden with adolescent fantasies. Le Brun had belonged to Erica; even if she chose, could she break that bond?

Heavy footsteps in the corridor.

Through the peephole in the door, she could see a man walking toward her room. A German soldier, young and fat. It seemed to her, from the angle of the peephole, that his shoulders were touching both walls as he lumbered forward. She couldn't see his face very well, if he looked determined and cruel.

He didn't stop at her door, but at the next one down on her side, 28. One sharp knock and the door was opened for him, and she heard a woman's high-pitched laughter.

There was talking then—the walls were not very thick—and then silence, and then the sound of more laughter and of the bedsprings squealing.

Finding a cuticle scissors, Sara stood up in front of the small mirror over the basin and began to snip at her hair, letting the long, silky strands fall into the basin, soon almost filling it.

By the time things had abated on the other side of the wall, she was looking a different Sara Jacobi. And she had permanently stopped the flow of tears.

Eleven

IT WAS THIRTY MINUTES before the last show of the evening when Sergeant Raeder arrived at Chez Jeannot. He had arranged with Colonel Bocke to call and make a reservation in his name, Bocke being more or less a regular at the club. But Raeder was under no illusion; he expected to be—and was—the only noncommissioned officer present, although there was a row of lieutenants shoulder to shoulder at the bar. Ignoring them, and being ignored by them, he was in a foul mood: Kröler had telephoned just before he left, canceling all surveillance of Le Brun, and in a tone that brooked no discussion. "Very good, sir," Raeder had answered. Of course he would comply, he added stiffly. Yes, sir, he'd inform Colonel Bocke, too. Kröler had hung up, evidently satisfied. *He shouldn't be,* Raeder had told himself, and was retelling himself now, thinking about it. *Wait until Goering hears about this, my dear Kröler . . . we'll see about this decision of yours —that bastard Le Brun knows where the Jacobi collection is hidden, I'd swear to it!*

But Raeder risked another step—a dangerous one, actually, but one worth the gamble. Following the Kröler talk, he had called at the Crillon, taking Colonel Bocke into his confidence: what he wanted from Bocke was minimal but important—an around-the-clock watch of the house on avenue Foch. No more than two men, on twelve-hour shifts. Plant them in a building across the way. Raeder wanted to know when Le Brun left and when he returned. No attempt to be made to follow Le Brun of course, just this simple, silent surveillance.

Bocke wanted to back away, but was in Raeder's debt on too many counts.

123

"If it blows up, Sergeant, it blows up in your face. I claim you passed on the Reichsmarschall's order."

"Agreed. I take full responsibility."

The men were already in place, Raeder had been informed. Luftwaffe undercover people. No noteworthy reports yet but Raeder was satisfied.

Tonight, he thought, *is for celebration.* He felt as if he'd earned a medal; he raised his head toward a waiter.

The waiter, instructed by Jeannot, gave Raeder no cause to complain about the location of his table or the service, treating him with the deference paid to brass. Hardly looking at the menu, Raeder ordered the most expensive champagne and, the waiter shrewdly guessed, would probably tip better than the generals he was serving.

A few minutes before curtain time the club was enveloped in a haze of cigarette smoke and brandy fumes, the noise escalating by decibels. The clientele, predominantly German, predominantly masculine, was aloft on alcoholic euphoria: this was the conqueror's due, this glorious ambience was the coin of victory. Those officers with Frenchwomen, conscious of the envy of the others, talked little to their companions, aware of being envied. The evening was still relatively young, the officers exuded charm, but not without the understanding of who was on top, and would be on the top by morning. The women, pretty, overpainted, but with the inborn chic of the French, had already drunk too much and talked too much. The handful of French civilians present were older, their wives presumably no longer desirable and therefore beyond risk. Their husbands were friendly with many of the more important army men and showed no need to hide it here; mere presence at Chez Jeannot was reasonable proof of amity.

The traditional foot-stomping backstage, and slowly the room began to quiet. A girl materialized out of the parting in the curtain, which now opened completely.

An audible gasp, then applause and a few raucous cheers.

She was long-limbed, with blond hair cascading to her shoulders. Her makeup was heavy but not vulgar;

124

her cleavage was deep and she was big-bosomed without appearing top-heavy. Her long black dress was split on the sides, revealing silky thighs. White teeth flashing out of moist red lips, she sang, "I am Germaine of Paris . . ." and began a slow grind in place.

The audience was aware of the joke, of course. They began to whistle and stomp and bay their approval. The song became bawdier, more explicitly scatalogical, Germaine's gyrations more pronounced. Laughter rolled against the walls of the tiny club like thunder. "I am Germaine of Paris, and you know what you can do, back, front, middle—where I make number two! But you'll still be number one with me!"

They gasped and howled, thumping the tables as she darted forward, kissed a colonel squarely on the lips, before disappearing behind the rapidly closing curtain.

This now pulled back again completely. Revealed on the postage stamp stage was a small band, Fernando at the piano, a drummer, an accordionist. The noise they made, however, was overwhelming; it served to rouse the most drunken. And on stage now, came the chorus line, six in all, including Germaine. There were redheads, brunettes, another blonde. Makeup superb, costumes rivaling the Folies-Bergère—Jeannot spared no expense—they sang more dirty songs, kicking, whirling, deftly executing the most intricate steps. A plump redhead with a particularly sexy manner captured, along with Germaine, the special admiration of the audience. At one point, a baby-faced Panzer captain, breaking away from his table companions, jumped up on the stage and grasped the redhead in a bear hug.

Squealing in mock fright, the object of his ardor slipped neatly out of the clumsy embrace, danced off with the chorus, which displayed superb *panache,* ignoring the captain completely. The curtain closed swiftly, and there was the young officer, alone, the spotlight deliberately on him, grinning stupidly at his hooting comrades.

From somewhere back of the stage, far back— *Could it be my imagination?* Raeder wondered— came the clear and distinct notes of the Marseillaise.

The anthem, which he could now swear he was hearing, underlay the ribald abuse directed at the Panzer officer, who was now jumping off the proscenium to join his companions.

Raeder decided the song had probably come from the street, a passerby, and settled back stoically at the table, contemplating the empty champagne bottle. He had neither enjoyed nor hated the show. Actually he had been disinterested except for the reaction of his countrymen, which he thought in poor taste and worse, displaying a lamentable lack of discipline. The Wehrmacht should not allow its leaders to debase themselves, especially in public.

Chez Jeannot had suddenly fallen silent.

In flesh-colored tights, spiked heels, a simple black band confining her breasts, Mallou had appeared in front of the curtain.

Not like the others, certainly. Very real. With a small, secret smile she began to sing. They quieted at once, listening respectfully. The song told of a lost urchin on the streets of a city—any city in any country —during an aerial bombardment, and she sang it effectively, without resort to sexuality.

When she finished they applauded with enthusiasm. She was a mother, a sister, a girlfriend, a whore. The Panzer captain was enraptured; later, at the end of her long act, he ordered the maitre d' to send a case of champagne to her dressing room with his compliments.

There Raeder waited for her when, wearing the flaming scarlet satin she used for her final number, she returned to the cubicle next to the kitchen that Jeannot had managed for her. She had closed the door behind her when she saw him, sitting quietly against the wardrobe wall.

"Who—" she began angrily, but Raeder was out of the chair at once, clicking his heels, bowing.

"Sergeant Hans Raeder," he said, speaking tolerable French. "Please forgive the intrusion, mademoiselle. I am here on official business." He smiled with all the charm he possessed. "That does not preclude the fact that I found myself captivated by your performance. May I—"

"You may get the hell out!"

She was standing very straight close to the door, eyes blazing, the red plumage of her costume giving her the ruffled look of an aroused bird of paradise.

He forced himself to remain polite, to keep from slapping that damned pouting mouth.

"You had better listen to me here or you'll listen at our headquarters and you won't be wearing such a pretty dress."

He was half-smiling and she could smell his sweat; his armpits were black with it. He was a dangerous man, she sensed at once, and became wary. She crossed to her dressing table and sat down, deliberately allowing the slit in her dress to widen, watching his glance plummet to her thighs.

Finding her cigarettes, she plucked one from the pack. He was at her side instantly with a lighter. She allowed it, thanking him with a nod.

"That's better," he said. "No reason we can't be friends."

"What do you want?"

He stood back a little, reaching into his tunic for a memo pad. "You are Margaret Hamilberg?" he asked, reading. "I am not speaking of your professional name."

Puffing the cigarette deeply, she leaned back, surveying him.

"So that's it?"

"That's it," he said with a full smile.

"You are Gestapo?"

"I am with the Gestapo and I'm not. I am a personal aide, you might say, of someone infinitely more powerful. You must disregard my rank. I'm in a position, Mademoiselle Hamilberg Dumont, to be very helpful to you."

He sat again, facing her, lighting his own cigarette.

She was rigid, watching him. She knew she must be careful, but she was not afraid. She had dealt with his kind so often.

"But why would I need help from you? Forgive me, Sergeant, I have many well-placed acquaintances."

"Perhaps not as willing as I might be to overlook certain . . . information."

He placed the pad back in his tunic. He was arrogantly at ease without being threatening.

"That I'm a Jewess?"

He crossed his knee, leg swinging.

"And, as such, in danger of being dispatched to a camp?"

"It would be inevitable, wouldn't it?" he said without emphasis.

"Unless you concealed the fact, I gather. And your price, Sergeant?"

"You know my price." He rose unexpectedly. "I've become quite taken with you, mademoiselle. From afar, naturally. I don't have to tell you how beautiful you are! I would value such beauty. The relationship could be kept private, secret if you preferred. I understand that. You would, in return, find me a powerful protector . . . I guarantee it. In addition," he said, hoarseness in his voice, "I think you would discover other satisfactions, shall we say, that might surprise—that you might even find exceptionally agreeable."

My God! she thought. *Quel salaud!*

She looked at him directly. His pupils were a dead white-gray, she discovered; they gave back nothing. "But you've made a mistake—a big one."

His jaw clenched, but he was unimpressed: Sergeant Hans Raeder made no mistakes.

"My mother's name was Marie Prieur. A good Catholic. My father, Gérard Prieur, also Catholic, died in my infancy. Joseph Hamilberg was my stepfather. I don't have a drop of Jewish blood, my dear Sergeant! It's all in the records. Baptismal papers—everything. I was born in the seventh *arrondissement*. I suggest you verify what I've said. Now, is there anything else you'd like to say before I call my *other* German friends and have you thrown out?"

It was unexpected, a possibility that simply hadn't occurred to him. Hamilberg, a stepfather! Making it worse, intolerable, was the contempt he read in her eyes—in the amused, theatrical way in which she suddenly pulled at a hook in the back of her dress, rose, turned and, ignoring him, actually began to disrobe.

He considered grabbing her—attacking her, killing her. The dress had fallen to the floor. Stepping out of the pool of scarlet satin, she wore nothing now but gossamer panties. Her body was superb, beautifully made, buttocks perfectly round, her plump breasts, nipples rigid, clearly revealed to him in the dressing table mirror.

Wanting to stay at any cost, furious, three-legged, he forced himself somehow to stumble out of the dressing room, slamming the door behind him.

The club was almost empty. A waiter directed him to a telephone where he called the Jeu de Paume.

A duty officer answered. Identifying himself by code, Raeder asked if ASIA, Goering's train, was still in Paris. It was, the man replied. Identifying himself by another code, in this case a name, Dr. Dürer, Raeder asked to be put through by radio telephone.

On ASIA, the communications corporal informed him the Reichsmarschall was incommunicado. "Just as well," said Raeder. "Connect me with Frau Thaler."

Waiting for her to come on, Raeder observed the cast of Chez Jeannot in street clothes beginning to emerge from the back of the club. To his surprise the men did not have any of the overt mannerisms of homosexuals; he could have passed any of them on the street without giving them another thought. God, how he hated faggots! Given his choice he'd drown them like cats in a sack.

"Yes?" came Maida Thaler's voice over the phone.

"Raeder," he said, successfully keeping his voice steady, "I see you're in town after all. Have a staff car take you to the Hotel Hamilton, rue de Rivoli. Room 48. Any problem?"

"You could manage to pick me up yourself," she said coolly after a moment.

"I'm busy. What difference does it make anyway? And it'll save time."

"In a hurry, are you?" she said suddenly, laughing. "All right. I'll leave right away."

She was gone, and he left the phone thinking what an arrogant bitch she was. The odd thing was she

129

appeared to enjoy the rough stuff, the slapping around. Well then, tonight she'd really be satisfied.

The ballroom at the Crillon was ablaze with crystal chandeliers, with the brilliance of the uniforms and the ball gowns, with the sparkle top brass automatically lent these occasions.

The wives, not all the clichéd image of plump, stolid German womanhood, looked almost smart. Some had already managed to be dressed by Parisian couturiers; a handful of the younger women were actually chic.

A military band, augmented by strings, was playing pre-war American popular tunes, but softly and with schmaltz, giving the music the quality of the old waltzes.

Von Banheim, nominally the host, was not on the dance floor but in a corner in conversation with Ernst Kröler, one of the few civilians present. The topic under discussion: Claude Le Brun.

Le Brun, according to Goering's instructions, was to be invited along on the expedition into the châteaux country.

Colonel Bocke, discreetly at von Banheim's elbow, ventured a suggestion.

Von Banheim turned to him with a nod. "Not bad, Bocke. An inspiration in fact. You agree, Kröler?"

"We give Le Brun an earlier date than the one planned for the trip . . . but why?"

"As a test, of course. Should he decide to try anything—inform the French, for example—why then his alleged disloyalty would be revealed."

"I don't see how . . ."

"We would assemble a false party to go down there, right, Bocke? Say, three limousines, with people dressed like you, me—even the Reichsmarschall. Should the unit be stopped on orders from higher French authorities, we'd know damn well that Le Brun had given them advance warning."

"A lot of trouble to test Le Brun," grumbled Kröler.

"Forgive me, sir," put in Bocke, "but it could well serve another purpose. In effect we'd be testing the possible French response as well. After all, when we

130

do go, we'll be risking the Reichsmarschall, won't we? In contravention of our agreement with Vichy, how will they react? As I see it . . ."

A beautiful blonde, the one Raeder has seen in von Banheim's apartment the day before, came up and the three men bowed slightly. She tapped a lovely, tapering finger on von Banheim's cheek. "Have you forgotten me entirely, *mon général?*" she asked with coquettish petulance.

"How would that be possible?" von Banheim said, mechanically drawing back. His disinterest was unmistakable, his look elsewhere. About to lash out, the girl thought better of it, following his glance. A tall, elegant civilian in dinner clothes had just entered the ballroom. The entertainer Mallou, in a clinging white sequin gown, was on his arm. For a brief moment, the blonde girl noticed, every eye in the room was on the two, even von Banheim's.

He had turned back to her.

"I'm busy now, *Leibchen,*" he murmured. "Forgive me. Later."

She was clever enough to smile and accept the proffered arm of one of von Banheim's aides, who led her onto the dance floor. Von Banheim, the girl saw, was heading to greet the newcomers.

Not too much later, the staff of the Kommandant of Paris arrived, without, unhappily, the Kommandant, who had unexpectedly been called to Berchtesgaden. But the tone of the soirée had been raised immeasurably. At least seven generals were now present and the evening was fast becoming memorable.

Le Brun early on found himself engaged in a conversation with Ernst Kröler on the relative merits of the fifteenth-century Italian painters. Kröler, who could be as pedantic as a textbook, tonight seemed deliberately so, until he casually mentioned the Reichsmarschall's intention of openly crossing the line into unoccupied France and paying a visit to Valençay.

"He was thinking of inviting you along," Kröler added, "but I talked him out of it. If the French stop us for any reason, your presence could prove embarrassing—for you, I mean, being allied with us so publicly."

131

"Yes, I see, of course," said Le Brun, wondering why he had been told in the first place. "But isn't such a journey unnecessarily hazardous? For the Reichsmarschall, you understand? Vichy wants to co-operate, as you know, but such an open breach of the treaty could put their backs up. And any raid on the art treasures would, I imagine, be insupportable."

"Oh, I agree," said Kröler. "But I hardly think Goering intends a 'raid,' as you put it. The trip would be more in the nature of a little sight-seeing, an inspection of the premises." Kröler grinned companionably at Le Brun—did everything but wink. "You know how he is when he sets his mind on something. I'm just telling you that you won't have to worry about us on Thursday. We'll be out of town."

Thursday! And he wants me to know, thought Le Brun. *Made sure of it. Why?*

Applause and a rumble of subdued laughter. Mallou had just left the floor with General Bauer, the ranking man in the room. Bauer, who had certain military stardom in the near future, was red in the face and wore a silly smile. Le Brun, who had had his back to the dance floor, guessed that Mallou, who possessed a fey sense of humor at times, had made the overstuffed general participate in some fancy maneuvers that had drawn the attention of the entire ballroom. The general was now quaffing one glass of champagne after another from a tray held by a waiter —that kid from the Crillon bar the other day, what was his name? McNulty?—while Mallou laughed and held out the final glass for the general. She herself rarely touched alcohol. Then von Banheim had joined them, the music starting once again, and Le Brun saw von Banheim and Mallou dance off together.

He held her lightly, very correctly; he was graceful without in any way being forward. He had not yet seen her perform, he told her at once, but would certainly try to do so in the near future—all he had been hearing from his colleagues and junior officers was Chez Jeannot and Mallou!

It was nothing, she answered, she was really not that good, but the supporting show was worth seeing; the boys were marvelous!

"So I understand," said von Banheim. "Fräulein, a command of ours in Paris is organizing a Berlin tour for performers—for the top artists in France—those who wish to show their . . . unity with the Reich. There will be many favors extended to these people, even, I've been told, an audience with the Führer. You can appreciate the golden opportunity it affords in these difficult times. If you're at all interested . . ."

She had been told von Banheim had a glass eye. It would be the left, she guessed, although it was difficult to be sure, the colors matched so perfectly. In any case, his gaze was glancing, almost indifferent; it was the smile he gave her now that was blunt, that told her exactly what he wanted.

"Will you think about it?" he asked.

"About the trip?"

"What else?"

He was the kind of man she knew perfectly—that patina of satiny manners on the surface, a rogue male, implacable as one of his Nazi tanks, within.

Well, Mallou was just as tough, a match for him. Appearing to stumble, she glided into him, and as she felt him react in surprise, reaching to prolong the contact, as quickly she withdrew.

"How stupid! Forgive me."

The good eye, the right one, was fixed on her, the fierce, predatory look naked. She had played with him enough, she guessed, although she refused to allow herself to be intimidated.

The music had stopped. He continued to hold her, if at a small distance.

"Yes or no, Fräulein? The list will be closed tomorrow."

"Yours is the second proposition of the evening— my second German offer, that is."

He was openly contemptuous, refusing to demand an explanation. "I imagine you'd have them all panting at your feet!"

"Is that a compliment, General?"

Careless of the picture they made together, he forced her to stand there with him.

"Yes or no?"

"I've heard how good a shot you are. Not one of

your staff has failed to give me full details; how you freed poor old Goering from the gardener's rope. I suspect they hero-worship you. But one bullet will not always do it, *mon général!*"

She had made him very angry. His face was dark with it. Satisfied, she slipped deftly out of his arms, making for Le Brun, who stood talking to Kröler. *How safe Le Brun makes me feel,* she realized.

Twelve

THEY WERE SPENDING their first night in the Jacobi mansion, in the Jacobi master bedroom, in Aaron Jacobi's huge, ornate bed.

Micha had been as good as his word; the room was furnished in the best the vandals had left; the linen the softest, finest cambray. No matter that the downstairs rooms were practically empty.

A moon hung over the garden and, having made love, they rose to look at their property—the expanse of greenery, the manicured hedges, the fountains gently playing.

"You must give a party," he told her.

"Yes."

"Invite your friends, too. I don't give a damn. It's your house now. Be the mistress."

She was far away, remote. It had been that way minutes before. Ordinarily her lovemaking was lusty and uninhibited; she might moan, even scream, but never cease skillfully to carry her partner to the edge with her. Only on occasion was she ever absolutely satiated, but not for lack of trying; there was no nuance of sexual provocation she didn't know and practice. She had missed her true profession, and her era, Le Brun had told her lightly but meaning it: she should have been a courtesan. She had only one weakness, he said.

"What's that?" she asked, for once curious.

"You'd give it away. You don't give a damn about money!"

"You're right, of course." She was laughing with Le Brun but actually she was deeply unhappy. There was something else she did care about which she could not, she had begun to realize, ever get from him: himself.

He was fond enough of her. And infinitely kind. And a completely satisfying bed partner.

Unfortunately, everything stopped there. Without, for all his intelligence, Le Brun's awareness of the depth of her need for him.

Tonight, uncharacteristically, she had turned away from him following the most perfunctory of performances, and after the moment at the window had gone back to bed. Soon he heard the slow breathing that indicated sleep. He assumed it was the new and strange surroundings. Le Brun, for his part, was wide awake, reviewing the evening at the Crillon, in particular what lay behind Kröler's revelation of Goering's contemplated Loire trip. It was something Le Brun absolutely had to work out. Or risk being caught in whatever trap the bastards were setting.

Something else had happened that evening. Before leaving the Crillon, while waiting for Mallou to emerge from the lounge, he had almost been run into by McNulty, the barman, emerging from the telephone room, face taut, hair rumpled, openly distraught.

"Forgive me, sir. Sorry," the boy had muttered in English, then, remembering, stuttered out an apology in French.

"Nobody's hurt," replied Le Brun. His calm had a quieting effect, and McNulty stared at Le Brun a moment—an idea, a hope of salvation obviously taking shape.

"Forgive me, sir, but you were in there with them. You are, you might say, friends?"

"No, not friends. Call it a business relationship," Le Brun replied stiffly. *Why in hell is it this boy's business? Why am I even bothering to answer?*

"You can help me! You must!"

"I *must?*"

The boy had lost all dignity. He was begging, incoherent: "Didn't mean it that way. No one to turn to . . . they've found her, the Gestapo, taken her away."

"Taken who away?"

"Anne, my daughter. She's only five."

"Why would they—?"

"Her mother was Jewish . . . died in childbirth. I've been living here with her parents. They've taken them, too. A few hours ago. I just called home. For God's sake, Mr. Le Brun, I'll never see her again!"

Music came from the ballroom, the pouring of thick syrup—*"Night and day, You are the one"*—and laughter, a woman's bawdy laughter echoing through the corridor. At the desk the night clerk's head shot up.

So that was what the boy was doing in Paris. Why hadn't he taken his daughter back to America? *Obviously because of the grandparents,* Le Brun answered himself.

Mallou came out of the other door fast; whatever was bothering her gone deep. She wanted to put the Crillon behind her. Grabbing Le Brun's arm, giving McNulty no more than an indifferent glance, she said, "Let's go—please!"

"In a minute," he said.

And to McNulty: "I don't know if I can help you. I'll try. Here, write down your full name, the one you go by in Paris, and the name of the child and grandparents. An address and a telephone number where I can reach you. I'm not promising anything, you understand."

"Christ, Mr. Le Brun, you don't know how much . . ."

"Write!"

The boy wrote on the back of the card. Le Brun pocketed it and marched Mallou toward the two uniformed men guarding the side entrance. He had to show his ID and his invitation, and both he and Mallou had to be checked off the list before they were allowed into the street. Security was always tight at these affairs—the reality of military occupation making itself felt—causing Le Brun to feel guilty for even holding out a wisp of hope to the young man.

Now he twisted in the bed, wondering what he could do, short of jeopardizing his own position. Which was too high a price. Absolutely! He'd call first thing in the morning and explain to McNulty that he could be of no assistance.

He fell into a restless sleep, and a dream in which the close-cropped blond hair of McNulty turned suddenly into Sara Jacobi's long black tresses, and he was holding her in his arms—then it wasn't Sara, but Erica, and they were making love on a beach while men in gray uniforms watched avidly.

Thirteen

ARNAUD WAS WAITING for him at the *concierge's* apartment, looking at his watch significantly because Le Brun was three minutes late.

The *concierge* had left a bottle of brandy and glasses on the table before disappearing. This time Le Brun poured himself a shot. He rarely drank anything so hard so early, but today he felt he needed it. He was not cut out for his new role. He was a novice in the sort of automatic deception it required. And with the Germans he was up against professionals. He said as much to Arnaud.

"You think any of us are born for deception?" Arnaud answered in his harsh, unpleasant voice. "No, I'm wrong; there are those who find lying congenial, even pleasurable—like masturbation, reinforcing a sense of superiority. Superior because they are doing it alone and dominating. It's not only society that needs violent reorientation, but individuals—their way of thinking."

"Possibly so," Le Brun said dryly. "Only I don't

want to dominate anybody. I just want to be left alone."

"To pursue your own quiet, devious capitalistic ways?"

Le Brun laughed, turning the conversation to Kröler's talk of Goering's projected expedition into unoccupied territory. He now had a definite date. It was to be Thursday next, Kröler himself had informed him.

"Of course it was told you for a purpose." Arnaud confirmed Le Brun's own suspicion. "They wanted to see if you'd report it to 'higher authorities,' as you have. Then, how would these 'higher authorities' react?"

"Well, how will they? By the way, where's Garnier?"

"Deliberately didn't ask him," said Arnaud, giving Le Brun a small smile. "In this kind of situation he might feel it necessary to do exactly what we *don't* want. And I also think it better if we allow him and his people to react 'normally,' without premeditation."

Beyond that, thought Le Brun, *you don't completely trust him, just as he doesn't completely trust you.*

"Finally," Arnaud continued quietly, "he might inadvertently drop your name to an associate, to someone who conceivably could give you away. Have you any real faith in the present government?"

Le Brun downed his brandy. "No."

"My feeling," Arnaud said, "is that this preliminary move be allowed to proceed without any intervention from us. In that way those bastards, who are shrewd enough, God knows, in sniffing things out, won't be able to get your scent. And that's what's most important right now—for us to preserve your cover."

Not because of any concern for my safety, certainly, decided Le Brun without bitterness.

"Not because we love you," said Arnaud, as if he'd been reading Le Brun's mind, "but because you are, in my opinion, in an excellent position. You are, perhaps, more capable than you think; I tell you frankly that I expect something extremely valuable to come out of your endeavors."

Le Brun did not respond.

Arnaud had risen, unsmiling. "If there's nothing else

. . . By the way, I *shall* inform Garnier—but *afterward*. In the meantime I count on your cooperation and discretion."

"Of course. But since you asked, Arnaud, there *is* something."

Arnaud, who had already clapped on a sort of workman's hat, a shapeless, dirty-brown velour affair, paused. "Yes?"

Quickly Le Brun told him about McNulty. "I'd like to help him," he said, supplying the details.

"Jesus, Le Brun, forget it!"

"Why?"

"How can we begin to concern ourselves with the Jewish problem? That's *all* we need! Like children try to hold back the tide with a wall of sand!"

"We must do what we can."

Arnaud smiled wearily. "You do what you can, old friend. Good luck! And don't call me a goddamn Nazi. I'll confess it to you, I had a Yiddish grandfather—that's why I'm so smart! Madame Chard, we're leaving!"

They went out into muggy midday Paris, Arnaud through the back as he'd arrived, Le Brun the front, the *concierge* pocketing the roll of francs they'd given her.

Sour with his dislike of the man, Le Brun crossed to the *café-tabac,* looked up a number inscribed in tiny numerals on a piece of paper in his wallet, telephoned. After a long wait he got the man he was after, Ernest Kröler.

"Le Brun here. Am I disturbing your lunch?"

"Just about to sit down. What can I do for you?"

"I've come across something. Would the Reichsmarschall be interested in a Géricault?"

"Perhaps. Do I know it?"

"One of his finest horses; I'll vouch for it. And I've heard of Goering's special liking for animals."

The briefest pause and Kröler was all business. "How much will it cost?"

"Not more than you can afford. There's just one catch."

"Ah, always a catch, isn't there?"

"Listen to me," Le Brun said. "The owner of the

painting has a particular friend. Last night this friend, his wife, and his granddaughter were seized—arrested, you understand? In any case, they've disappeared. For their return and safe transport to the unoccupied zone, the Géricault will cost the Reichsmarschall not one franc. It will be a gift."

There was hardly a pause on the other end. "Name of owner, please."

"Not available," said Le Brun.

"Look here, you're supposed to be working with us."

"Do you want the Géricault or don't you?"

Kröler sighed on the other end. "All right, just the names of the people taken."

Le Brun allowed his body to go slack with relief. But he was careful to keep his voice even, consulting the notes McNulty had scribbled for him. "Joseph and Frieda Mosse. Child, Anne Morgan."

"I will get back to you. Where will you be?"

Le Brun gave him the number of the *café-tabac*, hung up, took a table close to the phone.

Waiting, he ordered a ham sandwich in a *baguette* and a mug of beer. It occurred to him that at least he'd uncovered the mystery of McNulty's name: he'd been right in the first place—it *was* Morgan of course. Not that the difference mattered. How long since he'd spoken to Kröler? He checked his watch. Only twenty minutes. He felt he was back in school at the Beaux-Arts, waiting for the results of a critical examination.

He was still at the table an hour later when the phone finally rang. Motioning to the proprietor's wife that it was for him, he picked up the receiver.

Kröler: "That you?"

"Yes, go ahead."

"We are too late. They were in a group that completed a shipment. It left the country last night."

Everything was going on as usual in the *café-tabac*. A waiter was taking an order from an elderly man in an ill-fitting brown corduroy jacket. Three students were laughing over beers, and a pretty girl was sitting at an outside table drinking a *citron pressé*.

"You are certain?"

"Absolutely."

140

"Any idea of destination?"

Several seconds lapsed and then Kröler said. "Ravensbrück I should think. Perhaps Auschwitz."

The names meant little to Le Brun, but they didn't have to. "Goddamn it, what right—"

"Calm down, Le Brun. I don't decide our Jewish policy, and your cursing won't change it. I'll continue to make inquiries, but to be honest I can't hold out much hope. It's hardly the end of the world though. It's my understanding the two places I mentioned are nothing more than work camps."

You are not a very good liar, Kröler, Le Brun thought bitterly.

Kröler was still talking. "I'm afraid I've compromised you in another direction, however, my friend."

"Have you?"

"Goering happened to phone me from his train while I was awaiting your information. I made the mistake of telling him about the Géricault. He couldn't have been more excited. Turns out he has always wanted to own a Géricault horse. You see where that leaves us?"

"I see," said Le Brun, "where it leaves me."

"Exactly," laughed Kröler. "Oh, under the circumstances, I'm sure he'd expect to pay for it, say fifty thousand marks?" On the open market the painting is worth at least two hundred fifty thousand."

"I shall try and arrange it," Le Brun said. He placed the receiver carefully back in its cradle, then dialed McNulty's number. The boy's voice leaped at him before the first ring was even completed.

"Yes? Have you anything?"

"Not good news," Le Brun announced at once, thinking, *How do you give someone news like this?* Pretend you're a doctor—the patient is mortally ill; the next of kin must be told, but in a calm, efficient, civilized manner. "Your family is no longer in France. I'm terribly sorry. I promise to continue to do what I can. But in all candor I cannot hold out any hope. We all know the eventual outcome of affairs like this one. You're not alone right now, are you? Are there friends you can be with for the day? Perhaps talking with a priest . . ."

A sound came from the other end—it was, Le Brun realized, a raw, uncontrolled sob. The phone went dead.

Le Brun prided himself on being reasonably moderate in all aspects of life. Rarely did he violate this discipline. But now going to the bar, he cursed the Nazis, the war, his own damn futile role in it, and ordered the first of several double brandies.

Thomas Morgan did not spend the day drinking or crying or praying. What he did was contact a friend of his, a petty thief named Mathieu, who, having a magnificent body, modeled nude for Morgan during dry spells in his own work.

To Mathieu he gave practically all the cash he had on hand—it came to a considerable sum, five thousand francs—with instructions detailing what he wanted for his money.

This attended to, Morgan walked the streets of Paris. He walked the Right Bank first, seeing hardly anyone, perhaps giving some attention to the men in gray uniforms. He walked all the way from the Bastille to the end of the Champs-Elysées, then over to the river and across to the Champ de Mars. From there he tramped east, stopping only once for coffee—he had kept in superb condition all his life, having played football in college in Montana, and, except for an occasional glass of wine on festive occasions, was a nondrinker.

He walked through the Latin Quarter, past the Luxembourg Gardens and on and on aimlessly, ending up at the porte d'Italie; there he turned and retraced his steps, crossing streets in front of buses and private cars, immune to shouts hurled at him. He passed through a street market and plucked a peach from a stall, and when the owner, bellowing for the police, caught up with him, Tom Morgan slugged the man in the face. Ignoring the indignant cries of those who'd witnessed the blow, he proceeded calmly on, losing himself in the afternoon traffic.

Without consciously planning it, he arrived back at his apartment shortly before dark to find Mathieu waiting for him with his purchase. It was a 7.65 mm

Beretta automatic, and along with it was a box of ammunition.

Mathieu showed Morgan how to load the gun properly, how the safety catch worked, although it was all very simple, and, wishing Morgan luck—the disorder left by the Gestapo, ostensibly looking for subversive material, actually for jewelry or other loot, told Mathieu the story—left quickly.

Morgan followed him within minutes. Every second spent in the ransacked, empty apartment was agonizing.

At a restaurant nearby he had more black coffee, one after another, at least three cups. He paid and walked west, toward the Tuileries. He sat on a bench and waited until dark, one hand inside his jacket pocket on the gun, even while he fished out the coins for the bench collectors, watching lovers and older strolling couples and occasional loners like himself.

At one point he dozed, dreamlessly he thought upon awakening. But within him was the image of his dead wife, Elsa, and he felt vaguely comforted, though why he could not have said. From where he sat he could see activity at the far end of the gardens, at the Jeu de Paume, military trucks coming and going, hear the occasional bark of commands. He vaguely remembered being told that the Jeu de Paume was being used by the Germans as a warehouse for stolen art. The information did not interest him.

At about ten P.M. he was aware that the gardens had emptied, because of the nearness of curfew, he guessed.

It was what he was waiting for. He now began checking his watch.

Soon it was eleven and he was alone in the wide, black expanse of the park.

Two soldiers on patrol, or moving to the gate bordering the rue de Rivoli, crunched past him and did not see him. In the darkness that would have been next to impossible; by this time he was prone behind a file of iron park-chairs.

Rising, he yanked out the gun and fired into the back of the nearest soldier. He had been no more than four feet away; the range was practically point-blank.

The soldier went down once, mortally hit, the second man diving to the earth at the sound of the shot, groping vainly for his own weapon. He had hardly got his hand on it when Morgan's shot found him between chest and neck; then one more shot from the Beretta struck him in the temple and he died at once.

From far off, from the Jeu de Paume it sounded, came shouts—action would undoubtedly soon be taken —but for the moment the two dead men lay on the walk, blood seeping into the gravel like drops from a leaky faucet.

Morgan made off without undue haste toward the Seine boundary of the gardens. This necessitated a detour around the Orangerie, but he didn't hurry. Far behind him he could hear the grinding of vehicles; the Germans had, perhaps, found the murdered soldiers.

Without quickening his pace he walked to the pont de Solférino, and stood there behind a tree, watching ahead and also back toward the bridge spanning the river at the place de la Concorde. Cars were crossing at great speed; clearly there had been radio communication with the forces at the Tuileries. These new arrivals, troop carriers possibly, were zooming across the expanse of the great square.

Morgan wasn't very interested, his attention was drawn to an approaching foot patrol on the pont de Solférino. The regular custodians of the bridge, he guessed.

Two men. He could make them out clearly as they approached the Right Bank.

Waiting until they had marched to within a dozen feet of his position, Morgan fired at the nearer one, then at the second, emptying his gun.

One of the Germans managed a wild shot from his rifle, but Morgan was untouched and the soldier was mortally hurt, sprawling on the pavement only a few feet from him. The second man, bleeding horribly from his mouth, looked up at Morgan, his face caught in an overhead bridge light, and uttered what in his language must have been a terrible profanity.

Appearing not to hear it, without emotion, Morgan watched for several more moments until he could see the man was dead.

Unhurriedly, he started back toward the place de la Concorde. By this time military vehicles were speeding back and forth, the shots having been heard clearly, but no one had gotten so much as a glimpse of Morgan. Perhaps it was because he was walking alongside the Tuileries wall, cloaked in darkness. It might also have been that the Germans were looking for a group of men, a Resistance band, not for a solitary and quiet pedestrian.

Having walked the perimeter of the square itself without detection, he continued on to the Crillon, went around to the side entrance, and into the bar.

Roussilon, his boss, the chief barman, was furious. "Where the hell have you been? Are you sick? You look like you've been rolling in the gutter! No matter. There's a party going on in Suite 505. General von Banheim. Champagne. Take them champagne. But first, dammit, change! Take one of my uniforms. It's hanging over my locker."

Morgan, who had listened indifferently, nodded and obeyed. Killing the soldiers had, he realized, made no difference. He still felt like someone whose insides have been scooped out, a receptacle that would remain forever empty.

Fourteen

THE TWO STEAMER TRUNKS in Sara's top-floor cell belonged to her father, deposited there in Mischa's care before the family fled Paris. Time had been dragging for Sara; in order to carry on the deception for the *concierge's* benefit, or for any other curious occupants of the floor, she had to spend a reasonable time each day below in the Kilkanov flat ostensibly as the maid —the *bonne*. But she had also begun making discreet contacts with a few old friends. In the back of her mind was the idea of getting a job, perhaps with one of the many pro-Vichy newspapers that had sprung up in the city.

"Why one of those lousy Vichy sheets?" Mischa had demanded.

"I can write a little. I can fake some experience. They might even be able to use a photographer. And as a member of the press, it's possible to move around, Mischa. You have access to off-limits places . . . people tell you things. Sooner or later I can be of value to our side."

Mischa understood. At least it would be no more dangerous than any other activity she might seize upon. He worried about her constantly. "Just be careful whom you take into your confidence—whom you see! Dammit, why did you have to come back to Paris?"

She didn't blame him. The reality of the Nazi presence here was frightening. Just walking around paralyzed her at first. Now she took daily strolls, wearing an old raincoat the Princess Kilkanov had given her, a dark oversized knitted cap that came down to her eyelids, and torn woolen stockings that made her look like a rag woman.

She read constantly from the Kilkanov library of Russian novels. Civil disobedience, secret and continuing struggle against the oppressors, a fierce humanistic drive saturated the pages, making Sara more determined than ever to become part of the underground war going on in the city, to join the ranks of those whose hatred of the invaders was only exceeded by their scorn for those who, like Claude Le Brun, were collaborating with the enemy.

Sara had made a pact with Mischa. Strictly limited excursions outside until the job she was after was obtained—the new, safe identity established—one walk between eight and nine in the morning, when street traffic would be reasonably heavy; the second at six in the evening when the offices on the Right Bank emptied.

She was a good companion to herself and was not bored; rather she found herself living in a state of anticipation, of what she could not guess. The mere fact of being in Paris, close to the enemy, caused a powerful exhilaration.

And there was an unexpected source of interest.

In his haste to flee Paris, her father had deposited some of his private papers with Mischa—the two steamer trunks in the little room on the top floor—and Sara certainly had no compunction about an investigation.

Trunk number one proved of little interest, containing vellum ledgers noting her father's business transactions, mostly the buying and selling of paintings since his arrival so many years ago in France. Browsing over the yellowing pages would certainly have been a source of pride for Aaron Jacobi, proof of his acumen, his superb sense of trends, if ever he needed reassurance.

Following a brief amused dip into the ledgers, Sara replaced them carefully and closed the trunk. Not that she despised money or its acquisition. On the contrary, she liked being rich and was deeply respectful of her father's achievement. Within reason.

But fast automobiles could crash more easily than slow ones; planes with first-class sections regularly fell from the sky. Rich food brought on gout and heart disease. Those peasants living over a hundred years always seemed to come from impoverished villages in mountain fastnesses where they wore goatskins and lived on yogurt.

Trunk number two was another matter—crammed with Aaron's personal memorabilia. Old family photos, snapshots of the old country, old friends. Curious objects—a tarnished brass belt buckle with a royal crest, a woman's hatpin with a small, round, topaz head. A torn leather Florentine case filled with gold collar studs and single gold cuff buttons. A pearl-handled buttonhook. Yellowing suede spats. Two large, dog-eared stamp albums. A red-lacquered Chinese puzzle box, superbly crafted. Inside the final, tiniest cube a piece of paper no bigger than a fingernail. On it a woman's writing—or was it a woman's?—*I love you*.

She found letters from her father's first wife, which she did not read, love notes from her mother, which she did. There was a quickly scrawled letter from Erica, sent from Nice and postmarked several days before the plane crash. It told of her sister's excitement at meeting André Malraux, of the perfidy of France, of the world, in allowing Spain to fall to its knees before the Fascist knives like a valiant but stricken bull in the ring.

DEAR PAPA,

There is something else you must know: I am living in sin. With Claude Le Brun, whom I have seduced into my bed, you must believe me, against his will. I'm divinely happy. I want to marry him if he'll have me. You know him, I think, as a bright and faithful employee and perhaps a person with a built-in "feel" for art. But I have not chosen him (or fallen in love) for that reason!

He is, of course, a gentile, and although I know that you and mother are in that sense 'enlightened,' I can guess that deep down his being Christian will hardly influence you in his favor. Claude is also, unhappily, a snob. Something—with my own little ego—I hope to change. He cannot help it, coming from the family he does. (Whom for reasons he won't talk about he never sees!) He is also opinionated and secretive. And pathetically honest. He abhors fakery of any kind, or falsehoods— whereas you know what a terrible fraud and liar am I!

He is, in your terms—not mine—much older; I find this an advantage—you know how badly I've always treated boys my own age, or for that matter the slightly older ones who fancied me.

He'll keep me in line, I suspect, although for my part I shall probably make his life hell before we're through. I want so much, Papa!! I want to fight with everything I've got against those Fascist bastards! I want to help create a decent life for people everywhere! I want at least a half-dozen children!

I had to let you and mother know all this so that when I arrive in London the day after tomorrow, I will not have to stutter it all out and then (in frozen fear?) watch your faces.

Did I tell you before that I believe that Claude

loves me too? And that we shall undoubtedly marry whatever you and mother have to say about it!

Your loving daughter,
ERICA

That morning at eight sharp Sara took the back elevator downstairs, and with a smile to the *concierge,* ventured out. It was a dark morning, unseasonably cool, and as she strode to the Etoile and down the Champs-Elysées she kept her anger, a carryover from a sleepless night, at boiling point. What an unworldly child her sister had proved to be! "Pathetically honest" was Le Brun? How could Erica be so totally taken in? But then the most intelligent, most attractive women were the most easily duped, she'd heard—too often choosing fools or scoundrels.

She realized she'd been thinking of Erica as if she still lived, annoyed with her now as she'd often been in their petty, sisters' quarrels. But these had never lasted long, even the small jealousies, and now the love for Erica flooded over her, the knowledge of loss, and she was crying as she walked.

An elderly woman with a gentle face turned from a boutique window and peered at her, actually took a step toward her. "What's wrong, my child?"

"Nothing," she gasped. "Nothing! Sorry!"

Bolting, she finally reached the place de la Concorde. Here she slowed, her tears dried. The fallen plane could not be put together again, certainly not Erica's broken body. And God would visit his wrath on Le Brun—the Jewish God whose wrath was terrible.

Across the river in the grayness, the Chamber of Deputies sat ephemeral but majestic. As she looked far back, she could see the Madeleine, ghostly columns in perfect balance to the Chamber. On the other side the Tuileries, and to her right, the sweep of the Champs-Elysées, the Arc de Triomphe looming far up the boulevard, truncated in the gloom, ironic in its splendor.

As always, the Concorde was busy, both wheeled and pedestrian traffic surging around it, but she picked her way along the Seine toward the pont de Solférino, and then stopped. A small crowd had gathered in front of her, held back by police. Beyond she saw a military truck. She would have pushed by to get a better look but a man in coveralls, a young man with a brutish black beard, suddenly reached out, hauling her back. "Don't move," he warned her.

In a rift in the crowd, she caught a glimpse of what was going on. Civilians, men, women and children, about twenty in all, were being hoisted up into the back of the truck. "Hostages," the young man told her under his breath. "The Resistance ambushed a couple of *Boches* here last night, pumped them full of lead. And in the Tuileries, too, they say. Christ!"

A German officer next to the truck had a bullhorn in his hand. His voice boomed out suddenly, in crisp, correct French. "These people on the truck have been chosen at random; it will be their fate to pay for the cowardly attack on soldiers of the Reich peacefully trying to preserve order in the city. If the French do not want friendship, so be it. Four Germans have been killed. Forty of you will be executed by evening. Ten to one!" The voice was abruptly harsh, its rage making it barely comprehensible. "Spread the word—death to the enemies of the German people! Heil Hitler!"

The back flap of the truck was yanked down. Preceded by an open staff car, the truck gunned away from the curb, starting against traffic to the place de la Concorde.

Sara closed her eyes, not wanting to see it, not wanting to hear it go by.

Next to her the young man asked, "Are you all right?"

"Yes, thank you."

The cool of the morning was going fast, the sun breaking through. She did not like to see the overcast parting; she wanted the gloom to remain. She thought it odd that the city appeared to be carrying on as if nothing extraordinary had happened, that it was not weeping for its citizens. Why hadn't the people inside the truck thrust aside the tarp, broken out, scattering to the winds? Certainly a few would have made it, covered by the gathering crowds. The troops surely couldn't have killed them all!

And had she come along only minutes earlier would she had been one of those gathered up, one of the condemned?

Would she have jumped, run for it?

Fiercely she thought, *Yes!—and they wouldn't have caught me! I'd have outrun them.*

Mischa's wife, Sonia, was still very beautiful, a great lady. The Jacobi family had always thought that, treating her with great kindness and respect, insisting on Mischa's bringing her on festive occasions, insisting on paying the medical bills, the operations which were so painful and in the end unavailing, and eventually discontinued. She was always *the* Princess, while Mischa was rarely given his title, and when Erica's mother was away, the Princess was sometimes pressed into service as surrogate mother and, as the only one able to deal with the majordomo, her husband, the real boss of the Jacobi household and the girls.

But as time went on and the Princess' mobility, even in the wheelchair, became painful and limited, the sojourns to the Jacobis' became less frequent. Although the girls, who were genuinely fond of her, did visit her in the apartment, at least whenever their mother could shame them into it.

A tall woman with superb facial bone structure which years of physical pain had sculpted into an almost hieratic mask, the Princess now squinted at Sara, balancing a brandy on the wheelchair arm. "How can I advise you, dear? Mischa, *you* tell her."

Mischa made a noise in his throat. "We all hate him, but maybe this time he's telling the truth. It must be your decision, my girl."

Sara stared at them unwilling to make a statement. The apartment was not made for clear, forthright decisions. It was too small for larger-than-life people like the Kilkanovs. It was a hopeless clutter—paintings by friends; paintings of friends; ikons, a few immensely valuable; lace doilies; worn Persian carpets; and ashtrays donated by guests. Over a hundred perhaps. Those that were kept. Not a decent hotel in the world unrepresented. And mostly filled with stale butts; Sonia smoked like a fiend.

Mischa had only one rule: all ashtrays must be emptied twice a week. He wore an old embroidered shirt now—his favorite house garment. The giver had imagined it to be Russian (it was Romanian). Mischa tossed down his vodka and, standing above Sara, head close to the ceiling, continued: "I can only repeat what the man has told me. He claims your father had made him the gift of the Géricault as a reward for some successful deal he made—that he requested the Géricault remain with the collection until he decided what he wanted to do with it, keep it or sell it. In any case, he was frank enough to tell me he had not, at the time, wanted it returned to his family."

Sara was silent; Sonia lit a Gauloises caporal from the burning butt of another. Even the quality of tobacco had deteriorated since the war. Shifting from her bad right hip, she asked, "Why must Le Brun have it now? Why right now?"

"It may be a trick to get me to reveal the hiding place of the entire collection," said Mischa. "That must be considered. But all he would tell me was that he had sold it and wanted it back. Another lie, perhaps."

Sara shook her head.

"I could check it in Papa's records," she answered. "They're all in one of the steamer trunks. But I know he's telling the truth. I remember when it happened. He pulled off a coup involving a Monet, I think . . . you know that jewel—the farmhouse with the sunset. Papa was grateful and told him he could take back the Géricault, which was never one of his favorites anyway."

They did not try to contradict her. Mischa said, "It could still be a trick."

"He must have it back, regardless, since it belongs to him."

"Your house doesn't belong to him," commented Sonia sourly. "Still he's in it. With that cow."

"I hear she's very beautiful," Sara said.

Mischa, seeing the way things were with Sara,

merely said to her, "Have you thought about how you will handle it?"

"No."

"I'll tell you what you have to do," said Sonia, coughing—the cough accompanied everything she said, a litany to all the household sounds. Her lungs, Mischa had thought despairingly, must look like rotting Swiss cheese.

"All right, Princess Kilkanov," he said with a husband's knowing smile. "What must I do?"

The message Le Brun received from Mischa merely said that he should be waiting in his office at ten the next morning; he would receive a phone call telling him where to pick up the Géricault.

Le Brun didn't ask why the roundabout delivery. Why not simply, "Come and pick it up?" He was aware Mischa could consider the whole thing a device to track down the collection, starting with the premise that the collection itself was what everyone was really after. He had also been told by Father Gregory that Mischa visited the cave in the church regularly—to check on its contents. If he simply took the Géricault himself, Le Brun knew it would tip Mischa off that he knew the collection's whereabouts. All sorts of complications then. Better to go through with this rigmarole.

He was waiting for Mischa's call the next morning and it came promptly. "Go to La Madeleine. Ask for Father Brissault."

"Now?"

"Now, at once."

Le Brun obeyed, taking the Hispano.

Within thirty seconds he spotted somebody on his tail. A motorcyclist this time, a young, muscular man wearing a fancy checked cap. *Merde!* So Raeder finally couldn't resist! Should he tell Kröler, complain again? Or ignore it? Le Brun decided to wait.

He made no attempt to lose the tail, content to proceed with traffic along the faubourg, a left at rue Royale, and then across to a lucky parking place on the east side of the cathedral. His motorcyclist friend, Le Brun noted, had pulled in across the street, was hanging back behind a flower stand. No smarter than any of the previous agents.

Father Brissault had the cheerful look of a man at peace with God and the world. The war, it would seem, was no great inconvenience to him. Politely he asked for Le Brun's identification. Then: "In one minute," he said, padding off.

Le Brun sat on the bench in the last row, waiting. There were not too many people in the church, a handful of women in front. Behind him he could hear footsteps. Cap in hand, the muscular young man had entered, paused to genuflect, buy a candle, move in several rows ahead of Le Brun.

Father Brissault returned with a large, flat package done up sloppily in brown paper, tied with ordinary string. "This is what you have come for?"

"Yes, Father. Father?"

"Yes."

"It is possible you will be questioned."

"By whom?"

"By—certain police."

"About what?"

"About who left this parcel with you."

Father Brissault smiled. "But I do not know. I found it at the door to the vestry. On it was a note—which I destroyed—asking that the package be turned over to a Monsieur Le Brun."

Father Brissault's smile continued. "And, oh, yes. An envelope with money in it. A considerable donation. Too much for such a simple chore. That is my secret."

"I'll be going then," Le Brun said. He could see the motorcyclist watching them. He wanted to pat the smiling father on the shoulder. "Very good, Father, and thank you."

He didn't bother to check the package out until he got into the car. It was the Géricault all right. In perfect condition. Father Gregory and Father Brissault —two sides of the Catholic coin—must not be averse to occasional cooperation.

And then he thought he saw a familiar figure—a girl, standing on the other corner of La Madeleine. Sara Jacobi. Well, now she was sure he'd picked up the painting. And more than ever now, she would be absolutely certain of where Claude Le Brun stood with the enemy.

Kröler was openly jubilant.

The Géricault was superb, and he'd certainly gotten it from Le Brun ridiculously cheap. When reporting the acquisition to the Reichsmarschall, he would double the price, pocketing the difference. Even so, it was a bargain and Goering would be grateful. Of course they had paid a handsome sum for the Fragonard. But all things considered they had done good business. The French, he considered, were not as crafty as reputed. A smart German could get the better of them every time. Only Sergeant Raeder, certifying that the Géricault was indeed topnotch, was not as happy as Kröler.

First of all the Géricault coup was not of his engineering, nor would it redound to his credit. It would, on the contrary, undoubtedly be considered by Goering a point in the Frenchman's favor. Moreover, this was the night Colonel Boche had chosen to send the "supposed" caravan into unoccupied France to test, first, Le Brun's loyalty, and, second, the response of the Vichy government. Should it be decided that Le Brun had not informed his compatriots in advance, and that the French were too fearful to act positively against the expedition, then von Banheim, in conjunction with his superiors, would agree, if reluctantly, to Goering himself risking the journey at a later date.

What was eating Raeder was that at the last minute Colonel Bocke had informed him that he was to go along on this preliminary reconnaissance.

"Why me, Colonel? I have my own affairs!"

Bocke, who had the deceptively placid look of a parish priest, shrugged. "Someone's got to assume the identity of Ernst Kröler. If Le Brun had talked, they'll expect an art expert along—someone with the right answers. Otherwise they'll know we suspected Le Brun. Get it?"

Raeder got it. "But whom," he asked facetiously, "may I ask, will you send to double for Reichsmarschall Goering?"

Bocke looked sly.

"You know Frau Hilda Zetlin?"

"The Zetlin? . . . the art dealer from Berlin? . . . that monstrosity? What in the world? . . . oh, Christ!"

"Exactly," said Bocke with a laugh, enjoying Raeder's reaction. "Not bad, eh? And you know whose idea it was?"

"A madman's."

"Careful. Goering himself. Very amused. He's actually handing over one of his Reichsmarschall's uniforms. All we need now is a proper wig."

Raeder was incredulous.

"She's agreed?"

"What choice does she have? Actually, if there's trouble, I'm sure she'll wet her pants. That's the best of two possibilities that can happen to you. You'll be sitting next to her on the way down. Oh, a civilian suit—you have one?"

Nodding, Raeder thought to himself, *You'll pay for this, you bastard!*

The colonel was looking at his watch. "Herr Kröler has asked that you hop over to the Jeu de Paume to check on some painting. After that, Sergeant, you'd better get moving—the expedition leaves at sundown. Oh, I'm coming along, too. As commandant."

The expedition—three civilian vehicles—was stopped as expected at the control point separating the zones. A French gendarme, epaulettes indicating captain's rank, saluted smartly, asking for passes.

Bocke climbed out of the front seat of the lead vehicle. "Passes?"

"This is French territory. You must be aware of the regulations, Colonel."

"For certain people regulations are unimportant. I suggest you look in the back seat."

The captain opened the rear door and peered in.

Taking up almost the entire seat, except for a sergeant squeezed in somehow, great haunches clad in uniform trouser legs of silk-jersey, tunic in a darker shade, fully bemedaled, was Hermann Goering. Above the trunk of a body was a tremendous moon, a pouting moon it seemed to the Frenchman, from which a husky voice whispered, "Good evening, Captain. May we please continue on?"

The captain hung by the open door, still staring.

"Perhaps we should have supplied ourselves with the proper credentials," the Nazi colonel was saying behind him. "But it was such a lovely night, and the Reichsmarschall just took it in his head to drive down to this beautiful part of France—a breath of country air, a brief respite from the terrible tensions of war."

Bocke wondered if he'd laid it on too thick.

"With him, of course, is Herr Ernst Kröler, one of his aides. But if you should wish to check by phone with Paris—"

The Frenchman was still hesitating.

Now abruptly he came to attention, saluting Bocke.

"I would not wish to inconvenience the Reichsmarschall. I'm sure my superiors would agree. My compliments—and enjoy the trip."

Bocke returned the salute. "You are most kind. May I know your name."

"Captain Benoit Eglan; it is unnecessary, Colonel."

"Nevertheless—" Bocke scribbled in a notebook, watched a moment as the French man ordered the wooden roadblocks removed, climbed back into the front seat beside the driver. "Proceed."

The captain watched the cars until they had sped past the control point, disappearing around a bend in the road. His instructions from his superiors at Vichy had been explicit. He was to conform to what would be the normal reaction of a border commander in such a situation: rigid insistence on the rules, confusion when confronted with the presence of an important German leader, begrudging acceptance of his helplessness. Pass them through. He now tramped to the field phone to report the event.

The "Reichsmarschall" had fallen asleep, snoring loudly and leaning heavily on a grim Raeder. The problem was a particularly heavy musk perfume the "Reichsmarschall" was wearing. She'd laid it on generously, renewing it from a spray in her pocket whenever she woke up.

They had been driving steadily, watching behind.

No vehicles followed them, and monitoring their progress at night would have been impossible. Bocke was satisfied that security had not been breached; Le Brun hadn't betrayed them; and, in his view, the captain at the control point had displayed proper judgment in allowing them to pass. A promising officer.

Bocke intended to report that this small journey had indeed achieved its objective: Goering could safely make his own plunge into the unoccupied zone whenever he wanted. In all probability, Vichy would not block it.

For his part, Raeder had almost forgotten the purpose of the trip. The presence of this bloated female, stinking up the back of the car, swelling against him, had made him sick to his stomach. For one insane moment he found himself imagining what it would be like being in bed with her. As an antidote he began to think of the previous night with Maida Thaler. Reliving sexual episodes—or spinning sexual fantasies—usually succeeded in putting him in good spirits. He had done good work with Maida. He had given her so much she hurt badly, but still wanted more, unable to control herself, wanting his cock in every orifice. What it took to get her dressed and home to the train!

His thoughts shot to that other bitch, Mallou. What he wouldn't give to get between her legs, to make her crawl to him, whimpering . . .

Christ, he realized, his erection was growing, and he couldn't even get a hand in a pocket.

The "Reichsmarschall" was awake again, her sudden guttural question surprising them all. "Where are we?"

"Near Besançon, sir," Raeder replied. "Do you realize we're no more than two hours from Valençay?"

"So?"

"Why can't we go all the way, break into the château, take what we want?"

"The Winged Victory? Are you crazy?" Bocke asked.

"Not the Winged Victory. Entirely too big. But other masterpieces. Smaller. It's possible we could manage the Venus de Milo. Imagine the glory of bringing it back to Goering!"

Bocke wasn't in a mood to respond to such recklessness. "You fool, don't you realize you'd be depriving

158

the Reichsmarschall of his own triumph, his own foray down here, for all Germany to applaud his daring? Do you imagine for a moment he'd thank us?"

Bocke was right. Raeder knew it instantly and cursed himself for the proposal.

"Yes, of course," he growled. "Stupid."

"Very," agreed Bocke affably. The point he had just scored over Raeder put him in better humor. And they'd be back in Paris before dawn, the expedition a success, and that darling boy from Chez Jeannot waiting for him in his bed at the Crillon. Latins could be so extraordinarily passionate. . . .

House 71 : 1945

AFTER SEVERAL MORE DAYS of dialogue, resulting in more details of activities in the Jeu de Paume and in other areas that had been masterminded by Hermann Goering, word came from Munich: Goldfarb and Packard were to return immediately with their prisoner. Should any further information be required, Messrs. Jackson and Sherman, the original interrogators, would tie up the loose ends.

Munich, for Goldfarb, turned out to be a bore.

Trucks were arriving daily from the salt mines with treasures of incalculable value—the plunderer's booty. Goldfarb would have given his eyeteeth for a chance to evaluate the stuff, raw as it was, before most of it was shipped back to the individuals and the museums, the original owners. But this was G-5's job, Monuments, Fine Arts and Archives, and it wasn't about to invite the OSS boys to participate.

A Major Edwards promised Goldfarb an early trip to Berlin: Berlin would be sizzling hot with clues, Edwards said. And it was kind of a race too—get there and ferret out the stuff before the Russkies grabbed hold of it. "They're a fucking sticky-fingered bunch," Edwards said. They'll swear everything was stolen from *them*. Then, whammo—see you Sunday! Oh, by the way, a Captain Dante, Judge Advocate's Office, has been trying to reach you . . ."

Wondering what in hell he'd done to put the legal beagles on his trail, Goldfarb placed a call to Captain Dante, who asked him when could he drop over.

"This morning?"

"Fine. We're at General HQ. In the basement. Don't bother to knock."

No older than Goldfarb, a stringbean with sleepy eyes under heavy black eyebrows, Dante was behind a desk piled with thick yellow folders. "A mess, huh? Listen, in case you haven't heard, they're all going to trial . . . at least those we can lay our hands on. Place called Nuremberg. I'm one of a group of lawyers assigned to Goering. We've been tipped about his art activities—especially in France. We need filling in on details—names, dates. You know what we're after . . ."

"Sure," Goldfarb said. "But wartime looting . . . hell, isn't that a traditional sort of thing?"

Captain Dante was suddenly less sleepy. "Maybe. If no other crimes were committed along the way."

"Other crimes were committed, I'd guess," Goldfarb said. Plenty."

"We'd like documentation, Lieutenant. Packard tells us you've a special thing going with this Ernst Kröler."

"Captain Packard?"

"Copies of his reports on the salt mine art caches were sent to us."

"And that's why you picked me?"

"Another factor. Looked you up. Harvard. Me, too. Law School. Figured this operation needed a touch of Cambridge class."

"Definitely," said Goldfarb.

"You be smart with Kröler. If you can get him to really open up it'd be a help. We don't want any loose ends with Goering. We want to put it to that son-of-a-bitch legally, but right!"

Ernst Kröler had been placed in an improvised prison in Munich, actually a rundown hotel near the center of the city. A cot, a washstand, a window overlooking a small, dark courtyard. They couldn't consider Kröler a big threat to escape from there.

Goldfarb had brought C-rations with him, an apple, a pint of schnapps.

"Danke schön, danke schön"—Kröler actually broke out in tears when Goldfarb emptied his pockets on the soiled mattress.

"Forget it," said Goldfarb, acting embarrassed. "My problem, Kröler, is am I doing the right thing, coming to see you, sneaking this stuff in? Have I any right making it any easier for Goering's right hand, for all I know a killer of Jews?"

"I killed nobody! Didn't even know it was going on. My sister married a half-Jew!"

He would have seemed pathetic to the Goldfarb of a couple of months ago. But this new, battle-initiated Goldfarb wasn't at all bothered about Ernst Kröler's ending up with a noose around his neck. Kröler was regaining his courage from the schnapps. Replacing the cork, he unexpectedly sniggered a little. "So why have you come, Captain. And with such rare gifts?"

"Lieutenant. I'll be frank, Kröler. Your man fascinates me . . . the Reichsmarschall, the art lover, the obese, pushy, plunderer of life! And certain mysteries . . . that smashed Winged Victory at his chalet, for example."

Gnawing at the apple, Kröler didn't look up. When he did, he asked: "They've still got him, of course. Will they hang him?"

"He'll get a fair trial."

"If they hang him, they'll hang me."

"I don't think so, unless for some reason he drags you in to save his skin."

"No. He has many faults, but he is not small, not mean. Even when it started, in Munich, he was the only one with largeness—you know what I mean? A large, open spirit!"

Oh, for sure, thought Goldfarb—*for goddamn sure! That fat, smiling murderer!*

"Tell me about when it started . . . better, start with him."

"It's no secret. He liked to say he was of old Prussian stock—what's wrong with that? Who doesn't like to think he's in a straight line back to Frederick the Great?" Kröler paused, running it back in his mind. "His father, a consular officer, in his later years, was appointed to a prestigious but powerless post in Africa. A failure, I would say. . . . The family lived at the castle of von Epenstein, his godfather."

"Von Epenstein?"

"Yes, a Jew. Or part Jew. Very rich. It's whispered that Goering's mother was von Epenstein's mistress, that she'd slept with him openly, even while Goering's father was in residence. . . ." Kröler had finished the apple between slugs of schnapps; the C-rations he carefully placed under the mattress. "But you are not interested in gossip, in dirty linen."

"In *everything,* Herr Kröler."

"Goering had married a divorced Swede, the daughter of Baron von Fock. She'd been Carin von Kantzow —a beautiful woman and completely devoted to Goering. In Munich she became completely devoted to Adolf Hitler, that is, to the cause. She became, you might say, its heart and soul, its torch! Hitler adored her openly."

"And Goering rode her skirts to power?"

Kröler placed what was left of the schnapps with the C-rations. He looked at Goldfarb, his eyes showing a hint of anger. "Goering made his own contribution. He was a definite asset to Hitler in those days. A war hero. A man the industrialists could trust. And he believed in the movement, you must not doubt it! A patriot, no matter what you think, he could see no alternative for a country on its hands and knees, humiliated by defeat, by the weight of reparations, staggering blindly down a road leading only to disaster and degradation."

"The Beer Hall Putsch . . ."

"A bad miscalculation, in my opinion. A demonstration designed to show strength, and dramatizing weakness instead. The Bavarian party, the Bavarian government almost, had taken over this great beer hall, the grandest in the city, to announce its intention of seceding from the rest of Germany and placing

Prince Rupprecht on the throne. Frightened that the Bavarian leader, Ritter von Kahr, would steal his thunder, Hitler ordered his SA into action. Within minutes, truckloads of steel-helmeted Nazi storm troopers began to arrive, posting themselves at the doors. The beer drinkers almost choked on the stuff, I can tell you, and, in the height of the confusion, there was Adolf Hitler striding to the podium, Goering at his side, gun in hand."

Goldfarb looked skeptical.

"I wasn't there, Lieutenant. I've been told it was the most magnificent speech of the Führer's life! Unbelievably, he turned the whole meeting around; people were on their feet howling in support of the new government he proposed, shouting for him to take command. But even as he stood before them, the Bavarian government was reacting, ordering his immediate arrest along with the other Nazi leaders. A march to the city hall to defy the Bavarian Reichswehr was decided upon. It had snowed during that night, and there had been sleet. The streets were slick with ice in some places; in others, muddy. The march began at dawn, Hitler, Goering, Ludendorff, Alfred Rosenberg, Julius Streicher in the first rows, behind a party man carrying a huge flag with the swastika on it. Next, other party stalwarts, then the SA troops. But you've probably read what happened. Published around the world, no?"

"Perhaps so," said Goldfarb. "But we didn't pay very much attention. Another internal incident in Germany. And who had heard of Adolf Hitler?"

"Yes, who *had* heard of him?" Kröler said, "and they might never have! Reaching the Residenzstrasse, a narrow street, marching shoulder to shoulder, about to enter the wide-open Odeonplatz, the crowds cheering them all the way, the leaders were suddenly blocked by police and ordered to turn back. Of course they refused. Who would even think of firing on the august person of General Ludendorff, along with von Hindenburg, an idol of the entire nation? But the commander of the police gave the order and a volley of shots rang out. Sixteen marchers killed, the rest in disorder! A bloody mess, I don't have to tell you!

Hitler later insisted he was nicked by a bullet . . . I don't know . . . he was jailed, as you know . . ."

"And wrote *Mein Kampf.*"

Kröler hadn't heard; he was dreaming of the past like an old, tired dog, his eyes half-closed.

"Goering *was* hit," he said. "Perhaps that was what saved him from prison along with the Führer. But he paid in worse coin. It was during his hospitalization at Garmisch that the pain began to drive him to the use of drugs. Morphine to begin with . . ."

"And later anything he could get his hands on, right?" said Goldfarb. Kröler ignored him, lost in his memories. "Yes," he said finally. "Practically anything. But it was only after he was smuggled out of Germany to recuperate that the legends about him began to proliferate. He was always very popular with the people, you realize, which naturally made him very proud."

"More popular than Hitler?" Goldfarb asked, genuinely interested.

Kröler gave the question judicial reflection. "More loved, I would say. So when, later on, during the war, things began to come apart, when it was clear the battle for Britain was lost, when the Russian front was beginning to sour, when his relationship with Hitler started to deteriorate—"

"—he turned to his strength, the people, for support."

Kröler awarded Goldfarb a wisp of a smile. Kröler was still years back, at Goering's side escaping the small, foul room.

"More than anything he wanted to prove even to Hitler that when it came down to the final test he was the one to be relied on, the most loyal German of them all!"

"And the Winged Victory was to be the symbol of that truth?"

"More than a symbol—his statement to the German nation and to the Führer that despite the scurrilous attacks against him, he was still capable of leading the way. We would prevail!"

Flushed, Kröler abruptly stopped, seeing where he was, the man facing him. He realized he had been shouting. He began to laugh, laughter with an edge of hysteria; then he shut his mouth.

He was being foolish, he realized. And he was not with a friend. This American Jew officer, for all his apparent kindliness, was a deadly enemy.

Fifteen

THE "INCIDENTS" were occurring every evening despite redoubled vigilance and the beefing up of the military units in the area by order of the district commander. With apparent access to apartments on the rue de Rivoli, the assailant was marking up at least one gray-green uniformed soldier a night.

The "death patrols" they had come to be called by participants.

By virtue of convenience, most of the hotels occupied by Wehrmacht brass happened to be ranged along the rue de Rivoli either in the 1st *arrondissement,* as was the Crillon—or the 8th, contiguous—the Continental, the Meurice, and other smaller hostelries. Although these establishments were regularly searched, this vengeful criminal, something of a cat burglar as well as a superb marksman, ranged the rooftops undetected, to duck into unoccupied rooms facing the Tuileries and out again upon completion of his kill.

Should the patrols seek the safety of the colonnaded passage on the north side of the street, the sharpshooter would strike from the gardens themselves, perhaps from a treetop, before disappearing into the darkness without a trace.

Beefing up the patrols in the affected area worked briefly. But for how long could this enclave be so heavily reinforced? And reduce the patrols just slightly, and another sharp crack from a blackened window, another member of the Wehrmacht sprawled on the pavement, an ugly black hole in the chest.

No high-ranking fatalities as yet. The ranking officers were not impressed. It had become a bad joke around HQ. The Wehrmacht could conquer a continent; it could not eliminate one lousy sniper from the heart of Paris.

Ventner, commanding the district, had had enough. He had flooded the place de la Concorde with troops from front-line units. Men were stationed on rooftops. Throughout the Tuileries searchlights mounted on vehicles turned night into day.

For three days the sniper did not attack. The 1st and 8th *arrondissements,* Ventner discovered, became quieter than the Vatican. Knowing he was a laughing-stock, Ventner relinquished the extra troops and reestablished the smaller, regular patrols.

The following night Le Brun was at the Jeu de Paume with Ernst Kröler. In addition to selling the Fragonard, he had just been able to locate two very decent Corots, landscapes he knew Kröler would appreciate. Unheroic, they had the golden luminosity for which the painter was famous.

Asking a stiff price, Le Brun expected to be bargained down and was.

He still came out ahead and had managed to put Kröler in a splendid mood. Things were going well at the Jeu de Paume, if not in the war. "You French are remarkably stubborn people," Kröler complained. His master's words, one could be sure: "Do you have any doubts who will come out the winner? Why in the world not join with us as friends and allies? Why hold back your fleet?"

"I am a friend and ally. But you may just not come out the winner, Herr Kröler. What's the latest from Russia?"

"By Christmas we'll be in Moscow."

"Then by Christmas," Le Brun said, smiling, "you shall have our fleet. I'll demand it of Admiral Darlan personally."

Kröler laughed. "I'll hold you to it! By the way, watch it when you get into your car. That sniper'll catch you. Not much difference between a Frenchman and a German in the dark."

Le Brun had parked the Hispano on rue Cambon, across from the Tuileries. Leaving the Jeu de Paume, he walked slowly down the steps of the museum, enjoying the fresh, wet-grass smell of the late hour. Wispy clouds hovered over the city, doing a poor job of obscuring the moon. Too bright for the sniper. Le Brun found himself hoping the fellow wouldn't try anything tonight—the Krauts would fill him full of lead.

Past curfew. The Concorde was empty. At the far end, an armored car, barely discernible, cruised the western border of the square. Le Brun crossed the street at once, heading east. He had his identification, but to be stopped and interrogated could be a damned nuisance. And one could never anticipate the outcome. He could spend the rest of the night in a filthy cell.

The shot came, he could have sworn, from his right, near the corner of rue de Rivoli and rue Cambon —from on top of the Colonnades. A sentry tumbled facedown in the gutter.

The sound of the shot had carried to the place de la Concorde. Le Brun could hear an engine revving, a distant command. Lights were flaring in hotel rooms along the way. Men were running toward him, scattering fire as they approached.

He was a few steps from the corner, but caution warned him to stay where he was. A drum roll of bullets rattled past him. An open passageway near him led to a small inner court. While he hesitated, the option was withdrawn, more bullets sweeping the roofed-in walkway. A man had emerged from the court, rifle in hand. The sniper.

The sniper pulled out of sight, not seeing Le Brun, calculating his chances if he were to dodge back, find refuge in the building above. Bad odds, the sniper decided. Across the street, near the fallen sentry, was a Métro kiosk. If he could reach it, the man told himself, he could yet thumb his nose at them—miles of darkened subway track on which to lose pursuers.

Wasting no time, the sniper started his dash for

167

the kiosk. But the moon perversely chose that moment to break free, spotlighting him.

His luck having run out, the sniper had no place to go. Gunfire punctured the pavement around him.

He's hit! Le Brun realized, watching. *Get the hell out! Move!*

The sniper was trying. Clutching the rifle, he was shuffling—drunkenly it seemed at first—toward where Le Brun was hidden.

Let him go past, Le Brun told himself. But in the end he couldn't. He stepped out into the light, and the man brought up the rifle, ready to fire.

"Up the street!" Le Brun told him. "Rue Cambon. The Hispano. Get in and wait for me."

"Who in hell—?"

"For Christ's sake—don't ask questions! Hurry!"

"Yes."

"And I'll take the gun!"

The sniper, Le Brun could now see, was Morgan, from the Crillon bar, and it was his right leg that was bad—a bloody rag.

Reluctantly Morgan passed him the rifle, moving in slow motion toward the Hispano.

Hearing the armored car coming like the wind, tires rumbling past the Crillon, Le Brun slipped into the courtyard and, raising the rifle, deliberately let go a series of bursts. One at the sky. One at the treacherous moon. A final burst through the passageway, across to the park.

Then he dived back to the street, racing around the corner into Cambon.

Behind him the armored car had arrived. He could hear the first of the patrol hustling up, shouting at the other arrivals, tearing into the tiny courtyard he'd just left. The feint had worked, he complimented himself. The leader of the patrol was positive their man had fled back into the building, had been shooting at them from there. They had the sniper trapped.

"Throw your weapon down!" the leader shouted in garbled French. "It will go better with you."

Le Brun ran for the Hispano.

Morgan was in the front seat, but barely, unable to

close the door, blood leaking over Le Brun's fine Moroccan leather.

Le Brun hefted Morgan clear of the door, scooted around, and started the Hispano. Gently, as you wind a fine old watch, barely touching the gas pedal. The Germans heard anyway; they whipped into rue Cambon after him, but Le Brun was exercising full power now, the Hispano exploding like a meteor toward rue Saint Honoré. A screeching turn into rue Royale, then carefully, at ordinary speed, southwest until finally Foch and the Jacobi mansion.

Parking against the garage itself, Le Brun leaped out, holding a finger on the night bell. One of the maids was usually in the house, available for duty.

She was Violette, in spite of her name no delicate flower, but almost two hundred pounds of sleep-drugged beef. She stared without recognition at Le Brun. She could be forgiven. With Morgan slung over his shoulder, he was something of an apparition.

"Monsieur!"

"Open it, Violette! And quick, cloth for a tourniquet!"

Across the street, on the top floor of an exclusive apartment building, in a window under a mansard roof, the man who had been watching the Jacobi house for days now with no results, an absolutely boring stupid exercise, blinked at what his eyes were telling him. He'd dozed off only moments before, but the sound of the Frenchman's car awakened him. He now watched transfixed as Le Brun, staggering with his burden, disappeared through the Judas door.

Following his instructions, the agent picked up the telephone and called the number of Sergeant Raeder, who was to be informed of any unusual occurrence at the house under observation.

Sergeant Raeder was out, the hotel operator said. Try later.

Le Brun had Morgan placed on a bed in the servants' wing, not wanting to involve Mallou, who would be returning from Chez Jeannot after her performance. But, having regained consciousness, muttering a few words at Le Brun, Morgan was surely in need of medical attention.

Le Brun was in a quandary. There was small possibility of reaching Arnaud at this hour, and Morgan might just not make it by morning. The tourniquet Le Brun had fashioned on his leg had momentarily stopped the bleeding, but for how long could it be sustained?

He sent Violette for Mischa.

The Prince took forever, it seemed to Le Brun, to appear. Actually it was barely twenty minutes.

Calm arrived with him.

Filling the tiny room with his bulk, he took in Morgan, a broken animal in great pain on the bed, then scrutinized Le Brun.

"Who is he?"

"What difference does it make?"

"What am I expected to do about it?"

"You can see for yourself what shape he's in. And if it makes any difference, he's an American."

"I do not automatically love Americans."

"The point is, can we get him to a doctor?"

"Surely Monsieur Le Brun has enough influence with the occupying forces—"

"He's wanted by the Nazis. He's been fighting his own private war against them."

Mischa looked more interested. And in Le Brun, too. The older he got, Mischa realized, the less he found he really knew about people.

"Is he the one I think he is?"

"Perhaps."

"How did you come by him?"

Le Brun hesitated. "I've known him slightly. Tonight I just happened to be around. I think he became careless."

"They'll do anything to find him."

"Without doubt."

"Did they see you?"

"I went by them pretty fast."

Mischa shrugged. "Half of Paris knows your car."

Le Burn was losing his temper. "Listen you *merde* of an old man, I don't want this boy to die! If you're afraid to help, say so!"

Mischa thought he wasn't too damn old to stomp Le Brun into the ground. "It's not a matter of that," he said coldly. "Perhaps a question of faith, of trust."

"You know what you can do with your faith, your trust," Le Brun said, seething. Then he pulled himself together. "All right, Prince Kilkanov, I'll handle it myself! Get the hell out of here! Go back home to your bed!"

Mischa didn't move. "I know a doctor," he put in unexpectedly. He had modulated his voice. He even managed a smile, showing his big, yellow, horse teeth. "That is, he was a regular doctor. In Leningrad. One of our best. Here, he's a dental technician."

Mischa turned suddenly to Violette, speaking rapidly in Russian and she lumbered out of the room. "Violette," Mischa said, "is going for him. He lives close by. In my house, actually. How long has the tourniquet been applied? The bleeding, I think, has stopped."

Miraculously it had.

Le Brun loosened the knot.

They waited, watching the boy on the bed. Mischa lit one of those lousy French cigarettes, holding it between middle fingers, eyes on Le Brun.

"So you are not with them as we thought—"

"I'm with," said Le Brun not too clearly—he was very tired—"those I'm with. Don't have to give you an accounting."

"Wasn't asking for one," Mischa said. "Of course," he added, pointing to Morgan, "this could simply be a departure from normal practice—a touch of conscience, for example.

"It could be anything."

"But it isn't, is it? You've been cleverer than I imagined: you've been lying to us all as well as to them. You've been fighting them all the way."

"Have I?"

"I believe so. It also would not surprise me if it turns out you retain some basic loyalty to the Jacobi family. I repeat, it would not surprise me. On the other hand, I admit, I have problems understanding the French. It is not, as some think, that they're subtle; it's rather that they're so arrogantly oblique. They

171

suffer when they have to make a simple statement of belief."

"If you think so, Prince Kilkanov. Where the hell's your doctor?"

Eventually the doctor arrived. He brought two black bags, one with the stethoscope and whatever paraphernalia doctors carry with them, and a second bag containing splints and plaster to set Morgan's shattered bone.

He was Dr. Slovsky.

He was a short, broad man with a close-cropped beard and an easy smile that worked even at this hour, under these circumstances. No questions asked. No mention of what would happen to any of them should the harboring and caring for Morgan come to the attention of the authorities.

The bullet, Slovsky reported, had done its work and then exited. This while giving Morgan a shot of morphine and with Violette's help carefully cleansing the wound.

Then the slow, meticulous job of fashioning a cast. Rather like a sculptor, Le Brun thought, mentioning to Slovsky that the patient himself was an artist, a sculptor.

"So," said Slovsky. "But he'll still have his hands, correct? In two months, three, the leg will be scarred, not pretty, but for walking almost as good as new."

Mallou had come home; through a slit in the curtain Le Brun watched as the chauffeured car Jeannot supplied every evening deposited her at the front gate.

Mallou produced a key and disappeared inside. The chauffeur gunned the car away. Mallou would not find him in bed. She would say nothing, questions not being her way. What would he tell her in the morning? Increasingly Le Brun was having difficulty supplying Mallou with answers, and eventually there would be a price for it. How would he feel, he wondered idly, if he lost her?

Dr. Slovsky was finished, meticulously arranging things in his bags.

Le Brun turned to Mischa. "Would you ask Dr. Slovsky what I owe him?"

The Prince and Slovsky conferred.

"He'll give you his bill when his services are concluded, when the patient is on his feet." Mischa said, pointing to Morgan. "Do you plan to have him remain here?"

"That's a problem."

"With the number of people in and out of this house a danger! Suppose one of the servants drops a hint of something. They're not under military discipline, you realize . . ."

"Where could we take him?" Le Brun asked. "He'll need nursing."

"I know a young woman with nothing but time on her hands. And her place is, I think, reasonably secure. Should questions be asked, she could always be taking care of a sick lover . . ."

Sara.

About to indignantly veto the suggestion, Le Brun hesitated. What could it do but put her into deeper jeopardy? On the other hand, what else to do with with Morgan? And Mischa was certainly right about the Jacobi mansion—Mallou had mentioned holding rehearsals in the grand salon on occasions—they'd talked of a soirée, a grand garden party, with all her friends invited.

Morgan was twisting on the bed in pain; he gave the group in the room a long curious glance, aware for the first time, it appeared, of them, of his surroundings.

"Sorry to give you such trouble," he mumbled in English; then apologetically switched to French. "And thank you, Doc," he said to Mischa with a sad halfsmile, immediately dropping off to sleep, even beginning to snore with such ferocity they all began to smile.

"All right," Le Brun told Mischa. "You can take him to Sara, but it's only to be temporary. There are people I'll have to speak to about a more permanent place."

"Naturally," said Mischa complacently. "People you have to speak to. Understandable." He had bent over the bed, lifting Morgan, cradling him in his arms. "We'll go out the back, eh, Le Brun? Pick us up there in your car. Do you know what time it is? Not too safe in front at this hour. . . ."

The agent at the window across the street noted the time in his little book—5:36. The middle-aged man with the two black bags, the doctor, obviously, was just leaving the Jacobi house, walking north. Moments later, Le Brun could be observed leaving, climbing into his Hispano. No sign of the wounded man carried in previously, nor of the old, giant Russian servant who had entered the house before with the servant girl.

Was it too early, the agent debated, to call Sergeant Raeder again? Screw him, he decided. Raeder must have the softest job in the army, real heavy political pull somewhere along the line. Wake the son-of-a-bitch up! Let him scream bloody murder if he wanted to.

Raeder, who had spent most of the night with a woman he had picked up on the Champs-Elysées, answered the phone angry as a bear, ready to ream the man's rear end for him, when he started to listen carefully to what the agent was saying. "Very good," he told him, his tone changing. "I'll want a copy of your report. Keep at it. Who knows, you may end up with the Iron Cross."

More likely, the agent thought, hanging up, *with the double-cross, you bastard!*

Thoroughly awake, Raeder lit a cigarette and started thinking. It seemed he had really struck gold. A wounded man in the Jacobi house at such an hour? A doctor hurriedly summoned? And Raeder's heart jumped. Upon arriving at his hotel, not too long ago, the night clerk had been full of a story about an exciting shoot-out that had taken place earlier in the evening on the rue de Rivoli—a patrol had flushed "the sniper" out of a building; there had been firing back and forth, a German soldier had been killed. But in the excitement the sniper had escaped. Wounded, all right; there'd been blood. How was the escape managed? Raeder wanted to know. The clerk wasn't sure about that. It had been mentioned that there was an accomplice; a car had spirited the Frenchman away.

174

Raeder looked at his watch. It was a little past six, and the morning light was creeping into the drab little room, making the furnishings appear even more shabby. Should he have the Gestapo raid the Jacobi mansion? Suppose the wounded man, the body, whatever, wasn't there? Who would look the fool then? *No, he decided, I'll take my time, even if it's a month. Strike when I'm absolutely sure of my ground, when the evidence is incontrovertible. Then nail Le Brun to the cross.*

The first thing to do, he decided, later in the morning naturally, was to query Ernst Kröler. Kröler had mentioned Le Brun was to meet him at the Jeu de Paume that evening. At what time had Le Brun left? At what time exactly had the incident with the sniper taken place?

The garage under Mischa's apartment had a door leading to the rear and the service elevator. Le Brun drove directly into the garage, helped Mischa move Morgan out of the car, but that was all the assistance Mischa wanted, unless Le Brun wanted to go up with them to Sara's room, discuss arrangements with her himself.

"No," Le Brun said. "I'll leave that to you."

The elevator was there; Mischa opened the door with a free hand, Morgan's weight comfortably supported with the other. "She will know you're not the villian you've tried to make her believe," Mischa said, pausing, not the slightest hint of friendliness on his battlefield of a face. "Of course there are still many, many questions we have about you."

Le Brun had had enough that night. "You may ask them, Prince Kilkanov. Or you may not. And I may or may not answer."

He stomped back to the Hispano, heard the hum of the elevator rising, backed out into the street, and caught a glimpse of the sky: it had a slightly brown tinge to the east, he thought—the blood on his trousers had turned that color.

Sixteen

EMMY WAS SPENDING THE NIGHT in Berlin with friends; she hadn't expected him to return to Carinhall from a tour of aircraft plants until morning. It was just as well. It left him free to visit Carin's pavilion and her gravesite, where he placed a spray of hot-house pansies. It was a brisk night but he was bundled up nicely and could linger to ask his first wife's opinion of a political move he intended to make at the first opportunity.

Months ago he had presented an ambitious plan to the Führer, a detailed scheme to mount a massive three-pronged attack in the Mediterranean that would give Germany hegemony from Gibraltar to the Suez Canal. Then, only then, with one front to deal with, should the eastern gamble be undertaken.

Seriously examining the plan when first submitted, Hitler eventually rejected it, to embark on what Goering considered the suicidal eastern invasion.

His own power base rapidly deteriorating, Goering was now contemplating the resubmission of his plan: conduct a holding action in Russia, no more. Cancel every offensive operation there, using available resources to bolster this bold concept of his. With victory over the west assured, with England on its knees, resume the attack on the Soviets. Thus isolated, with all the Wehrmacht might directed against it, how long could the Reds hold out?

As he had anticipated, Carin's advice flowed into his mind with wonderful clarity. While the plan was undoubtedly workable, even brilliant, the voice from beyond agreed, the exact moment for its timing of resubmission must be propitious. Bormann and Goebbels would do their best to shoot it down as before.

"Its very audacity, and your courage in bringing it to the Führer again, will be used against you."

She was right of course. She was always right. The exact moment, otherwise he would make an unstable personal situation even more critical.

Kruger was rushing toward the pavilion, shouting "Reichsmarschall!" Kruger should know by now that his moments with Carin were precious to him. Frowning, he was about to give the adjutant a piece of his mind, when Kruger shouted again, "The Führer! You're to return his call at once!"

"So?" said Goering. Who was he to jump like a scared rabbit when the Führer snapped his fingers?

Kruger wasn't finished. "General Galland has also called, sir. Gelsenkirchen is under a bombing attack. Two, three hundred British planes!"

"Did the Führer mention Gelsenkirchen?"

"I'm sure he knew of it, Reichsmarschall."

Goering didn't run but he did hurry, out of breath almost before he started. "Go," he managed to say to Kruger, almost at the house. "Get Galland for me."

Kruger sprinted and Goering slowed. He had to be calm. There were two key oil refineries in Gelsenkirchen. If either of them had been hit—and how could they not be?—it would be a disastrous blow. He could imagine the scene over the small city, the huge British bombers, fire-breathing dragons filling the night sky, the lethal bombs falling, the terrorized people scurrying into the shelters. And if a refinery took a direct blow, my God, the terrible earth-shaking detonations! Flames sweeping through the city like a blood-wind.

Kruger had the phone ready for him in the den. Composed, but noncommittal as always, Galland confirmed the raid. "I'm sending up our night fighters, sir. I promise you they'll give them hell!"

"Don't hold back—and commit your reserves," Goering ordered him, sweating. He sweated a great deal under normal circumstances, but occasions like this brought forth rivers.

"As you say, Herr Reichsmarschall. All the planes I can possibly put in the air."

"The Führer has been alerted," Goering said. "He's very anxious. I want a bulletin every quarter hour."

Hanging up, he swabbed his face with a large linen handkerchief, gulped down two white pills without water, and saw the flashing light which indicated he was through to Hitler.

The familiar voice, rushed and exasperated of late, an engine pulling too many freight cars, was suddenly in his ears. "Do you know about it, Goering? Or have you been asleep as usual? Four hundred bombers, they tell me . . ."

"Three hundred. At most three hundred."

"Well, what are we doing about it?"

"We are doing plenty," Goering said, suddenly in an aggressive tone—a man could take so much. "We are going to knock them out of the sky . . . they won't be trying a trick like this soon again, I promise you."

"Very good, Herr Luftwaffe," the voice said, not attempting to conceal the sarcasm. "Then we shall celebrate the victory together in the morning. Do you hear?"

"I hear, my Führer."

The harsh voice was gone. Goering pushed the buzzer for his valet, Heinrich. He was drenched; he would need fresh clothes.

Galland reported as promised in fifteen minutes to the second. Air battles were in progress over the Gelsenkirchen sky. The Lancasters were not equipped to fight, many had already been shot down.

Goering had become cynical about early prognostications of victory. Yet Galland's voice had no bombast in it this time, but a calm, flat statement of the situation.

"About the oil refineries?"

"They're still untouched."

"Hold to this schedule of calls."

"As you wish, Reichsmarschall."

Speer was trying to contact him, as were Udet and Milch, all requesting up-to-date news of the bombing. This was the largest night attack to date by the British. One couldn't blame people for being nervous. Goering refused to speak to anyone outside of the staff in the field. Let the others sweat it out as he was doing.

Galland again on exact schedule. He was even more

confident. Lancasters were falling like flies to his night-fighters, the toll of downed enemy planes not to be accurately determined until morning. Gelsenkirchen itself was being plastered, but incredibly the oil refineries remained intact; it would seem the British bombardiers were highly inaccurate. "At the height the British are flying," Galland said, "I can estimate a minimum error of a mile. Perhaps even two."

This time when Goering put down the phone, he invited Kruger to have a glass of hock with him. If the Luftwaffe could control the night skies over Germany, it would mean that more units could be diverted to Russia—the result they all wanted so desperately—all in all of enormous benefit to the war effort and to him personally. Bormann and the others would crap in their pants from frustration when they heard. . . .

The next call from Galland, a quarter of an hour on the dot, was openly jubilant. "No question, Reichsmarschall, we've turned them back. They've been dropping God knows how many tons of high explosives and their primary targets are still undamaged."

"Tremendous."

"And our nightfighters have inflicted incredible damage. They won't forget tonight in a hurry!"

"Congratulations, General. I shall inform the Führer."

But Hitler had already been briefed when Goering finally spoke to him. The voice on the other end was calm, almost like old times, one could say even friendly. But then there was an interruption, someone talking to Hitler, Bormann, Goering guessed, and when Hitler came back on the line the familiar sharpness was present: "One more thing, Goering . . ."

My God, it's Emmy again. She's asked for special dispensation for some of her Jew friends!

"I want an exact count of downed Lancasters. Goebbels can use it. And of course our own losses. And needless to say, Galland will be rewarded."

"Exactly what I wanted to suggest, my Führer."

Another bottle of hock in his bath, in which he lingered happily, soaking, giggling a little to himself. How he'd turned things around!

Maida Thaler did not serve him while he was in residence in Carinhall—Emmy for her own reasons objected—and he decided to do without a rubdown. It would be self-indulgent to awaken the substitute masseur at this hour, and anyway he felt relaxed and drowsy from the wine and his pills and surely would have no trouble sleeping.

But later, in the huge bed, without Emmy's warm bulk beside him, he found sleep elusive. The fact was he was too excited, still savoring the evening's triumph; they'd come few and far between for him, particularly since the opening of the second front. Perhaps, he reflected, he ought to delay any further mention of his Mediterranean strategy at least for now—a turndown, and the fruits of Gelsenkirchen would be canceled. Smarter to withhold resubmission, as Carin had made him understand, until the propitious moment. So much in this world depended on timing!

Good. Decided. Thank you, Carin, my darling!

Sleep was beginning to come now, like a sweet cloud descending. What he needed was a break from tension; there were really too many burdens on his shoulders . . . the problems of arms production as well as the demands of a great air force. Perhaps Paris for a few days. Why not? Kröler certainly would have some new acquisitions. And there was that other project, the one that occupied so much of his thoughts; but he was asleep, snoring evenly without remembering what it was. . . .

Seventeen

THE DYING WINTER SUN, a great globe of citron, spread pale light over the Tuileries.

"It is very beautiful," said Goering, looking down the Champs, the Arc de Triomphe centered perfectly at the far end. He was wearing his favorite overcoat, butternut suede of a silky texture. The collar was dark mink; on his right breast he wore only one decoration, the large, diamond-studded star he had received from Mussolini.

It was cold this late afternoon, but brisk and dry: he breathed deeply and felt his body like a strong beast, his energies not dissipated at this early hour, alive with the juices of life.

"Bitte sehr, Herr Reichsmarschall!"

"Danke."

An aide had brought him a hot toddy laced with brandy.

Goering chose to drink it in the back of the Mercedes touring car. Its top was up and he was in high spirits, political worries thrust aside, looking forward to an evening's adventure.

Le Brun had received a call from Kröler less than two hours previously: "Come immediately," Kröler had said. "Bring your lady and a bag for overnight."

"What's up?"

"Goering's in Paris. He's invited us all on his train for a weekend jaunt . . . I think to Deauville." Kröler laughed. "He may have it in mind to open the casinos for a night of gambling."

"I can't speak for Mallou," said Le Brun. "She has performances."

Kröler's voice was steel. "The Reichsmarschall has heard much about her; his invitation was specific. Bring her, Le Brun, no matter what!"

"Do what I can," said Le Brun. He was hardly in the mood for such an outing with Goering and company. And how could Mallou break away from Chez Jeannot?

He called Jeannot and explained. Jeannot was furious, then adamantly negative, finally, by degrees, resigned. "What in hell can I say?" he growled. "If I bitch too much, the lousy *Boches* can close me down."

Le Brun didn't commiserate. "Let me speak to Mallou."

Mallou, surprisingly, was the only one who welcomed the news. "A night off," she said cheerfully.

181

"How nice. And how Jeannot must have bitched when you told him!"

"He bitched. Pick you up in half an hour. Oh, better take an evening gown. Deauville, probably."

He'd been at the office. Things to attend to. An hour lost before turning everything over to Lavoulière, then he hurried down to his car and set out for home. A thought had been buzzing in his head since Kröler's call. *Is this all it was supposed to be? Goering's sudden appearance? The abrupt command performance?*

He thought of trying to contact Arnaud, Garnier—they might have some sense of what was up, if anything. But by the time he reached the house it was too late. And he couldn't be sure his phone wasn't tapped.

Mallou, demure in a gray suit, was descending the wide staircase. Mischa was carrying her bag. Astonishingly, she and the Prince Kilkanov got along well. They were both eminently practical people and probably appreciated each other, Le Brun decided, because both were fiercely independent.

"You can close up till Sunday," Le Brun told Mischa. And, handing over an envelope filled with banknotes: "For the month. Yourself and the help."

Mischa grunted his thanks. His perception of Le Brun, of course, had changed radically since the night with the wounded American, Morgan. Not that he *liked* Le Brun now—liking was an entirely different matter. Also, he gathered, Le Brun preferred that the hostile tone be maintained between them: the woman evidently did not know of Le Brun's underground activities, and any change in the attitude between Le Brun and himself would be a tipoff.

Le Brun drew another envelope from his inside jacket pocket. "And kindly do me a favor. Give this to Father Gregory at St. Alexander."

"I don't understand," Mischa said after a moment. But then he did—Aaron Jacobi had entrusted the collection to Le Brun.

"The father will," said Le Brun.

Mallou had been looking from one to another. Outside, settled in the Hispano, she asked Le Brun what their exchange had been all about.

"Just a gift for the church. Aaron Jacobi always donated . . . thought it'd be *noblesse oblige* to keep up the tradition," he told her casually.

Mallou gave him a shrewd glance. But Le Brun had been no more than politely communicative the past months. *Has he another woman?* she wondered. She was so often furious with him, wanting to break through his control, to wound him badly. But he was scrupulously kind and considerate and gave her no opportunity.

Perhaps, she thought, *the weekend will be what we both need. And being with the Boches should be interesting; they'll all have their tongues hanging out for me. That in itself ought to be amusing. Might even twist the knife into this aristocratic son of a bitch. . . .*

Seeing Le Brun arrive at the parking area of the museum with Mallou, Kröler came over at once, kissed Mallou's hand elaborately, and told Le Brun that when they got under way he was to be third in line in the convoy, following after General von Banheim.

A large canvas-topped truck was stationed to one side of the parking area. Calling Le Brun and Mallou over, Kröler lifted the back flap and invited them to look inside. Cases of champagne, vintage wines, cartons of fruits and vegetables. And deeper within the cavernous vehicle, six men in white, crouched uncomfortably on benches. Stacked near them, dozens of warming ovens.

"Chefs from the Crillon and the Ritz," said Kröler delightedly. "And enough food for a dozen banquets. The Reichsmarschall travels in style, eh?"

"Travels where?" asked Le Brun.

Kröler grinned smugly. "I think I can reveal it now. Down to the Loire country—to scratch an itch, you might say. . . ."

Le Brun knew in a flash what was coming and contrived to match Kröler with a smile of his own. "To appraise the treasures! The Victoire de Samothrace!"

Kröler's triumph was open. "Château d'Albion. It appears the Reichsmarschall's interest in the sculpture became known to Vichy. And so they removed the lady—secretly, from her former hiding place, to d'Albion nearby. You're completely exonerated, by the way. Had you known, you would of course have informed us."

"Without question," said Le Brun promptly. "D'Albion, you say?"

"Correct, Le Brun. And I repeat, our faith in you remains undiminished. Witness your being invited along tonight." To Mallou: "Mademoiselle, I'm sure you agree—being with the Reichsmarschall is in itself a high honor. The weekend should be memorable." He left them and returned to his Mercedes.

"Did you know?" asked Mallou.

Le Brun nodded curtly. Not only had he known, he himself had suggested the d'Albion move to Garnier. *But how in hell did Goering's people find out? A traitor at the Beaux-Arts?* He'd never find out, he decided grimly.

Two additional Mercedes had sped up the ramp leading to the Jeu de Paume from the Concorde, brakes squealing on the gravel. Von Banheim and Bocke, plus three staff officers. And five young ladies.

Not the flower of France, Le Brun saw, but not obvious whores, either. Von Banheim, for all his military posturing, was not unsubtle. And Goering was a family man and could make things sticky for his staff if things were too obvious.

Kröler, the master of ceremonies, was beaming at the new arrivals.

Le Brun saw Sergeant Raeder; he had arrived earlier and stood apart, leaning against the commissary truck. Now he looked toward them, managing to turn a scowl into a reasonably polite nod of recognition.

"Couillon," murmured Mallou.

She had told Le Brun about Raeder's invasion of her dressing room, his proposition. "Don't fool with him," Le Brun had warned her. "When the time comes, I'll handle him."

When the time comes, you'll do nothing, thought Mallou without malice, sadly, *because you've stopped loving me, if you ever did.* Now she placed her arm in his, knowing other men were watching. She was easily the most beautiful woman present.

Von Banheim, swagger stick tapping boots mirror-shiny, strode over. He was an impressive man and knew it. "Mademoiselle," he said, "so happy you could join us. Le Brun, we shall feast our eyes as well as our stomachs, *n'est-ce pas?* You shall be our guide, I'm told."

"I was just informed, General. But more than happy to oblige."

"We shall reward you," said von Banheim, with the slightest mocking edge, "and not just with the gold you make selling us paintings. With a special medal, perhaps. Why not?" He was off to join Goering. Bocke was shepherding people into the cars, allocating the women. One of them, Bocke's apparently, wearing a sable coat and cossack hat, a strutting Russian Hussar, paused before entering the last Mercedes and winked at Mallou and Le Brun.

Le Brun nodded back perfunctorily before realizing Mallou's hand was over her mouth, muffling her laughter. "Marcel," she whispered to Le Brun. "Don't you see? It's Marcel! From Chez Jeannot!"

Marcel, without question, with a flash of silken legs, allowed Colonel Bocke to help him aboard.

On their way to the Hispano, Le Brun and Mallou passed Sergeant Raeder, who had left his position by the truck to cross toward the car with Bocke.

Where Raeder had been standing, Le Brun's eye was drawn by the glint of sunlight on metal—iron braces newly bolted to the front and back of the truck bed. Not essential surely for champagne, or food warmers, or chefs from the Crillon and Ritz, but damned important if you wanted to transport an exceedingly heavy object, say, a huge piece of ancient sculpture.

Looking up, Le Brun caught Raeder's eye; the man had paused, noting Le Brun's interest. Then Raeder quickly turned and got into the last car beside Bocke's driver, while up the ramp zoomed a final vehicle, a carrier packed tightly with élite Luftwaffe troops. At least forty men, Le Brun estimated, armed with automatic weapons. The convoy would not go like a lamb into enemy territory.

At the checkpoint into the unoccupied zone, the convoy came politely to a halt, while a captain of gendarmes appeared, accompanied by three soldiers with sidearms.

At once Bocke and a major from the troop carrier were running toward them. A brief conference; the Frenchman and Bocke seemed on friendly terms. Le Brun knew why, Garnier having given him a rundown on Bocke's previous expedition south.

Now the captain peered into the first Mercedes, saluting the Reichsmarschall inside. He then saluted Colonel Bocke, the Luftwaffe major, and issued a sharp command to his own troops. Barriers were hastily withdrawn, engines restarted, the convoy, gathering speed, swept into the soft, sweet, darkening terrain of Vichy France.

D'Albion lay in the center of a green meadow, a castle in miniature.

Two wings, walls serrated, a central rounded turret, it had been the love nest of one of the Louis', Le Brun recalled vaguely; a duke had built it for the concupiscent wife of a local farmer.

An embracing moat fed into a small adjoining lake. The convoy stopped in front of the drawbridge, then slowly drove through the portcullis into a parking area. Instantly the troop carrier emptied, gray-helmeted men leaping off, trotting toward doors, windows, as if breaking a siege.

A woman in a black, high-necked wool dress, a shawl over her shoulders, appeared in the entrance. Tall and thin as a willow branch, she waited stoically while Colonel Bocke made an attempt to account for the invasion.

The woman was Christine Chanton, curator at d'Albion, and Le Brun knew her only slightly; she was a quiet woman, he remembered, a spinster whose life was art.

Goering had emerged from his car, and as if unmindful of the exchange stood in the courtyard, clapping gloved hands for warmth, commenting on the château's architectural features to the staff gathered around him.

Bocke beckoned for Le Brun. With Mallou, he marched to the great front door and explained the situation to Christine Chanton: the Reichsmarschall, hearing that the Winged Victory had been moved here, had motored down for a look at it.

"A look?" Christine Chanton asked dryly, her glance taking in Mallou, the ranking officers, the women, the Luftwaffe troops who were trotting, weapons drawn, to throw a cordon around the estate.

Le Brun shrugged. Her eyes were boring into him with scorn. "And you, monsieur, are the guide?"

The current owner of d'Albion, a textile manufacturer from Lyons now living on the Côte d'Azur, had restored the château without counting cost. The Reichsmarschall was immediately installed in his chambers, formerly the duke's, splendidly furnished with authentic antiques.

The great long table in the banquet room was laid with the house's best linen, the frightened servants hurrying to oblige. Buckets of ice were brought from the ice cellar outside for the champagne. The chefs were already at work setting up the buffet.

Bocke's officers couldn't wait. They broke out the schnapps, installing themselves in the main salon, a great vaulted room of stone with a roaring fireplace at the far end.

Bocke had neglected nothing. Three Luftwaffe violinists, paunchy, elderly musicians, sawed away. Laughter began to fill the hall; the distance from Paris, from the general staff, swept away inhibitions. Fichner, a captain with a long, melancholy face and five children back in Hamburg, who had held himself rigidly aloof from the sexual practices of his fellow officers, felt suddenly young, released, the schnapps he had gulped down fire in his gut.

One of the women, Georgette, looked vaguely like his wife, but younger and much prettier. As she swung by, dancing with Major Tanlig, Fichner, on impulse, shot a hand forward, yanking at her bodice. A ripping sound and a breast escaped.

Major Tanlig, known to be resourceful, at once plunged his face into the softness. This struck everyone, including Georgette, as terribly funny. She pulled away the rest of the top, allowing both breasts to spill free.

Upstairs, dressed and ready to join the party, Mallou heard the commotion and decided against it; they'd be animals in no time at all. She rang for a servant.

A breathless, perspiring young girl eventually appeared.

"At madame's service."

"Champagne," Mallou told her. "Chilled."

"*Oui*, madame."

"A minute," a voice said. Von Banheim had appeared as if by magic in the corridor. He was bowing. That damned, absurdly correct, Teutonic exercise. But not the smile. The smile was warm, if his tone formal. "You look ravishing, mademoiselle."

"Thank you," she said, but coolly. She knew very well how she looked; she also knew how she felt.

"Champagne is not made to drink alone."

"Isn't it?"

"Rarely." That same nice, confident voice. "I gather you're not anxious to participate in the festivities downstairs. Can't blame you; on the contrary, it is to your credit. I, on the other hand, am banned because of my rank. It would never do, to . . . join in such activities with junior officers. A certain distance must be maintained. You understand?"

"Yes," she said.

"We could," he said, "enjoy our champagne together. In my quarters. Until Le Brun can join us, naturally."

"Naturally. Why aren't you with him and the Reichsmarschall?"

"Like you, I had the need for privacy, for quiet. And to be honest, I'm primarily a military man. And now a confession. You will not give me away, I'm sure. At times art bores me. This is one of those times, I think."

Von Banheim was quite a man, she'd heard. In

many areas. *To hell with Le Brun,* she decided on the spot. *To hell with him!*

"I believe you're right. About the champagne."

"How beautiful you are," he said, taking her arm.

"Very good," Goering said.

He was examining a child's head, third century B.C. Greek. There were four of them in the basement, not counting Christine Chanton—Goering, Kröler, Raeder, and Le Brun.

The stone-lined caves, running the length of the central structure, were filled with statuary—basically the overflow from Valençay, which held the cream of the Louvre sculpture.

Goering, Le Brun thought, was surprisingly mild and cooperative, sensitive to Chanton's situation, seemingly grateful for the bits of information she grudgingly offered on the tour of her domain. He had swallowed but two of his white pills so far as Le Brun had been able to observe; his speech was still unslurred. And his glance at the woman still managed amiability.

"All very interesting, mademoiselle. Is it not, Dr. Kröler? And mind you, this is not their best, which is at that other château . . ."

"Valençay," offered Kröler.

"Valençay. There we'll visit soon, too. A must, agreed? Now, if you don't mind, the beauty herself, the Samothrace; you have her, *nicht wahr,* tucked away in a secret corner?"

Christine Chanton hesitated, looking first at Le Brun, then at the Germans.

"I have it," she said in a thin voice. "This way, please."

A bricked stairway led up to a huge oak door—the door opened to the château's chapel. Towering over the nave, only vaguely outlined by moonlight filtering in through a stained glass window, was what they had come for.

The curator found a light switch.

The chapel was turned into a glowing jewel. Illuminated, her wings spread almost to the walls, the

Victoire appeared larger, more dominating than any of the visitors had remembered or imagined.

"*Du lieber Gott im Himmel . . .*" murmured Goering.

Out of breath from the climb, he moved slowly forward, standing at the base, gazing upward.

Several minutes passed. Finally, he joined the group. "I'll go to my rooms now. Thank you, mademoiselle."

Raeder noticed a second door and asked Chanton if it led to the sleeping quarters above. It did, she said. She had stopped looking at Le Brun. She switched off the lights as the group filed out.

The duke's chambers included a small sitting room with a fireplace and painted angels on the ceiling.

Goering sitting in the throne-chair which the owner had had copied from drawings of the duke's original throne, sipped brandy and admired a heavy gold inkwell on the Louis Quatorze desk next to him.

He was in an excellent humor.

"Make the arrangements," he told Kröler. "We leave in the morning first thing with the sculpture. And please, if possible, no trouble with that woman curator. You handle her, Le Brun. Explain that in exchange for the Samothrace, France will be given a fine piece from our own National Treasure."

Kröler had already motioned to Raeder, who slipped out.

"Surely she'll be reasonable," Goering continued. "Won't she, Le Brun?"

"I'm afraid not, Reichsmarschall."

Goering's brandy glass hovered, then settled on the arm of his chair. "Why not?"

"She's a Frenchwoman. The Winged Victory has been put in her charge. And she's no fool; she knows why you are here. You can be sure she's already sent word to Vichy."

"Impossible," put in Kröler. "The order to the troop commander was to seal off the château—no one to leave."

"Pigeons," said Le Brun.

"*What?*"

"The château has its coop; it would have been provided with a means of signaling out, you see. When they moved the Victoire here."

Goering was eating white pills; he rose from the chair, his bonhomie ebbing like the heat from the dying fire. "Why should I care about Vichy?" he asked Le Brun irritably.

"Forgive me, Reichsmarschall. Vichy will not take this without protest. They simply can't afford to. Even Laval has got to scream his head off. All sorts of delicate matters are involved. The fleet, the dispatch of workers to the Reich, for example. And with your hands being tied in Russia, will you want—will your Führer condone—such an action?"

Facing Le Brun, Goering had the inkwell in his hands, as if not knowing what to do with it.

"Dammit, are you presuming to give me political advice?"

"I'm simply wondering, Reichsmarschall, whether the risk is one you dare to take. For a piece of art?"

Goering knew Le Brun was right. He had come down hard on every sore point—to stir up the French, to create a diplomatic furor at this moment, with things so critical in so many areas, could be a ghastly mistake. What had he been thinking of? That meeting with Hitler next week could be his end. But his blood boiled with the knowledge—with the fact that every word this insolent fellow had said was true. And he *would* have the Samothrace—before the war was over he would have it! Nobody in heaven or on earth would stop him!

Raising his arm, he flung the inkpot not too far away from *dieser verfluchte* Le Brun, actually at the gold-flecked mirror over the hearth, shattering the glass into a hundred pieces.

Kröler was pale, motionless, waiting for an even greater outburst.

"Did you know, Reichsmarschall," said Le Brun with a smile, "that Napoleon was famous for flinging inkwells. It's really so! His aides got to be very good at dodging."

"I *will* have the Winged Victory, Le Brun," Goering said evenly. "Not now, but eventually! Before it's over! Now get out!"

He was not a fat clown making idle boasts—Le Brun saw it. Striding into the shards of glass, Goering himself picked up the inkwell and turned, facing Le Brun.

He might throw it again, Le Brun thought. *Like Napoleon. This time straight at me.*

"Where the devil's von Banheim?" he heard Goering demand as he left.

In the corridor the sound of someone shooting off a pistol in the grand salon below echoed, and drunken laughter mingled with the gunshots. Le Brun listened for a moment before finding the door to his room. It was empty, suitcases and clothes strewn about. Where was Mallou? Downstairs in that debauch?

In the long entrance hall, they had Georgette naked in a suit of armor and were taking turns firing their Lugers, trying to see how close they could come without actually puncturing the old metal. Le Brun noticed that Georgette didn't seem to mind, so why should he? Anyway, no Mallou!

Quietly behind them, he was able to feel his way down the corridor and to the chapel where he found Christine Chanton sitting in semidarkness, one candle on the stone floor beside her, in front of the Victoire.

"It's all right," he told her. "They won't take it."

She was silent, looking at him.

"Then you're not with them?"

"No."

"How did you manage it?"

"It doesn't matter, and it's only buying time. Goering will be back."

"With a division next time," she said bitterly. "He wants it badly."

"Yes."

"He can't be very happy with your part in this."

"It doesn't matter," Le Brun said. In the candlelight Christine Chanton's face was soft and ageless; it had its own sculptured beauty.

He took one more look at the Victoire, wings now spread protectively over the woman below, it seemed, and started for the chapel door. But then stopped. "Have you any means of getting messages out? Short wave, pigeons?"

"Radio? No. Pigeons?"

He laughed.

"A telephone," she said, "but it isn't working. It seldom is. You really ought to escape yourself."

"I'm not here alone."

"I saw her when you came. She's . . . stunning."

He nodded, not commenting.

"Goodbye," she said.

"Goodbye."

In the corridor he discovered that the shooting at least had stopped—the suit of armor stood empty. They were all in the banquet room, but the noise level had muted, like an engine throttled.

On the second-floor landing he hesitated: people were entering Goering's suite.

A woman came out and caught sight of Le Brun. It was Marcel, magnificent in a gold lamé evening gown. And he was beckoning, finger to lips.

"Le Brun, listen," Marcel whispered as they met halfway. "Do you know this Sergeant Raeder?"

"Yes, why?"

"He's sworn to Goering you're Resistance. He produced some reports linking you with that sniper who escaped after killing all those *Boches* around the Concorde. He swore you engineered the escape, brought the guy to a house on the avenue Foch. He had an agent in a place across the street. You're in bad trouble, Le Brun. Goering didn't need much convincing. He agrees you're untrustworthy, to say the least. You know what follows—" Marcel drew a finger across his throat. "You want my advice—beat it!"

Marcel moved off down the corridor, finger to lips once more, smiling.

Le Brun tried his room again. Still no Mallou. Exiting, he encountered Raeder leaving the Reichsmarschall's quarters.

"Oh, Le Brun," Raeder said. "I was looking for you. You'll be wanted by Reichmarschall Goering in a few minutes. As soon as certain other business is transacted. Please be ready."

Le Brun nodded, about to go on. But Raeder hadn't moved.

"Looking for your woman?"

There was an air about Raeder—an air of savage satisfaction.

"As a matter of fact, yes."

"She's in General von Banheim's room, Le Brun, in his bed, with her legs spread, with von Banheim showing her how the Germans do it. And she likes it, Le Brun, oh, how she likes it! Stand outside the door and hear it for yourself, hear her pleading for more!"

The moment of disbelief passed. Le Brun knew it was so, knew it because Raeder was twisting a knife in himself as well; it was Raeder's eyes, cold and tormented. The general, in a way, was cuckolding them both.

A grimace on his lips, Raeder lurched back into Goering's quarters, allowing Le Brun to duck into his own room.

Mallou's perfume still lingered, and he paused for a moment before crossing to his valise, ransacking it for the small .22 automatic pistol Arnaud had given him to replace his bulkier Luger.

No one at that precise moment was in the corridor, which permitted him to reach the servants' staircase at the other end, down past the huge old bricked kitchen—itself a world of shouting voices and banging crockery—to an outside door, which to his horror dropped off without warning to black-moated water.

Inside again. By now in Goering's suite they were asking for him. What was their intention? Execute him on the spot? Not impossible, knowing the Reichsmarschall's frustration.

Another door, finally, that looked promising and was—it opened onto the parking area.

Clouds were speeding across the sky, so he waited. Soon one caught the moon, embracing it. Le Brun took a breath and ran, reaching the portcullis.

Walking carelessly, automatic rifle held slackly, a Luftwaffe guard approached on his round, thinking, *What kind of stupidity is this assignment, anyway? The Reichsmarschall, they said, wants to steal a statue!*

Le Brun, behind him in the darkness, hesitated. Too long. When he got himself to swing the butt of the pistol at the passing head it was almost ineffectual, the blow merely glancing. The soldier went down, but with a clatter, echoing in the courtyard.

And then the man was on his knees, reaching for his weapon.

Le Brun fired and the man's face blurred away from him, smashing into bones and raw flesh.

Le Brun was across the moat, bullets cutting the air around him. *I can't last long,* he thought. And the château was awakened: lights were going on, he could hear shouting.

The moon had accommodated to the best of its ability. Racing from the clouds, it now hung clear above the château. Everyone could see Le Brun in the meadow, running for his life.

At a window, Mallou saw and held back a sob: beside her, von Banheim was cursing; where the hell had he put his gun? Why couldn't his men hit one easy target? How had the son of a bitch slipped through in the first place?

He had reached the fringe of the wood, his lungs bursting. Another minute or two, he begged himself, that would do it. *Keep running, Le Brun,* he told himself—*run!*

They had stopped firing at him now: he was deep within the wood and it would have been senseless; he didn't even believe they'd come to look for him. It would be dawn soon, and they would have to pick up and go—with their cars and trucks, with their women, with their Reichsmarschall.

He had stopped, exhausted, sinking to the ground in a small hollow, and here, after a time, he began to pull himself together. Eventually he got to his feet, realizing he was still clutching the automatic though the chamber was empty and he had no extra ammunition. He put the gun away, brushing wet, clinging leaves from his body.

It was cold. *A more experienced operator,* he told himself wryly, *would have put on a sweater before leaving the château; a bottle of brandy in a pocket wouldn't have hurt either.*

Curiously he felt exultant. Even thinking of Mallou and von Banheim could not take away this feeling. It ran through his body like a renewing flame. He was his own man, free.

There was a barely discernible lightness in the sky as he headed north, toward Paris.

PART TWO

Eighteen

THE *Concierge* OF THE BUILDING was Dr. Slovsky's wife, Elena, a dumpy, cheerful, but sharp-tongued woman. Since the job had been wangled for her several years before by the Princess Kilkanov, things were made relatively easy for Sara. No inquisitive darts hurled at her by other servants inhabiting the attic floor, hardly a second look by other residents. In France the approval of the *concierge* guarantees absolution from all crimes and total acceptance in the building under question.

Sara's fiancé, Elena Slovsky firmly let it be known, had been wounded in the last bit of fighting against the *Boches* entering Paris. A leg wound had refused to heal properly, necessitating a new and larger cast. Upon his recovery, the two would certainly marry. The girl, *bonne* to the Prince and Princess, was of exceptionally high character, witness her devotion to the poor boy, still unable to leave his bed.

A good deal of this was true. Morgan's wound was healing with agonizing slowness. Dr. Slovsky had redone the cast after several days, from hip to ankle, rigging a pulley from the ceiling to keep it in traction, which made Sara's job as nurse a punishing one. At first, hardly aware of where he was and what was happening, Morgan made things easy. Sara could think of him as an outsized child desperately needing her ministrations.

Her upbringing had not prepared her for this sort of thing. Not simply a question of emptying the bedpan. Immobile, Morgan could not fill it without the most intimate kind of assistance.

Following the initial shock, Sara performed bravely and efficiently. In the beginning of the third week,

Morgan, intensely embarrassed, began to be able to attend to these functions himself. By the fourth week, with the aid of crutches, he could hobble to the WC alone.

It was already getting on toward December, a cold, rainy, miserable autumn. The Parisians felt the cold more intensely than any other year. Fuel was at a premium, with the specter of a long, fierce winter ahead. Food was in even shorter supply than the previous year, the black market itself offering a skimpy larder.

Despite the difficulties her patient had brought into her life, taking even her bed—she slept these nights below, on the Kilkanov couch—Sara was holding up reasonably well.

Mischa had bought her a camera on the black market, a French make specified, even though she would have dearly loved a fast Zeiss lens. She'd taken to doing studies of the Kilkanovs, of prized objects in their apartment in black and white, color being almost impossible to obtain. And she'd recently made some portraits of Morgan—damned good ones; she was a hell of a fine artist, he discovered. She was also very beautiful and kind. Her presence made it possible for him to forget the terrible things that occasionally still sent wild, vengeful notions racing through his head.

Has he fallen in love with her? the Princess Kilkanov wondered, after five minutes in the tiny room with the two of them together.

It was her first visit since Morgan could be termed convalescent, still in the knee-high cast, traction discontinued, but stronger, beginning to move about, thanking the Kilkanovs for their generosity, for participating in this dangerous business of hiding him.

He was a tall, big-boned young man with rough blond hair that cascaded down almost to his shoulders, eyes not as blue as her husband's but blue enough, and a candid, shy smile. It could belong to a schoolboy but it belonged to a man who had killed, she knew, more than once, without knowing too much else about him.

"Cigarette?" she offered now, fishing a pack out of the wheelchair pocket.

He nodded and she tossed him the pack and matches.

His fingers shook as he lit up.

"Agreed not to smoke more than a few a day," he said, motioning to Sara. "Tiny room. Nice of her to put up with it."

"Nice of her to put up with you entirely," commented the Princess dryly.

He looked over at Sara again.

"Far beyond the call of duty. You all ought to throw me back, you know."

No comment from Sara, who brought him a small dish as an ashtray. Sara, the Princess had previously observed, was curiously contained these last weeks, petals often closed like a night-blooming flower. She hadn't returned to Paris to be confined to a cell nursing this young giant, the Princess could almost hear her saying—or screaming.

"The cast comes off tomorrow," she told the Princess now, sounding proud.

"Yeah, tomorrow," Morgan said. "And I'll be up and away."

"To where?" enquired the Princess in her usual growl of a voice.

A grin on his face, he said, "South with the birds. Who knows? But at least you'll be rid of me!"

His eyes were on Sara again, the Princess could see; oh, yes, he'd caught the bug all right! Sara was good about it, though, aware but not coy or pretending, and not feeding it, either.

"The first thing he'll do," she said quietly, "is get hold of a gun and start all over again."

"No," he said, angrily. "I promised, didn't I?"

Sara turned to the Princess. "If we could sneak him to the unoccupied zone—"

"We're not sure the building isn't still being watched . . . but if it's possible, Mischa will manage it."

"I don't intend to leave Paris," Morgan announced suddenly.

Sara started to speak, then checked herself.

"Suppose she comes back?" Morgan added, not looking at either of them, entwining his long fingers, studying them.

201

Sara and the Princess knew his story. At the height of his fever, it had spilled out to them in strangled bits and pieces. Mischa, via Le Brun, had supplied the rest. And then there had been moments, Sara confided to the Princess, when he confused her with his Elsa. He'd shown her his wife's picture from his wallet. Two women, Sara declared, could not have been more physically dissimilar.

That wasn't the only problem. Awakening from a nap the other day, Morgan struggled to get out of bed, reaching for the crutches, insisting he had to return to his old apartment. "Suppose they release the child and she comes back and can't find me!"

The next morning when Sara had come up from the Kilkanovs' with his coffee and croissant, he was spread-eagled on the floor, unable to reach a crutch which had slid away from him. For once very angry, Sara, using all her strength, got him back under covers, where he stared at the ceiling in surly defiance.

"The poor little child's almost certainly dead by now," the Princess said when Sara related the incident. "Mischa was talking to Father Gregory"—Sonia Kilkanov looked almost complacent for a moment—"at mass last Sunday. The point is, Father Gregory's reecived word from the Church in the east. They're death camps, whatever the Germans call them here. And for Catholics as well as Jews. No one who goes in comes out."

The two women were silent. The Princess finally smiled grimly up at Sara, twisted around in the wheelchair, and asked for the vodka. "Time for a drink, don't you agree?"

Sara had no words for the news of the concentration camps. How could she? Monsters!

"You must think of yourself," Princess Kilkanov said. "Your own safety."

But what answer could one make to that? And to-day, seeing Morgan after several weeks, the Princess had no special wisdom to offer. He was unexpectedly chatty, recounting Sara's struggles to get him up from the floor, where he had fallen trying to get to the WC, making a comedy out of it—his own incredible helplessness, like a turtle on its back, drawing a smile from the Princess. He could be charming, the Princess had to admit, and despite his pallor he was really very handsome.

Now, as if to preserve the favorable climate he'd created, Morgan held out for her inspection the photographs Sara had taken of him. "Damned good, aren't they, Princess? Look at the sharpness, the composition. And without adequate lighting."

This was one positive contribution Morgan had made, Sara was forced to admit—stimulating her interest in photography again. And it ate up the time between nursing chores as well as blocking off other concerns such as the war, her family, the fate of the collection. And Claude Le Brun. Almost making her forget Claude Le Brun. . . .

Lavoulière, appointed by the Nazis new acting head of Jacobi and Company, had, on the occasion of his inspecting the Jacobi mansion, revealed to Mischa at least part of the Le Brun Story. During a surreptitious foray by Hermann Goering into unoccupied France— the intention being to make off with a priceless piece of art—Le Brun had emerged in his true colors, thwarting the attempted theft. Then somehow, despite the efforts of the Reichsmarchall's troops, he had made his escape. And it had been Le Brun—no further need for secrecy about that, Sara knew—who had plucked Morgan from the rue de Rivoli, spiriting him to the safety of the Jacobi house.

All this information, completely unexpected, had the effect of making her totally miserable. How arrogantly she had judged him after her arrival in Paris! And how wrong she had been! How could she ever face him? Even if, as she said to the Princess, the poor man survived. The Nazis, Lavoulière told Mischa, had circulated pictures of him to all their headquarters.

The Princess, one of those foul-smelling *ersatz* cigarettes in her mouth as usual, squinted at Sara. "Who doesn't wear a false face in France? How could you have thought otherwise? And don't be too concerned— he seems passive, but he isn't. They'll never catch him!"

Sara nodded, the odd description of Le Brun sending her back years ago to an incident in the Jacobi garden. A summer night. Crouched behind a box hedge, Sara—how old was she then, seventeen?—with clinical interest in observing the amatory technique of her sister. Erica kissing, or allowing herself to be kissed, and responding shamelessly in what the family called "Josephine's Bower." (The queen had once been observed there with her hand in the emperor's trousers, so the story went, shortly before she was left for the Austrian woman.)

Le Brun, Sara noticed, was not acting like an emperor, more like a defeated general, but with sword still in scabbard. Almost able to thrust a hand through the hedge and touch them, Sara abruptly became certain her breathing was clearly audible in the garden's stillness. Discovery, she realized, would be utterly humiliating, calamitous—immediate suicide her only option. But any sort of retreat was bound to be discovered.

At this critical juncture, her sex-mad sister—shameless was too mild an opprobrium—finally coaxed Le Brun deeper into the garden, where the larger trees stood, bending the moon into deep lovers' shadows. . . .

Crying great tears, Sara remembered dashing back into the house. Were they tears of relief, or jealousy, or anger? she wondered now.

"No one's heard a word about Le Brun," the Princess was saying. "Gone to ground, Mischa believes, right here in the city. I think he's beginning to change his mind about Le Brun! Won't admit it. What a stubborn old bullmoose I'm married to!"

All that was required of Sara was a smile.

"I did tell you the latest about that woman, didn't I? Le Brun's woman?"

"No, you didn't. Princess, please!"

The Princess gave her the satisfied guffaw of an old campaigner.

"Where were you, child? How many light-years away? All right, they say she's cohabiting with a General von Banheim—quite openly. At least there's nothing hypocritical about that adorable little whore. They're living in an apartment the general's requisitioned in Passy. Just a sip more, dear. Thank you."

"How *could* she? With a German?"

The Princess sat back in her chair, contemplating not Sara but the room, her treasures, her favorite ikon. "Now you're feeling sorry for Le Brun. Cuckolded."

"No," Sara said. "Still—"

"Liar! Don't sell her short, my young lady! Mallou's a streetfighter. And Le Brun's a curious man—all inside like a walnut. She's cutting her losses, my guess. Same, in a different way, as you."

Staring into the hard, bright eyes across from her, Sara thought the Princess ought not sell *her* short either.

"A nut can be cracked! Who is von Banheim?"

"On Goering's staff. One-eyed. Which doesn't daunt the women evidently! Completely redecorated the place with fine antiques, good paintings. All plundered of course. And listen to this—black silk from China on the bedrooms walls. . . ."

Madame Slovsky had let Sara use a small storeroom in the basement—it had a rusted washbasin—as a darkroom. And being next to the furnace, it was warm. Whenever possible, often in the early-morning hours, unable to sleep, Sara would steal out of the Kilkanovs' dwelling, descend to the catacombs, and putter around, doing her best to transfer satisfactory images to the inferior photographic paper Mischa had managed to buy for her.

The night following the visit of the Princess to Morgan was another difficult one for Sara, dawn still in the wings, when she gave up, put her bedding away, and dressed. The same old litany—*Le Brun, Aaron, her mother, the collection, Le Brun. . . .*

She had left her latest roll of negatives upstairs, on Morgan's nighttable. She decided to risk retrieving it, take it downstairs for developing. Morgan, aided by Dr. Slovsky's pills, was sleeping soundly; she hoped she wouldn't wake him.

His face was turned to the wall. Closing the door behind her, she crept toward the table. But the floorboards creaked and she had to move with care, eyes on his sleeping form on the bed. Light was filtering in from a gap in the curtains, revealing evidence of his

205

restlessness, the blanket thrust aside, hardly on him at all.

Bending to fix it properly, she felt his hand move suddenly over her shoulder, then down, tightening over her chest.

He was sitting up. "Elsa," he said.

"Sara."

He was trying to pull her down. "Make love to me, Elsa. Dammit, how long's it been?"

"Tom . . . look at me. It's Sara. Let me go."

"Bitch!"

He had reached up, grabbing the collar of her blouse, pulling her down, suffocating her against his chest. Frightened, she tried to break away. It was the wrong move, the blouse and bra tore completely away. Naked to the waist, she was aware he'd abruptly released his hold. Gasping—rising, she saw that he was crying, wiping the tears with his forearm.

"It's all right," she told him, trying to gather the pieces of the blouse around her. "Was the dream very bad?"

"Yes."

He'd got control now, boosting himself to a sitting position. The morning light was stronger, had a carmine tinge to it that made the room seem warmer. From the facing building she could hear a shiver of wings, the pigeons conversing on the roof, cooing affectionately.

Morgan's eyes were fixed on her breasts, high, upthrust. "Do you think . . ." he began. "Oh, Jesus!"

"Elsa?" she asked.

"Sara Jacobi!"

Bending, she kissed him, letting him fondle her. "How will we? Your cast . . ."

"I'll slash the damn thing off if I have to. Don't worry about it!"

She gave him a small, sad smile, then sat on the bed and undressed. "My God," he said. The light was full on her, but still a dubious light, not yet quite real. Nor was she real for him—*No sculptor,* he thought, *could have fashioned such loveliness*—until she slipped atop him, a woman of flesh and blood, solidly in his arms.

But he was Prometheus, chained to a rock, and he cursed his cast and immobility.

"Let me," she said, rising.

"Yes," he said, already at the peak of tumescence but managing to wait while, gently, with a moaning as plaintive as the pigeons, she lowered herself again, and with a sudden harsh cry plunged him inside her.

Nineteen

THEY HADN'T GIVEN UP looking for Le Brun. Even after Lavoulière took over the Jacobi property they stopped by regularly at the apartment to question Mischa.

So they didn't know where in hell to find the fellow, Mischa gathered. *Good. Didn't like the man, no secret about that, but at least he wasn't the bastard he had appeared to be. Should have been smart enough to have known that,* Mischa admitted to himself. Aaron Jacobi made mistakes, but rarely about people.

Paris had gone into autumn, the war news not encouraging but not too bad either, the *Boches* stumbling on the front against Russia and the British slowly climbing to their feet.

The weather was something else—cold, rainy, punishing. Hot water available for limited periods only—a misery for Sonia—and food—well, it was war, what could one say? Mischa's bones ached but he'd be damned if anyone beside his wife would know it. He continued to hold himself straight as a tree in the forest.

They wanted Le Brun all right, wanted him badly. One day they came to Mischa's—the Princess fortunately was upstairs with Sara—and this time asked him to come with them. Gestapo. Two men, but uncharacteristically deferential. No, he need take nothing with him, he'd be home shortly, he could count on it.

An office building near rue Washington, off the Champs-Elysées. Very businesslike except for the uniforms. No screams, as he had feared, echoing down the corridor.

A Sergeant Raeder, one of Goering's men, was present, the session scheduled at his request. A handsome young man, Raeder, with strange eyes, reminding Mischa of winter-gray street ice.

Raeder participated directly in the interrogation. He was curiously knowledgeable about Le Brun, even up on the fact that little love was lost between Le Brun and the Prince.

Despite how he felt about Le Brun, Mischa would have allowed himself to be chopped into little pieces before giving anything to this smirking Nazi. It wasn't necessary. The dialogue, with the exception of occasional acerbic asides from the sergeant, was polite. Mischa, even had he desired to be, was of no use to them. He was absolutely ignorant of Le Brun's movements, or of his friends, acquaintances, and associates, with the exception of Mallou and Lavoulière, and Raeder was not interested in either of them, he stated.

Mischa, as he would learn later, was in relatively little danger, at least for the time being. Word had come down from higher authorities to question Prince Kilkanov if absolutely necessary, but handle him with kid gloves. Although the campaign in Russia was hardly proceeding as rapidly as hoped, it was assumed that one day in the near future the Wehrmacht would march into Moscow, proclaiming a new National Socialist government. When that moment arrived, a nephew of a grand duke, especially a man who had reputedly been a political rebel, a friend of Kerensky's, a truly democratic member of the royal family, the Prince Kilkanov, it was hoped, would come forward. If not to serve in a cooperative cabinet, at least to stand on a balcony applauding as the victorious Wehrmacht paraded below.

Dismissed with apologies from the Gestapo lieutenant, a deceptively bland junior officer, Mischa was on the way to the door when Sergeant Raeder, in a surprisingly sharp voice considering the previous tone of the meeting, stopped him. "Prince Kilkanov, a final question: one night not too long ago, a man your press called 'the sniper' was intercepted and badly wounded. Near the place de la Concorde. It is my belief this man was able to evade our patrol and escape with the help of Claude Le Brun. What do you know about it?"

Mischa stared down at Raeder.

"Why would I know anything about it?"

"Because," said Raeder with a sardonic smile, "a wounded man corresponding to his description—I speak of this sniper—was seen being carried into the Jacobi mansion on the night in question. You, yourself, my dear Prince, were observed entering the house less than an hour later."

Mischa's electric-blue eyes collided with Raeder's bleak gray ones. In his deep hoarse voice—he could, at will, make himself unintelligible—Mischa coughed and remarked, "Ah, you must be speaking of the night André Branoff, cousin of Violette Branoff—she's the cook at the house—was hit by a bus near the Trocadéro. It was just a short while before curfew. . . ." Mischa's glance drifted toward the lieutenant, who was watching him expressionlessly. "You must understand the panic all around, my friends. The bus barely stopped to make sure poor Branoff wasn't dead before continuing on. If it had pulled over, time wasted while the driver and God knows who else got out to examine the victim, everyone inside might well have been accused of violating the curfew and been arrested by your people. Rightfully. A regulation is a regulation."

The Gestapo man, remembering his instructions about dealing with the Prince, simply nodded.

"Poor André, a casualty of war, you might say, was left there in the street in bad shape, maybe dying, which, to give them credit, the people in the bus probably prayed was not the case. In time, André recovered sufficiently to crawl to the flat of a friend not too far off. This friend phoned me. My place being small —my wife, you may have heard, is an invalid—I suggested André Branoff be brought to the Jacobis', where there are rooms to spare. This was done. Happily, André recovered quickly, is now working somewhere near Bordeaux. To be honest, I'm not sure I could find him for you. . . ."

"Unnecessary," said the lieutenant at once with a warning look at Raeder.

"Agreed, Lieutenant," Raeder said in a stilted voice. *What about the doctor?* he wanted to ask this sly bastard of a Russian. *What about the man who showed up at the Jacobi house with the two black bags? Was he a registered medical man? If so, why hadn't his report shown up in the police morning dossier?*

The lieutenant was bowing the Prince Kilkanov out, Sergeant Raeder on his feet also, stiff as a bayonet, hostility as clear on his face as a street sign.

"You know, Lieutenant, he's a fucking liar," Raeder said when Mischa was gone. "I'd like to put some clamps on his balls. Then you'd get the truth, count on it!"

"No doubt," the lieutenant agreed with a faint smile, looking pointedly at the paperwork stacked on his desk. "Goodbye and thank you, Sergeant. We'll keep on the Le Brun matter—naturally, through our own sources. And we're always at your service, as you know."

Outside, in a cold, slashing downpour, Mischa strode along happily; he could hardly wait to get home and repeat what he'd told the Gestapo to Sonia . . . she'd want to hear every detail of the interrogation. As for the story he'd invented, she'd relish it but would surely find some aspect of it he could have improved on.

Aware that inevitably he attracted attention, Misach looked neither right nor left, but was proud of the way, even in this miserable soaking rain, people stared at him. No one, he thought, would have guessed his age, seventy-eight. He looked straight into the eyes of an attractive young girl whose glance had been drawn to him. But his mind, as he approached the Métro kiosk, was elsewhere. It would be necessary, he was thinking, to move that fellow Morgan from Sara's room as soon as he was able to get about. He wouldn't put it past that scum, Sergeant Raeder, to have a watch set on his apartment building, which could place Sara Jacobi in unacceptable jeopardy.

But where could he move Morgan? Not too far, the boy was still pretty sick.

Le Brun would have been able to take care of a matter like this. Actually he was aware he and the younger man had many traits in common: neither was a sentimentalist, not so one could notice, at any rate. Le Brun didn't go blathering about what he was going to do, but accomplished it quietly, without fuss. He was well mannered and no fool. Then why did he dislike him? A thought stirred uneasily in Mischa's breast. He even paused momentarily on the Métro steps before proceeding into the brightness below. Could it be he was jealous? Of Aaron Jacobi's feeling for Le Brun? Of the affection the Jacobi women obviously had for him?

In the Métro, Mischa moved to pleasanter thoughts. First the arrival home, the details of his triumph. Then, that evening, at the club—the White Russian club of which he was a founder—the final round of the annual bridge tourney. Dr. Slovsky and himself against Arymov, once a top Moscow lawyer, and the Count Anatole Drapin, close to being Mischa's equal. It would be a mighty contest, and Mischa considered it with anticipation, his blood quickening, but no question who would come out the winner.

Georges' wife, Arnette, a handsome redhead twice her husband's size, found a room for Le Brun on the same street as the garage; it overlooked a small courtyard which had geraniums in bright-green window-boxes, giving the cobblestoned courtyard a serene rustic quality.

The men in the building were, with the exception of Le Brun, heads of families and manual laborers; the women had enough to do queuing at food stores, cooking, cleaning, caring for their families, to worry about the new neighbor, especially when it was established he was a mechanic employed a few doors down.

In addition to affecting a stoop when out in public, Le Brun had dyed his hair chestnut-blond, grown a mustache, which he tinted the same color, and had even gone to the trouble to dye his pubic hair in case he was picked up and had to strip. Mostly he wore the overalls he worked in, although he bought a second-hand suit that fit him badly enough but not ludicrously so, he thought, although the trouser cuffs fell over his shoe tops. A faded, unpressed shirt and string tie completed the tailleur that sent Georges into a paroxysm of laughter when he first got a look at the outfit—Le Brun the impeccable dresser, never more than a breath away from Beau Brummell.

"Christ," said Georges, when he'd gotten over it. "No respectable working man would be caught dead looking like you!"

So Le Brun toned *up* the ensemble. A decent white shirt. A tie a little too loud. Slightly better fit to the suit. Reasonable shoes.

The most important thing, Georges advised, was the trace of black under the nails. "The grease," said Georges, "any good mechanic has trouble scrubbing out. Look at me . . . Arnette hates it."

Hating it also, Le Brun went a little heavier than Georges, having no woman to please.

He was not the man to brood over the defection— if one could call it that—of Mallou. He knew she regarded sex the way a man usually does, though she would not have cheated while they were together. "One at a time," she would have put it, demanding reciprocity from him. So fair was fair, no promises of eternal faithfulness had been exhanged, each was free to terminate without warning.

At least, so Le Brun thought, with the uneasy awareness that human relationships are rarely that neat or precise in practice. *Did I give Mallou as much as she gave me? Was the choice of von Banheim a woman's whim or a slap at Le Brun, the delinquent male, the adversary?*

In any case, a *fait accompli*. And he turned to other preoccupations—the collection. In his present state, on the run, the Gestapo hunting him, how could he protect it? Only one answer: stay away from it!

Sara Jacobi.

He found himself searching for her on the streets— the slim, naturally elegant easy-striding figure perhaps coming toward him—or standing at the light just ahead. On several occasions he walked up the Champs, or on Victor-Hugo, actually on the lookout for her. Or was it Erica's face he sought? He didn't know the answer himself. He was drowning in memories he couldn't sort.

Raeder and Company had already entered and cleaned out his Rond Point apartment. The fact that his small but decent art collection was now in their hands—his papers, letters, photos, cherished mementos—engraved gold cufflinks worn by his father, for example, caused him anger but no spilling over of bile. He would not weep over the loss of worldly goods. The loss of the cufflinks was regrettable. He had been eight when news of his father's death came. He had loved him very much, he remembered, a portly but elegant man usually awash with cologne, and with a delicate, ironic smile. . . .

On one of his Sunday strolls, killing time before a rendezvous with Arnaud, Le Brun found himself having an aperitif at an outside table at a café no more than half a block from the Seine. The Arnaud meeting was important to him, he had done some paperwork since going into hiding, résumés on the people in Paris associated with art, political sympathies, reliability, and so on—a sort of rundown on the art world for the future use of the Resistance. But a new, more important assignment, Arnaud had hinted, was in the offing: courier work, most likely between England and France.

It was a rare day, bitingly cold but wonderfully clear, and in the sun, bundled in the old tweed coat purchased in the flea market, Le Brun felt comfortable.

It was his birthday. He was thirty-five.

He'd be damned if he'd allow himself to indulge in self-pity. He was alone for now, perhaps more so than ever in his life. His leisure, what was left after work in the garage and the chores for Arnaud, was spent, despite his promise to himself, in concocting new schemes to rescue the collection and somehow transport it to England. A small idea, needing additional thought for implementation, had recently begun to stir in his mind. He had gone to school, the Beaux-

Arts, with a Jean Sard, who was director of a theatrical troupe called Players of the Night. By virtue of specializing in the classical theater—Racine, Molière—the troupe was permitted by the Germans to tour Versailles, Chartres, virtually all the towns on the perimeter of Paris. What if one of the vans carrying costumes, sets, props, also carried the Jacobi paintings out of Paris into the unoccupied zone?

Numerous obstacles would have to be overcome, even providing Le Brun could somehow talk Jean Sard into taking the tremendous risk. And not even for National Art but for a private collection! Even then, how to make contact with Aaron Jacobi for help from that end? Unless this courier assignment panned out, of course. Then it might all become possible. . . .

He checked his watch. Still an hour before the meeting with Arnaud. He ordered another drink. He tried to take pleasure in the view stretching out from the café, the elegant nineteenth-century building embracing the far corner, the sun touching the furrowed waters of the river, the structures immediately across from the Seine punctuated by the Eiffel Tower, the sweep of the Champ de Mars beyond it.

Thirty-five! My God, soon forty! Conceding that in this precarious time he'd survive. He would like someday, he thought, to own a small gallery somewhere on the Left Bank . . . exhibit only those artists he considered more than ordinarily talented, not having to worry what sold or not.

A melancholy notion intruded. *How many talented painters will be alive when the carnage was over?*

His father, Pierre Le Brun, had died in his thirty-seventh year, he recalled, only weeks after his, Claude's birthday. Killed near Verdun, by an artillery shell—an infantry major. Le Brun remembered imagining him dead and broken on the battlefield, a smashed bottle of cologne beside him.

The family, at its country seat near Troyes, actually close to the fighting at Verdun—they had been discussing evacuation—made immediate preparations to move back to Paris.

Guy, older than his brother, bossy as a drill sergeant, took charge at once. It was high time they left,

Guy asserted; the *Boches* could burst through any day!

Le Brun did not want to leave. On the day of departure, he was nowhere to be found, having taken off with his cat, Michel, a tawny tom who would perch on his shoulders like a bird and come upon call, like a dog. He wouldn't be allowed to take Michel, his mother had said; no pets to complicate life in the city.

With the caravan assembled in the great paved courtyard of the château, two touring cars crammed with mother, grandparents, Guy, servants, mountains of luggage, Claude's absence was finally insupportable.

"No problem," Guy told his mother. "In five minutes I'll be back with the goddamn rat."

"Guy!"

"Don't worry. You won't see a mark on him."

Claude's mother wasn't too concerned about that aspect of it; what Claude needed was a man's strong hand. There had been no real necessity for her husband to have joined the army, she thought peevishly; he should have foreseen the possibility of his being killed.

Guy knew just where to find the errant Le Brun, after which a little slapping around, he'd decided, would be appropriate—the little bastard was asking for it—not that you could ever get him to cry; no matter how hard you beat him.

But Claude wasn't at all where Guy knew he'd be, in the attic of the garden house; for that matter he wasn't to be smoked out from behind the feed bins in the stable. Which, if it left Guy frustrated, left the Le Brun family without its youngest member. "Too bad," his mother declared. *"Fichons le camp!* We'll go on without him."* At Troyes, Father Valvan would be briefed on the situation.

Watching them leave—he was on the château roof, concealed behind the great stone chimney—Le Brun could not now, so many years later, recall any positive feeling of loss. In the silence of the early afternoon, the sounds of the distant fighting were muted, hardly audible, the countryside green and inviting. It was late summer and still hot and full of good, familiar smells.

Le Brun really hated to leave his perch. On other expeditions up there he had witnessed German observation planes circling to the east, like chicken hawks lazily on the hunt for rabbits. Today he could waste no more time searching the sky, however, and sliding down the roof was tricky enough, even without Michel, hardly a lover of heights, digging his claws into his shoulder.

At a certain point in the descent, Le Brun remembered that vividly, Michel, with no more than a throaty goodbye, leaped to the ground, and a fiery swirl of color disappeared into the weeds of the herb garden. It was the last time Le Brun was to see his friend. "Well, so long, *mon vieux*," he called out, melancholy about the loss but not devastated.

The road leading past the Le Brun property ran several miles north before bisecting the main highway from Troyes, the road that eventually found its way to St. Dizier, Bar-le-Duc, St. Mihiel, and finally the fortress of Verdun, where, at the very least, he would bid a proper goodbye to Pierre Le Brun.

His thoroughfare was ordinarily alive with military traffic as well as the vehicles of people still living in the area.

The first ride Le Brun was able to get—on the back of a farmer's sputtering truck—took him to Brienne. He was to meet his mother in Brienne, he informed the man, who didn't believe a word of it. That night, with a tight-lipped Father Valvan on the seat alongside him in a second-class compartment, he took the long ride back to Paris.

As always, when the memory came back, as on this Sunday afternoon, he was touched with a sense of loss. If at least he could have looked on his father's face!

Leaving the café, heading for his meeting, he tried to shake off his sense of malaise. He was not one for fruitless brooding. Heading for the Champs-Elysées, he was suddenly stopped in his tracks. Just beyond him, not too far from the entrance of the George V, was an auto. An Hispano-Suiza. *His* Hispano-Suiza!

He shot a glance up the street. Nothing suspicious. No men leaning against buildings, newspapers masking their face. No one staring down from a balcony. Plenty of windows, of course, possibly with watchful eyes behind them.

He slouched forward, hardly looking at the car until he had reached it, throwing it no more than the casual, admiring glance of any passerby. He doubted that there were three more cars in Paris like it. The license plate numbers were unchanged—his car without a doubt! In superb condition, too. The metalwork gleamed. The mahogany side panels were alive with a sheen he had never achieved. And carelessly forgotten in the ignition slot the key! A man could slide in, be away in seconds.

Oh, no he thought. *Not that easy! A trap? Man and his car—the new century's lovers! Hardly a trap,* he reasoned. *Far fetched. Yet let us put nothing past Raeder.* Raeder would move heaven and earth to get his hands on him and, with a hot poker, dig out of him the hiding place of the Jacobi collection! But think a minute. Perhaps not Raeder at all. Perhaps von Banheim. His property now. Perhaps even Mallou. No, never Mallou! Whatever she might be, Mallou was not one to take pleasure in appropriating a former lover's property. In any case, Mallou thought an automobile no more than a convenience, like a bathtub. She preferred to be driven.

He walked swiftly toward the Champs, slanting one final look at the Hispano, smiling wryly. *Happy birthday, Le Brun!*

Crossing the boulevard, Le Brun had to catch himself. Almost walked into an old Citroën, a wood-burning attachment on the rear. More and more of those on the streets these days. Le Brun knew about them intimately. At George's garage installing them had become a specialty.

The shop was on rue de Berri. With the sugar shortage, nothing much in the window except what looked to be a stack of stale cookies and a pyramid of *baguettes.* Just two customers inside when Le Brun entered. He waited until they were served and ordered a combination of the cookies and several rolls. Not bothering to fetch them, the woman jerked a finger toward the rear of the shop. Slipping past

217

her, Le Brun went through the door and back toward the big ovens. Three men were already there. Garnier's assistant, Fauré, a rosy-cheeked young man with a bad leg, but very bright, and Stattin, tall, angular, with thick glasses, a Catholic. Finally a new man from the railroad workers, the SNCF, big-bellied, older, a railroad supervisor named Crossard. The Resistance had been augmented considerably in the past months, and the get-together today was to coordinate certain activities on the lower levels, although tensions were already building between political groups maneuvering for future power.

Fauré, munching on a *baguette,* grinned at Le Brun.

"And good day to you, sir. Would hardly recognize you, I admit."

"Go fuck yourself," said Le Brun amiably. "Garnier too busy to come?"

"Too important," said Fauré. "Should he get trapped, the whole damn Vichy government might be compromised. Which you bastards would regard as a stroke of good luck! But we do have our uses."

"Very few," Stattin declared sourly, looking at his watch. "Where's Arnaud? He's never late."

They lit up cigarettes and smoked uneasily. Sitting and waiting was always nerve-racking. No place was a hundred-percent safe.

"Do you have anything special for me?" Le Brun asked Fauré, whom he liked.

"Well, as far as we're concerned at the Beaux-Arts, just one thing that worries us. The bastards are back pestering us with that trade idea—a hundred of our best works for an equal number of theirs. And Goering's people are insisting the Winged Victory be included. You predicted that, didn't you? Only now they're getting a little less polite about it."

Crossard said, "Are you two serious? Who gives a shit about statues and paintings? Did you know they're beginning to move in their own maintenance crews for the locomotives—their own engineers! Think of what that does to our efforts!"

Stattin agreed "He lost a whole cell last week, eight

men, didn't you, Crossard? Accused of sabotage and executed right there in the yards."

"We're going to have to be goddamn careful," Crossard said gloomily. "There were good men in that crew." Crossard stopped and they all looked up. Arnaud had finally arrived, but he was jumpy, edgy, even for him.

"I may have been followed," he announced out of breath. "Didn't pick them up until I was almost at the shop—too late to turn away. I'm calling this meeting off. You'll be contacted when—"

He didn't finish. There were shouts from the front, a woman's scream, then a fusillade from a submachine gun. The door Arnaud had closed behind him was half blown away.

The men in the back of the bakery shop were already on the move, streaking past the ovens out an exit into an alley. Stattin didn't make it, however. Caught in the back by another blast of fire, he fell soundlessly, dead before he hit the floor.

In the alley, which was really just a narrow collecting point for garbage, the men split—a standard tactic, Le Brun and Fauré to the right, Arnaud and Crossard to the left, and into a courtyard at the alley's end.

Le Brun and Fauré ducked into a restaurant whose kitchen door was open. A heavily mustachioed chef, working alone over a stove, stirring something in a huge blackened kettle, looked up as they clattered in, eyes widening at the gun Le Brun had pulled from his pocket.

Nothing was said, the chef deliberately resuming his stirring while the two men entered the restaurant proper.

No more than usual customers and a woman at the cash register.

Making no pretense, Le Brun let the woman see the gun held against his hip. Her hand went to her mouth but she said nothing. Fauré grabbed a toothpick from a dish and smiled at her as they went out.

In the street, Le Brun and Fauré could hear more shots, like toy guns popping off, then silence. But since the bakery shop was actually back to back with the restaurant, they were a block away, and felt relatively safe.

"That was close," Fauré said, moving the toothpick around in his mouth. "How do you think they got on to Arnaud?"

"Your guess is as good as mine. Let's hope the others made it."

"Don't think Stattin did. Poor bastard! And the *boulangerie* woman!"

Le Brun didn't comment.

"Be seeing you. Garnier wants me to keep you *au courant* about Goering in case you have any idas."

"Give him my best and we'll be in touch," Le Brun told him as they parted.

House 71: June 1945

CAPTAIN DANTE of the Judge Advocate General's Office was interested in Goldfarb's account of Goering's activities but wanted something more concrete—real evidence he could use at the upcoming trial in Nuremberg.

"How about some Jewish corpses? You know, people Goering pulled in and used for target practice?"

"No need to be sarcastic. You're doing a good job with Kröler, supplying us with a lot of background material. That has its value. But what we'd really after is—"

"Good, solid evidence," said Goldfarb. "Like those Jewish corpses—"

Goldfarb had arranged for Kröler to be moved to a more comfortable room, still on the court but with some light occasionally filtering in. And Goldfarb never forgot to bring him his daily schnapps.

Kröler was actually beginning to look forward to the sessions; he'd become a historian, he felt, dictating his memories to this bright young American.

"By the late fall of forty-one things were not the very best for Germany, you appreciate that? For the Reichsmarschall as well. The advance was stalling in Russia, huge Luftwaffe losses there and over England, an enormous number of planes used up in the Crete victory. As head of the Luftwaffe, Goering was being held responsible, perhaps even a little lazy when it came to the boring organizational details—"

"I was told," said Goldfarb, "that Goering advised the destruction of the civilian population already taken in Russia so that these people would not have to be fed from diminishing German food supplies."

"Absolutely untrue," said Kröler indignantly. "It was Hitler who asked for it, maybe at Bormann's suggestion. I speak with authority on that point. Calling the Reichsmarschall in, the Führer ordered him to have the Luftwaffe made ready for sustained bombing attacks on Moscow and Leningrad—these attacks to continue until not a living soul remained in either of the cities.

"Bodenschatz, Goering's man at headquarters, verified that for once Goering stood firm, absolutely refusing to carry out such an order—which, as you can imagine, infuriated Hitler."

Kröler was at the schnapps. Then, wiping his lips with his sleeve, he looked across at Goldfarb. "That is the kind of information you want from me, Lieutenant?"

"Yes, fine," said Goldfarb, thinking it wasn't the kind of information Captain Dante wanted.

"A very bad period," Kröler said, shaking his head. "I don't believe the Reichsmarschall ever fully recaptured Hitler's favor. Then there was the tragic accident with Ernst Udet, his oldest friend from the Richthofen days. As supply chief for the Luftwaffe, Udet was really the one responsible for the growing production failure—plane production plummeted alarmingly—and what's more he was lying to Goering about it. Milch, part Jewish, felt the problem serious enough to lay before Goering. Aware the situation was beyond correction, Udet took the only proper course. After a night of carousing, he blew his brains out. Wait, of that I'm not absolutely sure! Perhaps it was a bullet to his heart."

"Either way it couldn't have helped Goering or the Luftwaffe very much," commented Goldfarb dryly.

But Kröler was lost in his memories.

"The affair had a touching coda. On a screen behind Udet's bed were two messages. The first: 'Iron Man, you have forsaken me.' The second: 'Why did you put me in the hands of that Jew, Milch?' "

"I'm sure Goering broke down when he heard of it."

"He couldn't function for days," Kröler said in a melancholy voice.

This session, Goldfarb figured, was surely wasted. Hardly any evidence for Captain Dante. Very little left of the schnapps. *And if I bring him a larger bottle tomorrow—a quart,* Goldfarb told himself, *he'll get drunk and I'll get zilch out of him.*

Goldfarb kept trying. "But when the Reichsmarschall got himself together, after he'd read the riot act to the production people, put things straight in that department, my bet is he turned to the one man who could pull him out of his depression—Ernst Kröler!"

Kröler's spirits rose appreciably. "You are remarkably perceptive, Lieutenant. And to the world where he was most at ease, where only I could transport him—the magical world of art."

"In a sense like Hitler, with his passion for opera —weeping at Wagner."

"No, not quite the same," Kröler said a trifle frostily. "However, I'd discovered a masterpiece, only waiting for his approval—a Holbein the Younger. A bargain at two million francs. He couldn't wait to get to Paris to see it!"

"And I'm sure, too, he hadn't forgotten about the Nike, the Samothrace sculpture."

"More than ever he dreamed of presenting it to Hitler—a symbol of faith in the Führer's star!"

Kröler went on to describe a party von Banheim had given for Goering at his elegant new apartment in Passy.

"All Paris was there. You should have seen the beautiful women! The hostess, von Banheim's current mistress, was perhaps not the most beautiful, but certainly the most exciting sexually—an entertainer called Mallou. Von Banheim knew how to pick them. I must admit that personally I found her rather cold, by that I mean somewhat uncongenial. It's possible, though," said Kröler wryly, "that she didn't like us Germans very much."

"The Reichsmarschall had his entire military staff with him, including Galland, as well as Rosenberg, Walter Hofer, a young art historian Bruno Lohse, Hilda Zetlin, Raeder, and yours truly. Immediately after making his entrance, Goering called von Banheim, Raeder, and myself into a private conference. He then revealed what was then still a military secret: only hours before, our army had withdrawn from the gates of Moscow! It was a terrible blow for all of us although plans were already being made, Goering assured us, for a new offensive in the spring. The point he emphasized was that the military situation had become unpredictable, fluid—it was therefore our job to gather everything of value and ship it back to the Reich as quickly as possible.

"At this point," continued Kröler, "Raeder jumped in: 'In the matter of Claude Le Brun, who I believe is still in Paris, find him and we put our hands on the Jacobi collection. Just permit me to use the Gestapo.'

"Goering," Kröler told Goldfarb, "fell silent at this. The Gestapo meant Himmler, and Goering did not want to tangle with him. He was sure, he commented slyly, that Raeder was smart enough to haul Le Brun in on his own. His ego stroked, Raeder admitted with braggadocio that he had laid some traps. Yes, he could certainly handle it on his own!

"We all returned to the main salon," Kröler went on, "where the party, as so often happened in these times, had gotten out of hand. If some of the Berlin wives could have seen their heroic husbands! But an unforgettable party in another sense! In the middle of the festivities, with the Reichsmarschall sitting in the center of the salon like Bacchus, regaling us with anecdotes of the Richthofen squadron days, the mistress of von Banheim suddenly appeared from a bedroom, holding a military radio aloft like a grenade.

In a theatrical tone, she demanded everyone's attention and turned up the radio's volume so high everyone automatically fell quiet.

"An English voice dominated the apartment—she had been tuned, strictly *verboten* of course, to BBC in London. An excited voice it was, and you can guess what it was announcing—the bombing of Pearl Harbor, the imminent entrance of the United States into the war against both Japan and Germany!

"Enough of us there were fluent in the language and sophisticated enough to understand the implications of the announcement. Despite our bravado— 'Good, now we can kick the crap out of those arrogant bastards!'—a chill penetrated many hearts.

"With a smug smile, Mallou placed the radio on a table, that damned British voice still blasting away, and marched back into the bedroom.

"The radio was quickly switched off and Goering rose at once, thanking von Banheim for his hospitality, asking for his greatcoat. As an aide hurried to fetch it, von Banheim remarked to the Reichsmarschall: 'Well, now at least I ought to be able to go down to that château again, *but in force,* and this time, sir, I won't come back empty-handed!'

"Goering's smile was bleak yet resolved. 'A little more patience, General. But you shall go down there again, and bring back the prize, I promise you!' "

Twenty

IT WAS DIFFICULT not to be exhilarated by the news. One could sense the new mood on the streets. The occupiers, too, were responding. In some, mostly younger, the response was even more swagger: "You think anything's changed? I'll prove to you who's boss!" In the older, there was a twinge of fear, like an oncoming toothache. "Life doesn't make sense . . . despite all the victories we can still lose . . . we did before!"

Le Brun, near the Opéra, on his way to a meeting with Fauré, stopped, disbelievingly.

The car was parked in a forbidden zone on a side street, but in the clear; one could literally spot it from four corners.

The Hispano-Suiza again.

It would have been smart, naturally, to ignore it completely. He did carefully survey the street before, as on the other occasion, strolling past it like any chance pedestrian. *Identical license plate but this time not my Hispano!* The wood side panels were recently installed, rubbed and polished to simulate the old wood. As before, the key was in the ignition. *Step in, Le Brun. Drive one block and find a half dozen Gestapo or Milice on your tail!* At the street's end was a garage. That's where they're waiting, Le Brun decided, Raeder and his friends. He took the Métro at the Opéra to the rue du Bac; no one was following him, he was sure. Let the bastard plant Hispanos like his all over the city; make a dozen copies—waste of time and money!

Ostensibly studying a second-rate Empire desk in the window of an antique shop where he was to meet Fauré, the idea came to him. *Difficult, complicated, the kind to be instantly discarded.* But the more he thought about it, the more it intrigued him. When Fauré tapped him on the shoulder, he whipped around, his hand already in his pocket on his gun.

Grinning, Fauré said, "Shoot if you must, but not in the crotch. That's where I keep my valuables."

The two walked slowly down the street, ostensibly interested in the antiques, the shops on the rue du Bac weren't as expensive as others in the city; on occasions one could find a bargain.

Le Brun told Fauré what he had been thinking.

Fauré listened intently, then responded as expected. "You're crazy! You'll never pull it off!"

"But if I can, it will keep Goering's big fat ass out of the Loire. At least for a little while!"

"You'd have to get Pierre Brazin. Don't know anybody else in France. And Brazin's in his eighties. How's his health? Christ, I'm no sculptor but I know enough—we both do—to estimate the odds!"

"Look here, granted it sounds impossible at first, but not when you start putting it together. All I'm asking of you is to place it before your people. As few as possible—I don't want leaks. I won't need much from them, you can tell them that. It all depends on Brazin, as you say. It can't possibly be accomplished without a master craftsman."

They continued walking, stopping to study a large ceramic Buddha, a beautiful piece. In other days Le Brun would have gone in and bought it.

They strolled on. "Another thing," Le Brun said, "I'll need 'The Sailor' out of the Louvre."

Fauré stopped cold, perplexed. "The Sailor" was a huge Greek sculpture, considered to be of such poor quality it was always placed in the darkest corner possible. Because of its sheer bulk—it was at least ten feet tall—and its pedigree, a product of the island of Paros, it was kept on in the Louvre, as a teaching tool. Teachers would contrast its shoddy quality with the sophistication and beauty of later Hellenistic sculptures, notably, of course, the Winged Victory. When, however, at the commencement of the "phony war" the finer works of the Louvre were crated and removed to the châteaux country for safety, "The Sailor" was left in place, forgotten.

"Of course, old Parian marble, like the Samothrace," muttered Fauré now. "But how in hell are you going to get it out of the Louvre without questions being asked? Another thing: how many tons do you think that piece of junk weighs?"

Le Brun knew roughly, and had some thoughts about moving it. What concerned him now was Brazin. "Can you find out where he's living? Let's hope he's somewhere near Paris."

"Give me time to get back to my office."

Brazin lived near Senlis, just north of the city, Fauré reported. Le Brun knew the town, having once visited its cathedral. Whether the old boy was in good health, able to function, Fauré couldn't say. "And yes, my boss will go along with you. Unofficially, it goes without saying."

Le Brun tried to reach Brazin by phone, failed. The trip to Senlis took about an hour. Once there, no transportation in sight, he started out on foot to the west of the small city, a cold, raw day, his feet in the cheap shoes already frozen. Thirty minutes later he reached a forested tract, the trees thinning out to reveal a house at the top of a hill, almost, by its size, a château.

"A copy of the Winged Victory?"

"Yes," said Le Brun.

"And that's why you've come? To recruit me for the job?"

The old man was gleeful. He had the look of a satyr, Le Brun thought, furry, coal-black eyebrows that peaked, a wide-mouthed smile, lips permanently turned upward, as if, like his work, it had been set in stone.

It was icy in the studio, the wind spiraling in from a myriad of open windows, but Brazin didn't seem to notice. He wore a flaming-red wool sweater, torn at the elbows, over skin. There was little of the octogenarian about him except the taut swoop under the cheekbones, a looseness under the chin.

Below the waist, he was a step away from being a dwarf, short, stocky legs supporting the outsized, muscular torso.

Noticing that Le Brun was shivering, he scuttled over to a big-bellied stove and generously tossed in firewood piled on the floor. Then to a long table on which a head of a bird had begun to emerge from a square of silvery marble—"Pentelic marble," Brazin said. Next to the bird was a bottle of cognac. A swig and the bottle was passed to Le Brun. As Le Brun took a pull, he said, "City folk! Can't stand a touch of winter. Shall we go in the house?"

"It's fine here."

Brazin pulled two chairs near the stove and placed the bottle at their feet. They sat together, Brazin suddenly silent, listening to the crackle inside the iron hearth.

For the first time Le Brun caught an impression of Brazin's years. The eyes were impenetrable, brooding. Not looking at Le Brun, Brazin asked, "Why is it so important?"

Le Brun told him. In lieu of the plan he was proposing, Goering would send troops down to the Loire to take the real Winged Victory and most certainly the Venus de Milo, and whatever else he wanted. Giving him the Samothrace—*what Goering thought was the Samothrace*—could forestall that calamity, buy time. And soon the Americans, thankfully now in the war, and the British, and the Free French, would come storming across the Channel, and the treasures would be safe forever.

Mocking, Brazin turned, "You believe that, young man, don't you?"

"Otherwise I wouldn't be here."

"And how many expert hands to accomplish this miracle in addition to my own?"

"The least possible. There is danger in numbers, danger that what we'd be doing would slip out. By the way, a former student of yours, an American named Morgan, is in Paris."

"Morgan? I didn't know. I'd need at least two more—my regular assistants. Can't even tell you where they are—they might not be in France."

"If they are, I'll find them."

"How do you intend to match the marble?"

Le Brun reminded him of "The Sailor." Parian marble like the Samothrace. And larger. It would serve as the block from which the "new" Samothrace would be hewn.

Brazin reached for the cognac again. "And what do we do about the aging process, the patina?"

The problem seemed insoluble. While "The Sailor" was weathered by age, as was the Samothrace, once the actual work was begun, once the "skin" of "The Sailor" was cut away, the marble underneath, while having the same golden sheen, would be without the pitting of the original, the ravages of time. Bronze sculpture could be weathered with acids; to Le Brun's knowledge no method existed to age marble.

"We'll have to find a way to get around that one,"

he said. "Or *you* will have to, *maître*. But what's it worth to you to deprive Hermann Goering of the Samothrace?"

Wordless, Brazin swung to his feet, walking the length of the studio, weaving between the blocks of uncut marble, unfinished pieces, the long, whitened tables, the cutting tools strewn everywhere. Then he disappeared into a toilet near the stove, leaving the door open. The sound of a strong, noisy stream. Buttoning his pants, Brazin emerged.

"Tell me, suppose Goering goes down and steals the damn thing. Why does it matter so much to you?"

"I'd feel for my country as a woman would—raped."

"It's a Greek statue; I don't even know how we acquired it. Why shouldn't it be in Berlin as well as Paris? The Mona Lisa is Italian—why shouldn't it be in Rome? For that matter, why not a complete international reshuffling? We return the exiles—our exiles are returned to us."

The satyr's smile again. "Tell me," Brazin asked abruptly, "have you any idea how long it could take to make a reasonable copy of the Samothrace? One that might fool the German experts?"

"How long, *maître?*"

"At least two years."

"I can possibly give you six months," said Le Brun.

He telephoned Mischa at his club—he couldn't be sure Mischa's home phone wasn't tapped. A heavily accented voice told Le Brun to call back, the Prince was expected shortly.

Le Brun tried later.

"Le Brun here. I must see you."

For a moment Le Brun feared Mischa was going to hang up. "About what?"

"If you don't mind, could we meet somewhere?"

Mischa said with a short laugh, "You know they're looking for you all over."

Le Brun thought Kilkanov and Pierre Brazin had something in common besides age; a sadistic sense of humor. "I'm aware of it. Can you spare me half an hour?"

"When?"

"Tonight."

A pause on the other end.

"At exactly nine o'clock hail a taxi in front of the Grand Hotel. A Biped. Young fellow with curly black hair. Don't worry. The doorman is a friend. He'll direct you properly. You are a trouble and a bother, Le Brun."

The Prince hung up, his irritability tangible over the wire. *I've probably screwed up his bridge hand,* Le Brun decided.

He looked at his watch. Time to kill. Many loose ends to work out with Fauré, but that would have to wait for the morning.

Leaving the *café–tabac* from where he'd phoned, he started for home—might be a message there from Brazin. Would the old artist go along?

He was walking too fast, too briskly. Slow down! Slouch! He found himself looking forward to the meeting with Mischa. Not too difficult to figure why. Mischa was but one step from Sara Jacobi. How was Sara doing? It had been months since he'd had a word. It occurred to him he couldn't separate Sara and Erica, the two faces had blended into one . . . he was walking faster again.

There was no message waiting for him from Brazin. It would have been in the form of a note from Georges, asking him to come to the garage for emergency night work. Brazin hadn't promised a quick answer. The project, he'd said, *en principe,* was absurd. . . . But when Le Brun was leaving the studio, half drunk, depressed, his mission unresolved, Brazin had unexpectedly slapped him on the shoulder, a mighty slap, then had stood in the open doorway, gazing intently at the slate-colored landscape. "It is not at all as simple a matter as I mentioned," he said. "I speak of our talk concerning the return of art to the country of origin. There's another point to be considered. For all their erudition, in their souls the *Boches* are, to my mind, barbarians. The French, with all their faults, are, to a point, civilized. To whose hands, is it preferable, then, the great

230

works of genius be entrusted? Our own. No question."

And Brazin was chuckling.

The young man with the curly black hair pedaled leisurely at Mischa's instructions while they sat back in the pedicab; they had no particular destination they'd told him, merely wishing to talk privately.

"Have you heard from Aaron Jacobi?" Le Brun asked.

"Have you?"

"He would not want to compromise either of us."

Mischa agreed.

The young man was pedaling them slowly along the boulevard des Capucines. There were many cinemas open, but few patrons, although the pedestrian traffic was weighted with gray-green uniforms.

"I assume you know Aaron told me you helped hide the collection."

"I guessed you'd been told."

Le Brun smiled. "You thought I sold out once, surely not now."

"No, not now," said Mischa, a stubborn thrust to his jaw, "but let the Gestapo get hold of a peacock like you, they'll squeeze you like a grape." He stared with his hard blue eyes over at Le Brun. "Hope and pray it doesn't come to a test. Now what's so damn important to take me away from my club? Got an idea how to save the collection? It can't stay in that church forever, you know."

Le Brun said he realized that fact. This meeting tonight did not concern the paintings. It concerned the Winged Victory.

"What in hell—"

Le Brun told him, explaining his plan in some detail. If Pierre Brazin went along with it, Morgan would be needed. And the Jacobi farm was not too far from d'Albion, the château in which the Winged Victory was deposited. If Sara agreed, he wanted to use the farm as the base of operations.

"Make your copy there?"

"Yes."

"I don't pretend to know how practical this plot of

231

yours is, but won't making Sara a part of it place her in jeopardy?"

"To a small extent . . . if eventually the Nazis overrun the zone. On the other hand, it has the advantage of getting her out of Paris, where she *is* in constant danger. I imagine nursing Morgan has kept her occupied, but that's got to end, doesn't it? How is he, by the way?"

Mischa sat straight-backed, eyes lidded. "He's starting to get around. What you have in mind would have the virtue of getting *him* out of Paris."

Le Brun remained silent, letting Mischa think about it.

"The girl's an angel," Mischa said abruptly, almost vehemently. "Doesn't deserve her."

Le Brun didn't know how to interpret that one. "Could we let her decide about this thing?" he asked finally. "Can you get her to see me?"

German soldiers were taunting a prostitute, who was screaming obscenities in return. Le Brun and the Prince were both reacting—each had the urge to jump off the pedicab, pile into the Germans.

The pedicab man took the decision away from them, swinging into the side street, leaving the distressed voice of the woman behind them, like the wail of a ship in a fog.

It had eaten into Mischa. "Are we men still?" he asked, almost of himself, then turned abruptly to Le Brun.

"You look rotten, boy. Kind of a disguise, eh? They hauled me in, the Gestapo, this Sergeant Raeder. Cold fish. Dangerous. He wants you, all right. We know why, don't we? Please remember that none of us is as strong as we'd like to think. So don't let him catch you, agreed?"

"Agreed," Le Brun answered soberly.

"I'll talk to Sara. God knows, my wife will miss her if you take her south. Good Christ, what time is it? Do you realize I'm in the finals of an important tournament?"

She had chosen it herself, Les Invalides, l'église du Dome, deciding that Le Brun would feel comfortable there, safe, at least to begin with. The ashes of the Duke of Reichstadt, l'Aiglon, Napoleon Bonaparte's son with Marie-Louise, were to be returned by the Germans—a propaganda move designed by Goebbels to win over the French populace. Les Invalides, as a consequence, had recently been in the news.

Along with the usual tourists, a small detachment of Wehrmacht troops not averse to shouldering close to her even here, she stood gazing down into the famous well at Bonaparte's tomb of red porphyry.

No sign of Le Brun yet.

Of course, she had told Mischa, she would agree to cooperate—he could set up a rendezvous at once. She had given Mischa her decision calmly. Whatever her deep, secret dreamworld, it no longer could include Le Brun—she had of her own accord removed that possibility. She considered herself tough, not simply the gentle wisp of a thing people thought her. But she wasn't tough enough to bid Tom Morgan goodbye. No more than she could have drowned a kitten in a sack.

She walked over to the roped-off area where workmen were applying the finishing touches to the catafalque on which the new, smaller l'Aiglon marble casket would rest. Others, French, stood with her—silent, absorbed in the mechanics of the job.

Behind her someone said, "Hello."

Turning, she saw a tall, chestnut-haired man, stooped, careworn, with a slight wry smile for her.

"So they're bringing him back," he said. "An excellent sign, don't you think? Our goodwill becoming so important?"

She nodded, unwilling to risk a break in her voice. The Le Brun she knew—he and Papa had carried on an open sartorial war—was barely recognizable in the man in front of her. But it was the tightness she saw in his face, not his shabbiness, that struck her to the heart. Huskily, she said, "You look fine."

"Then I'm a rotten actor."

A tour group, composed mostly of the Wehrmacht, was being formed. Le Brun took her arm and they joined it, dawdling in the rear.

The guide, a plodding man, had begun his recitation. Leading the way down the winding stairs into the crypt, he talked nonstop—a middle-aged Frenchwoman having made a last-minute appearance to translate for the Germans.

Sara had put her arm through his. "We should look like friends, shouldn't we?"

"Why not lovers?" he asked.

"Good friends," she said again. And then, quickly, "Will you forgive me?"

"For what?"

"For the last time I saw you—for doubting you."

"If you hadn't," he said flatly, "I'd really have been worried. It was the game I was playing."

"And very well," she admitted. "And very well now. Except that you look simply terrible."

He laughed. She loved seeing him laugh. He rarely did, she remembered, Erica vying with her to set him off, Erica easily the winner. But Sara had had her moments, too. Particularly when she could invent details of the steamy backstairs romance Angelle and Mischa were presumably enjoying. Le Brun had never believed a word of it of course, going along with it to please her. The Prince Kilkanov had never so much as slapped Angelle's ample *derrière* (as Sara had once caught Papa doing), even in playful admiration.

"Don't mind how I look," he told her as the guides droned on. "Mind how I am."

"Yes," she said, hooking closer to him as if to ward off a disturbing thought.

"But you, my dear little Sara, are far too thin! My God, almost fragile. Nothing really for a man to grab on to. I would have thought—"

Her fingers were digging into his arm.

"Well," he said. "Depends of course on the man. Now I happen to have sworn a vow of celibacy for the duration, so that as far as I'm concerned . . ."

Dangerous, she thought, releasing him, giving him the feeling of sharing in his joke. "Oh, Claude, if we could only go back to the old days—with Mama and Papa, with—"

"With Erica," he said calmly. "But we can't. Shall I kick him in the balls?"

"Who?" she asked, startled.

He gestured. It was an SS corporal, stocky as a bull,

staring openly, invitingly at Sara, completely unmindful
—or scornful—of Le Brun.

Le Brun appeared to stumble, landing on the German's boot. Grunting, the man automatically swung
hand to hip for a nonexistent weapon. The guide, de-
scribing the twelve colossal statues surrounding the
crypt, each symbolic of a Napoleonic victory, paused
with Gallic irritability, his rhythm broken.

"Please forgive me," Le Brun said in French, beaming at the corporal. "I'm a clumsy fool!" Taking Sara's
hand, he led her away from the group, toward the opposite staircase. On the main level they strolled slowly
under the great Visconti dome, grinning at each other.

Sara admitted that Mischa had given her some idea
of Le Brun's project. Of course the farm in the Loire
was at his disposal. She was sure that would have been
her father's decision. Le Brun thanked her. But the
project was still embryonic. Had Mischa made *that*
clear? Pierre Brazin, on whom all depended, was still a
question mark. Which reminded him . . . how was the
American getting on? In good enough health to participate?

"I think so," she answered. She'd forgotten Morgan
and the lapse dismayed her. "I've asked him to meet us
here. He's eager to thank you for what you did; I hoped
you wouldn't mind."

He did mind. Hated sentimentality of that sort. And
Morgan shouldn't have been told. Not yet. He was
about to scold her for the indiscretion when he realized she was suffering, for whatever reason, and he
couldn't understand why. Then he wasn't sure she was
suffering at all. She was checking her watch, cool and
possessed again.

"Shall we wait for him outside?"

Outside it was cold and bright, snow still on the
ground. The people here were well dressed, elbowing
one another as they walked. Nannies and children in go-
carts heading for the Champ de Mars. To the west, the
Eiffel Tower. The streets had a gay look today, Le
Brun thought. Very noisy. Very French. It was difficult
to imagine that Paris was occupied, a war going on.

They stood on the steps without speaking, feeling
comfortable together. Not a man passed, he noticed,

235

who didn't glance at her; she had a young girl's look with a woman's sexuality. She was saying something to him and he wasn't listening. "What?" he asked, smiling at her.

"It's good to be with you again, Claude."

On impulse, he bent, kissing her lightly. "Very good."

Sara saw Morgan approaching them, stopping to wave, hopping along with his cane. Suddenly she knew what was going to happen and stood waiting for it, helplessly. Climbing the steps to meet them, Morgan enclosed her in his arms before releasing her, smiling across at Le Brun and saying, "Hey!"

Le Brun had understood at once, Sara realized, at the same time shooting a lightning glance at her. Of dismay? Hurt? She couldn't know—probably never would —his face having closed so quickly. Morgan was pumping his hand. "Have you any idea how I've been looking forward to this meeting?"

His voice boomed in the wintry air. The Germans, leaving the shrine, paused to take him in. He had nothing but contempt for them; it was in his posture; he refused to budge, grinning, forcing them to go around him. Enraged, they muttered together, glowering. He was big, blond, handsome; he should have been wearing a Wehrmacht uniform. He was taller than anyone and he was with the pretty French girl.

The stocky one, the corporal, had retained his position on the steps, just above Morgan. The corporal had seen plenty of action, a killer. Unintimidated, Morgan held his place, returning the stare. A troop carrier waited at the curb and an officer in front of it murmured a command. The corporal hesitated, then obeyed, retreating slowly, dark with anger.

"Bastards," Morgan said loudly, watching the soldiers board the carrier.

Sara was speaking to him, softly, persuasively. The tenseness gradually ebbed out of him; he managed a weak laugh at Le Brun. "Can we go somewhere for a drink? What a day! Beautiful, isn't it? What a day to be alive! And Jesus, Le Brun, I owe it all to you!"

"It would seem," Le Brun answered with some irony, "you owe a little to Sara Jacobi."

He begged off the drink. He would be in touch with Sara about the other matter. He said it all lightly, cheerfully, he was very polite and sincere and Sara had the terrible feeling he knew exactly where matters stood.

Later Le Brun asked himself what right he had to feel betrayed because Sara Jacobi was having an affair with the American? Obviously, no right at all.

After several stops for refreshments, he had returned to his room. No message from Georges, which meant no decision by Brazin. He washed with cold water and went out again to Vernet's, just up the street. He wasn't supposed to patronize Vernet's. Since the meeting with Arnaud and Garnier, Vernet had reported the Milice was checking his bistro . . . several possible agents had been spotted.

Surprised to see Le Brun, Vernet said nothing but gave him a corner table slightly hidden from the other patrons. Le Brun ordered stew, probably the horse-meat special, and a bottle of house wine. By the time he finished off the meal, the wine, and a few brandies, he was beginning to feel less hostile toward Morgan. After all, hadn't he himself virtually put the fellow into Sara's bed.

Vernet passed several times to see if Le Brun was all right. Le Brun said he was fine. He paid his check, rose without difficulty, and went back to his room to find a note under the door from Georges: "Can you come in for some emergency work?"

He put on a heavy sweater under his coat—it was beginning to snow—and hurried over to the garage. Georges was waiting for him in his office. Brazin had telephoned. Le Brun could call him tomorrow.

"But did he give you any hint?" Le Brun asked Georges.

"Yes, he'll go ahead with it."

By the time the train pulled into the Austerlitz depot the snow was coming down heavily, almost a blizzard. Waiting at the station was a detachment of SS, a military band, the commandant of Paris, and everyone of importance in the Vichy government, including Laval.

As the snow continued to fall, the cortège formed behind the traditional horse-drawn casket, and the long, slow march to Les Invalides began. But the people of Paris were not hanging out their windows watching and applauding as Goebbels had anticipated. Quite the opposite. At the approach of the flag-draped coffin, the goose-stepping guard of honor, the dignitaries, windows banged shut, the procession winding through empty, ghostlike streets. No spectators. No cheers. Just boots crunching on the snow and the muffled beating of the drums.

In this fashion l'Aiglon, Napoleon's son, was returned home, to his father's side.

At Les Invalides, where wives and mistresses waited, a brief, strained ceremony and the interminable night was over. The French, it appeared, wanted their own back—but not at the price offered.

Outside the shrine, a large number of uniformed police as well as plainclothesmen were gathered, the usual barriers in place, a great reception by the public having been expected.

No more than several dozen Parisians, mostly Vichy office workers, huddled behind the barriers, miserable in the cold.

The doors of the church opened and Laval and the German general emerged.

As the lesser civilian officials followed, Le Brun, who was in the small crowd outside, shoved a barrier aside rushing toward one of the Frenchmen.

At first falling back at Le Brun's approach, the official seemed paralyzed, simply staring at him.

"Congratulations," Le Brun told him, pumping his hand. "France will never forget you."

A nearby colleague laughed sardonically. Several police closed in on Le Brun.

"It's all right," the official said. "He has a message for me."

The police saluted and withdrew.

"You son-of-a-bitch," Guy Le Brun said. "You haven't changed a bit!"

"You've changed a little," his brother said. "Ought to do something about that pot. Remember Uncle

Henri . . . he died young. Well, I'll be in touch. Good-bye."

Guy Le Brun walked immediately to one of the waiting limousines, and not until it was under way did he look at the note that his brother had placed in his hand: "When a Monsieur Marc Darle calls, speak to him."

Outside the shrine, with everyone dispersing, the police piled into the vans, which immediately took off. No more than a handful of men had been left to guard the shrine.

The snow continued unceasingly, making footing difficult, giving Le Brun trouble. He was trying to reach a Métro station and get home before the new, earlier curfew. This was one night he didn't want to get picked up.

Twenty-One

THE PLAYERS OF THE NIGHT were putting on Racine's *Alexandre* in Chartres, permission already granted by Vichy as well as the Military Government, and could the company please borrow several Greek busts, possibly a Greek statue, from the Louvre to dress the set? To be returned following the series of engagements.

The request was routinely approved. No works of any real value remained in the museum.

Weeks later, on a dark January night, the company truck used to haul scenery, possessing block and tackle for that purpose, appeared at the receiving dock of the Louvre, with papers authorizing Jean Sard, director of the Players, to borrow what he needed.

Sard, a small, confident man in his thirties, with an ingratiating manner, conferred with Diland, the young assistant curator, chose several busts from the sculpture storeroom, but then, pausing in front of "The Sailor," clapped his hands in delight. "Forget the smaller works,

Diland," he said. "This one will give me the exact atmosphere, the mood I want to capture." By its very immensity, Sard went on to say, it would catapult the audience into the Grecian period, as well as symbolizing beautifully the greatness of Alexander.

The young curator thought Sard typically a little crazy—"The Sailor," as far as he was concerned, catapulted him into nothing but deep depression—but Sard was welcome to it, he said. "And you don't have to be in a hurry to return it; I don't really think the statue will be missed."

Wasting no time, Sard had several stagehands wheel in a huge dolly of the type manufactured for industrial use. The curator did not think to question how it was that Sard was so well prepared. With the help of the museum staff, "The Sailor" was lowered to the dolly, strapped in, and wheeled outside. Here, using the block and tackle, it was raised to the level of the truck bed, and, with the assistance of the museum people, swung aboard.

The wind had come up by now, the cold getting to the bones, and no one was unhappy when, after signing the release—both the museum and the Players were, after all, part of the same organization, the Beaux-Arts—Sard gave the signal to take off. Lumbering out of the Louvre courtyard, the truck turned down the rue de Rivoli and was lost in the night. No one, especially Diland, gave it a second thought.

It was early evening and the traffic encountered was minimal. Munching a sandwich of cold veal, sipping on a bottle of burgundy, Jean Sard, in front with the driver, noted that the truck seemed to be handling the weight of the sculpture satisfactorily. The truck bed had been reinforced for the trip, specially heavy springs installed.

Just beyond the porte de Saint Cloud, the truck pulled off the road at a wooded area while Sard and the crew got out to stretch their legs. No more than a minute later, a black Citroën drove up. At the wheel was Le Brun.

Sard walked over to say hello and reassure Le Brun that things had gone according to schedule. Sitting next to Le Brun was a fierce-looking old man whom Sard thought he recognized as the famous sculptor, Pierre Brazin. In the back were two strangers to him, a young woman whose face he couldn't quite see, and a broad-shouldered young man. Le Brun did not make any introductions, and other than receiving Sard's bulletin with a satisfied nod, made no attempt to discuss the evening's activities. "Let's get on with it," he told his friend.

Almost at once, the Citroën moved back on the high-way, the truck following. The route had been carefully planned. Southwest, down the main highway to Chartres. Shortly before reaching Chartres, Le Brun swung onto an auxiliary road that worked its way further south and west. Close to the border of the unoccupied zone, he turned off to a still narrower road, a farm road, really, in very poor repair. Mindful of the heavily loaded truck behind him, he was forced to move at an agonizingly slow pace.

The farm was almost exactly at the zone line, Le Brun told his passengers. He had braked just short of the little group of buildings that lay dark and mysterious in front of them. But now a flashlight winked several times. "That means a patrol has just passed," interpreted Le Brun. "We'll have to wait awhile. Anyone who wants to pee, now's your chance."

"Thank God," said Brazin. "I'm ready to burst my bladder." He had been nipping from a flask and was first out of the Citroën, wading into a snowy meadow. Using his cane, Morgan joined him.

Appearing at Le Brun's side, Sara remarked with amusement, "Men can't hold it very well, can they?"

Immediately Le Brun swung around to her. "Back in the car, please," he said. "Unless you have a need." Offended by his tone, she complied immediately. She should have known better, Sara decided bitterly; put some people in charge and they become dictators. For his part, Le Brun was thinking that the girl must realize this was a quasi-military operation. Also, the men from the truck had descended, were drifting over, and he wanted as little fraternization as possible.

A factor, however, was that he and Sara barely talked, circling each other like sworn enemies.

Jean Sard had moved across to him in the dark. "What's the holdup?" he asked.

Le Brun explained. He wanted to be absolutely certain the nightly border patrol was well away, definitely out of earshot of their motors.

Just then, from the house, they could see a flashlight blinking again.

"Okay," said Le Brun. "We can move again in a few minutes."

Jean Sard moved toward the truck, then paused. He felt good out here in the country. The wine was warm in his stomach and he was doing something. For the first time since the war, actually *doing* something. "Claude," he said, "isn't that Pierre Brazin taking a piss over there in the snow?"

"Look here," said Le Brun. "You know what we agreed."

"Sure. I wasn't to be told any more than necessary. But for Christ's sake, this is getting damn silly. What is Brazin doing here? And that girl in the back of your car? And that blond giant with the cane? And what in hell are you going to be doing with that damn ugly piece of marble we've stolen? I'm taking a risk; I think I'm entitled to a little information."

"You're entitled to nothing," said Le Brun patiently. "Look, if you're picked up on the way back, if the Germans happen to get hold of you, put some electrodes to your testicles, how long before you'll be spilling everything you want me to tell you?"

"If that's all the faith you have in me—" Sard muttered sullenly.

"I have all the faith in you. Without your help, I'd be nowhere. And one day soon it will all make sense to you. You'll tell your grandchildren about it."

"If I'm still around."

"You'll be around," Le Brun smiled, smacking Sard's shoulder with a fist. "And it isn't Pierre Brazin getting back into the car now, is it? Now let's get started. I want you back in Chartres at your theater before dawn, otherwise we better worry about your balls."

The light was showing again, but steadily, as if held by someone riding a horse, and the Citroën and the truck followed it at a crawl down what amounted to a snow-encrusted path. The path led into the unoccupied zone, continued through a small forest, where the sides of the truck kept hitting against the trees, the snow on the branches shuddering to the ground like ghosts whispering. The path ended at a low stone wall that bordered a north-south macadam road. The stones in the wall could be removed, and the man with the flashlight —now revealed as a squat, bearded farmer—made enough of a gap for the vehicles to drive through.

The Citroën and the truck turned south on the road. Le Brun reminded Jean Sard to watch the distance guage on the dash, not wanting him to miss the space in the wall on his return trip.

By midnight they had crossed the Cher river beyond Vierzon and minutes later they passed through the gates of the Jacobi farm. They were met by a tall, raw-boned farmer, Ivan Povavna, almost as tall and massive as Mischa. Mischa had installed Povavna and his wife, Anna, as caretakers over a year ago, Sara reported; they could be trusted absolutely.

Everyone got to work at once unloading "The Sailor," lowering him by block and tackle to the dolly, which was then trundled, a dozen hands holding it steady, into the barn where another block and tackle on the rafters hauled the sculpture upright.

Several bottles of cognac were then produced and quickly dispatched: the tension of the night's ride and the cold had gotten to everybody.

Le Brun told Jean Sard he ought to be starting back. There was just enough time to cross into the German zone before the first light. But Jean Sard didn't seem concerned, or the stagehands with him; they'd make it all right, Sard said. But Le Brun didn't relax until he saw the truck on its way out of the farm, to the Vierzon road. Sard, however, had no intention of returning to the occupied zone. To hell with Le Brun! Once out of sight of the farm, he took the first side road toward the south and safety.

Twenty-Two

BRAZIN HAD ASKED for two men specifically, and they got lucky with the first, Charles Epernet. Epernet, it turned out, was a native of Bourges—less than a few hours from the farm—lived at Bourges with his parents. A telephone call delivered him. He was almost as tall as Morgan, in his late thirties, skinny as a sheet of paper, but, as Morgan who had worked with him testified, incredibly strong. Epernet had another quality; he rarely spoke. He had a stammer.

The second man Brazin had requested, Carlo Umbarti, was another story. A naturalized Italian living in Lille, far to the north, how was he to be transported across the zone? Providing indeed that he agreed to come. And as far as Umbarti's participation was concerned, Brazin was adamant. A craftsman of first rank, a genius with marble, he was absolutely essential to the project's success.

Le Brun had spoken to Fauré about Umbarti before leaving Paris. Fauré, hampered by having to operate within an organization composed mostly of open collaborationists, could promise nothing. But two days after their arrival at the farm, a smiling gnome, an inch taller at most than Brazin, elegant in a shortcoat topped with fur, showed up on a handsome motorcycle, a valise of fine-tooled leather strapped to the rear.

Taking in the Jacobi property—the farmhouse, the outbuildings, framed against the winter woods, the smile widened into a grin. "So—a working vacation in this lovely spot, my friends. With perhaps a *Boche* firing squad at the end of it, is that it?"

That was it, Le Brun told him.

The night of Umbarti's arrival they held their first

planning session. It was in the spacious workshop that Aaron Jacobi had arranged for Sara. What he had done was to take one of the barns, gut it, then double its size—in effect making a spacious studio-apartment for his daughter. Her photomurals decorated the walls, but the rafters still remained along with the original barnlike character, although a new mood had already been established. Standing exactly in the middle of the original structure, an immense, awkward, and as yet still unblemished figure, was "The Sailor." Living quarters were in the main house, a hundred yards away. Comfortable quarters, but far from the elegance of the Foch house. Aaron Jacobi wanted to "feel" the country. He had had the interior painted, modern plumbing installed, and little else. Brazin was awarded the master suite, Umbarti and Epernet doubling up in an adjoining bedroom, Sara and Morgan living openly together in what had been her room. Le Brun, although he would not have admitted to a subconscious motive, settled for the downstairs den, as far from Sara and Tom Morgan as he could arrange.

The night after Umbarti's arrival, the six of them crammed into the Citroën, and drove to the Château d'Albion.

It was one A.M., the kind of quiet winter night when the air itself seemed as fragile as the thin coating of ice on the lake. Parking up the road, they tramped in silence to the kitchen entrance where Christine Chanton, a priestess in a high-necked woolen robe, greeted them. While the château staff was small, and presumably loyal, Le Brun wanted to take as few chances as possible.

The chapel was lit with candles, but Christine had rigged a spotlight to illuminate the Winged Victory.

Critically they took it in as if for the first time, standing at the entrance studying the mass of it. Umbarti broke the spell. "What the hell," he said. "It's only a carved block of marble."

But now a different kind of knowledge of it was essential. Intent, detached—he hadn't even touched the flask on the half-hour drive over—Brazin alone did a slow walk around the sculpture, frowning, probing with old, wise fingers, making small, private sounds, finally indicating to the others to take their turn. They did so, Umbarti, Epernet, Morgan, aping the master's moves, whispering together, carefully stalking the great object, Le Brun couldn't help thinking, like the blind men trying to identify the elephant in the proverb.

Finished, they looked to the master.

Brazin hesitated for a moment, impassive: "Very, very difficult. Can we do it, Carlo?"

Umbarti was uncharacteristically stern, introspective, then the infectious smile crept to his face. "Of course not, *maître*. Impossible in the length of time. But we do it anyway, no?"

"Epernet?"

"Y-y-yes?"

"Morgan?"

"No problem!"

The tension was broken. They laughed. "You see, we're crazy," Brazin said to Le Brun. "But we'll do it, as Carlo says."

Christine Chanton appeared with two chilled bottles of champagne, and a tray of kitchen glasses.

They drank and toasted the venture, while Brazin scribbled a list for Le Brun of tools and equipment required. He had brought his own favorite chisels with him but additional ones would be needed. And plaster of Paris and strips of metal for the cast that would have to be constructed before they could even begin. And although Brazin preferred to work solely with hand tools —as did few sculptors anymore, whispered Morgan to Le Brun—an air compressor must somehow be obtained to speed up the smoothing process after the initial rough cuts had been made. And a pointing machine, of course, for the measurements. . . .

Where am I going to dig up an air compressor unit? Le Brun asked himself. *Why the hell didn't Brazin mention it in Paris? And a pointing machine! You'd think—*

Then Epernet was digging a finger into his ribs. "I h-h-have an air co-comp-pressor. And a p-pointing machine, too!"

Wonderful! Epernet also had a variety of necessary tools and knew where he could fill the rest of Brazin's shopping list. Get him a small truck. He'd run over to Bourges in the morning.

Sara had been studying the chapel itself, the lighting in particular. The idea she had gave her the courage to approach Le Brun. "I want to help, too, Claude."

"You *are* helping," he said trying to be reasonable. Had he been right to involve her in this? It certainly wasn't fair for him to become annoyed because she wanted to participate. "You'll be running the farm. We'll have to be fed, cared for." He smiled toward Brazin and Umbarti. "Prima donnas. It won't be a picnic. You'll have plenty on your hands—including a man of your own."

So that's what's eating you, she thought with satisfaction. *Jealousy! You're no different from any other male!*

"You've done wonders for him. Look at him, the way he's getting around," Le Brun went on.

It happened to be a fact: Morgan was almost ready to throw away his cane. A few weeks down here and he'd be good as new. "Yes," she said. If she could tell Le Brun about Morgan's nightmares . . . hardly a night passing that she didn't have to soothe and cradle him. But typically, of course, Le Brun was seeing what he wanted to, the sexual part of it.

It seemed as if they couldn't handle the anger simmering inside them. Morgan couldn't be conjured away. He was too visible, a big, amiable jungle cat, but not declawed.

Standing close to Sara Jacobi in the chapel, Le Brun realized, however, that her relationship with Morgan wasn't important; he was in too deeply for it to change or affect what in reality was the heart of the matter: he was in love with Sara, perhaps had always been, even when loving Erica. Not, curiously, did it affect what he and Erica had had together . . . she was part of him, of *it,* as was Aaron Jacobi. When you came down to the nub, wasn't love for one an amalgam of all other loves, like light fracturing off into reds and blues and yellows, the primary colors, or the in-between tones, magenta, pink, and so on, then re-forming into the unity of a spectrum? Or more pertinently, he came to decide later, it was as if Erica and her father and Sara had formed

247

a triptych, with Sara the center panel. As if the artist had planned it with the precognition of the way, one day, Le Brun would be looking at the three-sided painting.

She had moved back from the bright cone around the statue into the flickering shadows of the candlelight, which now picked up the soft sheen of her skin, the Italian look of her mother, the tilt to her head, proud and dangerous as a young hawk's. But then, sensing that in a way she couldn't know they had come to a peace, she half-turned, the large dark eyes luminous and sad. Giving him a small, unreadable smile, she suddenly extended her arm, touching her fingers to his cheek, a caress so light and fleeting he could hardly be sure he had felt it.

No one had noticed. No one had been paying them any attention. Umbarti had discovered several places on the Samothrace where bits of marble had been patched together with plaster. "An excellent job," Umbarti was saying. "But a bitch for us to copy. But what the hell, everything about this'll be a bitch—the only thing is to get on with it!"

Sara and Le Brun had turned from each other, innocently—children who had broken the jar of preserves, and were trying not to look guilty. But the others were at the sculpture again, Brazin concerned with detail on the original. "That's where the difficulty is," he declared. "We must get a good cast to work with."

Turning from Le Brun, Sara said, "I can make a series of photos and blow them up. You could work from them, too. Only if you think it will help, Monsieur Brazin."

"*Pierre,* please," said Brazin. "And of course, child, it will be an enormous contribution!"

He was beaming at her. He was forever making conquests. He loved all pretty women. He had already fallen for Sara, he declared openly. And tonight he had already begun his campaign to win the beautiful Christine Chanton.

"I can find you another spotlight," Christine told Sara. "For that matter you could come alone during the day. There's plenty of light from the clerestory windows, and one person taking pictures won't be danger-ous, will it?" she asked Le Brun.

Perhaps it would be wiser if Sara waited until Brazin had accomplished his preliminary work on the original, Le Brun said. They had to be careful, he warned them: despite the treaty, the unoccupied zone was infiltrated by German agents who knew of course that the Winged Victory was here. Any unusual activity could set off an alarm back in Paris.

It was close to dawn when they took leave of Christine. They were all a little drunk and sang songs on the way back to the farm. But at the foot of the stairs, saying goodnight to Le Brun, Umbarti suddenly grabbed his arm. "We sing and we laugh, Le Brun, but we know we are fools, eh? To make another lady like the first one, a lady good enough to fool that Goering, his bastard experts, is that possible? I do not really know."

"*I* know," answered Le Brun. "What the hell, don't I have the most talented sculptors in all France at my disposition?"

The pieces of steel Umbarti called fingers released Le Brun's arm. The grin was back. "You keep remind-ing us, *amico!* At the beginning of each day. At the end, especially. *Buona notte!*"

Morgan, coming out of the kitchen, his arm around Sara, waved goodnight, too. Sara gave Le Brun a swift glance, then tore the look away, climbing out of his view.

"Le Brun," a voice said.

Le Brun turned to find Brazin there with Epernet. "Please come with us," Brazin commanded.

Mystified, Le Brun followed the two outside and across to the studio where Epernet switched on the lights, revealing "The Sailor." A hammer and chisel in his hand, Brazin then pulled a tall ladder over, scram-bling up on his pony legs, torso level with the head be-fore he stopped and looked down at Le Brun. With a swift, graceful movement, he then brought the muscled arm down, cutting a fair-sized sliver out of the statue's shoulder. The blow had rung sharp and clear in the pre-morning silence.

Le Brun was aware that both Brazin and Epernet were watching him expectantly.

"All right," Brazin said. "Go outside."

"What?"

"Just outside the door."

Le Brun obeyed. The air was cold, as if it could be broken off into pieces. No night birds, not even a breeze to disturb the winter silence. From inside, Brazin struck the statue again and Le Brun suddenly understood what Brazin was demonstrating: the sound of chisel on marble was unique, traveling like a gunshot through the countryside.

Brazin and Epernet came out to join him. "In the city, naturally, it's not so bad," Brazin noted. "So many other noises to compete with it, drown it. But imagine what it will be here with four of us working simultaneously."

Le Brun could imagine: an anvil chorus! Enough, surely, to alert everyone within miles of the unusual activity at the Jacobi farm.

The rooms on the upper floor of the main house, Le Brun saw, had gone dark.

"Good night," said Brazin.

"G-good night," stammered Epernet.

What's good about it? Le Brun asked himself.

Twenty-Three

RAEDER HAD BEEN SENT UP to Antwerp for several weeks—dull weeks. He had no feeling for the city. With the occupation it was dirty and the women didn't catch the eye as in France. The prostitutes were heavy and old, and the young, pretty girls were kept inside, away from the German soldiers. Bruno Lohse, another of Goering's staff, was there and they had some nice dinners together, but Lohse was really all business. He had a deal going with a Jew dealer for a Frans Hals, a really superb painting that made Raeder's mouth water.

Goering would get the painting for practically nothing; the Jew would get safe passage to Switzerland. Raeder's job, when the interminable negotiating was concluded, was to transport the small masterpiece back to Paris. The job made him feel inferior to Lohse and he was glad when it was over and he was reinstalled in his room on the rue de Rivoli. It was important, he felt more than ever, to pull off some coup that would shoot him to the top of Goering's staff, not to speak of fattening the money pouch taped to the back of the bureau.

Two possibilities: the first, of course, was to somehow spirit the Winged Victory out of that damned château and onto a train for Berlin; the second, find the Jacobi collection. The Reichsmarschall would surely reward either accomplishment generously, and either would vault Raeder over Kröler, Hofer, Lohse, even von Banheim, for that matter, in the Paris hierarchy.

Unhappily there wasn't much Raeder could do about the Winged Victory, not at the moment anyway, with all the damned political maneuvering going on about the French fleet. The Jacobi collection was another matter. Raeder remained convinced it was still in Paris, which made him sure Le Brun wouldn't be far away. Had the collection been removed, word would have leaked out—the Germans were hated enough, God knows, and a feat like that, accomplished under their noses, would be shouted to the heavens.

Le Brun . . . find Le Brun he told himself, hammering at the stupidity of the Gestapo, the Milice, for failure. He had never expected the trick of placing the Hispanos around Paris to bring results, of course. Mostly it was intended to play on Le Brun's nerves, to inform him that he, Raeder, was implacably on his trail.

He would have thought that losing the woman to von Banheim would have had its effect. He had ordered the Milice to have a man put on Mallou, certain Le Brun would try to contact her, maybe win her back. No results. Le Brun never showed up. He must have ice water in his veins. A cunt doing a thing like that to *him* would be damn sorry, Raeder decided, fantasizing in detail how he'd take his revenge.

The morning after his return from Belgium, the

break finally came. A Milice agent having nothing to do with the Mallou case, but making a routine stop at a bistro called La Grandmère, had spotted a man he thought might be Le Brun. The agent knew Le Brun reasonably well, having been one of those assigned to tail him months ago. The suspect looked somewhat different—hair color, a mustache, walked with a stoop, but still—

The agent had followed his suspect to where he lived, learned from neighbors that he worked at a garage just a few steps away. All this, however, was weeks ago, the Milice desk man reported. They'd tried to contact Raeder but he was away.

Cursing his luck, the loss of time, unable to picture the immaculate Le Brun toiling as a mechanic, Raeder commandeered the Milice agent involved. Together they went to the garage, only to be told by the owner, a wizened little man who looked like a jockey, that a fellow named Tobier, possibly resembling the man they described, had worked briefly for him but had taken off one day without notice. And that was all he knew, the owner said.

"That's it?" Raeder asked incredulously.

"Sorry."

Raeder grabbed the little man by the front of his shirt. "Listen," he said. "What kind of idiots do you think we are? You employ a man off the street? No references? Not a fucking idea where he came from?"

The owner yanked himself free. He was surprisingly strong and wasn't intimidated by his visitors. "These days I'll take any help I can get. Anyone who can lift a wrench. No questions asked."

The Milice detective with Raeder came from the same neighborhood and knew Georges. He didn't want trouble with him later. At that point no one could be sure who was going to win the war. "I think he's telling the truth, Sergeant," the Milice man said soothingly.

"Oh, sure," Raeder growled. "All right. How long ago did this mysterious disappearance take place?"

Less than a month ago, the garage owner said. He had calmed down. He even told Raeder he was sorry he couldn't be of more help.

Raeder asked the Milice agent to nose around the

Prince Kilkanov's. If anyone besides Le Brun knew about the collection it would be the Prince. The agent came back to report that Kilkanov hadn't left town, hadn't departed from his usual routine, a daily walk up and down the Champs, the daily visit to that bridge club of his. Hadn't had any strange visitors. Nothing, nothing, the Milice man said positively. He'd spread Raeder's money around to the maids upstairs. If anything unusual had taken place he'd have been informed.

"I'm sure of that," remarked Raeder sardonically.

"One thing they did tell us," the Milice man said, resenting the German's tone, "although it's not at all what we want, is that Kilkanov's *bonne* left him. The Kilkanovs have another one now—one called Violette, the fat one who used to work at the Jacobi house."

Raeder's attention was caught. "What happened to the first maid?"

The agent shrugged. "She was living on the top floor with her boyfriend, a guy convalescing from a war wound. He recovered and they took off."

Raeder held his breath. "How long ago."

"About a month, I was told."

"Le Brun skipped out of that garage a month ago."

"You're right."

They were at a table at a hole-in-the-wall café near the rue Royale. The traffic here was fairly heavy and the men watched it. Raeder ordered a second gin. "I want you to go back and get a description of this boyfriend. And the exact date he and the woman left."

"What will all that have to do with anything?" the agent asked truculently.

"Find out for me," Raeder snapped.

The agent shrugged and left, but Raeder knew in advance what he would come back with: the boyfriend would have been big and blond, the description of the wounded man carried into the Jacobi mansion by Le Brun that night; the description would correspond to that of the rue de Rivoli sniper. Raeder gulped down the second gin without realizing he'd drunk it. And the day they took off, he was willing to bet, would tally with the day Le Brun took a powder from that garage.

A couple of streetwalkers, arm in arm, strolled past

253

the café. They wore the high wooden shoes the women of Paris had adopted these days to cope with the scarcity of leather; but as always the Frenchwomen managed to make the shoes look chic as well as flattering to their legs. And the legs were something! The girls lingered a bit, giving Raeder a quick glance. He thought briefly of responding: having the two together would be something . . . but today other things were more important. His particular pleasures would have to wait.

Lavoulière was more than polite; he was the soul of fraternity. He was sitting at what Raeder gathered had been first Aaron Jacobi's desk, then Le Brun's. He wore a handsomely tailored gray tweed jacket, obviously new, a silk shirt, conservative blue tie, and surprisingly ordinary cufflinks. Well, gold ones would come, Raeder assured himself; this fellow would waste little time.

He kept his left hand buried in his lap. Something wrong with it, Raeder guessed, and then saw that it was smaller than the other, and shrunken.

Lavoulière had clearly assessed the situation. He knew exactly where Raeder stood in the scale of things —his importance in the Jeu de Paume operation. Without being exactly obsequious, Lavoulière managed to let Raeder understand that with him in command at Jacobi's, cooperation was the key word. Now, what could he do for him?

"What I want," Raeder said, "is a rundown on Le Brun's activities immediately prior to his . . . disappearance. Social activities . . . if possible a list of his friends."

"He was not the one to confide in me. In anyone," Lavoulière added quickly with a wry smile. "A private person, as they say. So I don't know how helpful I can be."

"Try," suggested Raeder.

Lavoulière wore a smug smile. Swooping around to a shelf behind him, he pulled out a sheet of notepaper and placed it before Raeder with the air of a conjurer.

"What is it?"

"Le Brun planned a soirée at the Jacobi house before . . . well, *before*. This was the tentative list of his *invités*."

Le Brun's writing was bold but not too legible. Raeder could make out most of the names, however. He was not on the list. Otherwise most of the Jeu de Paume Germans: Kröler, von Banheim, Rosenberg, Bocke. At that moment in history, Le Brun was playing his cards shrewdly. Just a handful of French. Vichyites, mostly Beaux-Arts people: Garnier, a Robert Fauré, Garnier's assistant; several other names Raeder was not familiar with. Then some figures from the French theater. Most meant nothing to Raeder.

Folding the list, putting it in his pocket, he rose and thanked Lavoulière. They'd be doing more business, he promised him.

He tried Bocke at the Crillon several times before he reached him. Bocke had to lean on the Gestapo, Raeder announced. The last time Raeder had gone to those bastards with a problem they'd pissed on him; well now he had something only they could solve, and he wanted better treatment.

"What is it this time, Raeder?" Bocke asked snidely. "You ready to swoop down on the Jacobi collection, is that it?" Everyone in their group knew about Raeder's obsession with the Jacobi paintings. With Le Brun for that matter.

"Sooner than you think, maybe," replied Raeder coldly. "Can I rely on you or should I go directly to the Reichsmarschall?"

"No need for that," said Bocke in a more official voice.

Raeder said okay, and read him the list of Frenchmen Le Brun had compiled for his party. Required from the Gestapo: a rundown on everyone mentioned —their background and current status.

Later that day Raeder received a call in his cubicle downstairs at the Jeu de Paume. It was the Gestapo lieutenant who had given him the hard time with Prince Kilkanov. The man's voice was noticeably more friendly, Raeder was gratified to note. But he had nothing really hot to contribute, the lieutenant apologized. Those on the list attached to Vichy were for the moment untouchable, and actually all, with the possible exception of Robert Fauré, were reasonably clean. Fauré almost definitely had Resistance connections and sooner or later would be picked up.

Disappointed, nothing there he could use, Raeder was about to hang up when he realized the lieutenant was not finished. "I don't know if this is relevant, Sergeant, but one man on your list has disappeared."

"Who?"

"Jean Sard, the one connected to that theater group, Players of the Night."

Players of the Night didn't mean a damn thing to Raeder.

"Who the hell are they?"

The lieutenant explained, then went on, "What is interesting is that this Sard borrowed a statue from the Louvre for a performance in Chartres, went to all that damn trouble, mind you, then never showed up at the theater. Not him, or the stagehands, or the fucking truck! Probably escaped into the unoccupied zone."

Raeder felt himself going icy. "Can you give me the exact date, Lieutenant?"

"Friday will be four weeks. Is that any help?"

"Actually, yes," Raeder said, trying to hold down his excitement. It was an incredible development. A mountain had been moved. On that Friday, Le Brun, the sniper, the woman who shared the room with the sniper at the Kilkanov apartment, all three, and now this Jean Sard, had taken themselves out of Paris, decamped!

"What did this Sard take from the Louvre?"

"A gigantic statue called 'The Sailor.' That's what I find strange. . . . Sergeant—are you there?"

He was there all right, but hours later, despite all the promise the information seemed to offer, no closer to an explanation. He had once seen the statue in question. It was a piece of crap, a third-rate work at best. Why would Sard want it and then disappear with it to the south? What was the connection with this sniper, the woman, Le Brun? It made no sense at all. . . .

Twenty-Four

ON THE THIRD DAY, although Epernet would have to drive into Bourges for odds and ends unavailable on his first trip, Le Brun declared Project Samothrace officially under way. That night the Povavnas' truck was commandeered again to take the entire crew, plus sacks of plaster of Paris, buckets, extra ladders, to the Château d'Albion. As usual, Christine Chanton was waiting, had even managed to obtain additional spotlights, making the crucial area of the chapel as light as day.

Work was started immediately on the important job of making a mold of the sculpture, step number one in the process of copying it in marble.

Umbarti was in charge, Brazin sitting in a pew, watching closely but without comment.

Tonight Umbarti was also a master chef himself, preparing the special solution. The ratio of water to plaster of Paris, he explained to Le Brun, was a key factor in determining the strength and plasticity of the final mix. And the water used must be drinking water, containing minimal acid or alkali. And the quantity prepared at this point must be small. In a model of such size, the plaster would have to be applied in sections divided by strips of tin, enabling them to remove the sections later and reassemble them for the pouring of the cast. Finally, now, Umbarti added cement and a little lime water to the formula. Not too much of either, he said, but enough to make the mold harder, more positive. Creamy and smooth, it was ready, he announced, more stirring would "rot" the mixture.

Epernet and Morgan had begun to apply a thick coat to the Samothrace, starting at the top, balancing themselves on the ladders. "Be careful, watch for air bubbles," Umbarti, observing every move, shouted from below. "Remember that stuff expands in setting!" And to Morgan, "Watch it boy, fill every indentation —Epernet, every crevice!"

They had got through only the upper half of the sculpture that first night, the wings having to be done separately, giving them trouble. Although the plaster of Paris took a little more than a half hour to dry, Umbarti refused to be rushed. Beginning with the mix. In its own way this stage—with the necessity of ending up with the sharpest possible definitions—was most critical.

The mess they had left on the chapel floor could hardly be cleaned up in a hurry, and since the lumpy white bubble being formed around the upper torso of the Samothrace told its own story, Christine Chanton merely locked up when they had finished—no one would enter until they returned the next night, she promised.

Exhausted, they drove home in silence, Pierre Brazin snoring softly beside Le Brun at the wheel, dawn a faint silver spreading over the eastern sky. At the farm the Povavnas had fixed a hot breakfast which was demolished before, exhausted, they piled into their beds. All their meals were eaten around the long oblong oak table in the brick-floored kitchen, which contained an immense wood-burning stove, a fireplace, and great shining copper pots hanging everywhere.

Unlike the poor people of Paris, they could eat their fill here; the land was bountiful and the Povavnas more than competent farmers. And always the *vin du pays* set before them in big jugs: a decent red, but it was the white wines that excelled—the Sancerre, the Vouvray. This kitchen provided them a spiritual center offering not just nourishment but warmth and camaraderie—it was home and hearth.

By unspoken agreement Sara and Le Brun never sat together; they avoided looking at each other. It was obvious to everyone but Morgan, who worked obsessively, doted on Sara, and tried to spread his happiness around . . . Morgan's former life, his tragedy, had been tempered somehow, it seemed, by Sara's gentleness and by the euphoria of this task in which they were involved. His strength was prodigious; his stamina equaled it. As time went on, he insisted on the odious assignment of tidying up the studio each night, Brazin detesting disorder; he could even be found helping Anna Povavna with the mountain of dishes after the evening meal. He stoked the numerous stoves with firewood; in the studio, when the time came, he worked the air compressor, the dirtiest job. "No question," said Umbarti, "if the rest of the Americans are like him, the Nazis had better start cutting their throats; they've already lost the war!"

The following night they were back at d'Albion, the work going faster now, Umbarti knowing his mix, Epernet and Morgan applying it as fast as Umbarti could get it to them. They were now coating plaster of Paris to the lower folds of the garment, and soon to the pedestal. Proceeding with infinite care, they broke away the sections of the mold, fitting them together with the metal around an armature Le Brun had been readying on his own.

The mold was now ready to be filled.

Here Pierre Brazin suddenly sprang to life. Climbing a ladder alongside the huge mass of the mold, he supervised the pouring. "Slower," he pleaded. "Is the other bucket ready, Umbarti? Hurry, man—we always need more than we think. Good, good! The potage begins to set, thicken, see!"

Umbarti was using a barrel now for his mix, adding pieces of gunnysack for strength, Sara helping him. The mix normally did not have to be poured into the mold in one effort, but doing so minimized the danger of weakening the cast at the "joining" surfaces. And so Epernet and Morgan kept at it, until the mold had been filled to the neck. And since the sculpture was headless, their work for the moment was finished.

Back to the farm again to eat, to sleep, to wait restlessly for night to come to examine the results. A near perfect cast was essential. Without it, declared Brazin, as if they all didn't know it, he could guarantee nothing. But at the last minute, as usual, he found he needed something that hadn't been anticipated. Electric heaters, this time, to speed up the drying process.

Along with Epernet, Le Brun explored both Angers and Saumur, managing to buy, at scandalous prices, four heaters, two ancient, two reasonably new. The problem was that not more than one could be purchased at any one store: Le Brun was still worried about German agents; they hopped around like fleas in the unoccupied zone.

That night, at the usual time, they gathered at d'Albion while Brazin and Umbarti, working with hammer and chisel as precisely as surgeons, began to remove the mold. Slowly, a proud woman divesting herself of her garments, the new Samothrace began to emerge. Watching Brazin for a clue, Le Brun could see the satisfaction building on the old man's face. The definition they were getting was excellent, each fine sculptural line on the original Samothrace having been duplicated in the cast, the armature that Le Brun had fashioned holding the structure erect. Now the wings, which had been poured separately, were revealed. *Also damn good,* Le Brun thought. No need to look over to the professionals for their approval. They were busy in any case, seating the supporting iron of the wings, attaching the wings to the body.

Still not hardened, the cast was complete, standing chalk-white in the chapel, a pale but proud copy of her older sister.

The four heaters Le Brun had bought were set at different heights around her while Umbarti prepared hot washes of a borax solution; it would hasten the hardening process, he told them. The next liquid that concerned them was brandy; a bottle was consumed in several rounds, even Sara and Christine participating. There was no open jubilation—too much work lay ahead—but the first hurdle had been passed.

At the farm, Le Brun had gone around to the back of the truck where the cast had lain swaddled in layers of blankets before Morgan and the others had hefted it to the ground, transferred it to the dolly Jean Sard had left, and babied the dolly over the hard dirt to the studio. In the darkness, coming around the truck, Le Brun banged into Sara, felt her falling, instinctively grabbed for her. And then, as if there were no other choice, she was in his arms and they were holding fiercely to each other. She could have been a boy—the duffle coat she was wearing shielded her body too effectively—but the kiss, the kiss was a woman's. They were both lost then. Nothing, it seemed to Le Brun, could go back to the way it was. With a muffled sound that was not a sob as he thought, but a smothered obscenity, she had broken away from him. "Dammit," she said, legs apart, facing him like a boxer. "Damn you, Le Brun!"

His inclination was to laugh, not so much from the humor of it, but the sorrow, and because, in that moment, she was like any Jacobi, fists up, battling the world.

Lights had broken out in the studio behind them and they heard Morgan's voice, exultant in the stillness. "Look at her! Beautiful! Sara, where are you?"

Unsmiling, her eyes swept Le Brun once more.

"Coming," she called.

Except for the two cuts made by Brazin several nights before, "The Sailor" was still untouched, a colossus almost reaching to the rafters. But now, alongside it, pristine, stood the Winged Victory cast. Between them was the pointing machine.

The Greeks had known such devices, Le Brun knew, but it wasn't until much later that its use became general.

"I hate it—I despise it!" Brazin exclaimed. "It enabled copies to be made that lacked vitality, corrupting the soul of the original. It was a tool of the uninspired, the mediocre."

Only Umbarti was unfazed by the master's venom; he was already at work with the deivce. It was a movable instrument constructed of rods of varying length that could be turned from the plaster of Paris cast to the piece of marble, in this case "The Sailor," transferring the exact dimensions of one onto the other. Moving the rods back and forth from the model to the stone, marking off the desired depth, holes were then to be drilled into "The Sailor" to the depths the pointing machine indicated. When this rough marble was chiseled away, what would remain would be a crude but dimensionally correct copy of the plaster of Paris cast—and of the original.

Umbarti, having made his initial measurements with the machine, was ready to give the signal to begin the drilling, a delicate, time-consuming task. Hundreds of points would be required before they were finished. But Le Brun asked that the process be held up for a moment. It was early morning, not quite seven o'clock, and he was looking at his watch.

At exactly seven, from outside, came the clear and distinctive sound of wood being chopped. Le Brun walked to the studio doors, followed by the others.

A farm truck had been drawn up at the beginning of the woods beyond the fields. Three men, it appeared, were working there. And now, as a tree fell, a newer sound intruded. A donkey engine standing beside the truck had been started up, its staccato belching indecently in the quiet of the morning. The fallen tree was being carried forward, and a final culminating clamor ensued—it was the shrill whining of a chainsaw escalating in decibels as they listened appreciatively.

"Men from Bourges." Le Brun said. "Sara has contracted with them to clear ten acres in return for the lumber. They will work very slowly, believe me, keeping strictly to our schedule. Now, gentlemen, you can make all the noise you wish."

And he could soon hear them, working with sharp-pointed drills behind him.

But what a pity, he thought, still standing in the doorway, *about the little forest that's being demolished.*

"I'll build a house on that land after the war, don't feel sorry about it," Sara said. She had come up alongside him from inside, holding her camera bag. "And no man will ever be allowed to set foot there, to defile it. I shall live in it alone; I shall die in it alone."

He smiled.

"I hate you!" she exclaimed with passion.

Her eyes told him she meant it—momentarily at least. Not only Claude Le Brun the man. *All* men. He watched her as she got in the Citroën and drove west

262

toward Château d'Albion. He hoped letting her go there to photograph the Samothrace was prudent.

They would have worked around the clock except that Le Brun forbade it. For one thing there was the question of noise; they needed the covering sound of lumber cutting. And the master sculptor was hardly young; he needed his sleep.

Under Brazin's tight scrutiny, good progress had been made. The outlines of the Samothrace began to emerge, the torso of "The Sailor" slowly being obliterated. Le Brun, who had theoretical knowledge of the process from his days at the Beaux-Arts, was fascinated watching it performed by Brazin and Umbarti. And Epernet was no slouch. For that matter, Morgan, the American, for all his easy posturing, was highly talented.

The section of fishing dory on which "The Sailor" was presumably standing had been cut away from the body, a wooden platform substituted, and this heavy piece of marble given to Morgan to carve out the left wing. Known to be a reconstruction, the wing would be joined to the Victoire proper at a later date.

A good part of the preliminary clearing away having been accomplished by hand to the depths indicated by the pointing machine, the air compressor, with a bush hammer inserted in the nozzle, pulverized the marble, smoothing the crude cuts down to a few eighths of an inch. More delicate tools would now be employed, the claw or toothed chisel, as more delicate configurations were required.

Following days of photography at d'Albion, Sara disappeared into the back of the barn, morning to dinnertime. Since pre-war days it had been her darkroom-studio, and her equipment had remained there undisturbed. Late one afternoon she appeared, big rolls of blueprints under her arm. Not blueprints, it turned out, but immense blowups of sections of the Winged Victory, of the most minute details of the original.

Umbarti swung her around, hugging her. Brazin didn't seem so pleased—difficult to tell if he was faking. "Now you've given us more work; now we've got to include every damn refinement!"

But they anticipated that Goering's experts would examine the finished product with great care—enough photos existed. The entire venture had now become more than a wartime ploy: it was a captivating game, a challenge to their craftsmanship. . . .

To mollify the old man, Sara warned him he'd better look out—she'd invited Christine Chandon to dinner. "And from what my woman's instinct tells me, guess who's the attraction?"

"Who?" asked Brazin alertly, eyes sparkling.

Christine showed up the following night with disturbing news. The château, she reported, was under surveillance. "Last week inspectors came to check the foundations—at least that's what they told me, d'Albion being a national monument. But they were Milice agents, I would swear." And Christine laughed, rare with her—she was a solemn woman: "I made sure they saw the Victoire, which is all they wanted, of course. To make sure we hadn't spirited her to another château."

Does that mean Goering's move will come sooner than expected? Le Brun asked himself. No way to know, really. And unhappily no way to speed up what they were doing here.

In her quiet way, Christine, undoubtedly briefed by Sara, flirted with Brazin, who delighted in it. But it was Carlo Umbarti to whom she was attracted. And her interest was reciprocated. Umbarti took stage center, telling anecdotes of the great artists of the past. "You will think I'm inventing it, but Michelangelo, the Blessed, did not bathe for the four years it took him to paint the Sistine Chapel." The more Umbarti talked, the more Brazin sulked, drinking too much wine, nodding at the table. He had been Umbarti's teacher and mentor, and now Umbarti was his equal and Brazin was not ready to accept it.

Umbarti, himself, was not uncomplicated. He openly acknowledged the unpaid debt to Brazin but was unable to accept the old man's artistic dominance, a serious obstacle, it would seem, to the project. But when it came down to it, Umbarti would give way with grace, and it was his skill, his instinctive Italianate feel for marble, that was allowing them to proceed so rapidly.

Over coffee, Christine supplied them with news of the war they'd been missing, particularly the changing tide in North Africa. Then, almost as an item of gossip, the news she'd heard that André Malraux, under the *nom de guerre* of "Colonel Berger," was reportedly in the Périgord area to recruit a Maquis unit to harass the occupiers.

Sara said, "But Claude knows Malraux, don't you?"

"As does Pierre, I'm sure," said Le Brun.

"But the way you met him, the incident that followed—it was really exciting, wasn't it? Erica mentioned it in her last letter."

She is being a bitch, he thought, *but perhaps not —just self-punishing. All right. It wasn't so easy for me, either.* Quietly he began to recount what had happened at Nice, the attempt on Malraux's life, not hiding the fact that he'd been with Sara's sister.

Later, with Brazin marching off to bed, Morgan pressuring Sara into a moonlight walk, Le Brun, Umbarti, and Christine strolled over to the studio.

Inspecting the work in progress with a critical eye, clearly impressed but bothered by something, she turned to Umbarti. "You're working with old marble, but the new cuts are fresh, unweathered. How are you going to duplicate the Samothrace patina?"

It was the big unanswered question. Shrugging, Umbarti passed it on to Le Brun.

"Frankly," Le Brun admitted, "I've been praying that Brazin—or one of you—would have a brainstorm."

"The ancient sculptors would occasionally use soot to remove the gloss from the finished product. It would help," Umbarti said dryly, "until someone touched it with a wet finger."

"I was going to ask," Christine said to Le Brun, "if you would permit me to try and find an answer. I was pretty good at chemistry at school; it's possible that certain acids might be effective. I'd need some Parian marble from here to experiment with, large slivers if I could get them."

"How about an arm from 'The Sailor'? No use to us. I could bring it over to you tomorrow night," Umbarti told her.

"That would be fine," Christine said, smiling at him.

Why couldn't she take it with her tonight? Le Brun asked himself. *Stupid question!* They were off together to her car, bodies brushing as they walked, Christine saying that apropos of his dinner story about Michelangelo forgoing baths, she hoped Umbarti had no plans to emulate him!

Their laughter hung after them in the night air, and it was a long time before Le Brun could hear Christine's car starting up.

At breakfast Le Brun announced that the work had progressed to a point that made it possible for him to arrange for its future delivery to Goering.

"Don't be hasty," growled Brazin, "God knows how many problems lie ahead."

"You will conquer them."

"How in hell are you going to handle it with Goering?" Umbarti asked. "You simply can't let him come down and take delivery. He'd think it was fishy. Then the French would get word of it, they'd scream, and you couldn't deny it without giving away the whole business!"

"You have put my dilemma very neatly," said Le Brun, grinning. "But to use the cliché, there are many ways to skin a cat, and let's hope I can find one. I'll be going to Paris this evening."

Outside Morgan stopped him.

"I want to go with you."

"Impossible. You're needed here. And why would you want to go back? Do you think they've forgotten about you?"

"I have to speak to old neighbors, some friends. My daughter may have returned. One never knows. She's very pretty; it's quite possible the Germans—a few at least—are human. How could they harm a little girl like that?"

Morgan's face had gone rigid, his jaw tight; his eyes looked past Le Brun to the woodsmen. They were working away at a tree, their blows ringing out like a face being slapped without pity.

"I'm sorry," said Le Brun. "What I can do in Paris is to go where you lived and ask the questions for you. If by any chance the child's there, I'll bring her back with me."

Morgan thought about it, his eyes searching Le Brun's. "All right. You'll do your best, I trust you."

He scribbled his Paris address on a slip of paper, shook Le Brun's hand, and proceeded to the studio, where the sound of chisels on marble were already matching the blows of the axes. Then Le Brun became aware that Sara was standing outside the kitchen, watching them, and seeing Morgan disappear inside, walked over to Le Brun.

"You're not taking him with you?"

"No."

"He's really all right now, you know. It's only on that one subject . . ."

"I understand."

"When you go to Paris you'll be careful. As careful as possible."

Standing in the sunlight, they looked at each other squarely, honestly. "How much longer does it have to go on?" he asked her.

"I don't know."

She was as miserable as he was, but it didn't help very much. "I wasn't being truthful," she added now. "It's not only about his daughter. He's really hanging on by a thread."

"What he needs isn't a woman," he said bitterly. "It's psychiatric treatment."

"Perhaps. Will you see Mischa?"

"It depends on how things work out."

"Give him my love and the Princess, too. And, Claude—"

"Yes—"

"Come back quickly."

Spring had ventured a toe into the water that morning; the air had a lightness, the sun was warm, tiny lemon-colored buds were on the mimosa bushes. *Sara isn't just pretty*, he thought, *she's beautiful—slender yet hardly fragile anymore.* She didn't have to be told how much he wanted her.

At nightfall he took off in the Citroën, having changed its license plates and put the air compressor's bush hammer to a fender. Other than officials, few people, if they could wangle gas, bothered with body repairs. Disreputable-looking cars were common.

Le Brun followed the route they'd used coming down with Jean Sard and "The Sailor." At the border farm, however, he was forced to wait for several hours, not having been able to alert his friends there beforehand. And the Nazis had beefed up their patrols—more of them and they were staggered—difficult to time a crossing. He finally risked it, barely feeding gas, creeping down the black forest trail without lights, certain the Citroën was trumpeting its passage. After an eternity, he was in the clear, the farmhouse lights on his left, the Paris road ahead. At the road he stopped to smoke a cigarette and wait out his nerves.

From here into the city, the trip was uneventful. Cars were often stopped at random by Milice teams, but he was lucky and by midnight he was knocking at Georges' door, welcomed and plied with food and drink, and all but given Georges' wife to bed down with. He was easy with them, talkative, open. He was improving, Georges told his wife later; the snowman inside Le Brun was slowly thawing.

Midmorning Le Brun made a call from a *café-tabac* to the quai d'Orsay. "Guy Le Brun, please . . ."

A young, fluted secretarial voice—his brother hadn't changed much in his taste for women, Le Brun was willing to wager—answered. Who was calling, please?

"Marc Darle," Le Brun told her.

"I don't think—"

"Oh, yes. An old friend. He'll want to speak to me, I promise you."

A stubborn pause. "He's terribly busy. I'll try to interrupt him. One minute . . ."

The minute passed, and another—Guy Le Brun trying to decide how to handle this—then the familiar dulcet tone, soft and sly as a fiddle. Apparently the girl hadn't lied completely—Guy Le Brun wasn't.

"Yes, Darle."

"Rue St. Dominique. La Jardinière. Lousy food. You won't run into any of your fancy friends there. Not even any *Boches*. One o'clock. Inside. I'll be waiting."

"I don't know if I can make it today. Really. I may have to lunch with the minister. Another time perhaps, Darle. You understand, *mon vieux?*"

"Don't understand at all. And it has to be today. Or the consequences your end will be unfortunate, *mon vieux*. See you at one sharp."

He hung up and went to the address Morgan had given him, not too far from the place de la Republique. Entering the building, he studied the names of the occupants, finally deciding to ring the *concierge*. She was a comfortable-looking woman with bright red hair and wore carpet slippers. "I'm looking for the Mosse family. Don't see them listed."

"The Mosses?" she repeated, peering sharply at Le Brun. "They're—they've been taken away," she finally said. "Jews."

Le Brun made his disappointment emphatic. "Then I suppose the man I'm collecting for is out of luck. Out over a thousand francs, to be honest about it. He was their doctor."

The woman made a clucking sound.

"No chance of any of them returning, I suppose?" The *concierge* refused even to comment.

"There was a child. Perhaps you'd know who's caring for her? They might have information about her parents."

"The girl was taken, too."

Le Brun thanked the woman and backed out into the morning sunshine. With plenty of time before his meeting with Guy—if Guy showed up—he walked over to the Seine, across the pont Neuf, and down the quai Voltaire. The soldiers he saw on his trek looked older than those before he'd left Paris. Or very much younger—in their early teens. Obviously the prime-aged men were being sent into combat. The Russian front, Georges had confirmed, was turning into a disaster. Georges' other news wasn't that good. Fauré had been tagged by the Gestapo, had disappeared

269

from sight, probably executed. Also Arnaud, a few weeks earlier, along with some others picked up in a raid on the Left Bank, near St.-Germain-des-Près, in the flat of a *concierge*.

"Rue Visconti?"

"Yes."

Arnaud was a great loss, Le Brun would have to agree, but the news about Fauré touched him deeply. A fine, sensitive fellow. They could have become friends. The sons-of-bitches!

"What you ask is impossible. It would mean my openly being associated with you. To say that you are *persona non grata* with both Vichy and the Germans is putting it mildly. If you weren't my brother, there would be agents here to arrest you!"

His brother looked something like a successful pimp, Le Brun thought, with his round face, sleek black hair, tiny sleek mustache; with the Sulka tie and the manicured nails. He had refused to order anything to eat —he wouldn't be staying here that long, he had made it clear.

Being with his brother had brought back many painful memories. Le Brun asked him now about his wife, his children. All well, Guy replied impatiently, waiting for his brother to state what was wanted, which would be refused, so that he could leave and get back to his office.

Claude was in no hurry. "This is how it is, Guy," he said finally. "You're in a bad spot but you're really too stupid to see it. If it were someone else sitting here with you, say another member of the Resistance, and you showed your impatience so openly, why the fellow might just draw a pistol out of his pocket, put a bullet in your head, and walk out of here reflecting that another traitor to his country had been taught a lesson."

For a moment, Guy showed a hint of his old bravado. "You think I don't know you—you never could get yourself to squash a bug!" He laughed. "Get on with it, little brother."

"Feel the side of my pocket," Le Brun told him gently.

As commanded, Guy bent over and touched the side of Le Brun's jacket. The bulk of the gun could not be mistaken. Guy straightened, silent.

"Things are moving fast," Le Brun continued. "I speak of the war . . . the changing tide of the war. That is why I'm giving you this opportunity. So that the day the Allies enter Paris, I'll be able to speak up for you—we're flesh and blood after all—you see what I'm getting at? So that I'll be able to save my brother."

Guy asked a waiter for coffee. "You're fooling yourself if you think the Reich won't win in the end." His smile was distant, as if his thoughts were far away. He waited a bit until the coffee had been brought and he stirred with a spoon, although there wasn't any sugar. "But then you haven't changed much, have you, Claude?" He drank the coffee in almost one gulp, got to his feet, said, "Go to hell," and walked out of the restaurant.

Le Brun watched him go, thinking his brother hadn't changed much either, still an arrogant fool, a Le Brun characteristic perhaps, he concluded wryly.

Which left him in a difficult spot. A conduit was necessary for his purposes—a bridge to the enemy, but how—with Guy's refusal—to achieve it? There was a way—he had thought of it first then vetoed it. It held dangers and also happened to be personally difficult. He had no choice. With a sigh, he signaled for the waiter.

Le Brun walked into Chez Jeannot a little before six. They would just be stirring in the kitchen, but the waiters wouldn't yet have arrived, the entertainers either.

Jeannot was sitting at a corner table, sipping white wine and doing accounts.

"Jesus Christ," he said, seeing Le Brun. "Look what the cat dragged in."

She walked into the dressing room—Jeannot had agreed not to warn her—then stood without moving, staring at Le Brun. She was a little late, as always, and her hair was a mess. Instinctively her hand went up to it, then she pulled the hand down.

"What in hell are you doing here?" She hadn't

271

meant to be harsh or angry but that was how it had come out.

"I'm sorry if I gave you a shock."

"Damn Jeannot!"

"He didn't think you'd be so upset." He smiled. "Or, for that matter, did I."

She took a cigarette out of her bag and lit it herself. She made no apologies. She went to the oversized mirror, sat down, then worked at her hair with her long, deft fingers.

"You're looking better," Mallou said.

"Better?"

"Than you looked at Les Invalides that night."

"I didn't see you there."

"I didn't want you to." She'd turned, facing him. "I was tagging along with the other German women."

He chose not to respond to this.

"You must need something badly to risk coming here."

"Yes."

"Why should I do anything to help you?"

"Perhaps it isn't just for me."

The smile was sardonic. "For France?"

He shrugged, watching her stab the cigarette out on the dressing table glass. She wore a dress of some light jersey material that moved with her when she walked. She was a lioness in that tiny space.

"Von Banheim . . . it must have to do with von Banheim."

"It involves him."

She was in control, quieted. She sat down, crossing her legs, facing him.

"He's not a bad sort, you know. Decent in ways you wouldn't imagine."

Again he made no comment.

"And he loves me," she added, almost carelessly.

"Many people love you," Le Brun said, meaning it. She was outrageously generous; she could be a wonderful friend. But why in hell had she chosen a German? Perhaps, he thought, expressly because he *was* German. If he had a part in that—and he was afraid he had—he was extremely sorry.

"I know it pains you to be here. What is it, Le Brun?"

"It's very simple," Le Brun said. "I want von Banheim to contact Ernst Kröler for me. You must make him believe it's to his advantage as well as to Kröler's. He may resist you, disliking me as he does. If you can convince him, and I pray you can, the following message is to be delivered to Hermann Goering. . . ."

When Le Brun had left, she stood for a long moment, thinking of crying, but she knew that was not only silly but nonproductive. What she did was undress and stand naked in front of the mirror, examining herself critically. Here was her luck: she was still perfect.

Twenty-Five

THE AMERICAN BOMBERS, the sleek handsome planes called B-17s, were coming over northern France in waves, accompanied by their fighter planes, the P-46s.

"ASIA," caught between Berlin and Paris when the raid commenced, was drawn up on the tracks outside Aachen, actually within the broad path of the approaching air fleet . . . it could be heard high overhead, in a commingled distant roar, rolling away like distant thunder, gradually.

It was one of the first of the series of mass daylight raids considered suicidal by Luftwaffe Intelligence—even by the British—and Goering, slumped in his big chair in the salon car, sipping Médoc and eating sandwiches, was making Major Kruger run back and forth from Communications with news of the battle.

Kruger now arrived with a late bulletin. "Their fighter escort is already turning back," he announced ebulliently. "Galland reports Messerschmitts and Focke-Wulfs attacking in relays."

Reaching for a white pill, Goering merely grunted. He was no longer quick to snatch at early congratulatory communiqués. The Intelligence reports on these American bombers had told an ominous story: the new planes carried as many as ten .50-caliber machine guns, making them indeed what the Yanks were calling them—"Flying Fortresses." The German fighter pilots, for all their bravery and excellence, would be up against formidable obstacles.

But what made this new bomber an even more dangerous weapon was a small device it carried in its belly —the Norden bombsight. Galland's staff made no attempt to downplay its effectiveness. It could, they warned, pinpoint and destroy targets with remarkable accuracy. It posed a chilling threat to the future of the Reich's industrial output.

A Luftwaffe fighter zoomed in low over the train, the roar of its passage drowning out all conversation, even Goering's melancholy wanderings.

"Verflucht!" he muttered angrily.

Kruger, along with the Lieutenants Schpor and Eisenstadt, had run to the window facing the west. Goering, rising heavily, plodded after them.

Disappearing with a rush of air and a blast of engine over the troop car in the rear, the pilot dipped his wings in salute.

Lieutenant Schpor turned around to Goering excitedly: "A victory signal, Reichsmarschall—he's shot one of them down!"

"Freilich," murmured Goering, forcing a smile, unwilling to quell the boy's enthusiasm. "Marvelous."

Aides were now running back and forth between Communications and the salon car, bringing reports from aerodromes within France, within Germany, even from places as far-flung as Stuttgart, Frankfurt, and Bremen. All confirmed the fact that the Luftwaffe was exacting a terrible toll. The railroad car was thick with cigarette smoke, with loud voices and laughter. Perhaps now the arrogant Americans had learned their lesson: this slaughter of men, this costly loss of equipment, would surely create a backlash in the United States that no military commander could withstand.

Certainly no one would dare commit herself to another such disastrous adventure!

Certainly no one would dare commit himself to another

Goering heard Kruger's voice in his ears. "What we couldn't do if we had our full complement of planes, eh, sir?"

If the Queen had balls . . .

Kruger was referring to the fact that fully one-third of the Luftwaffe fighters were engaged in Russia—the new invasion he had so loudly, and futilely, deplored to the Führer's face.

"Is the target area ascertainable yet?" he asked.

"Galland guesses Koblenz, perhaps Düsseldorf. If they have any bombers left by the time they reach either city," Kruger replied.

Goering suddenly had a need to piss. "There will be enough left," he said dourly.

Kruger couldn't understand his commander's black mood—the Americans were being smashed. Break open the champagne, celebrate!

"I will be in my quarters," Goering said. "To be disturbed only when the final results have been confirmed."

Nodding, Kruger turned with a quick, harsh whisper. The room came to attention, remaining so until the Reichsmarschall had lumbered out and down the corridor.

In his private car, Goering passed Frau Thaler's compartment. The door was slightly ajar; he could see the woman in her slip, bent over a small ironing board, her rounded buttocks jutting toward him. He had never slept with her, though she occasionally performed other sexual services for him. Actually, he realized, he missed his wife, Emmy, not so much for the lovemaking as for the intuitive understanding she had of his worries, for the great spiritual comfort she was able to give him.

In his own bathroom, he urinated. He was beginning to do it more slowly, in spurts. His prostate—he must tolerate that damn doctor's fingers up his ass again! He put two of the white pills into his mouth, allowing them to dissolve slowly, like pieces of candy.

He buzzed for Heinrich, the valet appearing instantly, as if he'd been hovering beyond the door.

"I'm going out for a breath of air."

"Jawohl, Herr Reichsmarschall."

Heinrich disappeared to return moments later with a leather coat into which Goering struggled.

Outside the train the guard, spotting the Reichsmarschall emerge and move carefully down the steps onto the ground, saluted, then moved smartly forward to form a tighter cordon. Not too close, conforming to previous instructions.

Filling his lungs, Goering looked upward. It had been a stormy morning, but now the armies of thunder clouds had retreated and the sky, while clear, had not quite lost its menace, the early-spring sun giving it the dull sheen of steel.

Goering could see no planes, the activity had passed to areas in the east.

He began to pace back and forth beside the tracks, enjoying the bite of his boots on the coarse gravel, when Kruger appeared on the platform at the far end, jumping down to cross over to him.

"What is it?"

"General Galland, Reichsmarschall. Confirmed that the raid was designed for Düsseldorf. It is estimated that some seventy bombers got through."

Goering's glance moved up sharply. Major Kruger, he could see, had lost his euphoric glow; he had left without an overcoat and was trying not to shiver.

"Damages?"

"Extensive, sir. But, returning to base, the enemy will be at our mercy. Our fighters are already refueled and waiting. In my opinion this may be the last daylight raid attempted. The cost, they'll find, is simply too heavy."

"Thank you, Kruger, for your military wisdom. Now go in before you turn into an icicle."

"Zu Befehl, Herr Reichsmarschall."

It won't be the last enemy raid, Goering knew in his heart. *On the contrary, it's just the beginning.* He had had a long talk with Speer his last time in Berlin. In Speer's view, the production potential of the United States was unlimited; unless the war was speedily concluded on both fronts, they could find themselves overwhelmed in a global war of attrition.

Kruger had appeared again. This time he carried two dispatches in his hand, and made no attempt to hide his distress, merely saluting and handing Goering the communiqués.

The first was from Berchtesgaden and read: NEWS OF DESTRUCTION IN DÜSSELDORF HAS JUST REACHED ME. DEEPLY DISAPPOINTED IN LUFTWAFFE INABILITY TO PROTECT OUR GERMAN CITIES. LEAVING ON VISIT TO EASTERN FRONT. WILL RETURN IN TEN DAYS AT WHICH TIME REPORT TO ME. ADOLF HITLER.

Aware that members of the guard outside the train were watching, Goering stuffed the paper casually into a pocket and continued his pacing.

Ten days.

He could go home to Carinhall; Emmy would be a priceless companion, balm for his wounds. But a hard, practical streak in him told him, better not! Wiser to remain in the field, active, shoring up his defenses. For once he must face the Führer and not fall apart! *You can't bleed the Luftwaffe at both ends and expect results,* he would say. Yes, he would tell Hitler that. He would remind him of the failures of industry to meet minimum quotas. These insufficiencies could not all be blamed on Hermann Goering. Other heads would have to roll. *Tant pis,* as the French would put it.

He then remembered the second dispatch he was holding.

It was from Paris. IMPORTANT YOU RETURN HERE AS SOON AS POSSIBLE. OBJECT YOU HAVE WANTED ABOVE ALL OTHERS WITHIN REACH. ERNST KRÖLER.

Twenty-Six

THE MERCEDES TOURING CAR drew up to the Crillon at exactly two P.M. as Mallou earlier that day had informed Le Brun to expect it. In the back was Ernst Kröler; Sergeant Raeder was sitting alongside the driver.

"Please," said Kröler, leaning over, opening the door, beckoning Le Brun next to him.

Outfitted that morning by a tailor friend of Georges', mustache shaved, Le Brun looked reasonably respectable again. This was one occasion where if clothes did not make the man, they could help undo him; top Nazis did not willingly deal with beggars.

They sped at once into the Concorde traffic.

"You haven't changed much," Kröler said. "As a matter of fact, you look pretty fit."

"I've been in the country."

"We gathered you weren't in Paris," Kröler said with a dry smile. "At least if you were, we couldn't find you."

Raeder made a noise as if throttling a cough. "The sergeant doesn't think much of our arrangements today. He believes you're up to something. It's possible of course. For your sake as well as ours I hope not. Beyond the outline of your proposition, we were given no details."

Le Brun did not comment. From where he was sitting, Raeder's newly shaved head loomed squarely in front of him, a pimple at the base of the neck starting to blossom.

Le Brun swung his glance out to the city. They were moving fast, the driver paying no attention to traffic regulations. It was a day to treasure. There was perfume on a zephyrlike breeze; defiant of the invaders, Paris was flaunting her beauty like a coquette.

They were soon at the *gare,* and only slowing slightly, speeding down the access road to the yards, where ASIA sat, uncoiled on the tracks, a metallic serpent dozing in the sunlight.

The Luftwaffe guard converged, recognizing Kröler and Raeder at once, but still carefully inspecting their IDs. Minutes later, awkwardly silent, the visitors were in the third coach, the conference coach, awaiting Goering, who, before they realized it, had suddenly appeared in the entryway, standing there a moment, appraising them. "Please," he said to Kröler and Raeder, who had snapped to attention. Giving Le Brun a cool nod, he arranged himself in the end chair of the conference table.

They all took seats now, but not too close. No refreshments were brought. The Reichsmarschall was wearing a white silk Cossack shirt, balloonlike trousers, and seemed relaxed, almost sleepy. "I'm waiting, monsieur," he said finally to Le Brun.

Le Brun's throat was dry. So much depended on how Goering perceived him. For all his bulk, Goering wasn't soft.

"As Kröler was informed, I can deliver the object in question," he began matter-of-factly.

"For the moment we'll set aside your bona fides in that regard. What is your price?"

"The Jacobi collection."

Raeder couldn't help a sharp, indrawn breath. His glance spurted to the Reichsmarschall. Goering ignored him, eyes boring into Le Brun.

"So it is still in Paris?"

"Yes, Reichsmarschall."

"Why shouldn't I give you over to Raeder here—I can tell you nothing would delight him more—and sooner or later the collection would be aboard this train."

"That could happen. The flesh, mine particularly, I admit, is weak."

"But I'd lose out on the Samothrace, you mean?"
Le Brun shrugged and smiled and waited.

Goering remained immobile in his chair. They

couldn't really tell if he was awake. But then a ringed finger pressed a button. Almost instantly an orderly appeared with a pot of coffee and a large dish of chocolate pastries.

They were all served, Le Brun significantly immediately after Goering. Le Brun relaxed slightly. The man was talking: "I don't give a damn for those Jacobi paintings, Le Brun. Picasso, Degas, the rest of that degenerate crew—you can have them!"

The wide mouth snapped up a pastry. Le Brun, even at this vital juncture, couldn't help reaching for one himself. Raeder didn't dare, toying with a coffee spoon. Kröler was making notes on a pad.

Le Brun allowed the sweet taste to linger as long as he could. "I would want to be able to remove the collection from its hiding place in the city without fear of being impeded in any way," he said. "Of course it would not be transported across the zone until you, in turn, receive the sculpture."

"Agreed," said Goering, wiping his lips. He was staring at Le Brun moodily as if trying to penetrate his defenses, divine the game being played. "You're a Frenchman," he said now, slowly. "A loyal one, I gather. How do I account for your turning over to me one of your country's most important works of art?"

"Call it a trade-off, Reichsmarschall. I have a loyalty to Aaron Jacobi—"

"Greater than to France?"

"Jacobi was . . . *is* a surrogate father. I owe him a great deal. And I'll be honest; I believe Germany will lose the war. I expect that eventually the Samothrace will come home. But if the Jacobi collection is acquired by you—or let's say your people—inevitably it will be dispersed, scattered to the four winds, not ever to return, even in victory."

It was bold, nervy. He could expect an explosion. He got a silent one from Raeder. Raeder was furious, ready to shoot him right there at the table. Flushed, Kröler kept his eyes on Goering. But Goering was nodding; he seemed quite satisfied.

"When can this be consummated?"

"There are slight problems on my side. People I will have to persuade, perhaps buy. Nothing I can't handle, however, be assured of that. The time element is risky. Two months, I'd say. I'll be in touch with Herr Kröler for the final arrangements."

"Kröler, see that he has the necessary passes."

"Yes, sir."

"And that I'm not harassed in any way . . . by other German units," Le Brun said. He was looking at Raeder. "I could hardly function in your behalf, Reichsmarschall, should an accident occur," Le Brun added.

"No accidents will occur," Goering said, looking at Raeder, too. "Goodbye and good luck. Kröler, you and the sergeant remain."

Le Brun was ushered to the Mercedes by a lieutenant, who asked him where he wanted to be delivered.

"Anywhere near the Arc de Triomphe will do," Le Brun answered, smiling.

As soon as Le Brun was out the door, Raeder turned to Goering, his tone quiet and formal as usual, but with a touch of sugar in it: "Following the transfer of the Samothrace sculpture, Reichsmarschall, I take it we are expected—notwithstanding anything said to Le Brun—to secure the Jacobi collection?"

"Secure it?"

"For the Reich."

On his feet, Goering said witheringly: "You will secure nothing! I gave Le Brun my word. I am not a chameleon, Sergeant Raeder, nor a liar. I am an officer of the German armed forces, whose father was an officer. And his father before him. You, a Prussian, ought to know better!"

Raeder said nothing, his face becoming a sullen mask. But Goering's outburst, like an offshore squall, had spent itself; he walked over to the jar with the white tablets. A new thought, or an addendum to the principal question, struck him as something that must be verbalized. Turning, he said curtly, "We are not vandals, Sergeant. We are victors—a big difference: keep it in mind."

Raeder managed a smile.

"I was only thinking of the money the collection would bring—gold on the market. But you are right, of course, sir. Your orders will be strictly enforced. I will personally assume responsibility."

Like hell! Raeder thought. *And there are others who will listen to me, you fat-assed, doped-up mountain of lard!*

Le Brun had reached Mischa at his club, Mischa agreeing to meet him immediately. Le Brun had chosen the gardens of the Palais de Chaillot again. On a fine spring day like today there would be children and old people and ordinary citizens; he and Mischa would be nicely covered.

Actually, he expected to be shadowed, but for the moment it scarcely mattered. Later, before returning to Georges', though, the tail would have to be shaken.

He wasted no time with Mischa, briefly outlining the progress being made at the farm, recounting the morning meeting with Goering and the agreed-upon exchange. Mischa was impressed and for once did not try to conceal it. From beginning to end, he realized, Le Brun had acted with courage and audacity: Jacobi's faith in him had not been unfounded.

"But surely you don't expect the son-of-a-bitch to live up to his bargain?"

"Goering? I'm not sure. You see," Le Brun said with irony, "I'm hardly living up to mine, am I? Exchanging phony goods for the real thing!"

They strolled in silence for another moment. "No," continued Le Brun, "we will have to assume that somewhere along the line they will breach the agreement—or try to. At least we'd be fools not to anticipate that possibility. Which is the reason I wanted to see you today. Have you a channel to Aaron Jacobi in London?"

The old man looked up questioningly.

"I'd prefer not to go through the Resistance. Conflicting interests there. Someone might get the idea the collection could be quite valuable immediately, the funds going to *their* faction!"

"He always intended to give it to France," Mischa murmured.

"He still intends to, I'm sure," Le Brun said. "At the proper time. Right now there's a missing piece to the equation, a move I can't trigger from here. Don't know whether it can be worked from London either, but it's worth a try. Can you reach Aaron Jacobi for me, Prince Kilkanov?"

Mischa laughed. They'd come to two empty chairs and took them companionably, like old friends. "Not me, the Princess I think."

The sun was on Mischa's face, after the hard winter a blessing. He could feel the life force surging through him . . . this minute he felt he could live forever. He was even beginning to appreciate Le Brun, which was an unexpected turn of events. "The Princess is close to Father Gregory at our church. The Church, need I tell you, in war or peace, manages to keep its lines of communication intact. Yes, Father Gregory, I would bet, can manage London. What message would you have him send?"

Unshaven, unwashed, having driven most of the night, crossing at the usual place, having decided not to use Kröler's passes—much better that his point of entry into the unoccupied zone remain his own business—Le Brun arrived at the farm at breakfasttime. Instant pandemonium. Had he been successful? What arrangements had been made? Was Goering buying it? No, sit down first; eat! drink!

He ate and drank—hot tea laced with brandy—and demanded to know if the Samothrace was finished—or had they been sitting on their asses in his absence, enjoying the good country life?

"Ha, *funny!*" said Umbarti. "Those damn folds, the folds of her garment! Have you any idea how much work?"

But they were alert and excited, even Pierre Brazin. "Of course it isn't ready, but I'll admit, Le Brun, it's gone much faster than I expected."

And they had a surprise for him, Sara said. Her soft, dark eyes hadn't left him. But only after he'd bathed, rested. All right, he agreed, smiling at her.

He would, he had decided on the way down, give them no details of the exchange, not because of mistrust or any arbitrary desire to keep it to himself, but, one thing, the element of the scheme demanding Aaron

Jacobi's participation was still uncertain. For another—he was honest with himself—he didn't want this band of geniuses picking holes in his plan, coming up with artistic variations: better to let the mystery build—as well as their confidence in his wizardry—while they kept their minds on the job.

There was one at the table who had given Le Brun no more than a perfunctory greeting, sensing his arrival brought no welcome news: Morgan. "She's not there," Le Brun said to him. "I'm very sorry."

"You checked it out?"

Le Brun nodded. "The best I could. No Jews have returned."

In the silence, Morgan rose and left the kitchen. Wordlessly, Umbarti, Epernet, and Brazin followed him. Le Brun could see the four men through the window, trudging down the path to the studio.

"I'll fix your bath," Sara told him.

"No, please."

"I'd like to," she said.

They indeed had a surprise for him. From the waist up, with the wings already connected, the lady appeared a precise copy of the plaster of Paris model. From the waist down, not so precise; the finer details were still to be delineated. But what they'd done was to construct a scaffolding around her, roughly fifteen feet in diameter, which they'd lined with old mattresses, blankets, and burlap, even topping it with a ceiling. "Sara's idea," Epernet said. "See h-how the sound is mu-muffled."

He went beyond the improvised hut as they pounded away at the marble inside. Sure enough, one could hear them, but in the open air, with the studio doors closed, hardly at all.

"We sent the woodcutters away," said Umbarti. "Saved half the forest."

He watched them awhile, Brazin and Umbarti concentrating on the more difficult area, using fine-toothed chisels, Sara's enlargements of the original at d'Albion on the floor in front of them. Intent on each delicate blow of hammer and chisel, they could hardly be told apart, covered like ghosts with white marble dust.

Above them, Epernet and Morgan, on ladders, were polishing the areas Brazin considered finished. First wetting the torso, they were working it carefully with sandstone. It was imperative that the full richness of the marble be brought to the surface by hand polishing; Brazin had insisted on this tedious final process. Goering's experts would be quick to detect the traces of a machine polisher.

No one spoke of the final hurdle. How, when all else was accomplished, would they be able to weather the marble convincingly?

Another problem of course was—the following weeks as Le Brun used every excuse to stay away from the farm—Sara Jacobi. It was difficult not to keep watching her, her body, the way she moved, laughed, frowned, talked. Difficult not to build up a hatred of Morgan, in whose bed she slept every night.

He invented chores, some of them necessary. Find a vehicle sufficiently large and strong enough to transport the new Samothrace. Buy it from someone reliable, who would stifle his curiosity about the buyer. *Will weapons be needed?* he asked himself. *Not if the exchange goes smoothly.* Most rifles and sidearms had been confiscated by the police, but farmers were ever reluctant to give up this last symbol of independence. Shotguns could be had with ample ammunition, if one tramped around enough, pockets stuffed with francs. He bought one gun a week, gradually acquiring a decent arsenal.

Once, after dinner, Umbarti beckoned him outside. It was early May, and light was still in the western sky. The air was touched with the mint-smell of new grass and flowers budding. Le Brun could see Sara through the kitchen window helping with the dishes. She had filled out, still slim but sturdier, strong. "A real country wench," Morgan had remarked the other day, cupping her chin intimately, grinning. It was odd—following Le Brun's return, his Paris family seemed forgotten. Sara had instantly looked to Le Brun, then away, annoyed with Morgan, red staining her cheeks.

"I believe I have something interesting for you,"

Umbarti said. "But just for you and me, eh, for the moment?"

Le Brun didn't understand what Umbarti was getting at, but gathered that it necessitated a quiet trip to d'Albion. On the way to the château, Umbarti chattered about everything but the project. The British must be bombing the hell out of Germany; you could hear the Lancasters flying over almost every night. And wait till the Americans really got into it!

At d'Albion, Christine Chandon was waiting for them, looking younger, Le Brun thought, almost girlish. By the easy familiarity she and Umbarti displayed, it wasn't difficult to assess their relationship. She led them into the chapel where the real Samothrace stood, moonlight shining on the statue through the stained-glass windows, eerily beautiful. Christine picked up an object lying beside the pedestal. Removing the covering cloth, she now raised it up for them to see.

It was a muscular arm from "The Sailor," its surface chipped away as they had done at the farm; but the new, fresh marble underneath had been treated by Christine. She now held it against the Samothrace for comparison; it looked every bit as old and pitted and weathered as the original.

Christine and Umbarti were watching Le Brun, however. Having taken the arm from Christine, he was matching its patina with the Samothrace's—skin against skin, as it were, up and down, taking nothing for granted.

Behind him, Umbarti couldn't hold it any longer. Over Le Brun's shoulder he said, "Good, huh? *Magnifico!*"

"*Magnifico, Carlo.*" And to Christine, embracing her. "How in hell did you do it?"

She was smiling at the two men, delighted by their approbation. "Just an old family recipe my mother taught me. Grime and soil, mosses and lichens, I think some leeks, definitely garlic, and oh, yes . . . acids, not too caustic—they'd eat at the marble. The acids were a bother, I admit. A hundred batches before the final one." She held up long, graceful fingers, the tips stained and blistered, which Umbarti would have kissed, holding back in time, remembering Le Brun's presence. "And then a long soaking—at least a week. Don't worry," she added, "I've had a tank built in Bourges big enough for the Samothrace. To clean it, I've told everyone."

"My God, she's clever, isn't she?" declared Umbarti.

"A true heroine," said Le Brun, meaning it. "Look, why don't I take the arm back with me right now to show Brazin? Carlo, you might as well spend the night here, I'm sure Christine can find a bed for you—have her give you the exact formula—forgive me, recipe. We'll need to have a large enough batch of it made up."

They beamed at him, happy at his reaction, also smugly pleased he hadn't divined their secret. Heading out of the chapel, Le Brun could hear their smothered laughter. Children! Love, then, and sex, too, he had no doubt, could come at any age and make one any age! Christ, what a philosophic giant he was! Considering Christine's success with the marble, his mood should have been good; instead it was rotten. Slamming the Citroën into gear, he felt more frustrated, more cheated by circumstance than ever.

Twenty-Seven

SHE HAD FINALLY BEEN PRONOUNCED completed, her pristine body immersed in Christine's outsized tub, steeped for a week in the foul-smelling brew Christine had concocted, allowed to dry in the studio, which stank of her for days; but now cleansed and properly aged—uniquely enhancing her beauty—she stood proudly before them for inspection.

There were critical areas: the joints where the wings had been attached, the joint to the pedestal. But the pedestal marble had come from Rhodes, Umbarti pointed out, and so the difference there was authentic. The pittings, of course, did not exactly match those of the original. But Goering's experts, in the unlikely case that their suspicions were aroused, would not have Pythokritos to consult with or the original to check against. And ordinary photographs would hardly reveal such details.

She was superb, they thought, trying to be as objective as possible. Even the French experts, should the copy instead of the original be returned, would be fooled. And what was marvelous was that Christine's magic solution had not dulled the golden sheen characteristic of Parian marble; all in all, the four sculptors and Le Brun agreed, she was a dead ringer for her d'Albion sister.

Under Le Brun's whip, they'd been working night and day. Now they were too damned tired to celebrate. They looked at their Samothrace, one by one, and then walked to the farmhouse for dinner. It was special that night, with a fine old Romanée-Conti that Sara had gotten for the occasion, but they hardly were aware what they were eating or drinking. And besides, they knew that perhaps the most delicate part of the affair remained to be concluded: the transfer of the sculpture to Reichsmarschall Hermann Goering.

Le Brun telephoned Paris from the hotel room in Vierzon, a number Kröler had given him. The person receiving his call took his message. Within minutes he received a call back. Kröler. "This line is safe," Kröler said. "What have you got?"

"I am ready to deliver at this end," Le Brun said without preamble. "How do you want to accept?"

A short pause and Kröler said, "The receiving party will send his personal train."

A moment elapsed, Le Brun trying to keep the relief out of his voice; his entire strategy had depended on Goering sending ASIA to pick up his treasure. "Will he be aboard?"

Kröler's voice went cold. "I cannot predict his intentions in that regard."

"Just curious," said Le Brun. "There is one further stipulation: the Prince Kilkanov has been designated by me to collect the Jacobi paintings and truck them to the point of exchange. Should any attempts be made to harm the Prince, to intercept his vehicle, in short, should that part of the bargain, inadvertently or even accidentally, be aborted, the exchange is off."

"I believe," Kröler said stiffly, "that my principal gave you his word in that respect."

"In any case I wanted to make my position clear," conceded Le Brun. "I will be prepared to deliver at 2100 hours in the marshaling yards of the railroad depot of the town agreed upon—exactly three days from today, the twenty-third. Is that satisfactory?"

"I'll get back to you within the hour," Kröler said.

Twenty-Eight

IT WAS TWILIGHT, one of those transitional evenings in late spring when the earth smells pungent though it is not yet summerdry. The horizon had turned from gaudy purple to tame violet-gray.

Le Brun had crawled to the top of the railroad water tower on the unoccupied side. Perched there, he could see over to the occupied section of the station even without his binoculars. The station straddled the border and was a junction, with large marshaling yards. From there, in normal times, freight was switched to Brittany and Normandy, as well as to the south. Not too far away was the city of Vierzon.

There was no visible kiosk as at most borders. A large hut served as a border station on the highway that ran parallel to the main tracks. This hut housed both German and French guards, one German for the moment in view, leaning against the building, smoking a cigar.

Although some fifteen minutes still remained before the rendezvous, Le Brun could see the ASIA's unmistakable prow, a snake's head, rounding the turn into the yards, slowing to a stop. Immediately behind the engine was the armored car with the usual Luftwaffe detachment. Since Le Brun had last seen the train, turreted machine guns had been mounted on the roof, fore and aft, gun crews visible at each. Behind the armored coach something else caught his eye: an empty flatbed car, clearly designed to be the private chariot of the Samothrace. As Le Brun continued to observe ASIA, several squads disembarked, setting up the usual mobile defense along the tracks.

Some distance away from the water tower, an ambulance, markings indicating a nonexistent hospital in Bourges, waited on the road leading to the border hut. Standing alongside the vehicle were Morgan and Epernet. They were supposed to be waiting inside the vehicle. But Morgan as usual had casually shrugged off his orders. Le Brun hadn't wanted to take him along, but had no choice. Behind the ambulance was his black Citroën, the driver inside the car, out of sight.

Le Brun swung his binoculars across the zone again. Despite Goering's assurance, he had the firm conviction that the plunderers would not allow the Jacobi collection to escape them, one way or another, by whatever stratagem. But would the grab come from the ASIA command, in direct and blatant contradiction to the Reichsmarschall's promise? Le Brun doubted it. From where then? Yet, other than the Luftwaffe patrol, the train itself, sitting on the tracks in the fading light, its menace open, unconcealed, he hadn't a clue. A rustic springtime landscape . . .

He hated them. The hate knotted his stomach; he hated the bucket-helmeted men in jackboots patrolling the marshaling yards beyond. Most of all he hated their masters. But hate alone would not work for him now. . . .

Another last sweep of the binoculars and he climbed down from the tower. Like naughty children, Morgan and Epernet immediately dived back into the ambulance. When Le Brun arrived, they were crouched inside alongside the Samothrace, grinning at him. Both were big men, and with the statue, there was hardly an inch to spare.

"The train's here," Le Brun informed them. "Just pulled in. Morgan, you remember what I told you?"

"I'm not to open my big mouth; my accent might give me away."

"If somebody like Kröler hears it, yes. But that's not all . . ."

"I'm to watch out for my temper. I'm to tell myself those bastards are my friends; I'm supposed to be picking up a lot of pocket money out of this caper."

Nodding, Le Brun turned to Epernet.

"Okay?"

"O-k-kay," Epernet replied.

Le Brun closed the door of the ambulance and turned to the Citroën behind it. Sara Jacobi was at the wheel; she wore a dark brown sweater and no makeup and was putting out a cigarette as he crossed over to her. He had tried to keep her from coming. Useless. Beneath her soft-spoken insistence was the singlemindedness and discipline of a French Legionnaire. "It was my farm you used," she had told him. "My father's paintings will be delivered—"

"We hope—'"

"All right—'we hope.' But I've a right to come along. A vested interest. And another thing, you can't really anticipate what will happen, can you? You may need the Citroën badly. And I'm one helluva driver!"

And she had smiled, looking for an instant the way Erica had looked, but another kind of humor in her eyes. *Don't tell me about life, I'll tell you,* the smile said. And without warning she had leaned into him, kissing him on the lips, letting the sweetness linger for both of them before pulling away as he reached for her. "That was wicked, wasn't it? Forgive me, Claude?"

She gave him no chance; she was flying up to her room.

"We're almost ready," he said to her now. "You'll stay here as you promised. If we need you, you'll know it. But even then you're to wait where you are—"

She gave him an obedient nod, possibly reliable, possibly not, and he checked his watch. About now, the Prince Kilkanov, with two trucks, ought to be pulling over to the side of the Paris-Tours road, two miles short of the depot and the border. The Prince, unless Goering's orders had been countermanded, would have the Jacobi collection with him.

Le Brun's instructions had been transmitted to Mischa directly by phone and necessarily had been terse. The afternoon of the twenty-third, he was to be at his Russian church with helpers. A large furniture truck would arrive. The man driving it was named Georges and could be relied upon absolutely. The Jacobi collection was to be removed from the cave below and placed inside the truck, which would be outfitted with racks to receive the paintings.

Item number two: once loaded, the truck, with Mischa accompanying the driver, was to proceed to a point outside Paris where it would rendezvous with a second truck. From here on, Mischa was to surrender all initiative to Georges.

Mischa had exploded. "Why this Georges character? And what's going on? Dammit, Le Brun, don't you trust me?"

"What you don't know at this point, dear Prince Kilkanov, can't hurt us and can't hurt you."

Mischa had hung up, bitter. *And just when I'd begun to think better of Le Brun!*

The arrangements had worked out as Le Brun had said they would. With Father Gregory's help, plus the men from the club he'd dragooned, Mischa supervised the move. The paintings were carried up through the empty church while the other priests gaped, and placed inside the maw of the huge van. Seventy-seven masterpieces, Mischa counted with Father Gregory, not believing they'd get them all into the single vehicle. But the racks had been cleverly constructed, and by God, the paintings all went in.

Outside Versailles, at the exact spot Le Brun had indicated, another truck awaited them, remarkably the twin to theirs, even to the numbers on the license plates. The two trucks had then proceeded through a flaming sunset, Georges timing their speed so that they arrived at the designated spot near the depot checkpoint almost exactly on schedule.

Mischa, Georges, and Henri, a good-natured young fellow who had said hello to Mischa and that was that, got out to stretch their legs, smoke, and wait. Puffing his cigarette furiously, Mischa looked down at Georges —he could have picked the little man up and hurled him like a ripe tomato at the nearest tree. "Well, what happens now?" he growled, trying to keep it civil. "Or am I supposed to drive to my death not knowing the secret?"

Georges looked at the Prince towering above him and laughed. It was a heartier sound than anyone would have expected. He ground out his butt in the dirt. He glanced at the sky, searching for something that wasn't there, then back at Mischa.

"No reason you shouldn't know." he said. "In a little while—the way Le Brun explained it—all hell may break loose and we'll be in the middle of it. Let me give you the timetable. . . ."

The ambulance was waved through the checkpoint without either the Vichy guard or the one German guard in sight even bothering to ask for identification of contents within. Clearly orders from above and/or intimidation by the Goering faction.

There was a side road leading from the checkpoint to the marshaling yards. Unwilling to risk damaging his cargo, Le Brun drove carefully until he came abeam of the train, two sets of tracks intervening. Braking, he turned the ignition key and got out.

Three Germans were already striding across the tracks toward him; they were Kröler, Colonel Bocke, and Sergeant Raeder. Reaching the ambulance, Kröler and Bocke shook hands with Le Brun. Raeder hung back, making a vague gesture of greeting.

Bocke explained his presence: "Colonel Urquhardt, commanding the train's military complement, is sick. I volunteered to replace him. Don't mind telling you, Le Brun, I consider it a lucky break for me. An exciting moment."

"Why the ambulance?" Kröler asked. "Couldn't you find a larger vehicle?"

"Sure," Le Brun answered. "But people might question a truck; an ambulance supplies its own answers." He flung the doors open, the Germans crowding around, looking over his shoulder. Morgan and Epernet were revealed sitting beside the Samothrace.

"Two of the men who helped me swing it," explained Le Brun. "Step back a minute if you don't mind."

The Germans retreated slightly as Morgan and Epernet kicked and pushed out the canvas sides and top of the ambulance. It was obvious that the chassis had been removed earlier and nailed lightly back. In hardly more than a minute the top and sides were down, knocked clear to the tracks, the Samothrace lying open to the night.

The Germans now pushed forward, flashlights beamed at her. Le Brun scarcely breathed. "The Reichsmarschall will be very pleased," Kröler said finally.

"Then I'm pleased," said Le Brun.

"Who'd you have to bribe, a curator?" Bocke joked.

"Just about," replied Le Brun, as if Bocke had hit the nail on the head. "Curators like money, too."

"What will happen when it's discovered she's gone?" Kröler asked. "Will they blame it on us?"

"Possibly, but they won't be able to prove anything."

"Will you get in trouble, Le Brun?"

"I think I've covered my tracks pretty well. Of course, one never knows. . . . However, it's getting late, gentlemen. No offense, but I'd prefer not being seen here with you. May we make the transfer?"

Bocke looked at Kröler, who did not demur. Bocke shouted a command toward the train. Immediately two Luftwaffe squads, at least twenty brawny men, came running, pounced on the Samothrace, and with much grunting and swearing—she was heavier than they anticipated—manhandled her across to the flatcar, where a wooden cradle had been built to receive her. Then with superb efficiency, as if the maneuver had been practiced by the numbers, chocks were placed and the statue secured with heavy rope. Men were ready to throw a large tarp over her when Kröler shouted, "Wait!"

They held back as he barked another command, and a huge searchlight on the roof of the armament car swiveled down, bathing the sculpture in dazzling white light.

It was as though the curtain in a theater had been

294

suddenly drawn, the surpassing beauty of an actress center stage silencing the audience's restlessness.

They were hanging over her, those who had brought her, others from the machine-gun turrets, half a hundred war-tempered men, riveted by whatever the artist had managed to capture in the marble; by the sheer power and mystery of the truncated figure.

Aware of the theatricality of the moment, Kröler moved forward, wanting to prolong it, savor it. But Raeder had joined him, and fear pricked at Le Brun. Not of Kröler: Kröler wanted success too badly for his own career ends. Fear of Raeder: Raeder was young, with a good, solid art background; with a suspicious mind, a suspicious eye. Raeder was now pacing the length of her and, abruptly, without reason it seemed, paused and knelt.

Aware of the men watching, the spotlight on him, Raeder took his time, playing up to them, making them wonder what he was up to. Probing the base of the left wing with his fingertips, a master safecracker at work perhaps, he rose suddenly, strode to Le Brun, and announced, voice parade-ground harsh, carrying over the flatcar: "Were you aware that the left wing is a restoration?"

Insects fluttered against the searchlight glass; otherwise the silence was absolute.

"No, I was not," Le Brun said humbly.

"I'll show you the proof of it," Raeder said in a leading man's baritone. "In Berlin! When you come to visit!"

The tension broke, a roll of laughter sweeping over the troops. A corporal slapped his thigh. Raeder delighted in it, hands akimbo on hips like the Führer, grinning at Le Brun.

Le Brun was smiling automatically, but his eyes had taken in a face just above the level of the flatcar—Morgan's. The white light from above exaggerated Morgan's blondness, but also the anger in him: he was a grotesque dummy placed there to register unholy rage. Deliberately, Le Brun took several steps toward him, backing around, hoping to at least block him from the others.

"Jesus, Morgan!" he hissed.

Morgan's face disappeared.

Bocke's voice had cut through the merriment. "Put the tarp in position, please. Secure it properly."

Men jumped to obey. Le Brun turned to Kröler. "Now for your part of the bargain, Herr Kröler."

"Where are your trucks?" Raeder intervened. "I don't see them."

Bocke moved next to Raeder, Le Brun noticed. The two men were tensed, like runners at the start of a race.

"One truck, a big one," Le Brun said. "And just up the road. Two shots in the air will fetch it."

Without comment, Bocke reached for his service revolver, yanked it out of the holster, and fired twice.

He, Raeder, and Kröler twisted around to the north, where the truck with the paintings would appear. It was night now, but not too dark, the moon almost full. The road had a silver sheen on it; an approaching vehicle would be picked up at once. Then they could all hear it, and several moments later see it, speeding toward the checkpoint. But abruptly a half-dozen uniformed men darted out of the checkpoint hut. They paused, then fired a warning burst in the air from their submachine guns.

"What in hell's going on?" Le Brun demanded. The truck had screeched to a stop a thousand or so yards from the soldiers.

The checkpoint Germans were moving slowly, weapons at the ready, toward the truck.

"Did you really think you'd get away with it?" Raeder asked.

"I have the Reichsmarschall's word," Le Brun said to Bocke imploringly. He was talking into the wind, playing for time and knew it; the Luftwaffe troops, having secured the tarp on the Samothrace, were moving back toward their armored coach, ignoring the action at the checkpoint.

"The Reichsmarschall is not a part of this," Bocke said quietly. The Luger had not been replaced in the holster; it was directed at Le Brun.

So it was Raeder and Bocke! For proof, Kröler had disappeared; Le Brun could see him climbing into

296

Goering's bedroom car. Kröler wanted to hear nothing, know nothing.

"If you obey directions, you'll come out of this alive," Bocke said.

"What do you want me to do?" asked Le Brun with a shrug. He had managed a glance at his watch: 2100 hours in thirty seconds.

"Call off the men you brought with you. Order the driver of the truck and anyone else in it to turn around and head back for Paris."

"Where in Paris?"

"He'll be escorted," Raeder said. His voice was slightly fluted, breathless; he was like someone who had just laid down his cards in a poker game and was preparing to rake in a giant pot.

"So just the two of you . . . a private undertaking, I gather," Le Brun said. "The paintings will end up in Switzerland, temporarily. When the war is over, where will they be sold? South America? The United States?"

Bocke was silent; he had a classic soldier's face, thin, regular nose, lean cheeks, a slit of a mouth. He could have given orders to hold at Thermopylae. "The money will buy you plenty of pretty boys, Colonel," Le Brun said.

The Luger, butt first, sailed up like a mailed fist at Le Brun's head. Le Brun ducked, hit the floor of the flatcar, rolled over, and spun to the ground next to the car wheels.

They could have killed him where he stood, but there was a sudden rumbling above, quick claps of thunder, that seized their attention, startling them. The sound came from the west, from out of a great cloudbank trapped in the moonlight. Then the first of the planes burst free, heading toward the marshaling yards and the train—a Lancaster bomber. Behind it, in V formation, two additional Lancasters.

Gun crews were rushing their posts, and several antiaircraft guns from the rear coach began to chatter.

Under the lip of the flatcar, Le Brun, mesmerized, watched it. Although he had planned it, called for it, he could scarcely believe it was happening, that Aaron Jacobi had pulled it off.

Above him a Luftwaffe captain was shouting, "Colonel, have I your permission to get us out of here?"

Bocke was staring upward, transfixed. "They must think Goering is on the train," he said, the thin mouth twisted. "They've been tipped. Your Le Brun tipped them, Raeder."

Le Brun was on his feet; the lead bomber, unusually low, released its load. The woods on the far side of ASIA exploded, the forest appeared to lift into the air, falling back on the train.

"Signal the engineer," Bocke shouted to the captain.

The second and third bombers roared over on their run. Two more explosions in the woods; flaming branches, earth, debris, raining over them on the flatcar.

"Listen to me, Bocke!" Raeder was screaming. "They've found out we've got the Samothrace aboard!" They don't dare hit us! They just want to bracket us, stop us! My God, don't you see?"

The guns on the train were doing their best, puncturing the sky with tracers; the Lancasters were seeking altitude; the Luftwaffe captain was bellowing into a walkie-talkie, trying to make sense to the engineer. Within seconds the train bolted forward once, and then again, like a dog pawing the ground, then edged backward, but with painful hesitations; the armor plate above and below made the engine's load extraordinarily heavy and difficult to get under way.

"At least leave me a platoon—a squad," Raeder begged. "There are millions involved. The war will be over, Bocke—we'll lose; we'll be shit on again! Then what will happen to us?"

The Lancasters were forming for another run. Bocke stared up at them and back to Raeder. There was a doubt about what was going through Bocke's head. "You may be right, Sergeant. They may not want to hit us, just trap us, demolish the tracks ahead. Sorry about the paintings, but the train is my responsibility. I'm in command. Captain, when in hell are we going to move?"

The train lurched forward yet again and Bocke toppled, but it wasn't the unexpected movement—his chest looked as if it had been splashed with blood, and Le Brun saw Morgan scooting toward the ambulance with his shotgun smoking.

The train was beginning to back up at a steady but slow pace while a machine gun on top of the armament car above Le Brun combed the area between it and the ambulance. Le Brun was certain Morgan would be caught in the sweeping fire, but he saw him reach the ambulance, dive under it. And then Le Brun, with the train moving past him, backing out of the yards, had his own safety to think about. About to make his own dash to join Morgan, he saw that Raeder had jumped from the flatcar and was running for the truck with the paintings, at the same time waving to the soldiers from the checkpoint to follow him.

The train was past Le Brun now, while the Lancaster eggs broke a final time in the woods, spewing dirt and fire on the yards. Gathering speed, the train was almost gone. So were the Lancasters. They'd be heading for home, Le Brun knew, mission accomplished.

He made the ambulance, flung himself under it, and grabbed a third shotgun Epernet pushed at him. Morgan was cursing, fumbling with his gun, reloading it. "Why doesn't the damn fool get going?" he asked in English, indicating the truck.

Le Brun asked himself the same question. The driver—whom would Georges have chosen, Henri?—had been instructed in a situation like this to go screaming into reverse. Anything, just disappear!

Henri knew about the contingency plan. But just for a breath he panicked, hands frozen to the wheel, and the lousy bullets from the approaching *Boches* had filled the cab and he knew he was bleeding in the legs —he couldn't get them to put pressure on the clutch. And then more bullets smashed around him. He thought he could see them approaching, almost on top of him, the dirty gray-green sons-of-bitches, then, like a shade being drawn, he couldn't see anything at all.

From under the ambulance, Le Brun had to constrain Morgan and Epernet. The shotguns had only so much range. "A few more seconds," he pleaded with them.

They could see Raeder and the two border guards circling the truck, Raeder hurrying around to the rear, yanking open the truck doors, expecting to see an Arabain Nights treasure within, prepared to confound everyone and drive off with it. But the inside of the truck was empty, bare as a ransacked tomb, and from where he watched, Le Brun could see the astonishment, the agonized frustration, in Raeder's face.

Raeder had turned, straining to sight up the road where Mischa and Georges waited with the second truck. Le Brun knew what was in Raeder's mind: he was realizing how he'd been fooled, but even then was frantically trying to devise a way to turn things around.

In that brief period, however, the Germans forgot the men under the ambulance, and that was all Morgan needed: wriggling forward, he jumped up and, racing forward, was almost upon them when he fired. The shotgun's accuracy was poor, but the blast felled one of the guards, blowing his stomach away, and Raeder was flung down as well.

Untouched, the second guard pivoted toward Morgan, triggering his submachine gun. The charge caught Morgan in the chest, a bullet even creasing his head. Morgan refused to die easily. Waving the shotgun at the guard, blond hair reddened about him like a casque, he sought to bring the gunbutt down on the man's head. There was no need to—a shot from Le Brun killed the German outright. Trying a smile toward Le Brun, Morgan barely managed it before toppling in front of him, falling like a tree.

It was then that Le Brun became aware of the quiet. The train was out of sight, just a faint hum on the far rails, and the Lancasters were well away, a throttled drumbeat in the west.

Epernet was groaning. "It's all right," he said without a stutter when Le Brun reached him, "just my leg." He was pulling up his trouser leg to investigate the wound.

A new sound was intruding. From the woods above came the second truck, Georges driving it. Georges and Mischa had seen the train moving past them, the Lancasters disappear, and that was their signal. Now Georges braked behind Henri's truck, which was canted across the road, blocking it.

Raeder was still alive. Part of the hail of pellets that

had blown the first guard away had torn into his hip, but he was conscious and the pain was not unbearable. A bad sign, he thought; he remembered being told once that if the pain from a serious wound was not severe enough to be felt, it meant that death was in the offing.

His mind was as sharp as ever. He saw the second truck arriving and instantly understood how Le Brun had planned it, the first dummy truck to waste the attack under cover of the bombing. And the Lancasters. Of course the British would have sacrificed the Winged Victory in order to destroy the Reichsmarschall, but it was not by happenstance that all the Lancaster bombs had missed the target. They'd known that Goering wasn't aboard, and so they hadn't wanted to hit the train. What they wanted to do—arranged by Le Brun and Aaron Jacobi—was create a diversion, save their precious paintings. In British eyes, and to the French in London as well, the collection was a museum in itself, a National Treasure because it was truly French, of more importance even than the Samothrace.

Raeder, by moving ever so slightly, could see the driver of the truck, a little man with his head out of proportion to his body, slide out of the driver's seat and walk toward Le Brun. Following the little man, whom he now recognized as the garage owner he had questioned once about Le Brun, was a bald giant, the Prince Kilkanov.

Raeder discovered that he could move. He was sprawled almost directly across the dead guard, and in front of him was the submachine gun.

Reaching for the stock, he pulled it slowly toward him until he had it firmly in his hands. He would fire at the gas tank of the truck; a short burst into the tank would send the Jacobi collection sky high. But even with the truck squarely in front of him, he found he couldn't pull the trigger, couldn't, when it came down to it, wantonly destroy this incredible store of art. What else in the world beside art had he respect for?

"Raeder!" a voice shouted.

It was Le Brun, Raeder saw, who was advancing, gun pointed at his head. Le Brun was another story. Raeder twisted around, firing. But in amazement he saw that he had missed Le Brun almost completely, nothing more than a small red blotch showing on the Frenchman's forearm. And worse, that familiar, arrogant face was now over him, the barrel of Le Brun's gun at his head. He heard Le Brun curse, a vicious stream he couldn't understand, and Le Brun had swung his gun away, the ending shot Raeder had tensed for never coming.

Sara Jacobi was running through the checkpoint with the captain of gendarmerie, a Captain Benoit Eglan, two more gendarmes, and Frenchmen from the railroad depot. They'd all been under cover during the bombing by the Lancasters, and then had waited until the firefight on the other side of the line had subsided before coming over to investigate.

A real ambulance would be arriving any minute, Captain Eglan told Le Brun; he'd phoned Vierzon for it—that arm could use attention. The arm was nothing, Le Brun said, but the German sergeant was another matter: he was in extremely bad shape. Epernet needed medical attention, too. Morgan and the two Germans from the checkpoint were beyond help. And of course the driver of the first truck.

"I can see that," said the captain calmly. "In the meantime," he said, looking Le Brun straight in the eye, "if you don't mind, you can speak to the people in that second truck. If they could move the first truck out of the way, and then go wherever they're going so that the road is clear. You see, that road is what the ambulance must use."

"Very good, Captain," said Le Brun, wondering what Sara Jacobi had told this man, for obviously he was very efficient and wasn't allowing the Jacobi collection through the checkpoint by carelessness or oversight. Most probably, he decided, Sara—whose thought processes ran in a straight line—had simply told the truth, and Eglan was a patriot.

Le Brun walked over to Mischa and Georges, who had pulled Henri out of the cab and were arranging his limbs neatly on the ground with great tenderness. Le Brun transmitted the captain's message.

"Okay," said Georges, "but Henri comes with us."

"If you're taking him, take Morgan, too," said Le Brun. "He's the other man we lost."

Sara was standing by Morgan's body when Le Brun went over to her. She was crying, but softly, as one does when tears are not enough. But then she caught sight of Le Brun's arm, and with indrawn breath plucked at his sleeve. "It's nothing," he told her. "Nothing."

Mischa came over and patted Sara's cheek before bending to pick up the American. The rear doors of the second truck were open to receive the bodies, but Le Brun wanted Georges and Mischa to hurry. *For Christ's sake, do they think they have all night? And how long before troops arrive from the German side?*

At the farm, Brazin and Umbarti helped to remove Morgan and Henri, and laid them out in the studio. Christine Chandon was also at the farm, and when Le Brun and Sara arrived in the Citroën, Christine doctored Le Brun's arm. It was really the slightest of wounds, as he'd said, Raeder's bullet having sliced off a piece of flesh the size of a fruit pit. Then Le Brun and Georges, politely refusing Mischa's offer to accompany them, returned to the truck and drove north and east, to the Brittany coast.

There were still several hours to go before dawn when they coasted into a little beach town near St. Malo and Dinard. It was called St. Lunaire and had a long, beautiful beach with a resort hotel sitting above it. After sending Le Brun's message to Jacobi in London, Father Gregory had received a message in turn for Le Brun: BEACH AT ST. LUNAIRE. EARLIEST, 0200 HOURS: LATEST 0400.

It was hellishly tight, Le Brun thought, *London assuming that everything would go down smoothly, like a fine red wine.* It had in a way; they were actually at the beach twenty minutes ahead of schedule.

It was low tide, which was unlucky, for the walk from the water to the road where they had to park the truck was endless. The two men waited on the sand, shivering not so much from the raw Channel wind, but from the work of the night. And gloomy, massed clouds hid the moon, which was better for their purposes, of course, although the hotel was shuttered and the beach deserted.

At exactly three o'clock they saw a large rubber dinghy slide into the sand almost a quarter mile from them. The men that came toward them, tramping the wide expanse of beach, were armed and wore dark woolens; they might have been British navy, or civilian for that matter. Out beyond the surf Le Brun and Georges could see a large shape hovering, engines throttled.

In command was a short, compact young man who wore shorts, and carried sidearms. He eyed the two Frenchmen sharply. "Le Brun?"

"Right."

"First name, please."

"Claude."

"Very good. Now, where are your goddamn paintings?"

From the farm, after picking up Henri's body, Georges went straight to Paris, taking Brazin with him. There wasn't the same trouble getting back into the German zone as there was leaving it. Mischa was to depart the next day, after the funeral for Morgan. They buried Morgan in the newly cut area above the studio, Sara reading a passage from *Candide,* which she said Morgan had loved. It would only be temporary burial, Sara noted. When the war was over, she'd contact Morgan's family in Minnesota; they'd probably want him home.

In the morning Le Brun drove Mischa to Vierzon, to the bus station. The Prince was tired, his bones ached, but his shoulders remained straight, the blue eyes were undimmed; he wanted to get back to the Princess. He told Le Brun not to wait. He stuck out his hand toward him. Mischa's smile came awkwardly; he had never before given it to Le Brun. "You accomplished it, Le Brun. Not only the collection, but the Victoire. I congratulate you."

"It was not accomplished alone, Prince Kilkanov."

Except for brief salutations mornings and nights,

Sara did not communicate with Le Brun for three days. For three days she walked the country back of the farm. It was raining almost constantly, a soft, warm rain that gave the countryside the bouquet of lilacs. Umbarti had disappeared with Christine Chandon—bicycling around the Loire, a note said cryptically. The real Victoire had been secretly removed the night the false one was delivered, in case anyone came snooping. The real one had been trucked back to Valençay, hidden in the deepest dungeon of the château, and there was official wailing to Vichy that somehow it had been spirited out of d'Albion. Vichy said it would investigate, but could Valençay present evidence of German involvement? It couldn't.

On the fourth night, following supper with the Povavnas—Sara had eaten a bite earlier, they said—Le Brun strolled over to the studio. The rain had finally stopped, the sky had a melancholy cast, fitting Le Brun's mood. He could not be sure Goering's experts in Germany would accept the Samothrace as the original, but he had done his best. A letdown was natural, he supposed. And he did not know what the future held for him—even what he wanted of it. Go back to Paris, let the Resistance decide his role?

The studio looked as it had before he arrived months ago. The floor and the walls had been meticulously scrubbed so that all traces of marble dust were gone. Sara's photomurals had been put back; they were better than he remembered. She had striven not for effect but for truthfulness; the people she had caught with her camera might have been trapped by life, but they were not resigned to it. Unfailingly, they stared back into the lens with defiance.

Before leaving, Pierre Brazin had remarked on it. "When it's over, all over," he told Le Brun, "I'd like her to come to Senlis and do a series of my works for a book." The old man, Le Brun noted with an inward smile, had no doubts about his stature in the art world. "She sees with an honest eye," Brazin said, "and then such a pleasure to look at her, eh?" Clasping Le Brun's hand, he added, "We'll get together and laugh and talk about these days—if I'm alive."

It was the first time Le Brun had heard him express

305

a personal doubt. "You'll be alive, *maître*. You've created the second Victoire!"

Immensely pleased, Brazin had kissed him on both cheeks, climbed into the truck with Georges.

Turning off the studio lights, staring down the path to the house, Le Brun paused. Sara was coming toward him. "They said you'd be here, Ivan and Anna..."

"Admiring your pictures," he said.

She'd hardly heard him. "Walk with me, Claude?"

They turned and side by side walked the path that led above the house into the woods—or what remained of the woods—and where Morgan was buried.

It was a warm night, the wind restless, the harbinger of an early summer storm. They reached a crest, not too high—at best this was hilly land—overlooking the farm. It had been Aaron Jacobi's favorite spot, she had told him once before. From here, by day, one could see the far reaches of the valley.

"Do you remember Christine telling us about 'Colonel Berger'—André Malraux?" she asked suddenly. "That he was down in the Périgord, forming a Maquis unit?"

He nodded. What light there was touched her face like a candle; her loveliness was palpable; he wanted terribly to imprison it.

"And that years ago Erica wanted to enlist with Malraux in Spain?"

"Yes."

"I want to join Malraux, Claude. There'll be work for me with him, don't worry. And it will be almost as if Erica..." She paused, the rest of it in the air. But she knew he understood her.

"Agreed," he said with enthusiasm. "Périgord. Malraux. Both of us."

She looked at him with great seriousness, then smiled and took his hand, entwining their fingers. They walked slowly down toward the farm, not in any great hurry to reach it, not in any great hurry to get anywhere.

House 71: June 1945

"FORGET KRÖLER," Captain Dante said. He was snowed under with paperwork; his unit was being moved to Nuremberg to prepare for the trials. And as it looked now, Dante told Goldfarb, they wouldn't need any further proof of atrocities relating to the plunder of art. They had enough on Goering to hang him a dozen times.

"Then the stuff I got out of Ernst Kröler wasn't of much use."

"Hell yes, Lieutenant. It verified a whole shitlist of sources, filled in the big picture, you know what I mean?"

"Sure," said Goldfarb.

Goldfarb had learned he was being transferred to London; chances were he'd be sent home.

He went to see Kröler for the last time. Kröler, he philosophized, was like a crotchety old uncle you knew was a miserable son-of-a-bitch, but you kind of enjoyed him all the same.

He couldn't tell from Kröler's reception whether the German would miss him or the regular ration of schnapps. Probably the latter. Kröler said querulously, "I don't understand your superiors. Do they want the whole Goering story or don't they? There's still enough left to fill a book!"

"I believe you," Goldfarb said, rising to leave. But a thought struck him and he suddenly said, "You never gave me all the details about the Winged Victory . . . how it eventually landed in Goering's hands . . . why I found it in that condition in his gymnasium."

Kröler had the bottle of schnapps to his lips. Putting it down, he smiled at Goldfarb, an elfin smile interpreted one way, a devilish one, another. "No, I never finished that story, did I? All right, I see you're in a hurry to say goodbye to old Kröler—I'll make it brief. After the bombing raid on the railroad yard— and I don't mind saying that Raeder and I were lucky to come out alive, even if Raeder's hip was shot away —Goering had his prize."

"I thought he planned to present the Victoire to the German people. To my knowledge it never—"

"Yes, yes! As a symbol of their eventual triumph. So he had it brought to the chalet, set up in the garden where he could admire it daily while he waited for the Wehrmacht victory, the Luftwaffe victory, the proper dramatic moment, you understand, to make the supreme gift."

"A moment that never came," said Goldfarb.

"Exactly. Defeat after defeat. Stalingrad. El Alamein. Sicily. Italy. The air attacks on our cities. The breakdown of our production lines. What was worse was his fall from grace with the Führer. He was seldom consulted anymore. . . ."

The schnapps again. Kröler coughed. "There was an especially dreary period the following winter. Rotten weather. Snow, sleet, rain. The Reichsmarschall was living on his white pills."

Did Kröler expect Goldfarb to bleed for his Reichsmarschall? But Kröler was oblivious to Goldfarb— lost in his memories. "Raeder, just discharged from the hospital, joined us for a visit. The weather had cleared, for a little anyway, and he went out to look at the Samothrace—after all, it was the cause of all his grief. Also, I think during his hospital stay Raeder had begun to get a fix on what Le Brun had pulled off. In any event, he hobbled back as fast as he could to the chalet, insisting Goering return to the garden with him."

Kröler sensed he had captured Goldfarb now. His voice had grown a little hoarse; he was even ignoring the schnapps.

"Go on," Goldfarb said.

"There, in front of the Samothrace," said Kröler, "Raeder pointed out to the Reichsmarschall a small area on the stomach, just under the bellybutton. It was lighter in color than the rest, actually looking as if the patina had washed off! Yes," said Kröler with a wry smile, "even while Goering stared, eyes popping out, Raeder applied caustic acid, fuller's earth. Slowly a larger portion began to whiten, the marble underneath emerging fresh and new. It was abruptly clear as death to Goering that the Samothrace was a copy, that Le Brun had duped him, that he was as much a victim as the many he had robbed during the war!"

Goldfarb was smiling; he couldn't help it. "But by then," he said, "the French had scuttled their fleet at Toulon. All France was occupied. Why in hell didn't Goering march into the château, snatch the real Samothrace—the whole damn National Treasure for that matter?"

"By then," said Kröler sadly, "Bormann was top dog. He'd completely taken over the Jeu de Paume operation. And with the invasion imminent, the generals did not want the French stirred up more than they already were. Then there was the fact that Hitler believed the invasion would be turned back, that France would become the playground of the Reich. Why not let the French curators care for the art, saving the Germans the trouble?"

Goldfarb was still eager for more about Goering and the phony Samothrace in the garden. "What did he say when he realized she was a forgery? How did he react?" he asked Kröler.

"First," said Kröler, "he ordered the sculpture carried to the gymnasium where you found it. Then, asking for a sledgehammer, he smashed at it with all his strength, again and again, the sweat pouring off him, laughing, weeping, a madman! For his own health's sake we finally had to haul him off. . . ."

He sat in the dock and listened to his fellow accused, Schacht, Schirach, Speer, Doenitz, von Ribbentrop and the others lie and beg and prostrate themselves to save their lives. A wall of hate sprang up between them and himself. "To piss in front and crap from behind just to live a little longer!" he cried. "Do you think I give that much of a damn about this lousy life?"

When it came his turn, he tried to show that he had acted out of patriotism, with honor. To questions about his theft of art, he declared indignantly that he had paid good money for every piece, bought each work legitimately, or was the recipient of gifts.

The court didn't seem to believe him. Summing up, one of the justices called him "half-militarist, half-gangster" and asked for the death penalty.

But he was of the blood of Teutonic princes, Goering told himself. He would not allow his body to be humiliated; they would never hang him, he swore.

In New York, leaving the recently refurbished Jacobi Gallery off Madison Avenue to have dinner with Sara and his in-laws, Claude Le Brun saw the headline: the night before his scheduled execution, Hermann Goering had swallowed a vial of cyanide somehow concealed in his cell, cheating the hangman.

The best
n modern fiction from
BALLANTINE

The most fascinating people and events of World War II